DEEP DARK LIES

AVA CORTES: CRIME THRILLER SERIES
BOOK 1

RAQUEL BYRNES

AVA CORTES: CRIME THRILLER SERIES

Deep Dark Lies

Dark as Pitch

Fade to Dark

"Art is the imposing of a pattern on experience."
— Alfred North Whitehead

ONE

Eighteen Years Ago

Her mother's scream tore through Ava's dreams, waking her. She sat up, heart ramming in her chest, pulling her rainbow blanket up to her chin. The room was dark. Wind chimes tinkled softly just outside her window.

"Ava, did you hear that?" Her brother Tomás whispered from the bathroom they shared. His face looked pale in the dark doorway. "What's happening?"

Though older by ten minutes, Tomás always came to her during loud storms, or when the wind sounded like howling. He stared at her with frightened eyes and scurried over to her bed. They listened in the darkness to a strange voice. Heavy boots. Mom sobbing. Ava's stomach tumbled at the sound. Something bad was happening.

She crept over to her door and peeked down the hall at her parents' room. The door was open, the light on. Her parents' bedspread lay wadded up on the floor. It trailed almost out the door, like her father had run with it wrapped around his legs or something.

1

She looked the other way toward the kitchen. A man walked back and forth in front of the sink, and she yanked her head back into the room. She didn't know him, but she knew he was dangerous. He had a knife in his hand. A big one. And his long, tangled hair and dirty clothes made him look like he lived in the woods just past her neighborhood.

The man raised his voice again. He shouted, telling her father to shut up. Ava's heart thumped so loud she feared the man could hear it. Tomás moved closer and bumped into the dollhouse next to her door.

"Be quiet," she whispered. "He'll hear us."

Tomás pulled nervously on the buttons of his new pajamas. He'd just gotten them a week ago on their tenth birthday. "What are we gonna do?"

"We have to call 911."

She couldn't see her mom and dad. The wall hid half of the kitchen table and Ava took another step out into the hallway. Something made a loud scraping noise, like a kitchen chair on the wood floor. Then her father jumped at the man. They wrestled on the floor and Ava ran toward the kitchen screaming for her daddy. Tomás ran past her to their mother, who sat huddled in the corner. The blood on the floor turned Ava's stomach. Her father's face burned red as he and the stranger fought. The big knife skidded under the fridge. They punched each other, and the horrible sound of her father's pain pulled strangled cries from Ava. She ran to the phone near the microwave. The charger was empty. No one ever put it back.

The man jumped onto her father, wrapping his hands around his neck. Ava's mother tried to help. She grabbed a nearby cutting board and hit the man on the back. The man spun and punched Ava's mom, sending her flying back into the wall. She landed on the floor and didn't move.

"Mommy!" Ava cried. The man glared at Ava. He had spit on his beard and blue tears tattooed on his face. He smelled gross. Like garbage and dirt. She backed up, flattening herself against the wall next to her brother, trembling.

Her father pushed the man off him, and they got to their feet and faced off across the table. Hope radiated through Ava. Her father used to be a marine. He was strong. But the man didn't look scared. He smiled, and then he pulled a gun from a pocket at his knee. Her stomach dropped.

Her father's gaze locked on her. "Go, Ava! Run!"

Ava grabbed her brother's hand and yanked him from his knees. They ran along the side of the kitchen counter to the back door. Her father shouted again, and Ava hesitated in the yard. She looked back at the dark open door and then a flash lit up the night. A shot so loud it pushed her back. She turned and ran, dragging Tomás with her. Another gunshot sounded from inside the house. Her breath crowded in her throat, but she didn't stop. Past the swing set, through the chain-link gate, across the sidewalk and street to the field of tall grass that butted up against the woods. The long blades of drying grass sliced at her arms. Her face too. The cuts stung with her tears as she pulled her brother behind her.

They stopped to listen. Crouching in the dark field, the bright moon overhead. Ava worried the man could see them.

"What about Mom and Dad?" Tomás cried. "What if that guy—"

"Oh, no..." Ava said, cutting him off. She'd chanced a look back at her house, hoping to see her father waving for them to come back. That everything was fine. But what she saw instead made her teeth chatter. The bad man. His long hair blew around his head as he moved in their direction.

His voice floated to them in the inky night. Scratchy and mocking. "Where are you going, little girl? Did your daddy tell you what he knows?"

"Go, go, go," she whispered, pushing Tomás out in front of her. "Stay down or he'll see us."

They ran in a crouch across the field until the cool wind whipping through the trees made her stop at the edge of the woods. She'd heard they were haunted at night. That's what her friends at school had always said. The sound of crunching grass spurred her to move. She'd rather face a ghost than a man with a gun.

They crept carefully into the woods. She moved them from tree to tree, hiding like when they played tag with friends. The dirt and rocks bit at her feet and she shivered. The man had neared the edge of the field. He stood there looking into the trees, panting, and she could see from behind a trunk that he still held the gun in his hand. Tomás must have seen it too because he backed up. With panic in his eyes, he turned and ran. Ava tried to follow but couldn't see in the dark. She got turned around. Lost. She had no idea where she was. Her head swam with fear.

"Tomás!" Ava whimpered. She moved as quietly as she could, the moonlight peeking down between the trees as she searched. "Where are you?"

Leaves crackled to her right, and she froze. It was the man. She spotted his shape between a couple of tree trunks. He looked back and forth. And then he raised his gun and fired at the sky. Ava didn't move, but white pajamas flashed to her left as Tomás ran out from behind a tree. The man took off after him. She remained frozen. Not even breathing as she tried to think what she should do. She crouched down, sobbing as she searched the ground with her hands, she closed her fingers around a fallen branch. Lifting it with both hands, she hoped if she just hit the man hard enough, they could get away.

Sirens blared across the field, and she looked up. Blue and red lights flashed in the distance. Help. It was grown-ups coming to help! Ava looked back into the woods. She couldn't see Tomás. She couldn't see the man. Maybe if she went to go get the grown-ups, she could show them where her brother ran. Then she wouldn't have to go back into the dark where the bad man was. Ava ran toward the flashing lights. As fast as she could, back toward her house. Almost there. A crack of gunfire ripped through the night.

Everything seemed to freeze at that moment. Shaking, she stood motionless in the moonlight. Her breath came out in cloudy puffs as the night cooled. Policemen and women ran into her house and toward her. Others went past her to the woods, guns drawn, their flashlights slashing the dark. She stood in the field, listening to the whisper of the grass in the wind and waited for Tomás to come rushing out. She shouldn't have run. She shouldn't have left him.

A woman officer came up to her, picked her up, and took her to one of the cars before offering her a warm drink. Ava didn't look at her. She didn't move. She just stared out the window at the woods. When an officer tried to ask her questions, Ava didn't speak. Not when the men carried a small bundle wrapped in one of their coats out of the forest. Not when they gave up looking for the bad man with the gun. Not when her grandma came and got her from the hospital, her eyes swollen from crying.

Ava didn't speak until almost a month later when the counselor pulled her into her office at school.

"Ava, your teacher and I are concerned for you," the counselor said. "We're worried you still won't talk to anyone. Not even your grandma. She says you're moving with her to Oceanside next week. What do you think about that?"

Ava glanced from the brightly colored wall clock she'd been staring at to look at the counselor. The woman's gaze held pity, and it made Ava's stomach hurt. Everyone had looked at her that way during the funeral for her family.

The counselor continued, "Are you still having nightmares?"

Ava shook her head.

"That's good. Do you think that's good?" Her counselor tilted her head down to catch Ava's gaze. "It seems like you've made some progress, huh? What do you think changed? Was it the journaling we talked about?"

"No," Ava whispered. "I promised myself something."

"What's that, honey?"

Ava looked out of the counselor's office window. She could see a stretch of woods at the far end of the school playground. It was late in the afternoon, and the sunshine peeked through the rows of trees. It looked pretty and the kids out at recess made shadow puppets against the handball wall. They were Tomás's friends. He used to play four-square with them on the blacktop. A flash of his smiling face, so much like her own, burned behind her eyes.

"I promised myself I wasn't going to run away from anything ever again."

TWO

White crime scene floodlights sliced through the near black night as Ava drove up the increasingly rugged forest road. Her phone rang again, and she answered it with her earbud while bouncing over the rutted dirt toward the row of cabins up ahead. She hated driving, let alone doing it in the middle of the night on the way to a crime scene.

"If you keep calling, you're going to make me run into a tree." She parked her SUV behind an ambulance that looked about fifty years old. "I'm already here anyway."

"You're going to have to walk the rest of the way." Special Agent in Charge Nora Vincent sounded tired, not surprising given the hour. Nothing good ever happened at three in the morning. "The team has a space set up just outside the residence. And thanks for coming so quickly. I know you were on vacation."

"No, no, I'm sure I would've *hated* a tropical vacation with my friends. I mean, who wants to bask in the sun in February?"

"That's the spirit."

"Hearing my name over the airport announcement system was fun too."

"They tell me they caught you *right* as you were getting off the plane in Hawaii," Vincent said.

"I can hear the amusement in your voice. You know that, right?"

Ava pushed the driver's side door open, and the scent of pine trees hit her. Located in the mountains between LA and Palm Springs, the town of Black Oak sat atop the San Jacinto range overlooking Coachella Valley. It might have been warm enough for a heavy sweater in Oceanside where she lived, but up on the mountain, it definitely still felt like winter. Whereas her vacation suitcase had bikinis and cute dresses, the go bag she'd barely had time to grab at home was less beach paradise cheery, and more winter murder dreary. She grumbled inwardly, shrugged on her black wool trench coat, pulled her long dark hair out from underneath, and grabbed her leather messenger bag. A white field tent stood in the distance, and the flurry of movement underneath it caught her eye. She trudged toward it.

"We're tucked in a bit."

"I see it." Ava's phone gave its final low battery warning, but she swiped it aside. "Be there in a few."

She ended the call and stood quietly, getting the feel of the place for a moment. The smell of incoming snow brushed her nose. Wet ground. The narrow road wound through the woods with several homes lining one side. Snow dusted the high pointed roofs of the cabins. Dark windows, some boarded up, gave the street a haunted aura. Except for one house. It was lit up like a pinball machine with what looked like a half dozen officers standing around. Crime scene tape strung between the surrounding oak and pine trees fluttered in the frigid mountain air. An overhead bank of clouds blotted out the sliver of a moon making it nearly impossible to see the path. She tried her phone flashlight but realized it had already died. Not surprising given the hours of research she'd done on her flight back. She couldn't find the charger she normally kept in her SUV either.

The chatter grew louder as she slowly made her way toward the tent. Garbled conversations with a distinct agitated tone. Coping with death never looked normal to people who hadn't experienced it as much as most law enforcement had. Ava lifted the tape to walk under, but a burly deputy hurried over.

"Hey...hey! What do you think you're doing?" He put his hand out, blocking her with his body. Face twisting with irritation, he snapped the tape back down. "No one's allowed in. Especially press."

She'd passed news vans on her way up. They sat parked behind a roadblock she just talked her way through. There's no way he could think she'd hiked up a mile of rutted mountain road in the dark. Her oversized sweater and jeans didn't exactly scream anchor desk.

"You think a reporter would wear this on camera?"

"You could be with the paper or have a podcast or whatever."

He looked to be in his early thirties. Getting some gray at his temples and crow's feet, likely from smoking though he didn't smell like it now. His name plate read Deputy Chutney. They usually lived locally. He must be scared to have a death like this invade his town. She took a step back, trying to ease the tension.

"I'm not press. I was invited." She felt around in her bag and then sighed. "Look, my credentials are in the car. I barely made it through those woods without falling on my face. Can you just radio Agent Vincent? She asked me to come."

"I don't care if the governor himself sent you an engraved invitation. I'm going to have to see I.D." He stepped closer, trying to crowd her back.

"What if I call her?" She pulled out her phone before remembering. Ava nodded to the field tent. "She's right in there. Just radio her."

He crossed his arms. "Go back to your car and get it."

Ava tilted her head back and yelled, "If I have to walk back to my car, I'm going back to my vacation!"

Chutney reached for her. "Stop shout—"

"She's with me," Agent Vincent called from the opening of the tent twenty yards away. "Stop screwing around and let her pass."

"But she—"

"Chutney, get out of the way!" A grizzled voice shouted from the same tent. Ava couldn't see who said it, but the deputy jumped.

Moving aside, Chutney flashed her a dirty look. "You could've just said you were FBI."

"I'm not. I'm CBI. We're state agents." She brushed past him making sure she forced him to move aside. "And you could've been nice."

"I thought you guys were Feds."

"We are and we aren't."

Chutney shot her a skeptical look. One she got often. California had the fourth largest economy in the world and boasted a population of nearly forty million. It was bigger than most countries. To police a territory of that size, California had its own vast law enforcement agency, the Bureau of Investigation, with agents reporting directly to the Department of Justice. But most people didn't know about it and therefore never knew what to think about CBI agents, unless they were getting arrested.

Vincent met her at the edge of the tent. Her sensible silver bob disheveled and bags under her eyes. She shook her head as Ava approached. "Sorry about that. Local law enforcement is spooked and ready to spring."

"Probably best you don't let them anywhere near the press."

"We're all a little tense. We were trying to keep a lid on the murders, but the press just got wind of them and started a ruckus. We had to call in additional patrols. The heat is going to turn up on this fast, so I needed you here as soon as possible."

"Who scooped the story?"

"Some reporter from the LA Times wrote about it this morning on the newspaper's blog. All hell broke loose shortly after." Vincent led her into the tent. A group of agents stood around a table set with coffee cups and secure tablets. "Everyone, this is Special Agent Ava Cortes. She's the expert I was talking about."

The discussion going on in the center of the room stopped abruptly as four people turned to face her with blank faces. But it was the man they all seemed to have been listening to who made her catch her breath. Agent August Blake stood in the corner, his gaze resting intently on her. She hadn't seen him for two years, and the look on his face when she'd told him goodbye remained burned into her mind.

"I hope working together won't be a problem." Vincent motioned him over. "We need all the help we can get on this one."

"Of course, it's not a problem." Ava plastered on a serene expression. Vincent didn't even have the decency to look apologetic for not giving her a head's up. "Did he know I was coming?"

"He does now."

"That's not awkward at all," Ava muttered as he approached.

August looked good in his polished, intense kind of way. His dark brown hair, longer in front, fell into stressed amber eyes. His expensive polo and dark field jacket, however tailored, did little to hide his athletic frame. He'd played rugby at university and never lost the muscle. Of course, her outfit suggested she'd spent the day drinking wine and watching reality shows on the couch just before she came.

"Hey, Ava," he said with a puzzled look. "Are you joining us?" His gaze slid to Vincent.

"She is," Vincent answered and checked her watch. "Now that you two can get rolling on this, I need to head out. I have to get back to the LA field office and deal with the fallout from this. The Attorney General wants a call. Keep me posted. Hourly updates."

She nodded and left Ava and August standing and staring uneasily at each other.

"I see everyone's comfort is still her priority," Ava said with a forced smile. "She could have warned us."

August nodded with a smile. "Well, uh...welcome."

"Is working together going to be a problem?"

He looked at her for a beat and then shook his head. "No, no...We need the best. He's already killed four people. We need you on this."

"Great." She smiled despite what seeing him again did to her.

"Good." Clearing his throat, he motioned toward the murder house. "Did Vincent read you in?"

"I read what you have on the flight back from Hawaii. Vincent uploaded the case onto my secure tablet."

"Oh right. It's your friend group's Faux Summer February thing." His dark brows furrowed. "Sorry about that."

"Don't be. Four deaths in seven weeks is a brutal pace." She nodded in the direction of the house outside the tent. "These victims were discovered two days ago?"

"Yes, by the daughter, Lucy Thompson. She was supposed to get married this weekend and when her parents didn't show up to prepare for the rehearsal dinner, she came to see why. She's under observation right now. They had to sedate her."

"Poor woman. This was supposed to be the happiest time of her life. Does she live here too?"

He shook his head. "She lives in Irvine. She's a paralegal."

"Anything point to this having to do with the wedding?"

"We spent some time talking to the would-be guests the day after the parents were found. This doesn't seem to be related as far as we can tell. The fiancé was cooperative, but clueless. He's with Lucy now."

"The Thompsons were the only couple though?"

"Yes, the two prior victims were single males. Both live in other towns not far from here. Actually, Agent Rondeau has all the up-to-date stuff." He nodded at the group of people pretending not to watch their conversation. "Come on. Let me introduce you to the team," August said as they walked over. He motioned to an agent leaning over a laptop. "This is Agent Martin Rondeau. He is our digital guru."

"Agent Cortes," Rondeau said with just a hint of a West Virginia drawl. Slight, but there. He was a tall, sinewy man, lithe but strong, like a farmer. Pale blond hair styled short, if not a little shaggy. Light, intelligent eyes. A well-worn hunting jacket hung open revealing a misbuttoned flannel. He moved with relaxed ease. Friendly, but tough. Rondeau shook her hand with a nice smile. "Glad to have you."

She nodded. "Thank you."

August gestured to an older man in a tan uniform. "This is Sheriff Granger. He's our liaison with the Black Oak Sheriff's Department. He made the call to us after the second victim. He's been tracking this killer from the first murder."

Granger looked close to retirement age. A hairy man everywhere but his head, it even grew on his knuckles and sprouted from his ears. He had more gray hair than he needed and didn't seem to mind. He smiled with straight, white teeth, and his eyes never left hers. She liked him.

"What kind of special agent are you, exactly?" Granger leaned a hip on the table, hands in his pockets like he was questioning a person of interest. "Vincent said you're some sort of expert from White Collar crime?"

"That's right."

"This is a far cry from chasing hedge fund criminals. I mean, the carnage..."

"Details are details, Sheriff. I thrive in the minutiae." Ava tilted her head, sizing up the older man. He liked August... was watching out for him. "I'm only here to help."

Granger gave her a crooked smile. "So I'm told."

The fourth person, a woman, looked young. Maybe late twenties. Natural hair, root beer-colored eyes, intelligent gaze. Needlessly gorgeous. She extended her hand. "I'm Dr. Talia Clay, forensics and crime scene analysis."

"Pleased to meet you," Ava said. "I'll want to pick your brain later if that's ok."

"Of course," Dr. Clay said with a smile.

"Let me know what you need." Rondeau motioned to the laptop and files on the table. "Do you want to review all the updates now or you want it back at the station?"

"Back at the station, please. I'm just walking through the scene for now." Ava pulled a pair of nitrile gloves from a box on the table and started toward the cabin. She called over her shoulder, "If you don't mind, Agent Blake, the scene isn't getting any fresher."

August caught up with her within a few strides, and they walked together down the path to the murder house. About twenty yards into the woods, the sizable home stood crowded with brush and brick-work. Log siding, Adirondack chairs on the large porch, and a wrought iron bird feeder arched over a dry, stone fountain in the small yard leaned into the cabin-in-the-woods vibe. The portable lamps set up by the forensic crew cast a garish white light onto the front of the house.

"What's going on?" Ava peered back over her shoulder at Granger as he followed behind at a distance. "We don't speak for two years, and suddenly Vincent reaches out of the ether to pull me back into PIT?"

"I hear she's under a lot of pressure from above. The story is gaining traction and people want answers." August pushed a branch out of their way, letting her pass. "To be honest, we could use your help."

"Looks like you've got a good team."

"I do." He walked with his hands in his dark field jacket, eyes on the trail. She recognized it as the one he wore to ride horses on his father's property. August grew up with money, which he tried to hide, but couldn't. Even his cologne conjured images of him lounging lazily on a yacht. Breeze tousling his hair. "We've just hit a wall."

"Give me the run down on the team. Who does what?"

"We've consolidated. The PIT team, me, Agent Rondeau, and Dr. Clay, travel together and work with local authorities. Dr. Clay sets up in the nearest medical facility or lab to run forensics. We also still use the California DOJ forensic services when we have a lot of evidence to process quickly. Agent Rondeau works out of the police and ranger stations to handle our tech and communications. I go out into the field with the liaison. A sheriff or detective. Regional law enforcement helps with manpower and other heavy lifting if there isn't enough local staff. The set up keeps us nimble, but when we get a case like this, one that needs more specialized knowledge, we run into trouble."

"And you're in trouble?"

"That we are."

Ava nodded, glancing over her shoulder at the tent. "What's the sheriff's office look like up here?"

"It's just Sheriff Granger and his deputy, Chutney, who I believe you met. Both are good guys, trained to handle small town issues. If you were lost out in these woods, they'd find you, no problem. But this..."

"Yeah." Ava looked out at the dark pushing back from just beyond the trees. She hadn't camped since she was a child and forgot how incredibly still it could be in the woods at night.

"They're competent," August continued. "They've just never dealt with anything like this."

"And no leads?"

"Nothing new from this most recent case, which you probably gathered from the case files. We drilled down into the forensics, had our shrinks write up a profile, looked at every scrap of evidence we processed. You name it. All I have to show for it is two more bodies. Vincent wasn't even convinced the first two crimes were related until recently."

"Why not?" Agent Vincent was a strong investigator. She didn't rise to the top of the CBI by not catching what most people missed.

"The first victim died by stabbing during a home invasion, but the second was found at the bottom of a cliff. Other than Granger's gut, there was no concrete connection."

"What changed?"

"They found the second victim on state grounds and after Granger's multiple calls that the two were connected, I came to meet with him. Turns out he was right. During the autopsy of the second victim, the one who fell, the medical examiner discovered he'd been stabbed. A week later, the killer hit this couple. When the news reported the nature of the murders, things started getting ugly. Brass wants the connection to the first two murders played down to avoid panic. But this area has heavy tourist and temporary rental traffic, which could complicate things. After the storm blows through, families will come up to visit the snow. That's a lot of potential victims in a concentrated area."

"What storm?"

"There's one a few days out. Doesn't look like anything we can't handle."

"Messy *and* complicated. Remind me to thank Vincent for involving me." She caught his gaze. "I'm not here to step on any toes."

August shook his head. "I'm not about to turn away reinforcements. This case needs someone who knows this kind of monster. Has hunted them before."

"I'm not the only one on that list, August. There are other excellent agents Vincent could've called—"

"No one can see what you see, Ava." His gaze held hers, magnetic as it always was when he was desperate to stop bloodshed. "You know it's true."

"Don't do that. I got lucky."

"The first time, maybe. But you've tracked down three of these monsters when no one else could find a thread on them. That's not luck. It's something, but it's not chance." He looked away, shaking his head. "Look, you're here. Just walk the scene. Tell me what you think. I don't care about the past or what happened between us. I just can't have any more people dying on my watch."

She regarded August silently in the police lights as they walked. His tick had come back. The tiniest quiver at the corner of his left eye. A stress indicator for him. Dark circles under his eyes meant he wasn't sleeping very much. Probably eating even less. A thread of concern pulled through her. "Show me."

They mounted the river rock steps to the home where the most recent murders had taken place. It was incongruently adorable, like a post card log cabin. A wreath of artificial pine boughs adorned with painted wood hearts hung on the front door. Ava walked up to the picture window and cupped her hands around her face. The dark interior offered no clues to what had happened inside. Sheriff Granger caught up to them and came to stand next to her on the porch.

"Did you know the victims?" she asked him.

"I've seen them at town meetings and such. My wife and I knew them enough to say hello but that's about it. Three towns share me and my deputy. The other guys you see out there are from neighboring departments. Chutney and I cover Pine Cove, Fern Valley, and here, Black Oak. They're small by most standards, but that's a lot more people than you'd think. Then there's the weather tourists."

"Come again?"

"The homes in these towns are mostly owned by snowbirds who live here during the hot summer months and leave for the beach during cooler months. They'll also have Christmas here in the woods with family and whatnot. But most of them don't stay year-round. A lot of them rent out their property while they're gone, too. We've got people coming and going out of these towns regularly. Around this time of year, we're full of families looking for a winter wonderland vacation."

"So, no one would really notice a stranger in town?"

"Honestly, not anymore. Then there's the people from all over the Inland Empire who come stay a few miles down for the art festival in Idyllwild. That's the biggest town on this part of the mountain. It's pretty famous."

"There's also Suicide Rock," Ava offered. "I used to hike the trail with my friends in the summer. We'd drive up from Oceanside, take pictures posing off the rocks like we were dangling over a cliff. We'd always get pizza at that Italian restaurant...Donatella's?"

"Ah, it's some fancy gastronomy place now." Granger frowned. "So, you're from around here, then."

"Give or take." In Southern California, you were essentially an hour or so from everything. The beach, the desert, the mountains with lakes... Even theme parks and movie stars. 'From around here' encompassed a lot more territory than most places. "I used to have family in Oceanside."

Granger nodded. "Well, we call it Lily Rock now, but yeah... hikers and picnicking families are up here a lot too."

"Their mayor is a dog," August said absently as he sliced through the tape with a key. "A Golden Retriever."

"Yeah." Granger chuckled. "Anyways, most people visit Idyllwild to see the snow, do some sledding, eat at the little cafes in town. Day trippers. But some do make it all the way up here to these smaller towns on occasion. We get a lot more snow, but fear of getting stuck up here keeps it from getting too crazy."

Ava pulled the nitrile gloves on. "So you're saying there're a lot of unfamiliar people wandering around."

"In a nutshell," Granger said.

She walked the length of the porch, taking in the surrounding landscape. Wet leaves and twigs squished under her shoes. Pine and the scent of log fires drifted to her from distant cabins. The marked absence of insect sounds gave the woods an eerie quiet. If she hadn't looked at the maps, she might've believed there were no other houses around for miles. The darkness beyond the police lights hid even the shape of the roofs from view.

According to Vincent's files, the murdered couple, the Thompsons, had owned the two-story log cabin for over a decade. Ava could tell it had been built in fits and starts. Some of the construction appeared older than others. The perfect place to hold Thanksgiving dinners and Christmas parties, big and cozy. Overgrown hedges shrouded the front of the house, and a lattice of dead honeysuckle shielded the entrance from view of the other home down the way.

Granger nodded to the dried plants. "The Thompsons probably used the plants to block the afternoon sun from coming in through the window in the spring."

"Well, it also provided a nicely hidden alcove for the killer to work." She broke off a piece of the dried honeysuckle, smelled it, and dropped it into her pocket. "Did forensics already clear out?"

August walked over to stand next to her. "They moved the bodies. We also had the power fixed. After our little tour, we're going to shut down the rest of the scene, but I'll keep it sealed for a while." He pointed to the ground just below the front-facing window. "We found shoe prints over there."

Ava's mind flashed to the photographs taken by the crime scene team that she'd seen in Vincent's files earlier. The boot prints in the mud. The image of the casts floated to mind, a black ruler next to it in stark contrast to the white plaster. Size twelve shoes on the Bannock scale stood side by side right beneath the front window, putting the wearer somewhere in the six-foot or taller range. Tread like a work boot, oval label where the arch would be. A series of possibilities ticked behind her eyes, and she settled on black, rubber-soled work boots used all over the country by blue collar workers. Not enough to shed any light on the intruder. Not yet.

"He watched them," Ava said and squinted at the shadows cast by the floodlights. "Let's kill the lamps. I want to see the house like the unsub did that night."

Granger did and she stood still, letting her eyes adjust.

"The killer walked in through the front door. The back door appears untouched as far as we can tell," August said.

"Bold. He doesn't crouch in the shadows." She glanced back toward the other houses. "No one would have seen him working here, even if he had a flashlight. The lattice and hedges would've absorbed the light and blocked the view."

"The only other neighbor is about a hundred yards to the north, through the stand of trees. The residents were home that night, but they didn't see or hear anything." August offered her some of his menthol gel for under her nose. She took some, as did Granger.

Ava pushed through the squeaky front door, and then the smell hit her. Despite the menthol, the copper sweet scent of a kill assaulted her senses. She slid her hand along the inside wall and found the switch. The lights of the foyer and stairs flicked on. Ava's gaze went to the wall opposite the doorway and found it empty. "I thought there was an alarm?"

"Yeah, but Thompson built this cabin bit by bit through the years until they retired up here. Rumor is he didn't pay much attention to actual permits." Granger moved next to her, knocking on the wall. "He put the alarm here instead."

"That's a bad place for an alarm." Ava stood in front of the panel and then looked behind her. The living room's picture window gave a clear view of the keypad. "Anyone watching could see what they punched in."

"We don't think it was on anyway," August said as he strolled toward the living room. "The killer cut the power, but even if they hadn't, the system is a cheap one. It isn't wired into the house. It runs on batteries, but Thompson's daughter said he sometimes would forget to replace them."

Ava peered at the alarm's keypad. "Most alarms trigger an alert if the power is cut. Does the security service have a record we can check? I don't remember one from the files."

"That's because there is no security service," August said from down the hall. He walked back, typing something on a field tablet before looking up. "If the alarm trips, the phone line automatically calls the police. That's it."

"Thompson probably felt safe with his gun anyway." Granger's hand went to his waist in a subconscious tick. He didn't seem to notice.

The small front entrance gave way to a large living room to the right and a den with a fireplace to the left. Mrs. Thompson must have been a fan of sage green and used it at every opportunity in couch pillows, throw blankets, and curtains. Big box store art on the walls depicted duck-filled ponds and horses running through misty glens. An anniversary card stood on the mantle over a river rock fireplace. Family photos hung on the wall between brass sconces. The Thompsons with their daughter, Lucy, at a park when she was little. Her graduation photo from college. A vacation of some sort in the desert, large boulders in the background as they stood with arms linked, smiling at the camera. They looked close.

Ava wandered into the den. Bloody boot prints spanned the light beige carpet, five to the desk to grab the laptop, five back out. Large stride, consistent with a six-foot male. No prints were found on the desk or evidence that any of the drawers had been opened. The bottom right drawer to Thompson's desk remained untouched despite having over a thousand dollars and some important papers still in it, according to the daughter's initial interview with the police. Pictures of the drawer lock showed no attempt to jimmy it open.

She turned to August. "He only took the laptop? We're sure?"

"First responders got a little information out of the daughter, but she wasn't in a good place. We'll have to reinterview."

"I want to do that."

August nodded. "I figured. The killer left all the jewelry and a lot of small, expensive electronics."

Ava's gaze drifted to the bloody boot print on the floor. They had come down the stairs, across the rag rug in the foyer, and then into the office. Another set of prints overlapped the first on their way out the front door. But none led into the living room. He hadn't bothered. The kitchen was down the hall and had also not been entered, at least not after the killing. Pictures she'd seen of the knife block on the counter had shown all the slots filled. "The killer brought his own blade?"

August nodded. "Preliminary notes from Dr. Clay's autopsy report said the knife bore a serrated top edge."

"A hunting knife," Ava said as images of jagged blades flickered behind her eyes, but she let them fade. Not important right now.

Slowly taking the stairs up to the second floor, she avoided the killer's boot prints as she let her gaze travel along the wall and banister. No bloody smudges, no crooked picture frames. A step creaked under her foot, loud.

Granger looked down at it, frowning. "You know, I didn't notice that till now."

"It was probably loud when you processed the house. Lots of talking, movement, nature noises, but you'd think the victim would have noticed it," she said and glanced at August.

"I thought I read that Mr. Thompson was a cop. They're usually light sleepers. Did he have any history of hearing loss?"

"He did. Lost a lot of hearing on the job. It's why he retired." August checked the field tablet. "The wife did not. Perfect hearing."

"She still wouldn't have heard," Ava said and climbed further.

She stepped onto the landing and headed down the hall. The thick carpet muffled her steps, and she stopped, listening. More bloody boot prints snaked along the carpet from the door of the master bedroom. None leading into any other room. A singular purpose. A mission not to deviate from.

August walked up and stood next to her. "Why wouldn't the wife hear the step creak?"

"She was out cold," Ava said. "Sleeping pills."

"I don't think so. We don't have the tox screen yet, but there weren't any pills on her bedside table or in her medicine cabinet," Granger countered from the landing.

"I saw a bottle in the photos of the kitchen counter. She had a prescription for them, a current one." Ava stood in the doorway. "She probably took one with dinner or shortly after, so she kept them downstairs. There weren't any kids to keep them from."

Granger shook his head. "No, those were all vitamins and supplements in that basket."

"Not all of them." Ava stepped into the room and flicked the light switch. A drum ceiling light glowed on. The quiet of the cabin somehow sharpened the terror that had taken place in that room. She took in the violent streaks of blood on the walls, the mottled pools on the carpet, and a familiar chill gripped her spine. She walked further into the room, her gaze on the bed. Dark spray arched along the back wall and headboard, onto the lampshade and sheets. She swept her gaze slowly, deliberately moving across the scene to look at details.

"Agent Rondeau and Dr. Clay used a 3D mapping drone to capture the scene. She's working on solidifying the attack choreography via blood spatter."

"That's new," Ava said absently.

"PIT has all the bells and whistles now," August said, watching her.

The room looked cramped and cluttered as most old people's rooms do. Small tables with knickknacks sat tucked into several corners. A child's wicker rocking chair held a creepy antique porcelain doll with eyes that never left Ava's face. The wife's night table, also with plenty of personal clutter, sat less than a foot from the bed. Brushes, shabby paperbacks, reading glasses. The litter of living one leaves behind.

Ava nodded at the window. "Two days ago, the moon was a waning crescent. That's two to six percent illumination. Plus, it was overcast that night, I checked. The cloud cover brought light flurries, like this morning. Add in the absence of streetlamps, there'd be no extra light to the room." Ava glanced around, looking at the outlets. No night lights. "And the killer took out the power before entering. So, how did he not knock over the lamps in the attack?"

"Flashlight?" Granger offered.

"Maybe," Ava muttered.

August kept his focus on Ava. "Tell me what you're thinking."

She stepped over to the side of the bed that Mrs. Thompson slept on and raised her arm as if holding a knife. As she approached the bed, her head bumped against a small shelf jutting out from the wall next to the right side of the bed. Far too many figurines sat crowded on the surface. Reaching out, she gave it a little shake. The figurines clinked against each other. It hung high enough for the five-foot Mrs. Thompson to pass under, but head-height for Ava's five-foot five frame. According to his boot size and stride length, the killer stood over six feet tall. The shelf would've caught his shoulder.

"Sheriff Granger, can you please hit the lights downstairs? The ones in here too, August."

He flicked the room switch off. Ava let her eyes adjust to the darkness once again. Granger's footfalls receded and the downstairs lights went out. She stood in the nearly total dark of the woods.

"August, you're what – six two?"

"Last I checked."

"Could you walk over to me?"

A moment later, August hit the shelf, and the contents clanged against each other. "Ow."

"Weird right? He didn't knock *one* thing over?"

"Maybe he got lucky," August said. She heard him fumble his way back to the doorway before the room light snapped back on.

Ava touched the wall behind her guessing maybe twenty-four inches were between it and the bed. "And maybe he walks in the shape of a seven which is the only way he'd have missed that shelf if he didn't already know about it."

Granger propped his back against the threshold. "You think he was in this house before the murder? Knew what to avoid even in the dark?"

"No, I don't think he was in the house before. I think he had night vision goggles," Ava said, her gaze still on the delicate figurines.

August nodded. "We considered that. They would've helped him to navigate the woods at night. Like you said, with the waning moon, it would've been nearly pitch black."

"And he couldn't have avoided all the noise an old place like this makes. The terrain outside leading up to the door would be noticeable in the dead of night. I've stayed in a cabin before. A raccoon lumbering outside on the sticks and leaves woke me up. The front door is squeaky and there's that stair that creaks. Was the killer just lucky that none of these things woke up an armed cop? Or did he know it didn't matter? Did he watch them and figure out their security system sucked or that Thompson was bad at arming it? Or did he just cut the power and hope for the best?

Either this guy is the luckiest killer I've ever come across, the stupidest, or..."

Her gaze drifted to August.

"Tell me what you're seeing," he asked.

"Incongruity. First there's the patience. The planning. That level of control doesn't match the frenzy of an attack like this. Look at the walls, August. The ceiling?" She hooked her thumb toward the stairs. "And then just like that...back to cool and collected? Take the laptop and leave? Don't disturb any other rooms? One of these two aspects of the killer isn't true."

"Staged?" August pulled at his chin, a sign he wasn't convinced.

"Not exactly," Ava murmured. "But something."

"What are you guys saying?" Granger looked from Ava to August. "You think he faked that kind of viciousness? Why?"

"I don't know yet, Sheriff. I just got here." Ava smiled at Granger, and it seemed to startle him. "But don't worry. These guys, they're my specialty."

Back down by the cars, Ava waited as August locked up the house. Granger sat in his cruiser with the motor running. The interior light on and bright, and he spoke on his cell while looking at her from behind the windshield. His breath came in puffs of vapor. He shook his head and ended the call.

"What's up," August asked, walking over. "Who's he calling?"

Ava shrugged, snapping off the nitrile gloves and stuffing them in her jacket pocket.

Granger made his way over. He shook his phone, looking at her with the same unsettled curiosity her teachers often had. "I just called Deputy Chutney and had him check the photos."

"Which ones?" August buried his hands in his jacket pockets.

"The ones of the counter, right?" Ava smiled. "The vitamins."

"One bottle of sleeping pills prescribed to Mrs. Thompson. It was mixed in with the other bottles in a basket. You were right." Granger folded his beefy arms. "So that's what you do? Remember stuff?"

Ava blew hot air into her cupped hands. "What I do, Sheriff, is grind. Every piece of evidence you guys process, I pour over. And then I pour over it again. The avalanche of data that comes in goes through me. Again, and again, until I dream it. And yes, I remember. All of it."

"So, details," Granger said, his brows furrowed.

She shrugged. "I know. Not glamorous, but yeah. Every life has a flurry of minutia that tells a story. Details and little throw away facts that aren't important most of the time. Things people miss because they're commonplace or insignificant. Like the way you lean on something every chance you get or how you keep your gun belt loose despite having to hike your pants up all the time. You don't have a limp yet, but I'd bet you a steak dinner you have arthritis in one, or both, of your hips."

Granger hiked his pants up, looking at August uncomfortably. "Doesn't affect the job."

Ava nodded toward the cabin. "These devils are always found in the details. Always. You just have to look long enough and close enough to find them."

"Yeah, well...you think you can find this killer then?" Granger asked.

"I might not have to."

August's gaze snapped to hers. "What's that supposed to mean?"

"If he's the hunter I think he is, then he probably watched the entire crime scene process from somewhere out there. So, he knows we're onto him. The question now is...what's he going to do about it?"

THREE

They broke for the night, and Ava drove back into Black Oak's town proper to check into the Timberline Inn where the CBI had rented rooms for the whole team. August stayed back with Rondeau and Dr. Clay to close down the scene. By the time Ava left, the fatigue of two flights and a long drive caught up to her. The thought of a nice warm bed was the only thing that kept her moving. The inn, a refurbished Victorian Painted Lady, boasted six rooms with clawfoot bathtubs and an enclosed solarium with a 'garden experience.' After hours check-in consisted of scanning a QR code on their door, entering your reservation number, which she'd found in her email, and waiting for the system to text back the front door's code. After hearing the lock unlatch, she entered the home. It smelled of potpourri and candles. A glass jar on the check-in counter held fancy match boxes with the inn's name on them. She grabbed one in case she needed a candle. Ava wandered about in the dimly lit foyer and dining area before locating her room upstairs.

The flowery blue wallpaper in her suite matched the house's outside paint, and the upholstered furniture, with gold and burgundy accents, rounded out the vintage feel. She sank onto the sleigh bed and contemplated the wicker fan spinning above her on the ceiling. Though her body screamed for sleep, her mind raced with the details of the case. After locating her phone charger, Ava showered, changed into sweats, and went to bed, exhausted.

She dreamed of dust and heat. Bright sun and the smell of blood. A rodeo she had seen as a kid, only this time she was in the arena, not watching it. She clung to the bull's harness with shaking hands, the rope tearing into the soft flesh of her wrist as the beast roiled and bucked to throw her off. Stark white horns tore through the air, their points razor sharp. In a panic, a scream erupted from her, the shrill sound echoing through the dark arena. Pinprick camera flashes blinded her, and still the beast wrenched her back and forth. Ava's head whipped painfully, teeth snapping shut on her tongue. Cowboy clowns ran in slow motion toward her, their arms waving, mouths frozen in pained grimaces. They shouted for her to let go.

The bull twisted sideways, careening toward the metal fence. Ava lost her grip, the force of the jolt enough to throw her from its back. She screamed again, hands shooting out as she flew at the ground. The scene slowed, her gaze locked onto the shredded skin of her arm, her breath catching in her throat. She froze mid-air, her body hovering over the dirt as she stared at the angry rope marks on her skin.

Mr. Thompson had no ligature marks. He hadn't been bound.

Ava jerked awake, a gasp pulling at her chest. Tangled in the sheets, she staggered out of bed, sank onto the floor, and inspected her arms. The burn of the rope still lingered. Thompson was a big man, a strong one. Her messenger bag lay on the floor near the bed, and she dug her tablet out, swiping through the file to the Thompsons' autopsy photos. She couldn't find any of his wrists. Grabbing her phone from the bedside table, she dialed August.

He picked up on the first ring, his voice a rasp. "Agent Blake."

"It's Ava, listen... Mrs. Thompson's hands were bound, yes? I remember the crime scene photos."

"Uh," he yawned. "Yes, her hands were bound."

"But Mr. Thompson's weren't?" Ava flipped back through the case file on the tablet. "I don't see any photos of his wrists."

"That's because we found no evidence he was restrained. Dr. Clay is running further tests."

"Something doesn't fit."

His bed squeaked and then he sounded louder. "Where are you going with this?"

"When you ride a bull, you wrap the rope over your wrist. The glove protects you, but sometimes there's tearing—"

"Wait, what?" His bed creaked as he shifted. "What are you saying?"

"I was dreaming, I think, about bull riding and it occurred to me that Mr. Thompson was a hefty guy. Dr. Clay's autopsy report said the angle of the knife wounds points to the killer striking from above with Thompson on his back."

"Yes, dead on. No defense wounds on his hands. We found it consistent with a blitz attack mid-sleep. He didn't have time to react."

"But then why bind the wife's hands?" Ava countered.

"I... don't know."

"The photos show her hands tied in front. So he had rope. Why not use it on the large male victim?"

August remained silent for a moment. "We'll get you connected with Talia—Dr. Clay in the morning. She did the autopsies."

The clock on Ava's phone screen read five in the morning. "How soon can I meet with her?"

"We have a seven o'clock meet time at the sheriff's station."

She debated pushing for a moment but decided to let him sleep.

"Okay. Sorry I woke you up."

"No, no," he said with amusement in his voice. "Just like old times."

She let him go and tried to go back to sleep herself but couldn't. Instead, she brewed some coffee with the small machine on the side table and started jotting down thoughts and scenarios in her leather notebook. Mr. Thompson had to have been drugged too, right? She kept going over her notes, struggling to envision what had happened to the Thompsons. After she finished her coffee, she gave up. Not enough information yet.

Needing to move, she dressed in a dark blue cable knit sweater, hiking pants, and rugged black trail runners. It wouldn't get cold enough for her trench coat until tonight, so she went with the average tourist ensemble. Pulling the hem of her roomy sweater over the clip-on holster at her waist, she made sure it covered the bulge completely. The inn provided a plate of pastries near the coffee carafe downstairs and Ava grabbed one of each on her way out.

Black Oak Sheriff's Station, a squat rectangle decorated in shades of gray and beige, sat in near silence given the early hour. The lights were on, and Ava knocked, flashing her CBI badge to the cleaning crew who let her in. Once inside, she grabbed more coffee from the break room and then went to find a place to work. The conference room sat between the public intake area and the inner office as a sort of neutral zone. Large windows gave the occupants a wide view of the goings-on in the station. Long, thick blinds offered privacy if needed, though they were wide open when she entered.

August had a tendency to ask the local law enforcement agency to gather all evidence in one easily accessible location for the CBI team. Granger's office had set up everything they had so far on all three cases in the conference room. Settling in, Ava sorted the piles of evidence from each crime scene on the long conference table. Then she poured through the bags containing bloody clothes, broken objects, photos of smears and drops of blood. The detritus of dying. Fatigue caught up with her, and she leaned forward on one of the chairs, elbows on her knees. She set her head on the edge of the table as she contemplated her shoes. A thread of tension vibrated through her at the thought of someone watching them at the crime scene.

"Lose a contact?" A woman's soft voice said from the door.

Ava looked up, surprised. "What are you doing here, Dr. Clay?"

"Please, call me Talia. My father is Dr. Clay. Besides, I can't let the new guy show me up on the first day." She strode over and handed Ava a mug. A gold sheriff's star emblazoned the blue surface. "It's just regular. Two creams, two sugars. You'll need it. We only have so much time before the next storm comes through. The sheriff warned me that the weather's turning again."

"Thanks," she said as she slid the pen she was using behind her ear and took the coffee. It tasted glorious. "I think he's sore I outed him about his hip."

Talia chuckled. "I heard about that. Hey, the guy asked." She leaned against the wall and sipped her coffee. "From all the talk, I think he was worried you were a flaky psychic or something."

"There was talk?"

"Your reputation precedes you," Talia said.

"I deny everything unless it makes me look good."

Talia smiled and nodded at the table. "What are you doing with all of this?"

"Just laying out the evidence, getting familiar with it." Ava stood, stretched out the stiffness in her neck, and pointed to the eight-by-ten crime scene photographs lying face-down on the end of the table in rows. "I'm playing the most disturbing game of memory you've ever seen."

Talia strode over to the corkboard with the phone records pinned to it in three groups. "Most people pin the pictures up."

"Sometimes the violence hides the truth." She cupped her hands around the hot coffee mug and blew across the surface. "When we catch the killer, it will be because of something he couldn't account for."

"What do you mean?"

"Fate hinges on little things. A broken switch. A missed call. A step too far. Chance lives in those moments. That's where we'll get him."

"You're already the strangest psychologist I've ever met, and that's saying something."

"That's probably because I'm not a psychologist."

Talia raised a brow. "But Agent Vincent said you were an expert on finding these monsters."

"I have two degrees, one of which is the study of complex systems. Now, that can be anything from ants to meteorology to the economy, but I specialize in people. Criminal activity to be exact."

"So you're a scientist?"

"Not voluntarily," she said with a grin. "I needed a scholarship and the one I qualified for was for a STEM degree. So, I got one in complex systems science. But what I really wanted to study was criminology. They dovetail nicely, it turns out."

Talia took a sip of her coffee, eyeing Ava. "How'd you end up hunting killers?"

"If I'm being honest, it was two things. My big mouth and numbers, or rather, patterns that pulled me onto the PIT task force."

"What'd you use, some sort of advanced math to figure out where a killer lived or something?"

"If I could do that kind of math, I'd work for NASA." Ava laughed. "No, I was at a seminar at the CBI academy. Agent Vincent was running the Violent Criminal Apprehension Task Force at the time and presented an open case for our class. I wanted the extra credit, so I went. During the Q&A period afterward, I noticed something, brought it up, and didn't think anything of it until three days later when I found myself on a jet to a crime scene."

"Just like that? What did you notice?"

"The way the killer had arranged some artifacts at the scene. I'd seen it before in a medieval etching. And there were other things. Patterns that led us to realize not only why the killer had done certain things, but why the times were important, and what he might do next based on that assumption."

"You caught him?"

Ava nodded. "We did."

"After how many bodies?"

"He'd killed five women before the team took him down." She cleared her throat. "He died in a supermax. After that, Vincent assembled the Priority Investigations Team around August, who'd led the investigation."

"So, if you were one of the original members, why did you leave?"

Ava grinned. She liked Talia. "You're just all up in my business, aren't you?"

"Sorry. Inquisitive minds." She stirred her coffee. "But really... PIT is the all-star team of crime fighting. What would make you leave?"

Ava shrugged. "I got too into the chase, I think."

"Meaning?"

"I don't like to lose and at some point, that became a problem."

Talia looked at her askance. "And now?"

Ava walked over to the papers on the corkboard and closed her eyes. The streams of numbers scrolled behind her lids. Nothing spoke to her yet. "And now I'm back."

Talia checked her watch before changing the subject. "Are you waiting for the medical examiner's office to open? I can walk you through the Thompsons' autopsies."

"I read your report. It was incredibly thorough." Ava turned to Talia. "I'd like to have both Mr. and Mrs. Thompson's blood checked for a sedative."

"Not just the wife?"

"I'm ruling something out. Are we able to do a tox screen on him?"

"Sure, I'll get the paperwork started when we go see the bodies."

"I actually want to speak with the town's medical examiner first. The one who did the autopsies on the first two victims."

Her delicate brows furrowed. "Really? Why?"

"When I join an investigation, it's usually already in progress. I find starting from the beginning, talking with everyone involved, gives me a better handle of what's going on."

Talia narrowed her gaze. "You mean what's going wrong?"

"And right. I'm just getting the whole picture of the situation." Ava gestured to the evidence on the table. "Your observations about the blood spatter were interesting. We should talk about them later."

Talia nodded, "I can get behind that. Oh, by the way, cell phones are spotty out here. The sheriff's receptionist, Gale, can set you up with a patrol radio."

"Thanks for the heads up—"

August strode into the station, shrugging snow crystals from his field jacket. He caught sight of them. "Are you headed out?"

Talia nodded. "I'm going to Riverside this morning. The tox screens on the prior victims weren't a priority, but given Ava's idea about Mrs. Thompson's sedatives, I'm going to run some more tests."

"Sounds good. Keep me posted."

"Will do," Talia said. She nodded at Ava, gathered some supplies, and left.

While August hung his jacket by the space heater to dry, Ava put the empty sheriff's station mug into the messenger bag by her feet.

He turned around and nodded at the table full of evidence. "Settling in?"

She smiled. "I am. Lots to see. Your team's been busy."

"Hasn't done any good," August said as he sank into the chair opposite her. The navy long sleeve hiking shirt, dark field slacks, and hiking boots fit his personality better than the suits. "Anything pop for you?"

"Well, I've seen the files, read the reports, and looked at the photos. But those aren't what's interesting." Ava slid an open map of the area between them. "Tell me if I have this right. It appears the killer has been operating for seven weeks. But no one knew that for sure until two days ago. The first murder was not reported to the CBI because it looked like a home invasion gone wrong."

"Yes. Hold on." August got up, walked to the end of the table and flipped over photos until he found what he was looking for. He returned and handed them to Ava.

The first showed a DMV photo of a man in his thirties, dark curly hair, strong brow, a hint of a smile.

"Victor Suarez," Ava said.

"Someone fatally stabbed him in his cabin in Fern Valley. That's the next town over, about ten minutes out. His house appeared ransacked. His brother found him when he didn't show up for a planned fishing trip."

She set his photo down. "Arrest records showed a history of bar fights and speeding, if I recall correctly."

"You do. People described him as a hothead, in and out of jail for fights, mostly. He lived on the outskirts of town and worked as a mechanic at a place called Spiffy Oil. When we interviewed his boss, he was a fan. He said that other than losing his shirt and caps all the time, Suarez was a great mechanic."

Ava frowned. "Just a regular guy, then."

"The second victim, Tone Marley, couldn't be more different." August tapped the other photo in her hands. It was of a younger black man. Polished, with a great smile in his college ID.

"The student," Ava said, shaking her head. "He was just a kid."

"His death appeared to be an accident at first pass. He was twenty years old and an A student at the community college down in Hemet. No arrests, not even in his juvenile record. Hell, Granger even said the kid was a shoo-in for the junior deputy program they have going on up here. We found no drugs in his system. Marley didn't have a job that would put him in contact with Suarez by chance. Nothing to suggest he even knew who Suarez was, much less had anything to do with him."

"Suarez was stabbed, and Marley was..." Autopsy photos she'd seen earlier flickered behind her eyes. "Discovered to be stabbed later?"

"Correct. A few weeks after Suarez was killed, hikers found Marley at the bottom of a cliff at a state park in Pine Cove. That's another little town near here. He'd been reported missing by his mother a week before, after she came home from work and he wasn't in the house. She called but he didn't answer his phone." August slid a nearby file toward her, opened it, and pointed to another photo. "When they retrieved his body, the injuries supported an initial finding of death by fall. The mother reported her son mentioned working on a project for science class. Granger posited the kid went out to find samples for it and lost his way once night fell. At the time, it looked like an accident, and it happened over a weekend, so they waited three days to do the autopsy."

"Ah man," Ava said. "They had no idea they were working against a clock."

Augusts shook his head. "No one did. The following Monday, the medical examiner here found evidence of stab wounds on the victim's chest and side. She listed his death as a homicide. And it looked like the killer used the same hunting knife that he'd used on Suarez. That's when Granger had started calling the CBI repeatedly. Once we heard they'd found Marley on state land, I came out with Agent Rondeau the next day."

Ava leaned back in the chair. "The victimology is all over the place. One victim was black, the other Hispanic. But... both males. Both found in secluded areas. Both stabbed and possibly robbed." She eyed the towns on the map. Both areas miniscule. "Doesn't seem like enough people in each town to support a sheriff's office and an ME's office. Granger said they all shared him and his deputy?"

"Yes, the cluster of small towns up here, Pine Cove, Fern Valley, and Black Oak all share the station and morgue here in Black Oak. That's why Granger caught both victims."

Ava shook her head. "The authorities are spread thin on a good day."

"So are we." August traced his finger along the map. "This whole area is on the edge of my territory. They don't even have their own hospital up here. Just a medical clinic. We're way out in the boonies." August sat back, exhaling heavily. "As far as evidence, the victims didn't seem connected."

"Other than the knife."

August nodded. "We came out here to work with Granger and,

not a week later, the killer hit the Thompsons. That was two days ago."

"Three weeks between the first victim and the second?"

"As close as their ME could get with the week of decomp and predation on Marley, yeah."

"Then what, seven or eight days between the second victim and the Thompsons?"

August nodded. "He's moving fast."

"Yes but..." Ava shook her head slowly, her eyes going blurry as she looked at August but didn't see him. The recklessness of it piqued her interest. The map of the area she'd studied on the plane slid into focus as the killer's route burned a path along the image in her mind. Ava reached for the pen behind her ear and traced a trail of ink across the paper map laying between them. Over and over, she drew the chaotic route. "Doesn't make sense."

August stopped her hand with his. "What is it?"

"The crime scenes span three towns. But they don't follow any logical path. At least not one I can see. I mean, he doesn't seem to be moving through the area on his way somewhere else like a transient-type killer." She pushed the map toward him, pointing as she spoke. "First, he went north, then southwest, and then east? Why is he zig-zagging?"

"I don't—"

"He wasted time on the road," Ava continued. "Risked getting pulled over, chanced being remembered by locals. That's chaotic behavior."

"But yet he's organized enough to bring his own weapon, control two people, leave almost no trace..."

Ava nodded. "And these aren't big cities, either. Their populations are what, maybe ten thousand at the high end, seventeen hundred on the low? That's nothing."

His confused gaze met hers. "This is significant because..."

"You're a killer who likes to stab people to death. That kind of crime pulls attention. A lot of it. There are already news people gathering at the scenes and outside the station. That's a lot of people looking. Why not hit LA where you can hide in a population of ten million? Instead, you go to a little forest village? It's at least fifty miles from any significant trucking or train routes. What would even draw him here in the first place?"

"Do you think he lives around here?"

Ava shrugged. "He's definitely staying here. Not sure how permanent that situation is though. I wouldn't bet on a rental. It leaves a trail, and people talk. If you're murdering people in a small town, you'd need to lay low. My guess is he's staying in the woods, which means he's an avid hunter and camper. The temperatures alone would take out most people."

August nodded. "He'd be trained in some capacity to be able to hide out for this long."

"Of course that's just conjecture at this point. He could be blending in. Just walking around town plain as day if he's bold enough," Ava said, sketching a pinecone in the margins of the map. Something bugged her about it all, but she couldn't quite see it. "What did the shrinks say? I didn't see the report in Vincent's file."

"She didn't want to taint your first look at the scene."

Ava raised a single brow, waiting.

August sighed and leaned back in the conference chair, swiping through his tablet. "The shrinks say he's older, maybe late thirties. Likely a skilled worker, like a welder or other technical blue-collar jobs."

"Why'd they say that?"

"I don't know, actually. Our Behavioral Science Unit wrote it up after the second victim." August flipped through the file before handing his tablet over.

Ava skimmed the report. Dr. Seth Masters, the head of the CBI's Behavioral Sciences Unit, often worked with PIT. She'd taken his classes at the academy and thought of him as a sort of mentor. Familiar with his methods, she found him spot on most of the time.

"At first, we thought we were looking at a local who went off the rails or a newcomer in town. We checked out every known trouble-maker in all three towns with the sheriff's office. Nothing came of the interviews and alibi checks."

Ava chewed on her pen. "He's killing in three separate towns. Who knows which one he's staying in."

"What we do know is that this killer is organized and meticulous. He leaves no trace behind. We're still processing evidence from the latest scene right now, but he hasn't left us anything to go on so far. No prints, hair, DNA of any kind."

Ava nodded. "He's intelligent. Aware of forensic countermeasures. A planner."

"Yes." August sighed and rubbed his face with both hands, tired. "I'm still wracking my brain to figure out the connection but I'm just not seeing one. It appears to be random."

"It's not random."

August's brows furrowed. "Tell me why you think that."

"I wouldn't pick these people to try and kill for fun. They're not vulnerable enough." She tilted her head from side to side. "I mean, they are on some level, because, you know, they're dead."

August glanced at the door and Ava smiled. Her morbid sensibility always made him nervous in public, but he leaned in.

"Okay, keep talking."

"These recent victims, the Thompsons, were an older couple, but in great shape. The wife was a nurse, the husband a cop."

"He was retired."

"*Just* retired. Not sitting in a rocking chair on the porch, retired. He also wasn't a pencil pusher. He worked the streets as a beat cop and then ran patrols as a sergeant. He could handle himself. The autopsy protocol paints a picture of a big guy. One who isn't afraid to throw a punch if you consider the amount of times his nose was broken. The murder book said there was a gun in the nightstand next to him. Loaded, but never touched. The alarm system wasn't tripped, the daughter stated that he sometimes forgot to set it, but she also said he always did a perimeter check of the doors and windows before turning in every night." Ava showed him a social media account on her phone. "The wife's posts talk about how she did a 5K run last year. That's fit."

August nodded, picking up the glossy photo from the table. "The first victim was a tough guy. Got in a lot of bar fights."

"Also, not an easy mark. And the second victim doesn't make sense to me either."

"The college kid?"

"The six-foot athletic hiker? Yeah." Ava held up the photo of Marley. "He looks like he lifts weights."

"You're saying they appear different on paper."

"Yes. But maybe they do have a connection. It's just a negative. Something they *don't* have in common."

He sat back. "Walk me through that one, Ava."

"When you choose your victims, you pick weak people. Vulnerable people. I wouldn't pick a young fighting age male or a runner. Let alone a street brawler and a retired cop. And why chance facing a gun any cop would surely have on hand?" She navigated her phone to the Census Bureau Stat's page and read the entry. Then she showed it to August. "Black Oak is mostly a retirement community if you look at the numbers. Thousands of rickety old fogies nearby, probably with more money, who would be way easier to murder. They wouldn't even make me break a sweat. Their bones snap like toothpicks."

"Alright, take it down a notch, Jane the Ripper."

"I'm just saying... Why risk attacking these people unless you have to? Better, easier victims lived right next door." She held up the photos of the victims like playing cards. "Don't get me started on cross-race predatory practices."

"That bothered me as well. You think there's a reason beyond victimology for his attacks?"

"Maybe. Could be ideological, but we've not found anything like a manifesto or iconography. No symbols or messages at the scene. No positioning of the victims for display. No indications of sexual assault. Given the locations, I can't say they're crimes of opportunity either. He left the Thompsons' house pristine, stealing only a laptop, but displayed wanton violence with the victims themselves. It's interesting."

"Interesting as in you learned something?"

"I think it's significant." Ava rubbed her eyes, mind racing. The rush of the chase humming in her head. She glanced at the maps again, the crime scene notes from the first responders, the testimonies of witnesses—until they filled her mind. They whirled around each other, still so nebulous in their significance. "I just don't know why yet. For now, I'm waiting for the medical examiner's office to open."

August checked his watch. "You should wait for Dr. Clay to get back to go over the bodies."

"I want to speak with the local doctor first. She saw the first two victims."

He made a face. "I don't know if she'll be all that helpful."

"Because...?"

"When the Thompsons were found, we didn't call Dr. Wren. She's the ME for these towns. We had Dr. Clay do the autopsies overnight." He shrugged. "I think it offended her."

"And rightly so."

"We cleared things with her boss."

"You cut her out of the investigation completely? As in bodies arrived at her morgue, with our forensic pathologist in tow, and you didn't give her a heads up? Plus, you called her boss and basically said she's not good enough?"

"She missed stab wounds, Ava. What did you want me to do?"

"Doesn't matter. You know I always talk to everyone."

"Do what you have to do but do it fast. We need a clearer picture of him before he strikes again. People are terrified." August stood and she looked up at him. He shoved his hands in the pockets of his slacks and tried for a reassuring smile. "No pressure or anything."

FOUR

The ME's office, located in the small medical center, sat a few blocks away from the station. Akin to a small hospital, it handled emergencies, minor surgery, and other light medical care. August needed to interview the daughter of the most recent victims, Lucy Thompson, but her doctor seemed resistant to letting her speak with the CBI so soon after her breakdown. August headed over there to try to smooth things over, so Ava decided to walk.

Early morning mist hovered over the worn asphalt road, the moisture sticking to weathered wooden fences and metal signs as she strolled. Flurries drifted around her, disappearing before they hit the ground. Overhead, power lines sizzled in the misty air. Quaintly painted shops with red and blue roofs butted up against Black Oak's main road. Old-timey street lamps lined the road with a soft orange glow that seemed to warm the chilly streets. Somewhere, the scent of cinnamon floated in the air. A beautiful retreat... except for the killer running loose. The woods encroached on the edges of the sidewalk in places. The tree line thick enough to shroud the dark forest beyond. A crack of twigs from within pulled Ava's gaze, and then a flurry of birds scattered noisily into the sky. The hair on her arms rose as she scanned the foliage. Nothing. Pulling out her phone, she continued past the stand of trees.

Ava dialed a number from memory and was picked up after one ring.

"Well, where have you been?" An amused voice drawled. Smooth and low, the Tennessee accent brought a smile to her face. "How can I serve lady justice?"

"Hey, Denny. I need a data scrape on some names."

"When?"

"Yesterday." Ava gave him the names of the victims so far. "Same parameters as normal. Legally available information only. Nothing black hat."

"No funny business. I know the drill," he said with a chuckle. "You into something deep?"

"A killer. So, I need that information stat."

"Copy that," Denny said, and was gone.

Ava found the medical clinic a few minutes later, a two-story boxy building clad in dark wood siding and glass. She dug her credentials out of her bag and showed the intake nurse at the front counter. She also asked for directions and followed them to the far side of the first floor to the morgue. It was still closed when she got there, so Ava waited against the morgue's double doors and checked her watch again. Only eight in the morning, but after hours of going over the physical evidence it felt like midnight. She turned toward the sound of clicking heels on the linoleum.

"Dr. Wren?"

The medical examiner, a lanky woman with a blonde pixie haircut, nose red from the cold, hesitated with a wary look. "Yes?"

"I'm Special Agent Cortes with the CBI," Ava flashed her badge. "I'm not a grieving next of kin or a reporter, I promise."

"That's great, but I don't know how I can help." Wren shrugged, her walk stiff as she led them into the morgue. The lights flashed on automatically. She set her bag down on the workstation against the wall then turned, hand on her hip. "I'm sure you guys got the post-mortem report from your ME."

"I'm not interested in a report." Ava held up the file in her hand. "I'm sure our doctor did a bang-up job, but sometimes perceptions can be... blunted by distance and timing. You were at the first two crime scenes. You handled the bodies. Which is why I had a few questions, if you don't mind."

Wren smiled ruefully. "Me? I'm not sure what I could add that a *federal* ME didn't already include."

"Plenty. Your first impressions."

"Are you serious?"

Ava shrugged. "Things sometimes don't have a place on official reports. Doesn't mean they aren't important. I really just hoped to get another opinion on the Thompsons' injuries."

"I didn't do their autopsies."

"But they were here, in your morgue. You must have looked at the bodies before our forensic pathologist showed up. They were fellow Black Oak residents. I would've at least taken a peek."

Wren hesitated, her lips pressed into a straight line. "What if I did? Your team has made it very clear they don't need my help. They said I missed the knife wounds but the decomp on the Marley boy was—"

"Doctor, you have the ruffled bearing of someone who was unfairly pushed off their own turf."

"I beg your pardon?"

"And it's completely justified. You assessed Tone Marley's body in the field. He looked mangled. You gave a professional opinion that changed after the autopsy. There's no shame there, but here you are all aggravated like I called you a quack or something."

"Your fellow agents might as well have."

Ava tilted her head at Wren's insulted expression. "What if *our* doctor missed something? Two more people died after we took the case out of your hands." Wren looked uncertain so Ava pushed. "Five minutes. Let me pick your brain. Off the record."

Wren sighed. "I guess I don't have anything on the books this morning." She nodded toward the cooling beds on the far wall. "Did you want to see the bodies?"

"Oh, please, no. I'll just go by the pictures."

"Okay..." A look of confusion crossed Wren's face. "My office then?"

"Perfect." They skirted the metal tables and cooling drawers on their way to the one room office in the back. Mounted pictures of Wren with her family showed two equally blonde kids, and a handsome, if not a bit chubby, husband. Shelves behind a gray metal desk held more pictures of family occasions, school portraits, and a tropical vacation with the husband in an eye searing Hawaiian print shirt. Ava motioned toward the photos. "You like to sail?"

Wren looked at the picture of her family on the bow of a boat with fishing poles in hand. "No, we rented it last summer. It was kind of nice, you know, to see how the other half lives for a few days."

Ava smiled, sizing up Wren. A proud mother. A loving wife. "So, this killer, are you worried about him?"

"I... what?" Wren's brows furrowed. "That's your question?"

"Who would know better than you? You were one of the few people at the first two scenes. You handled the bodies initially. You also aren't law enforcement. You're a scientist, a doctor. I already read our report. It's all the technical details. I want to know your gut reaction."

"My gut, huh? I'm a general practitioner. I got the ME job here through an election. My experience is in family medicine—in a tiny town. I mean, I've seen stabbings before, but this killer is..." She shook her head. "I don't even know where to start."

"You saw the Thompsons' bodies?"

Wren crossed her arms over her chest. "I did. Your medical examiner did the autopsies, but I was in the room."

"Did you read the after report?"

"Yes."

Sensing hesitation, Ava said, "How about this. I bounce my thoughts off of you and you tell me what you think?"

"I'll try my best."

Ava paced back and forth in front of the desk, collecting her thoughts.

"Okay, let's start with the Thompsons. I look at the damage to the male victim's body and initially think the attacker was full of rage. But the more I think about it, the more it doesn't seem quite right. The number of stab wounds, there's at least seventeen on Mr. Thompson. His blood was thrown all over that room. Sprayed across the ceiling, the walls, on the carpet... But only one strike to the wife? She was stabbed only once, in the heart. That's a quick death, efficient. No rage at all. Does this match what you found with the first and second victims?"

"Not really. Mr. Suarez died of exsanguination from the wounds to his body, but he didn't look... beaten."

"And the Marley kid?"

"Again, I couldn't tell because falling off a cliff causes a lot of damage, but he had two stab wounds. One to his liver and one to his chest."

"Just like the first victim," Ava said mostly to herself. "Suarez and Marley. Both with two wounds each."

"Yes, the liver and then the heart, which was the killing blow. Pretty efficient really."

"Why is that?"

"Both wounds would have killed them, but one would've taken longer."

Ava stilled. "Wait, they were going to die either way?"

"I mean, if they didn't get medical help and surgery right away, yes. Both liver wounds were lethal in terms of blood loss."

"Okay, but then the killer attacks the Thompsons in a completely different way."

Wren shook her head. "I think they were pretty similar, actually."

"What do you mean? What's efficient about almost twenty strikes at Mr. Thompson? The wounds are all over the place. His chest, neck, stomach... even his arm. This is anger.”

“You’re right. Never mind.” Wren pressed her lips into a thin line.

“I’m sorry, Dr. Wren. Argument sometimes helps to solidify facts in my head.”

“The Socratic Method.” Wren nodded and settled back into her chair, her shoulders dropping. “We learned it in medical school.”

“Exactly. I’m open to any thoughts you might have. They won’t make it into any report, so nothing you say will blow back on you, right or wrong. I just need a fresh perspective, and these technical terms and sterile observations are not what will help me.”

“Okay.”

“You said something about the wounds before. They struck you as efficient?”

“Sort of. I mean, Mr. Thompson had the same liver and heart wounds the other victims had. The outcome would have been the same, but...” She shook her head. “I’m veering into supposition and theory. Not my area.”

“Look, I asked if this guy worried you because I know with a family out here, you’d be thinking about this case constantly. Has anything come to mind?”

Wren bit her lip, gaze traveling Ava’s face, and then put her hands up in surrender. “Fine. But I have nothing to back it up. It’s just an errant thought.”

“So, share it.” Ava shrugged. “Worst I could do is think it’s dumb.”

Wren chuckled. “Okay, well, Thompson’s brachial artery, the one in his right arm was severed. He should have bled out in less than a minute, but he didn’t. There was clotting along the wound track. Which isn’t strange in and of itself. Blood thickens with adrenaline and the body’s fight or flight reaction, which can cause it to clot faster. The body battles to survive and sometimes the wounds just overwhelm it. What was strange was the indentation just above the wound."

"Where?" Ava dug the photos of Thompson's wounds out of the file she'd brought, and Wren stood, walking around to her side of the desk.

"Right here, it's a straight-line bruise, something he'd get if he was flailing around and his arm hit the edge of the night table."

"That's what our ME put," Ava said. "But you think different?"

"No, that *is* the logical conclusion. My professional opinion is in line with your CBI doctor. I stand by what the report says."

"But...?"

Wren hesitated, then walked back over to her chair and slumped down. "I got my medical degree from the military ten years ago. I served in the field for a few months and out there, you use drastic measures to save lives."

Ava sat in the chair with her hands on her lap, waiting.

"A few weeks before I came back, there was an explosion. An IED took out a transport vehicle and shredded the guys inside. One kid, he was hit in the leg, the femoral artery, and had tried to stop the bleeding. It didn't work. He died. But he'd had the same straight-line mark above his wound as Thompson. It was from the belt he'd used as a tourniquet." Wren rubbed her eyes as if trying to wipe the memory away. She leaned back, opened a drawer in the desk, and pulled out a length of medical tubing. She wrapped it around her bicep just above the crook of the elbow. "Like this. The mark on Thompson does indicate something with an edge, like a nightstand, as your ME asserts. But it's possible it could be from something else."

Ava blew out a breath. "A tourniquet?"

"See what I mean?" Wren threw her hands up. "If I hadn't seen it with my own eyes before, I'd think I was reaching too. Because why would the victim use a tourniquet on his arm if his entire body is riddled with holes, right? The straight line could lend itself to being a belt, but where would Mr. Thompson get the belt if he was in his pajamas? Why not reach for the phone to call 911 instead?" Wren shrugged. "It doesn't make sense, doesn't fit the scene, but boy, that image of the kid's leg keeps popping into my head."

Ava looked through the photos. There wasn't one specifically taken of Thompson's arm. "Wouldn't the wound go all the way around?"

"It would, but sometimes those bruises don't show up like they would if his heart was still pumping."

"How would I see if it's there?"

"Alternative lighting. Maybe reflective UV photos." Wren shook her head. "Like I said. I have no proof."

"You thought the wounds on Mr. Thompson were similar to the other victims despite the vastly different number. Why?"

"Well, if you wanted to stab someone a bunch of times without killing them, then this would be the way. Most of the wounds weren't immediately fatal. Eventually, yes, but not like a severed artery would be."

"So, like the first two victims, a slow death or a quick one."

"Yes, and to be clear, no tourniquet or belts were found near the body," Wren said with a grimace. She set the tubing down on the desk. "It's just weird that the one fatal injury to the wife is dead on with no hesitation, but the man sustained almost twenty wounds only to die of a final one to his heart. It's almost as if the killer dispatched the woman right away and then toyed with the man, just torturing him before ending it."

Ava sat back in the chair, her brows furrowed. "I think that's probably close to what happened that night."

"Why?"

"That's the million-dollar question, isn't it?" Ava bit her inner cheek, thinking. "I'm also wondering if there were any signs of binding on Mr. Thompson's wrists. I didn't see any in the CBI autopsy photos. If I go out and look at the body, will I see anything?"

"We can check if any markings have emerged over time, but you really need photos taken with reflective UV."

"Can you do that? If I had the equipment sent over?"

"I can ask my colleague in Hemet to come up with his kit."

"You don't have to—"

"If this helps, then I'll know I did everything I could to stop this killer, regardless of my delay to declare Tone Marley's death a homicide. If there are markings, I'll find them."

Redemption. One of the hardest things to achieve, especially in one's own mind. Ava nodded, pulling the length of tubing toward her.

"Let's do that then." She stood. "Thank you for speaking with me. I appreciate your insight."

"Listen, I have no proof of the tourniquet thing." Her face pulled into a sad smile. "I was just speculating, but I sure appreciate you asking. Maybe I'll be able to sleep now."

"I hope so," Ava said and left with a picture of a young, dying soldier in her mind. Once outside the medical clinic, Ava dialed August's number, biting her thumb nail as she waited through the rings. It went to voicemail. "I just got done with the ME, and now I *really* need to know what was on the laptop stolen from the Thompsons. Also, I'm right. The killer was watching them."

FIVE

Delano Kester sat on the bar stool, his calloused hand encircling the bottom of his beer bottle. He slid it back and forth over the puddle of condensation, ignoring the clack of pool balls and the twangy music overhead while he watched the news.

Video of a woman standing beneath police floodlights played behind a platinum-haired reporter as she spoke in front of the sheriff's office in Black Oak.

"Members of the Priority Investigations Team, the CBI task force behind the apprehension of the Ghost Town Killer two years ago, arrived at the scene of the grisly double murder that shook the small mountain town of Black Oak earlier this week." The television cut to the reporter. Her movie-star face took on a fake sorrowful expression. "Rumors continue to swirl that the CBI was called in to assist with the murders due to a possible connection to others in the area, adding more fuel to the panic surrounding the town as details of the attack continue to emerge..."

Delano ignored the reporter, gaze fixed on a woman in the video playing silently during the broadcast. Long dark hair, small stature. The news camera zoomed in through the trees and showed her speaking sternly to one of the deputies near the cordoned off area, who then let her past. What they didn't see was how she'd behaved in the room with all that blood. How it hadn't seemed to affect her like the others. She didn't puke like the deputy who'd arrived first on the scene or rush out for fresh air. Through his scope he'd seen her stand in the center of that carnage, her gaze wandering the walls like she could see him in all that blood.

"The Ghost Town Killer, huh?" He tossed some stale mini pretzels in his mouth from the communal bowl on the bar, thinking. She stood out from the other CBI agents. He'd seen them huddled together in front of the sheriff's station. All suits and sunglasses. As if they would survive out in the woods for more than twenty-four hours. But this new chick... She wore civvies and looked like someone's hot mom.

He took a swig of his beer, finishing it, and then slid off his stool. Delano passed people who were already dazed despite the morning hour. They ignored him as he exited the dive bar. The cloudy sky cast a hazy light to the day, and he took a deep breath of the frigid air. It smelled like diesel and dog crap. Evening would bring a lot of traffic going up the mountain. Families looking to sled down the fresh snow in the morning. He intended to slip back into town with that rush hour crowd, so he had plenty of time to kill until then. Walking out to the parking lot, his eyes danced along the foot traffic. Hemet was buzzing already. He climbed into the truck he'd stolen and pulled a U-turn across traffic. A soccer mom in an SUV honked and yelled something out of her window. He flipped her off as he sped ahead. Delano squirmed in his seat, trying to ease the discomfort at his side he could never quite escape. The beer would help, he told himself.

The new agent bothered him. He hadn't seen her before. She didn't look like them, act like them. Hell, he'd already seen her wandering around in the early hours of the morning by herself. No telling what could happen to a person alone like that. Still, in his experience, when someone gets called in after the initial team, they're usually the big guns. If that was true, then the CBI was desperate. Tiny thing like that was probably a shrink or something anyway. Maybe he'd pay her a visit. See what she thinks she knows about him.

Delano smirked. He'd panicked when they'd found the kid, but this could work in his favor. He could send them chasing their tails if he wanted to. Something to think about.

He pulled into the back parking lot of a small hardware store. The owner, a guy who looked older than dirt, couldn't see shit. Hopping down from the truck, Delano pulled a list of supplies from his pocket. Time to get back to work.

SIX

Ava strolled the downtown area after her meeting with Dr. Wren, looking for a place to eat. She needed to find a hub. Most places, especially small towns, had areas where certain groups gathered. The stay-at-home moms, car dudes, old ladies who liked to gossip, professionals, retirees. Even people who hated people usually ended up somewhere. There was always a hub, and it was typically a place to eat breakfast. She passed a ceramic studio with tinkling mobiles hanging from the ceiling, a souvenir shop with sweatshirts flapping in the chilled breeze, and a small market at the end of the street. Baskets of fruit and flowers sat outside the bustling store. Colorful flags on the street lamps honored those serving in the military, and the remnants of Valentine's Day decorations clung to the store windows. It felt too quaint to hide such horror beneath the surface.

Still thinking about the young soldier and the tourniquet, Ava jumped when a loud crack sounded behind her. A man across the street picked up the A-frame sign he'd dropped in front of a café. The corner of Ava's mouth lifted as she noticed the decent crowd milling around just outside the establishment.

The Riot Brewing Café's sign, a sleepy-looking owl wearing combat boots and holding a steaming mug of coffee, sported the same black and yellow as the umbrellas that covered the metal bistro tables and chairs peppering the front sidewalk. People wrapped in thick coats and wearing beanies ate pancakes, cinnamon rolls, and other breakfast goodies. Steam rose off the plates into the chilly air, mixed with the scent of excellent coffee. She went inside and grinned from ear to ear. Punk band posters, a graffiti mural depicting a mohawk-wearing guitarist leaping into a sea of jagged neon decorated the far wall. People sat inside eating and talking over the alternative music playing in the background.

"What can I get you?" the cashier asked. Her name tag read Maisy. Curvy build, bright blue eyes, a wad of jet-black hair with a stripe of purple sat in a loose bun atop her head. Extremely long fake lashes and a lip ring went great with the totally black waitress uniform. She smiled at Ava with dark purple lips.

Ava smiled back and squinted at the chalkboard menu behind Maisy. "What do the locals like?"

"We have the Morning Maverick that's really popular. It's a full, lumberjack style breakfast. Two of everything. Hot cakes, sausage, eggs..."

"I'm sold. Let me get that." Ava deliberately spilled a few of her CBI business cards onto the counter while taking out her money. Maisy's eyes widened, but she said nothing. Ava scooped them back up without a word.

"It'll be a few minutes," Maisy said, handing back her change. "I'll call your name..."

"Oh, it's Ava."

"Are you here with anyone else?" Maisy asked, failing to hide her curiosity.

"Just me for the moment."

Maisy nodded and Ava took a turn around the café while she waited. A bulletin board sat against the far wall between two bookcases. She checked it out, standing close enough to hear a few of the hushed conversations. Everything from a storm brewing to someone taking their dog to the vet and complaining about the prices. The bulletin board itself held advertisements for tree removal services, horse boarding, babysitting, walking groups, and book club invites. Ava tore a few of them from the cork, pocketing them. She spotted a pen lying on the shelf and used it to twist her hair up, then moved on to the far bookcase. The volumes of history and art and music looked interesting, and Ava grabbed one on the punk artist, Jamie Reid, leafing through the vibrant images while she slowly strode along the wall of the bustling café. People seemed more morbidly curious instead of freaked out, as August had asserted. Whispers of a serial killer floated to her as she feigned interest in the variety of sugar offerings at the condiment bar. She grabbed a few napkins, a butter pat, and a wooden stirrer, listening.

I heard the CBI is going door to door to find this maniac... I heard the Thompsons were butchered... Why hasn't there been any kind of press conference... Is the killer still here in Black Oak?

The usual concern and curiosity of a shocked public. The fact that the CBI joined the investigation sent a tremor of worry throughout the community according to what Ava heard. Out of the corner of her eye, Ava saw Maisy huddled with one of the waitresses at the front counter, both glancing at Ava surreptitiously.

Here we go, Ava thought.

The other waitress's fire-engine red bob matched her lipstick, and she glanced at Ava while hurrying over to a table where a young couple sat. All three of them watched Ava walk to an empty half-booth near the window and settle in. She ignored them and fiddled with her utensils, waiting. The waitress with the red bob then scurried to another booth at the far end of the café filled with older couples. One of them, a woman with short, jet-black hair, eased out of the far booth, grabbed Ava's order from the counter, and made a beeline for her table. She wore no uniform but must have been the one in charge because most of the conversations trailed off as the patrons watched her approach.

She wore a black band T-shirt of the Smiths with green and black plaid pants. Both arms covered in tattoos depicting botanical and animal life. Eyebrow piercing. Older, maybe late forties with laugh lines that crinkled at the edges of her eyes as she smiled.

Setting Ava's coffee mug and plate down she said, "I heard you were with the CBI."

"Direct, I like it," Ava said with a smile. The bacon smelled divine, and she took a bite of one of the strips. "Are you the owner... Miss...?"

"Phillips, Velma Phillips. My husband Cole and I own the café," she said and nodded to the seat opposite Ava. "Mind if we join you for a second?"

"Your joint," she said with a shrug. "I'm Ava."

Velma glanced over her shoulder and waved over the man she'd been sitting next to. He made his way to the table. Deep green sweater frayed at the cuffs, long espresso hair going gray at the temples, belt chain dangling against his faded black jeans. He wore black rimmed glasses and smiled when he walked over. Despite the snake tattooed on his neck, he gave off a friendly vibe.

"Cole, this is Ava," Velma said quietly. "She's with the CBI."

He eased into the booth next to his wife with an awkward smile "Sorry to disturb your meal, but everyone here is losing their minds wanting to talk to you."

"No worries. What's on your mind?"

Velma glanced at Cole and then said, "Listen, Ava, we were all wondering what's going on. Are you really one of the agents investigating the Thompson murders?"

"I'm more of a helper, really." Ava sipped her coffee, and the dark roast felt like a caffeinated punch to the face. Perfect. "But yes, the CBI is assisting Sheriff Granger with the investigation."

Velma's shoulders relaxed. As if the idea of speaking with a member of the staff wasn't as intimidating as speaking to a full-fledged agent of the CBI.

"We all feel so bad for Lucy," Velma said. "Finding her parents like that must've been awful. Is she okay?"

Ava nodded as she poured maple syrup over her entire plate, eggs and all. "She's safe. They have her under a doctor's care."

Cole leaned in, his voice low. "Do you have any idea who did this?"

Ava tilted her head, considering the obvious concern on their faces. "Did you know the Thompsons?"

Cole nodded. "Since Jack retired. Stephanie was planning on doing the same next year."

"And Lucy?" Ava asked with another sip of coffee.

He looked at Velma, who answered, "She was marrying some boy she met at college. They live up in Irvine, but the wedding was supposed to be down in Carlsbad. On the beach, I think."

"Oh, how lovely. Were you guys invited?"

Velma shook her head. "Nah, we didn't know them *that* well, but several families around town were going. Mostly friends of Lucy and Stephanie... I mean, Mrs. Thompson. Maybe some of Mr. Thompson's old friends from the Temecula police department."

An older guy who could've been on the cover of a senior hunting magazine, sat in the next booth over and peered over Velma and Cole's seat before adding, "They brought Lucy up for the holidays. Jack and Stephanie moved up to Black Oak permanently only a couple of years ago. Before then, they lived down in the valley."

Velma's eyes widened. "Oh, my gosh... how is Deputy Chutney handling things?"

Ava sat up straight. "Chutney?"

"Yeah, he and Lucy dated for a year or so before she met her fiancé."

"Really?" Funny she hadn't heard that from Granger.

Cole nodded. "Yeah, about five years ago now. She was working in

Irvine by then. She'd gone to court reporting school or something like that. I think it was the distance that did them in. They never seemed to be fighting anyway." Cole looked at Velma, worried. "He must be torn up."

"He's doing his job like a pro," Ava said, digging into her pancakes. "So, what are people saying about all this?"

"Pardon?" Cole asked.

"Scuttlebutt... rumors... speculation." Ava finished off a piece of syrup drenched bacon. "What's the buzz around town?"

"Uh... fear," Velma said. "People are afraid to go out at night."

"That's good, actually." Ava mopped up more syrup with a bite of eggs.

"Really?" Velma's eye grew wide.

"Well, yeah," Ava nodded. "Until the CBI finds the killer, caution is absolutely a good idea."

"Do you have any suspects?" Cole pressed.

"Do you?"

"I—what?" Cole shook his head. "Shouldn't the CBI?"

"You live here, Cole," Ava said as she set her utensils down. She leaned back, full. "Anyone you think might be good for it?"

His brows furrowed. "You want me to give the authorities some names of my fellow Black Oak residents?"

"I'm asking if anyone popped into your head when you heard what happened," Ava said with a smirk. "I'm not the man, Cole. We're here to help."

"Calm down, honey," Velma said and patted his arm. To Ava she said, "I mean, surely no one in Black Oak could do something like that."

"Really? No one?" Ava smiled. "You must live in a utopia."

"I don't know..." Velma looked around the café. A woman seated at the counter mouthed something. Velma sighed and said, "There's a cabin in the woods out by Beggar's Lake. It looks like a group of guys. Not exactly a gang, but lots of partying and loud music. They ride their motorcycles at all hours. It's bad for the cabin rentals around there. People want peace and quiet, not a motorcycle gang next door."

Ava nodded, pulling the pen from her hair to write down notes on her paper placemat as they spoke. People liked to see that, it made them add more. They sometimes even checked spelling on names and streets, which Ava found helpful. The trick was not to seem like she was taking notes about the speaker themselves and definitely not on an official-looking police notebook.

She looked up and smiled. "Any idea who lives in the party house?"

"We don't know," Cole said. "It's part of a clutch of cabins owned by a rental company. They don't seem to care about the complaints we've emailed. No one wants to go and talk with them, but sometimes we see them in town. Mostly at the market buying beer."

"What did Sheriff Granger say?"

"Well, nothing really. He said he was going to give them a noise disturbance ticket or something like that," said the senior hunter. "Useless. They don't cause trouble in town so, no one can do anything."

"When did you see them at the market?" Ava asked Cole.

"I don't remember."

"When do you usually go to the market? Is it sporadic, daily, Fridays?"

"Fridays," Velma said. "We always do a big meal for movie night."

Cole nodded. "Must be Friday, then."

"Anyone else?" Ava asked, her peripheral registering multiple faces turned her way.

"I mean, Morris Walton could," an old guy in a booth said.

Velma's eyes widened. "Oh my gosh, yes. Remember Diane's car?"

"Oh, come on," Maisy said with a wave of her hand as she walked up to the table to refill Ava's coffee mug. "Old man Walton can barely get around now without his cane."

"What about the car?" Ava asked.

"He took a butcher knife to the rag top and the hood," Velma said. "They had to total it."

"And Colleen Baker," a woman said from a table of four. Twenties, ponytail, running clothes. "She nearly shot somebody's head off last summer."

Ava jotted down the name. "Whose head?"

"Some drifters she said kept walking through her field."

"They weren't drifters," the old guy in the booth shot back. "They were Bill's kids, they were doing some sort of Eagle Scout project..."

Once they got started, the café's customers had no issues lobbing out names and suspicions, even an alien conspiracy. The forensic tents had brought up questions about another plague. And Granger's silence had suggested something far worse than what they'd been told. Ava wrote it all down, taking in names as they spoke to one another. Just normal folk jumping at shadows until someone said the magic words. Rio Suarez. The first victim.

Ava's gaze snapped up. "What's this about—you said Suarez?"

A middle-aged man stood next to a nearby table, mug in hand, wearing a puffy blue vest and fishing cap. He looked at her with intelligent brown eyes.

"There was another murder before the Thompsons'," he said. "A resident named Rio Suarez. He used to hang out with the Milford boys, remember? I heard he was stabbed too."

"Yeah, Doc, but that guy was always fighting with people," someone said from the back.

Ava didn't catch who but let it go. She looked at the puffy vest guy and wondered what kind of doctor he was. "What makes you think they're related?"

"We get fist fights here, maybe someone brandishes a gun before peeling out of the bar parking lot, jackassery at best," he said. "This is different."

"I heard they'd been stabbed multiple times," Velma said. "Is that true?

Ava nodded.

"That there is homicidal rage if you ask me," Maisy said, her voice rising as she poured coffee for another table.

"Okay, enough with your true crime ghoulishness," Cole said, irritated. "Have some respect for the dead—"

"It's literally *true* crime. As in stuff like that happens," Maisy shot back, gesturing with the coffee pot. She looked at Ava. "I heard they were stabbed like a hundred times. The killer is a deranged maniac, right?"

The entire café turned in their seats, watching.

"No one was stabbed a hundred times," Ava said. Though seventeen wasn't any better, she thought. "Look, usually the citizens of the town have some ideas as to where the danger might be coming from. Sheriff Granger said plenty of people who don't live here move through Black Oak on a daily basis. That's a lot of strangers. It might not be a bad idea to look out for people who seem out of place." She paused for effect. "On the other hand, who would know the Thompsons were even out there? Their property isn't in town. Not along a popular road. Hidden by trees. Could a tourist accidentally happen on the residence... sure." Ava finished off her coffee. "But how likely is that?"

Murmurs moved through the café, a well of anxiety opening up.

Velma drummed her black painted fingernails on the table, her gaze out the window. "It has to be one of us, then. Who else would even know to go and look for the Thompsons' house way out there?"

Ava shrugged, wiping her mouth. "Private road. No lights. I see what you mean."

"So, was it someone the Thompsons knew?" Maisy asked.

"That's what we're here to find out." Ava's phone dinged, and a message from August popped up on her screen.

AUGUST

Where are you? We're cleared to speak with Lucy.

She typed out her location, rose from the booth, and folded her placemat. Stuffing it in the leather notebook in her purse, she pulled out a few business cards and set them on the table. "If you guys think of anything else you want passed on... give me a call."

When Ava got to the door, Velma asked. "What are we supposed to do until you catch this guy?"

Ava turned to the concerned faces watching her and said, "Watch out for each other."

SEVEN

Lucy Thompson had a breakdown the night she'd discovered her parents. Understandable, but given the town's size, inconvenient for first responders. The medical clinic in Black Oak didn't have a psych ward and there were no beds available at the hospital in Hemet, so the Thompsons' family doctor had improvised. He'd admitted her to Shady Acres Recovery Center, a rehabilitation center which catered to patients with substance abuse issues, brain injuries, and other conditions that required a safe, peaceful environment with round-the-clock mental health care. Nestled in the woods, it provided seclusion and privacy. Ava had looked up the website, surprised to read rumors claiming sightings of troubled celebrities strolling the grounds.

"Looks expensive," Ava said as they took a meandering path made of paving stones to a building that reminded her of a turn of the century mansion. Made of timber and river rock, the patient rooms offered terraces that overlooked the grounds and a winding stream. A pristine, manicured commune with nature. She'd read on the website that at one time, Shady Acres had served as a hunting lodge for the Victorian upper crust.

"It is. Rondeau checked it out." August cracked his fingers as they strode, his go-to tension release. "The fiancé wanted to move her closer to their home in Irvine, but the doctor didn't think that would be wise given her state of mind."

"What's the deal with Agent Rondeau?" Ava asked.

"He's a genius when it comes to anything tech. He grew up in the rough country of West Virginia. Got into tech in high school. Then in the military, Rondeau worked with high value target security, so he knows all about the latest ways people try to kill each other," August said. "He's a smart guy. Tough."

"Good to know," Ava said.

Birds chirped in the towering trees, white wrought iron furniture arranged in conversation circles under large oaks, trimmed hedges, the cool air of late winter held a crispness to it that stung Ava's cheeks and made her nose run. They checked in at the front desk, and the nurse told them they were waiting for Lucy's family doctor to arrive from the town further down the mountain, Idyllwild.

Luxurious, tasteful furnishings gave the waiting area a spa-like atmosphere. Original paintings and peaceful music encouraged calm. The interior of the facility appeared restored to its former glory with soft velvet and wood chairs and settees.

Despite the decor, after thirty minutes of waiting, Ava paced in front of the seats. "If this guy doesn't get here soon, I'm going to lose it myself."

"I had to talk him into letting us speak with her," August said, glancing at the nurse behind the counter. "Please don't piss off the staff. They're already doing us a favor by letting us see her."

She sank back into the chair next to him. "Who's paying for this luxury stay, by the way?"

"Her doctor arranged it," August said, seemingly calm except for chewing on his gum like it had done him wrong. He read her notes on the paper placemat from the café, squinting needlessly, in her opinion.

"What's wrong with your face?"

"Your handwriting looks like an EKG." He pointed to something on the paper. "Does that say aliens?"

"Just... let me give you the run down." The small table between them sat littered with all the mini origami figures Ava had made out of pages from a nearby fashion magazine. A nervous habit she'd picked up in college to keep herself focused. The valleys and grooves of the paper, the edges and flat surfaces, points and curves, all combined to make something unexpected. She folded another shape while recounting what she'd learned at the café. Names, conspiracies, vibes. Possible suspects. Unsupported suspicions.

"Wow. They're all over the place," he said, folding the placemat and handing it back to her. "I'll ask Granger about the party house. We'll find out who's living out there and run their names."

She dug in her bag for her notebook, slid the placemat between some pages, and dropped it back into the jumbled depths. "They're spooked. Either way, I got a lot of names and accusations. Mostly local bickering. We can check them against what the canvass provided. I haven't read the notes on local interviews from Granger's deputies."

"I have them. Gale made copies."

"You're not doing the CBI any favors with those forensic tents by the way. They're freaking the town out. They think you're hiding an Ebola outbreak or something."

He smiled at that. Ava placed a fox made out of a perfume ad on his leg. It slipped, but he caught it. "Any theories after your town hall at the café?"

"The citizens of Black Oak offered some interesting connections but nothing solid. It's weird though..."

"Weird how?"

"I'm getting the feeling we're not looking in the right place."

"You mean the town?"

"Maybe. Do you think it's possible to check the trail cams around the Thompsons' home?"

"You think the killer is camping?"

Ava shrugged. "Isn't that what other hunters do? Stay close to their prey?"

He looked at her for a beat, then said, "I'll ask Granger about it. You don't have to register cameras on your own property, but municipal land cameras should have a record of installation."

Checking her watch, Ava sighed. "We're playing catch up with this guy and they're wasting hours."

"The doctor has other patients besides Lucy Thompson." August muttered as he unfolded the origami fox, frowning as he tried to put it back together. "He'll be here soon."

"Meanwhile, the killer is out there, plotting." Ava stopped folding for a moment, thinking. "We need to make him feel pressure. Like we're snapping at his heels."

"Problem is, we're not." He put the paper fox down, but it fell over. "Do you really believe he's watching us?"

"I would. This place is a fishbowl. Everyone knows we're here and they're all talking about it. Specifics of the case are going to get out."

He turned in his seat. "Then you better be more careful. No more strolls in the dead of night without a partner. You keep saying the word 'hunted' and that's not sitting right with my gut."

"I'm a black belt in karate and armed," Ava countered.

"Don't give me a hard time. The partner thing goes for everyone. You, me, Dr. Clay, and Agent Rondeau. We follow protocol."

His eye quivered ever so slightly at the corner. Ava put her hands up in surrender. "Fine."

"Listen, the stuff from the café is good. You've been here less than twenty-four hours, and the town's people already talked to you more than the rest of us combined. I appreciate it."

"That's because I lied through my teeth about who I was," Ava said. "Don't paint me as noble."

August grinned. "Did you say you were a helper again?"

"I did. No one seems to know anything except for this one guy they called Doc. I think he's a vet though, he was wearing rubber boots and looked tan. Lots of horses and farm animals up here."

"I'll ask Granger who he is." August tapped on his tablet. "What did he say?"

"He connected Suarez's death with the Thompsons'. They're starting to say things like 'homicidal maniac'. I tried to brush it off, but the events speak for themselves. There is in fact a killer running around in the dark killing people they know."

"You think we should talk with the vet?"

"It wouldn't hurt, but I think he's just smart and medically trained. He might've heard about the wounds and figured it out. Either way, people will start to panic soon."

August leaned back, chewing on his gum even harder. "That's the last thing we need."

"If it gets out that we think Suarez and Marley's deaths are connected to the Thompsons' it might make the killer go to ground. While also causing said panic."

"Yes, serial killers tend to do that," August nodded. He opened his mouth to say more but an older, flustered-looking man in a brown suit pushed through the lobby doors from outside. He took a look at them and extended his hand.

"I'm Dr. Craig, the Thompson family's—Lucy Thompson's doctor. Sorry for the wait. I was checking on a patient down in Idyll-wild." Ava noticed his silver hair, damp with the flurries falling outside. Dark circles under his eyes. "Shall we?"

"Are you transferring Ms. Thompson to a hospital when a bed becomes available?" Ava asked.

"I don't think I'll need to. She's doing so well that I don't imagine her staying more than a few days total. I've had patients stay here for various reasons. I believe this is the best environment for her right now," Dr. Craig assured them.

He led them into the facility, to a grand staircase and up to the second floor. Portraits along the walls of haughty-looking strangers watched them as they strolled the lush carpet to Lucy's room. She sat on a rocking chair in the corner, gazing out the large window over the writing desk. Small, a blanket over her shoulders, arms crossed over her chest like she was trying to hold herself together. Dr. Craig peeled off his coat and knelt in front of her, whispering. After a few moments, he reared back, surprised.

He stood, anger furrowing his brows. "She's been sedated."

"What?" Ava stepped back outside the room and grabbed the patient file from the metal pocket on the wall. She took a few steps into the room as she scanned it. "I thought you said you weaned her off the meds?"

"I did." Dr. Craig said and hit the call button near the bed. "I'll ask the nurse what happened. Put that down, agent. You can't look at her medical record."

Ava finished skimming the first page and then put it down. Less than a minute later, a woman in blue scrubs came into the room. Early thirties, red hair in a tight bun, makeup that couldn't hide the myriad of freckles. Ava took one look at the tension on her face and knew something was up.

"Yes, Dr. Craig?"

"Debbie, what did you give to Lucy?"

"I—you ordered Versed."

"Not today," Ava said.

Debbie wrung her hands, shifting on her feet despite the defiant face. "It was a standing order in the event of another panic attack."

"Why wasn't I called?" Dr. Craig demanded. "Versed affects memory. How are the agents supposed to speak with her?"

"I didn't have time to call, doctor. It just happened."

"Apparently, you didn't have time to add the dose to the chart either," Ava said and pushed the medical chart toward the doctor.

He looked at it, then up at the nurse. "What is going on, Debbie?"

"You're saying she was agitated?" August asked.

"Yes. When she found out you guys were coming to interrogate her," Debbie snapped. She turned to face Dr. Craig. "That's what set her off. As soon as I told her they were coming she—"

"Why would you tell her we were coming?" Ava asked.

"I had to get her ready, okay? She was a mess." Debbie looked at Ava like she was dumb, but the anger hid something more. Fear.

"Her hair isn't wet," Ava said. She walked to the trash can. "I don't see any kind of wipes or dry shampoo containers, not even those giant Q-tip thingies for cleaning teeth. What did you do to help her get ready? Other than sending her into a panic and dosing her."

Debbie planted her hands on her hips. "What are you accusing me of?"

"I think my colleague was pretty clear," August said, moving into her space. "Why don't you want us talking to her?"

"That's not—how dare you suggest—"

"I find it odd that according to Dr. Craig she was fine an hour ago when he said we could come and speak with her," August said.

"I told you, she got upset about speaking to you guys!" Debbie blinked with indignation, her neck flushing. "If you have a problem with my care—"

"I do," Ava said.

"Thank you, Debbie," Dr. Craig cut her off. "You may leave."

She turned and left in a huff, closing the door behind her.

"Look, she's a good nurse." Dr. Craig shook his head, gathering his things. "I've known her since she was a child. I'll go and talk with her. We'll straighten this out. Maybe we can try again tomorrow."

"I'm not waiting until tomorrow doctor," August said and pulled the desk chair next to Lucy. "The killer is still out there. I want to at least try."

"I don't think she's going to give you much," Dr. Craig said, but put his coat down. "As soon as I say, you stop with the questions. I don't want her having another panic attack."

August's gaze went to Ava. "I'll start. You jump in if you have any questions."

She nodded, taking notes while he talked with Lucy, leading her through the rehearsal dinner preparations that day at the restaurant. How she hadn't heard from her mom, which was weird. Clearly sleepy, Lucy seemed present enough to nod and verbally answer August. She and her mom were close. Heavily involved in the wedding planning...

Ava circled the room looking at the personal effects. An overnight bag on a stand at the end of the bed still filled with folded clothes and toiletry bags. None of it disturbed. She passed the bathroom. Standard hospital dispenser. No personal toiletries out or used. The lunch tray on her bedside table looked untouched. An unopened container of chocolate pudding. A can of ginger ale with a straw next to it sweated on a paper doily. An uneaten turkey sandwich. Lucy wasn't doing well in terms of self-care. Not a great sign. Ava slipped the doily out from under the can and dropped it into her leather notebook.

"Ms. Thompson, you picked up the wedding dress from the cleaners and you went to drop by your parents'," August led her gently, his voice soothing. He was good at that. "Then what?"

"They steamed the wrinkles out of the silk." Lucy pulled the blanket around her shoulders to her chest, her fingers caressing the satin edge. "It has Italian lace," she said softly. "My dress, I mean. The boutique made a crown with the same kind of lace for me."

Ava spotted a wedding binder on the side table. The kind that helps you plan and organize every aspect of the event with folders and pockets. She picked it up, leafing through it. Various satin and lace swatches stuck to a cardstock page, along with bridesmaid dress colors and flower ideas. All of it had been stabbed with a pen. The blue ink marks trailed into dozens of punctures through the material, the pages, all the way down to the back cover. As if Lucy had taken out her grief on the binder.

Interesting, Ava thought.

"You told Sheriff Granger that you parked near the house and walked in through the kitchen." August tried to circle back to finding her parents again. "You had a key. Was the door locked?"

"It was locked," Lucy said, a frown pulling at her lips. "I let myself in and knew right away something was wrong. It was like the air was different."

"It probably was," Ava said from across the room. "Did it smell metallic? Like pennies?"

"Yes, that's what it was." Lucy nodded slowly. "And then I saw the shoe prints on the carpet."

"You went upstairs?" August started. "To their room?"

Lucy smiled, her face slack, eyelids half-mast. "My mom wasn't sure about the ivory color, but as soon as she saw the dress..."

"Do you have any idea who might want to hurt your parents?" Ava asked. "Did your dad have trouble with someone from his work?"

Lucy shook her head. "Everybody loved my dad."

"What about your mother?" August asked. "She was an ER nurse, right? In Hemet? Maybe—"

"You can't get it here in the US," Lucy said, holding the satin edge of the blanket out to August. "Hand woven lace."

Ava moved closer, opening the wedding binder in front of Lucy. "Why did you do this?"

Lucy stared at the pages and her lips quivered, eyes filling. After a few seconds, she whispered, "I don't know."

Ava squatted next to Lucy, holding the damaged pages between them. "Most people have sorrow first. Disbelief. This is rage, Lucy."

"There was so much—" Lucy gasped, her breath catching. "There was so much blood and I—"

"Are you mad at the killer?"

Lucy nodded. "Yes."

"Then why destroy *your* wedding planner?" Ava pointed to the silk wedding dress swatch.

"I... I can't." Lucy shook her head back and forth, her tears falling.

"Just tell me why you did this," Ava pushed. August put his hand on her shoulder. A warning to back off.

"I don't know," Lucy said, her voice rising. "I was just... I felt so bad." She started crying.

Ava scooted closer. "Bad that they died or about something else?"

"I think we should take this up again later," Dr. Craig interjected.

"Bad about what?" Ava pushed. She reached out and moved Lucy's hand to the binder. "Why did you do this?"

"I killed them!" Lucy shouted suddenly. She collapsed into sobs, her face buried in her palms. "I killed them! I killed them!"

She crumbled into hysterics and Dr. Craig rushed forward.

"That's it," he growled. "That's enough."

Inconsolable, Lucy devolved into gasping breaths. Her face red, body tense.

"You know who did this, don't you?" Ava asked over Dr. Craig's shoulder. "Or you know why?"

Lucy covered her ears with her palms, crying with anguish. "I did it! I did it!"

Nurse Debbie rushed in, and Dr. Craig shouted for her to get them out of the room. She shooed Ava and August out the door. Shutting it behind them.

"What was that about?" August snapped when they walked into the hallway. He shook his head. "Why didn't you back off?"

"She's not telling us something." Ava paced the floor. "That nurse drugged her for a reason."

"You don't know that!"

Ava pointed at the door. "I want information on that nurse. The card on her lanyard said her name is D. Whitmore. I want to know why she sabotaged our interview with Lucy."

"You know she didn't kill her parents," he said, gesturing at her with the tablet. "There wasn't a drop of blood on Lucy when the deputies arrived. Granger said she was just standing in the hallway outside of her parent's room screaming. She never touched them."

"*She* thinks she did."

"Grief and shock do weird things to people."

She stopped, facing him. "Did you see that wedding binder?"

"If I recall, you once took a bat to an offender's car."

"Okay, that was strategic. I'm never not in control."

"Mmhmm." August held her gaze with his. "When I tell you to back off, you back off."

Ava shook her head. "This is why I'm here, August. And I want to talk with her again."

Lucy's sobs emanated from behind the door.

"You're here at Vincent's request, but I still lead this team," August shot back. "You don't speak to her again until I say so. That's if Dr. Craig allows us to again."

"She has a fiancé, maybe we can get him onboard. Interview him even."

He held up a finger between them, his jaw clenched. "Listen to me. We've done enough to that poor woman. Besides, she wouldn't stop talking about her wedding dress. She's not going to be much help."

Ava looked at him for a beat, then said, "I want to exhume Suarez and Marley."

"Exhume—" He gawked at her. "What? Why?"

She rummaged in her bag and pulled out the length of medical tubing she stole from the ME's office. "Because of this."

EIGHT

By the time they left Shady Acres, a bank of clouds had moved in and darkened the afternoon. Ava's weather app predicted a turn in the weather. A chill sharpened the air, and her cheeks burned as they made their way to the car. They stopped at a nearby deli and then drove to the sheriff's station. They chose to eat in the car with the heater running, and it reminded Ava of when they'd been out on cases together as partners. There'd been a weird silence since they left the recovery center, and she didn't know if he was pissed, thinking about her exhumation request, or something else.

She busied herself with stuffing potato chips into her turkey sandwich. The added crunch was needed after not eating all day. Lucy and the stabbed binder kept coming back to her as she ate. She knew there was something there. Denny hit her back with the data scrape she'd requested that morning. He'd put together a light dossier on all four victims. Not bad. She perused the files on her phone while she ate.

August finished off his sub, chewing slowly before wiping his mouth. He turned to her, his gaze intense. "What are you doing, Ava?"

She stopped with her sandwich halfway to her mouth. "I feel like that's a trick question."

He narrowed his eyes at her. "You know this is a small town. People will hear that you bullied that woman."

"I hope so," she said. "Anger is more motivating than fear."

He leaned back, staring at her for a moment. "You put a target on your back. On purpose. You want the killer to hear about what happened and wonder if Lucy told you anything."

She took another crunchy bite. "The investigation is stagnant. It needs a shot in the arm."

His gaze traveled her face, resting on her lips for a moment before he turned away. He looked out the window at the steel gray sky. "I thought I was done worrying about you."

"I know what I'm doing."

"Have you ever thought *I'd* like to know what you're doing? Maybe even before you do it?"

"You've mentioned that before, I believe."

"And yet..." August shook his head as he finished off his chips. Crumpling the bag, he said, "Tell me about the tourniquet thing."

"Remember I talked with the ME this morning?"

"Yeah. Was it fruitful?"

"Well, you were right. She was pissed about getting booted from the investigation, but she had some interesting things to say." Ava told him about their conversation. How Dr. Wren thought the mark on Mr. Thompson's arm could be something other than a bruise from the nightstand. Their discussion about the knife wounds and why their placements might be significant. "It's just a theory, but Dr. Wren's working on the UV images with her colleague, so we should know soon if it holds any water. The wound placement matters, I think, but I don't have anything to back it up yet."

"It's something when we had nothing yesterday. I'll send Rondeau over to help the medical examiner with the UV photos. He does amateur photography so he's good with cameras," August said, rubbing his eyes. "What next?"

Ava checked her watch. "We've got a few hours until it gets dark. I'd like to see Suarez's cabin."

His gaze rested on her face. "Have you slept yet?"

"I'll sleep when I'm dead."

He huffed. "Okay. Granger saved the crime scene, so I'll ask him to meet us there with a key."

"We should put a guard on Lucy's door. That place didn't look very secure."

"You think he'd go after her? She arrived at her parent's house hours after he left. She's not a witness."

"Like you said, if it gets out that I bullied her, then it gets out I talked with her. And I wasn't kidding about the nurse. She's off somehow."

August nodded. "Well, your gut's usually not wrong. I'll talk to Granger about setting it up."

———

Half an hour later, they pulled onto a property located on the outskirts of Fern Valley, the next town over. Dust kicked up on the dirt road as they drove along a winding, rutted track to a shabby cabin. Since Suarez lived on the edge of the small town, nothing but thick forest extended behind the cabin. Granger leaned against his patrol car, waving them over as they walked up the incline to meet him. A tall, rugged man stood next to the sheriff. He wore old jeans, a hunting jacket, and a sour face.

"Wind picked up," Ava said to August as they approached. Trees bowed as a chill breeze moved through the woods, rattling the bare branches and whipping up dirt. "Who's the guy with Granger?"

"Suarez's brother." August's breath came in clouds. "He's not a fan of ours."

"Boy, you just ruffled all the feathers up here, didn't you?"

"I'm not a social chameleon like you," he grumbled, pulling out his tablet. "What you see is what you get."

"Mmhmm," Ava said with a grin. "Let me talk with him first. You'll just piss him off."

Granger greeted them both. The brother stood with his hands shoved in his coat pockets, beanie pulled down over furrowed brows. When she offered her hand, he gazed off to the side, his lips pressed into a thin line.

"Alonzo wants to start packing up his brother's cabin," Granger said. "I thought I'd have him come and talk with you. Maybe speed up that process."

"Mr. Suarez, thank you for coming back up the mountain," Ava said. "I know it must be difficult to be here again."

"What's difficult," Alonzo said, turning to glare at her, "is that it took you all weeks to give a shit. It wasn't until that Black Oak couple was butchered that the CBI bothered to show up."

Granger shook his head. "Alonzo, I already told you—"

"I know what you said," Alonzo snapped. "And I know what actually happened. Which was nothing. Until that couple got murdered, then, all of a sudden, things need investigating."

"Been running your mouth, Mr. Suarez?" Ava yanked the length of crime scene tape blocking the steps up to the cabin, snapping it off. She shoved it in her pocket and stepped closer, getting in his space. "Who did you say that to?"

"Say what to?"

"You just linked your brother's murder to the Thompsons', twice." Ava put some steel into her voice, matching his energy. "Who have you been telling that to?"

"Why?" He looked down at her, squaring up. "It's a free country."

"Sure, but you're putting a target on your back spreading that around. What if the killer is still here?"

He froze, gaze scanning the area. "You saying he is?"

"I'm saying you should help us," Ava said. "I get you're angry. I don't blame you. We messed up by not putting it together as fast as you did."

He nodded, unconsciously agreeing. Feeling heard. "Yeah, alright."

"Mr. Suarez, I know you already spoke to Sheriff Granger," August cut in, "and I know you've been waiting over a month for answers. But—"

"I haven't heard *jack* about my brother, despite leaving several messages." He shook his head at Granger. "That's messed up, Sheriff. For real."

"Are you done?" Ava checked her watch. "Wanna get a little more feelings out before you talk to us?"

His face twisted and he stepped toward her. "What the hell did you just say?"

"You heard me." Ava snapped. "I get that you're upset. But I'm out here *now*, Mr. Suarez. Freezing my ass off, investigating multiple murders, and you're gumming up the works."

"Gumming—Dude, who is this chick?" Alonzo asked Granger.

"I'm who you want hunting this asshole, Mr. Suarez," Ava shot back. "And I don't have time to waste holding your hand. I know you're resentful and outraged by how things have gone down so far. You have every right to be." He looked away, shaking his head, but she stepped into his line of sight, softening her voice. "Things will go differently. Now, will you speak with us or not?"

His red-rimmed eyes met hers. "That cop and his wife got more interest in days than my brother got in weeks. I don't even think Deputy Chutney knows his first name."

"Well, I do. I know your mother named him Rio Isaac after your father. I know he was a veteran. Iraq," Ava said. "He was wounded in action and still managed to save himself and a couple buddies. He ended up with PTSD for his heroic efforts. At least according to his file with Veterans Affairs." She caught August's look. He hadn't provided that information. "And I know you were close. Mr. Suarez, I'm truly sorry we didn't realize that your brother's death was a part of a larger investigation, but as I said, I'm here now. Asking you to help me find who did this."

"You aren't saying it was a drug deal gone wrong anymore?" Alonzo asked. "Because that's killing my mom, you know? He might've smoked some pot now and again, but he had a straight job. Rio was a mechanic in town."

"No drugs were found in his system," Ava said, the autopsy report flitting behind her vision. "There's no reason to think he was killed for that reason."

"You're the only one who thinks that." Alonzo shot an angry look at Granger. "Just because he had trouble when he left the military doesn't mean he's a criminal."

His extensive RAP sheet sort of meant he was, Ava thought, but smiled with sympathy. "You're right. So, walk me through what you think happened."

"What I think?"

"You knew him better than anyone."

Alonzo looked at her for a beat, his shoulders relaxing. "I did. He was my little brother."

Ava kept going. "You told Sheriff Granger that Rio was supposed to go fishing with you. Was it a special occasion or..."

"No, uh. I live down in Hemet by the reservoir. Rio would drive down with some food and beer, and I'd rent us a boat. We'd go fishing at least one weekend a month on Diamond Lake." Alonzo shook his head. "We didn't go the weekend before because I had to work. He was supposed to meet me that morning around six."

Ava nodded. "But he didn't show up?"

"No. I called but he didn't answer. That wasn't like him. So I drove up and..." Alonzo sniffled. "His truck was still here but the cabin was dark. Quiet, like in a weird way."

"You had a key?"

"Yeah, for emergencies."

"Did you call out?" Ava moved, shifting so the door of the cabin was in his line of sight. Alonzo shook his head. She motioned with her arms. "You got in. Saw the scene. What was the first thing you thought?"

"I didn't understand." Alonzo shook his head again. "It looked like a hurricane tore up the place."

"Okay, you're inside the cabin. What then?"

"I looked around for him, calling his... name," Alonzo sniffled, wiping his face on his jacket sleeve. "Uh... I went down the hall to the bathroom and h-he was there." He started hyperventilating.

"Come back with me to when you entered," Ava said. Pulling him from the horrific memory. "You're by the door again. Can you do that, Mr. Suarez? Think about your first look inside."

"Okay."

"What else registered in that moment while standing in the cabin? Any particular smells, sights, fears?" He looked at her askance. "Fears?"

"Humans have a survival instinct too. Our subconscious mind processes information much faster than we can think it. So, we feel it. Patterns, subtle signs of danger, things that don't ring true. What did your gut tell you when you walked into your brother's cabin?"

"It was just so still. But when I saw my brother, I was afraid of the killer."

"Because you thought he might still be in the cabin?"

He thought about it for a moment. "No... because my brother didn't have one bloody knuckle. Not one mark on his arms or face. Like he'd been ambushed. The cabin looked gone through, you know, ransacked?"

"Yeah," Ava said. "Which meant..."

Alonzo's eyes flitted off toward the woods. "My brother, a trained marine, didn't or couldn't put up much of a fight. Like he was hurt or stabbed from the get-go."

Ava nodded, taking a slow breath. "Like the killer lay in wait and stabbed him as an opening volley, not as part of a fight that got out of hand."

"Exactly," Alonzo squinted his eyes at her.

"You think it means the attacker had training of some sort?" August asked from the stairs. "Military, maybe?"

Alonzo shrugged. "I heard the ME said it was a hunting knife. One of those Ka-Bar ones like the military has. I've heard they're a favorite of operators... you know, SEALs. Those guys know how to ambush."

"Do you think it was someone your brother knew from his days in the marines?" Ava asked.

"He didn't keep in touch with any of them and as far as I know, none of them had beef with him. Listen, Rio was always into things he shouldn't have been, but he didn't deserve this."

Ava led Alonzo back around to finding his brother, asking if he remembered any kind of trouble he might have been in, but didn't get much more out of him. She and August thanked him, and he headed out. Granger handed her the keys and went to speak with Alonzo about the cabin's future.

"Still working with Denny, I see," August said. "Knowing the victim's service record was a nice touch."

"He comes through now and again," Ava said, then nodded at the sheriff talking to Alonzo down the hill. "Granger's station is leaking like a sieve. We didn't release the serrated edge or make of the hunting knife, did we?"

"No. It might have come from the ME's office."

"Maybe," Ava said. "Have you been inside?"

He nodded. "Unfortunately, they didn't preserve the scene very well." He handed her a pair of nitrile gloves and offered her menthol. She took both. "When Granger got through to me, I had him seal it. I think that's part of what's fueling the brother."

She smiled ruefully. "It's not even a little part of what made Alonzo mad. He called the Thompsons, 'that Black Oak couple.'"

He turned to her. "Yes, and?"

"Black Oak is both richer and whiter than Fern Valley and Pine Cove combined. His brother got a small-town deputy and victim blaming, and they got the full force of California's elite crime-fighters."

August shook his head, unlocking the rusty doorknob. "We didn't know."

"I'm not saying he's right. Fairness loses meaning in grief." She took a shallow breath of the menthol at her nose. "I'm saying he's not mad about the cabin."

Ava pushed the door open and, despite the minty vapor, the smell of death hit her like a fog bank, engulfing them in the violence spread out before them. Suarez's one-room home managed to include both a full kitchen and a decent living room despite the low square footage. A potbelly stove stood in a brick-covered corner. The fold-out couch sat extended, revealing dingy sheets and flat pillows. He'd built an impressive cinderblock and wooden plank shelving system that held a large screen television, a sound bar, and a speaker system. All of it smeared with bloody hand and boot prints.

"That's all from Suarez," August said and pointed to a handprint on the wall. He handed over his tablet with the forensic report on the screen. "He was bleeding, stumbling for the bathroom, falling. Dr. Clay says the killer likely wore gloves. Some kind of canvas work glove. She found fibers consistent with the kind used for construction."

Ava nodded. "Dr. Wren said the liver wound was first. Deep. Rio panicked with the pain and blood, probably tried to stem the flow, slipped and slid to the..."

The only other space was a small bathroom with a toilet, sink, and small tub with a showerhead. She walked toward it. The forensic report contained photos of blood smears on the wall and rim of the tub in which Suarez was found. Some drops on the floor leading into the bathroom, some smeared on the small window. Not a lot, but enough to show the victim had tried to get it open, possibly to escape. It seemed to be big enough. The bulk of Rio's blood, however, had gone down the drain.

"Suarez's brother found him around nine in the morning. He let himself in, found his brother in the tub, ran outside to vomit, and then called 911."

"That's horrible," Ava murmured.

She turned away from the tub and checked the medicine cabinet. Standard over the counter cold and pain relief supplies lined the shelves. Some razors, aftershave, band aids as well. He even had a half-full bottle of daily vitamins. Black fingerprint dust made dark smudges on the glass, the sink, the door.

She walked the cabin slowly. Too much mess and debris littered the floor to really see the path of the fight. Drawers pulled out, cabinets empty, clothes on the floor, shoes thrown. Everything had been photographed. She'd seen it before, in the report Vincent had sent her, but standing in the chaos, she understood the desperation and fury that clashed here. August waited by the door as she wandered the kitchen, looked in closets, and peeked under the foldable bed.

Fishing rods, a tackle box, and a life jacket sat wedged against the wall underneath the sofa bed. A boat trader magazine had slipped against the wall. She found several dog-eared pages inside containing various fishing boats for sale. A shiny shape clung to the blanket's edge, hooked like an ornament on a tree. She unstuck it and held it up to the window. The silvery blue plastic of a fishing lure reflected the late afternoon sun. Ava glanced over her shoulder, spotted August looking out the cabin door, and pocketed the lure.

"I've seen what I need to see," she said as she stood, dusting off her hands.

"I'll let Dr. Clay know. She has final say on releasing a crime scene," August said, lifting his phone as they walked out.

Suarez's cabin sat in a clearing surrounded by pine forest and a riot of crows flew out of the trees, squawking with irritation. They circled overhead. August stood next to her on the porch watching.

"I like her. Dr. Clay," Ava said, eyes searching the bushes across from the gravel parking area. "She's sharp."

"She is. I poached her from the FBI to come work with me on PIT. She recently published a paper on cutting edge evidence retrieval for victims with advanced decomp."

"Huh. And where did you meet this forensic powerhouse?"

"What are you doing," August asked, his gaze wary.

"I'm trying to learn about the team," Ava said, grinning. "Why so touchy?"

After a few moments he said, "I met her in San Francisco. I was working with the FBI on a human trafficking task force a couple of years ago. She was their forensic expert."

"And she just left the FBI to come work for you?"

He looked away. "She did."

Ava nodded. "Did you two have a thing?"

August kept his gaze out on the horizon. "I don't date colleagues anymore."

A small truck drove up the gravel path, pulling her attention. It parked on the property. An older man wearing bib overalls, a straw hat, and construction boots leaned heavily on a cane as he made his way up to them.

"Names Doug Fetterman," he said. "I'm the landlord. Sheriff Granger asked me to pop by and speak with you all again."

Ava stepped down while August locked up the cabin. "I appreciate it. Do you live close by?"

"Yup. A mile down the road."

Ava raised a brow. "I didn't see any other cabins on the road coming up."

"Yah, no you wouldn't." Fetterman pointed his cane in a vague direction down the hill. "Most of the parcels out here are set back from the road."

He was polite, and sharp, but after a few questions he didn't seem to have much more to offer past the initial interview. Suarez had paid his rent late on occasion but always paid it. After two years of living in the cabin, Fetterman said it looked well kept.

"No complaints from you or anyone else?" Ava asked, narrowing her gaze. "Really?"

He hesitated for a moment. "I mean, it was nothing."

"What was nothing?" August, in the habit of holding back to let her talk to witnesses, finally walked down the cabin steps to stand next to Ava.

Fetterman rubbed his chin with his weathered hand. "Someone filed a noise complaint. Maybe a month and a half ago."

"How loud was the party to get a complaint way out here?" August asked.

Fetterman shook his head, pointing with his cane at the cabin. "It was music. He started blasting music all hours lately. Margie Dulles down the way called me. I thought things might get a little heated, so I told her I'd stop by. He answered the door drunk, but he was apologetic. Turned the stereo off right away. Never had a problem with him before and hadn't had one since."

"What kind of music was he playing?" Ava asked.

"Uh... Pink Floyd, I believe." Fetterman furrowed his brows. "Does it matter?"

Ava shrugged. "Well, I don't play 'Comfortably Numb' when I'm in a good mood."

"I guess you have a point," Fetterman said. "I'm thinking he did look kind of bummed."

August tapped out notes on the tablet. "Was the music system new?"

"Couldn't tell you. I hadn't been inside since I rented it to him." He opened his mouth to say something but then stopped.

Ava leaned in. "What is it?"

"It's just rumors. I don't want to speak ill of the dead."

"I think he'd appreciate you helping us find whoever did this to him," Ava said.

"Okay, well, I'm over at the Prickly Pear, it's a dive bar at the other end of town. Locals mostly. I used to go a lot but now that the doctor scared my wife, I go to the café and drink tea with her." Fetterman chuckled like he didn't mind. "Anyway, last time I was there Rio was buying rounds for everyone. Dream Taylor, the bartender, said he did that every time he came in. He also promised to buy her a fur coat."

"When was this?" August asked.

"Oh, I'm not sure. A few months before he died, I guess. Dream called him a regular, so I guess he went there a lot after I stopped going."

"On a tab?" Ava asked, glancing down the drive at Granger and Alonzo talking.

Fetterman shook his head. "No, she said he paid cash."

August's gaze slipped to Ava's. "Sounds like he came into money recently."

"Suarez was an okay guy. Not stupid, anyway. But since this all happened, I heard he was always getting involved with get-rich-quick schemes. Maybe it was something like that."

"Maybe," Ava said, though the money thing definitely piqued her interest.

They finished with Fetterman, and he left, a cloud of dirt lingering in the air behind him. Granger, done with Suarez's brother, ambled back up to his patrol car.

August gave him a nod. "Appreciate you having them meet us here. I'll have Dr. Clay give Mr. Suarez an update on releasing the property. I know he's anxious."

"Appreciate it," Granger said. To Ava he asked, "You good?"

Ava nodded. The sun hovered low on the horizon, and a chill moved on the wind. "I'm gonna take a turn around the property and then I'll be ready to go."

She strolled the gravel, eyes up in the trees, listening for the crows. They'd settled back down. Walking the perimeter of the cabin, she familiarized herself with the grounds, the sight lines and blind spots in relation to the terrain. She stopped at the rear of the home and faced the encroaching forest. Her gaze traveled the brush, the setting sun sent shards of orange spires through the trees. Ava caught a flash as she turned to leave. A slip of light reflected back to her.

"August!" Ava shouted, pulling her gun and striding toward the location. "On my six!"

His heavy footfalls sounded behind her as she moved forward, weapon down at her thigh. "What is it?"

"There's someone out there," she said, walking toward the tree line.

"Where?" August ran up behind her, his pistol drawn.

The brush shifted and a form shot out from behind a stand of trees. Tall, bulky, black watch cap – camouflage coat. Sunglasses. Gloves.

"There!" Ava yelled and took off after him.

The suspect trampled through the brambles, struggling with the terrain, nearly going down. Ava chased him, gaining, as his wheezing breaths sent puffs of vapor into the air behind him. He moved wrong, Ava thought, favoring his right side.

Raising her gun she shouted, "Stop, CBI!"

He twisted, his arm coming around, a gun bucking in his hand.

"Gun!" Ava threw herself to the ground, continuing to fire as she fell, her arm burning.

Three rounds blasted toward her and August, chewing up the tree bark and ringing in her ears. August hit the deck next to her, then popped up, returning fire. The assailant crashed through the dry brush. They tried to follow, but the low light obscured his path, and they lost him in the woods.

August looked at Ava, his face smeared with dirt, pupils blown wide with adrenaline. "You said he was watching us."

"He had a gun," Ava panted, holstering her own.

"I caught that detail." He looked her over and then pulled at the sleeve of her sweater. His finger went through a bullet hole under the armpit. "Dammit, Ava. He nearly hit you."

Granger ran over to them, his eyes wide as he took them both in. "What the hell is going on?"

"He had a gun, August," Ava repeated. "He had one and didn't use it."

"You're getting ahead of me. Tell me what you mean." August peered at her with confusion.

"He had a gun but killed them with a knife. He stabbed efficiently." Ava shook her head. "I've been looking at this all wrong."

August dusted off his clothes. "Meaning?"

Her eyes fixed on him, but she wasn't seeing him. She saw the wounds, the blood, the jagged knife, and knew. "I don't think it's just about the victims."

NINE

Sheriff Granger, Ava, and August did a search of the area, but it proved too dark to see anything. Dr. Clay and Agent Rondeau arrived at Suarez's property shortly after. They brought floodlights from the Thompson house as well as Dr. Clay's forensic equipment. Ava walked her to where she'd last seen the shooter and let her work.

Agent Vincent came down to deal with the shooting.

"You just got here, Ava," Vincent said stiffly. "This must be a record."

"Technically, I haven't shot anyone yet," Ava argued.

The CBI and Granger's office signed off on an interdepartmental investigation. Agent Vincent used her supervisory discretion to allow Ava to continue with the investigation given the ongoing threat of the killer at large. A CBI investigator who'd arrived with Vincent took Ava's statement, then August's. He collected their weapons and released Ava from the scene around eight that night.

She stayed for another hour, watching Agent Rondeau help Dr. Clay collect the bullet that had nearly hit her from the tree trunk. While they worked, she used the Identikit program on a CBI tablet to get out details while they were fresh in her mind. He'd worn a mask,

95

one of those neck gaiters that pulled up and covered his mouth and nose. His sunglasses had obscured his eyes, and the knit cap had hidden his hair color. She tried working out his basic body type, but the brush and his bulky jacket made it impossible to tell if she was right. Running a hand through her hair, she shut down the program. She had nothing.

On top of that, with the adrenaline burned through, she couldn't stop yawning. Since she had been involved in the shooting, she wasn't going to be any good at the scene, so August sent her back to the inn.

"Sleep," he told her. "I mean it."

She drove his car back to the Timberline Inn, took a shower, and changed into sweats. Hungry, she wandered back down to the lobby looking for something to eat. A young woman, brunette, with big brown doe eyes smiled at her from the reception counter. Her name tag read "Theresa."

"Can I help you, Agent Cortes?"

"Oh, uh, I'm not sure," Ava said, startled at the familiarity. "Have we met?"

"No, but you've been on the news."

"I have?"

"Oh yeah." Theresa's eyes grew wide with excitement. "Not the national news, but our local station for sure did a story on the CBI being here."

"Well, let me know when I hit the big time." Ava leaned on the counter. "I understand the kitchen's closed, but is there any place open right now?"

"Oh, no," she said with a sympathetic smile. "Everything around here closes at like, six."

"I see that. What about the gas station?"

"I can send up a snack platter if you want," Theresa offered.

"What's that?"

"It's slices of meat from dinner, in this case, roast beef. And some cold sides. Some bread..."

"Any dessert?"

"We've got cake."

"Oh, my goodness, I'd love that," Ava said, craving the sugar. She hooked a finger over her shoulder. "Can I still use the solarium?"

"Oh yeah, that's open all night. I can bring you the platter in there if you want."

Ava thanked her and then wandered through the inn toward the back patio. She stood in the dark, letting her eyes adjust, feeling the bite of ice on the wind. Walking about twenty yards down a mulched pathway, she found a glassed-in structure. The metal door opened easily, and the steamy warmth of the solarium surrounded her. It was essentially a fancy green house with seating. Exotic plants crowded together on hand wrought wooden tables. Rows of orchids delicately swayed in the artificial breeze of the room. A small pond with bright orange koi fish gurgled in the far corner. A circle of cushioned bamboo lounge chairs rested beneath the muted glow of a pendant light. The roof, made of glass panels, let in the vast dark of the night sky overhead.

Ava sat in one of the chairs. The overstuffed cushions a welcome comfort to her sore body. She listened to the trickle of the irrigation system, the hum of the koi pond's aeration bubbler, the sound of the wind rustling the branches outside. She took her leather notebook out of her sweatshirt pocket and let the day's information play in her mind. Pulling the cap off her ink pen, she drew several large circles and wrote down every person she'd spoken to and what she'd learned, connecting the bubbles to each other with lines. She needed to get ahead of the killer's path, not keep following in his wake.

She couldn't speak with the closest thing they had to a witness, Lucy Thompson. Whitmore, the nurse at the Shady Acres Recovery Center, had acted suspicious, but that didn't prove anything. What she had learned was that the killer was likely strong, trained, and not working out of some psychotic rage. Which would explain why he hadn't left any evidence. He was also, as Suarez's brother asserted, likely ambushing his victims, yet with the Thompsons, it appeared he hadn't dispatched the largest threat, the male, first. Which Ava found dissonant. Like a wrong note on a piano. His erratic path through the towns also presented a problem she couldn't stop chewing on.

But it was Suarez's cinderblock and plank shelving unit that bothered her the most. It seemed obvious he'd come into money and had been spreading it around like he'd won it, not earned it. Buying rounds. Promising furs. Shopping for boats. The landlord had said Suarez was into schemes so not entirely out of character. However, when she and August had tried to interview Lucy, she wouldn't stop talking about the Italian lace of her dress, how you couldn't get it in the states. That sounded expensive. And Velma, from the Riot Brewing Café, mentioned the wedding was on the beach. Also costly.

Despite the fact that the murders had taken place in Lucy's family home, Ava wondered if the contents of her bridal suite at the hotel would be more informative. She needed to see that dress. Ava remembered the image of Mrs. Thompson's calendar from evidence. She was older and used a spiral-bound paper calendar she kept on the counter.

Whispered numbers raced through Ava's head, a jumble of gathered information calling for her attention. She closed her eyes, relaxing, and let the day fall away. The calendar pages flipped before her as dates and scrawled notes scratched across her vision, telling the story of a mother planning a wedding with her daughter. Dress fittings, catering menu ideas, seating arrangements, reception details, they all faded to nothing—unimportant. The information tumbled through her mind, chaotic and untethered. Then, one number burned brightest through the noise, and she focused on it. A circled number and letter on a Friday. Mrs. Thompson had written, "Château Lane deposit," with "25K" circled in red next to it. A small detail written a month before they died. It wasn't mentioned in anything she'd read so far.

Ava's eyes popped open. A retired cop and nurse put a twenty-five-thousand-dollar deposit down at the most luxurious beachfront hotel in the area on top of all the other expenditures.

"How could they afford that?" She asked the empty solarium.

The image of Tone Marley's battered body from the photos she'd seen of the autopsy came to mind. He was in college according to Granger's interview with the mother. He'd been working on an assignment when he went missing. But it was community college. Ava shook her head. Why, if he was an A student, would he not have gone directly to a four-year on scholarship?

She dug her phone out of her sweatpants and texted August's number.

> Tomorrow, I need to see Lucy's dress and I want to interview her fiancé. And I need to see inside Tone Marley's home, and I want to run financials on all the victims. Still waiting on the exhumation too, so… Also, goodnight.

She set her phone on her lap and leaned back into the cushion, thinking. August would want to know what she'd meant about the killer not really being after the victims. She knew this like she knew direction. By feel, and experience, but August needed more. A trail he could see and document for trial. Ava re-lived the walkthrough of the Thompsons' house. Flashes of images merged into a full rendering of the room. Bloody boot prints emerged from the lush carpet, glistening in the brightness of her mental reconstruction. She moved through the house, up to the bedroom. The bodies of Mr. and Mrs. Thompson in bed, as they were photographed by the ME, superimposed on the bare mattress. She walked to them, going to Mr. Thompson's side this time. Photographs of his wounds flashed in strobe, focusing on his chest, his stomach. The wounds looked torn, due to the jagged blade, but something that *should* be there, wasn't. Understanding tightened in her mind, like a long, slack line finally catching on a snag. Dichotomy, duality. A choice of some kind?

Dr. Wren had theorized the victims really had two ways to die. A slow death via the liver wound. And a fast one, the heart. And now, impressions on the skin told the same story. One steady, the possible tourniquet bruise on Mr. Thompson's arm, and one sudden, like the hilt of a knife during a frenzied killing. Only she didn't remember seeing any sign of bruising around the wounds and she hadn't come across how deep they'd been. Ava wrote a reminder in her notebook to pick Dr. Clay's brain tomorrow.

Theresa came in with plates of food. One piled with sliced roast beef, a couple of dinner rolls, and a small cup of coleslaw. The other with a large slice of carrot cake. Ava thanked her and dug in, enjoying the peace of the solarium as she ate.

Halfway through the meal, her phone trilled, and she answered. "That was fast," she said, expecting August.

A low, gravelly voice answered her. "Did I get you? I saw you jerk as you were falling."

Her heart sped up, and she grabbed her pen and notebook, jotting down impressions.

Caucasian? No accent. California native?

"Who is this?" she asked.

"You know who it is, Ava," he said, and she could hear the amusement in his voice. He was having fun. He didn't consider her a threat.

"Where did you get this number?" She put him on speaker, then texted August that she was on the phone with the killer.

He drank something because the ice in the glass tinked in Ava's ear. "You left your card all over town."

"I guess I did." Ava wrote down "high risk tolerant, possible gambler." Her phone lit up.

AUGUST

Rondeau running trace.

"What do you want?" Ava asked.

"I want to know where I hit you."

Her fingers found the spot under her left arm where the bullet had seared her skin. "You're not that good. Then again, it's hard to shoot straight when you're scurrying away like a rat."

He chuckled, a congested, cackling sound. "How'd that dirt taste? Did you bang up that pretty little face?"

Smoker. Feels superior enough to tease.

She forced the same mocking tone into her answer. "Did I hit *you* or do you naturally favor your right side?"

"I don't favor anything but taking out hypocrites and liars."

"That's gonna be a big job," Ava said, noting the elevated language. Slightly slurred speech. "Why start up here in the mountains?"

"I saw you in the Thompsons' bedroom. When that fat deputy first showed up, he ran back out and puked. But you... you looked right at home in all that bloodshed."

"Why did you butcher them?"

The killer remained silent for a beat. "They know what they did."

"Why did you do this, Mr...."

"They must be culled," he spat. "They must be punished."

Ava paused, surprised by the sudden vehemence. "Is that what you're doing? You're punishing people?"

"Yes." The killer let out a weird cackle that made the hairs on Ava's arms stand up.

"What did Tone Marley and Rio Suarez do?" When he was silent, she continued. "I've seen your signature at every scene. You can't hide it."

After a few seconds he said, "They were punished for their sins."

"How so?" Ava asked. "Tone Marley was a child."

The killer laughed. "He didn't fight like one."

Her gut knotted. "Why would you—"

"The shadow of judgement falls on them all!" He cut across her, his voice rising to a shout. "They will die by my blade!"

"Tell me what you want..." Ava began before realizing he'd ended the call.

She sat for a moment in the dark, listening to the blood rush in her ears. The call made her gut churn. It felt incongruent. None of his behavior thus far suggested a delusional killer or any kind of mission-based psychopathy.

AUGUST

What's happening?

He hung up

A second later, her phone rang.

"What'd you get?" he asked.

"Well, he's a liar and a hypocrite," she murmured, her gaze falling on the dark windows. "And he wants us to think he's crazy."

"Is he?"

She thought about his taunting words. His comment about Marley not fighting like a kid. His brutality to Mr. Thompson. The humor in his voice.

"He is, just not the kind he wants us to think he is." She rubbed her eyes, exhausted. "Did you get a trace?"

"Agent Rondeau captured a number and general location. He's checking the tower maps to see which cell service providers cover this area. We'll put a tap on your number tomorrow." August yawned and it made Ava do so as well. "Get some sleep. We'll attack this in the morning."

"This guy's cunning, August. Mean." Ava stood and started back toward the inn with her plates. Outside the solarium the temperature dropped. A strong wind coming out of the woods pushed a shiver through her. She wondered if the killer was watching her. "He's not going to stop."

"Then we'll do it for him," August said. "And we're moving you."

"You think he might go after me?"

August sighed. "As you always say, 'I would.'"

TEN

The next morning, a wake-up call Ava never asked for woke her for a meeting she never knew about. Squinting at the time on her phone, she called August.

"Is there a reason the front desk woke me at the butt crack of dawn?"

"I requested it last night," he said, with the gall to sound chipper. "We need to regroup. And relocate. So pack up."

Half an hour later, she met him in the lobby of the inn wearing a light blue ski sweater, dark jeans, and her trail runner sneakers. She'd moved her backup weapon from her ankle to her hip holster for the time being. Her go bag sat at her feet. August wore a collared sweater and black slacks, and she thought he almost looked relaxed. He held a carrier with four coffees and a bag full of muffins in his hands and gave her a tired smile when he saw her. A couple of deputies nodded to him on their way out.

"Did you seriously have a guard duty set up?"

"The killer called you last night," August said with furrowed brows. "I know stuff like that doesn't really register with you, but it does with me. I pulled them in from the Riverside Sheriff's Office."

"It registers," she said, taking the coffees from him. "It just doesn't change anything. I have a job to do."

"Rondeau put a trap and trace on your number in case he calls again."

"He'll be in touch." August raised a brow and she sipped her coffee before saying, "He was fishing for information."

"Feeling the pressure." He nodded.

As they drove to the station, the stillness of the town seemed artificial. Like the silence of the woods when a predator is afoot. Late February had one more cold front in it, according to her weather app, and the encroaching dark clouds blotted out the warmth of the sun. They talked about which hotel the CBI had moved the team to, but Ava balked when August mentioned it was a few towns over.

"I'm not leaving the area. The killer is here."

"Literally why we're moving." He turned into the station's parking lot. "It's just down in Idyllwild. Bigger town, more places to stay, larger number of people—"

"To hide in, I get it, but he didn't know where I was staying. He called a number I gave out to the public. I was alone and unarmed in a greenhouse when he called. If he knew that, he would've taken his shot." She shrugged. "He didn't."

August's gaze slipped to hers. "You might not believe this, Ava, but despite what you think, you are not, in fact, bulletproof."

She shrugged. "I mean I have been so far..."

They went back and forth on the hotel issue, not coming to a conclusion by the time they parked so she changed the subject, nibbling on her muffin as they walked inside. "Any movement on where the call came from?"

"Agent Rondeau is working on it. We'll hear from him and Dr. Clay at the meeting." August pushed through the station's front doors, letting her in.

"What about my requests? The exhumations and financials. I also need to speak with the fiancé."

"I called Vincent about the exhumations," August said, leaving a coffee and muffin on the front counter for Gale, the receptionist. "Aside from the town ME's hunch, there's no reason to submit that type of request just yet. She wants us to wait for the photos of Mr. Thompson's arm to move ahead with that one."

"They're waiting for you," Gale said. Middle aged, tortoise shell glasses, and fuchsia lips, she pushed fly-aways from her updo back into place. A mix of worry and curiosity on her face. "Did something happen?"

"Can I get Agent Cortes a patrol radio and earpiece?" August asked instead of answering.

Gale nodded and headed toward the supply room. When she left, he led Ava to the gun locker in the back of the station. He used a key to open one and reached in.

"You're cleared of the shooting at Suarez's place," August said, retrieving her weapon and handing it to her.

"That was fast," Ava said, switching her ankle piece back to the holster on her leg.

"Vincent lit a fire under them," August said.

"Can she do the same with the exhumation orders? We don't have time to wait for bureaucratic nonsense." Ava checked her main weapon, reloaded it quickly, and slipped it into her hip holster. "We should be looking at the first two bodies right now, not waiting."

August motioned for her to walk with him. "Either way, Suarez was cremated, so that's a bust."

"And Marley?"

"Dr. Wren did the autopsy, collected evidence, and then the body was released to the funeral home. He's buried in Riverside. Glades Cemetery."

"I want to speak to his mom."

August stopped just in front of the conference room doors. "Not about digging up her son. Not yet."

"What if the photos of Thompson's arm show bruises?"

"*Then* we have reason." He gave her a warning look. "No rogue operations, Ava. You're on a team."

"Rogue operations?" She smirked. "Is this about Denny? Are you peeved I used him?"

"Agent Rondeau is our information guy, not a friend from your college days who may or may not be a black hat hacker."

"He was sixteen and he did his time in juvie." Ava rolled her eyes, pushing through the door. "He's at an AI start-up now making more than you and me combined."

August pointed his tablet at her as they strode in. "I don't want the complication at trial. Stay in-house."

"Fine," she said, irritated with his stickler attitude.

Dr. Clay, Agent Rondeau, and Sheriff Granger stopped talking when they entered. They stood together next to the long table, watching her and August as they set down the coffees and muffins.

August looked at Agent Rondeau. "Let's get down to it. I want to hear from you first, Martin. The killer's call. What do we know?"

"All right, well, the killer called the public CBI number Agent Cortes keeps on her hand out cards," Rondeau said while everyone found a chair. He clicked a mini remote control. The wall display lit up and a basic flip phone appeared on the screen. "He used a burner phone like this. Low tech. You can pick one up at the local Walmart. I used Agent Cortes's logs, as well as available cell tower mapping services to pinpoint the call's location. Unfortunately, the program only narrowed the location down to a twenty-five-mile radius."

"That would include all of Black Oak, Fern Valley, and Pine Cove," Granger said. "Probably Idyllwild too."

"So not overly helpful yet." Ava pulled out her notebook, jotting down thoughts. "The identikit I did on him doesn't create much of a picture of what he looks like either. He covered himself from head to toe."

"I'll add it to the physical profile," Rondeau said. "Every bit narrows the profile down."

She smiled. "Thanks. And call me Ava." She turned to August. "What do the shrinks say about the language the unsub used?"

"I spoke with the head of Behavioral Sciences last night. Dr.

Masters agrees with you that the hints of religiosity and paranoia are atypical. Chaotic and vague. Their unit is still working on a profile."

"That's because Seth knows it's bullshit," Ava said.

Talia tilted her head. "You think the unsub is trying to throw us off his trail."

"More like hide his motive."

"Which is?" Granger asked.

"I don't know yet." She caught the sheriff rolling his eyes and wondered what that was about. "Also, we shouldn't release the call. He was enjoying it too much and I think the religious stuff is total crap."

"Sheriff?" August asked.

"She's right, I guess," Granger harumphed. "Releasing the contents of the call would send the whole town into a panic with the stuff he said. He sounds like a religious nut on a mission."

"I think he told on himself a little," Ava mused. "I think he is after something."

"We'll keep an open mind until we hear different," August said and nodded to Rondeau. "Anything else?"

Rondeau clicked his remote again. "Agent... uh, Ava requested I look into trail cameras in the area." The screen on the wall displayed a map of California with hundreds of red dots.

Her jaw dropped. "There're that many?"

He nodded. "Three years ago, the US Forest Service started a camera and microphone share program. They networked National Park Service equipment that had been placed in parks for monitoring wildlife migration with other trail cameras approved for use by university research programs, conservation projects, weather stations and the like. The idea was to widen available data to everyone by sharing access to the various feeds via a Forest Service network. I've used information off it for hunting."

August pointed with his pen. "And that's every national park?"

"Ideally, but the network started in the Joshua Tree National Park and spread from there. It's mostly California and parts of

Oregon at the moment," Rondeau said, zooming in on the map. "There are cameras and microphones in the Mount San Jacinto State Park and the San Bernardino National Forest, here. A few expanded out toward the towns, but they're mostly on hiking trails. If the killer is wandering around at the edge of town, we may have a recording of it."

"I had Gale give Neil Yaeger a call," Granger said, taking one of the muffins on the table. He avoided Ava's gaze. "He's sort of the go to guy for hunting and trail cameras. He runs a fishing and game club with members all over the region. He's reaching out to owners of private trail cams around where the Marley kid was found, the hiking trails behind Suarez's cabin, and the area around the Thompsons' home in Black Oak."

"Keep us posted," August said. "What else?"

"We've been looking into the information Ava gathered at the Riot Brewing Café, the party house in particular, and the suspected veterinarian." Rondeau turned to Ava. "Smart move, by the way. I heard you're popular."

"Enough to get shot at," Ava said with a smile. "What'd you find out?"

"Deputy Chutney and I went out to speak with the people at the party house, but the place was empty. The company that owns the home confirmed the guests were supposedly vintage motorcycle enthusiasts. Mostly older couples in their fifties and sixties. No trouble other than classic rock being played too loud. But that was for a retirement party, and they turned it down by nine."

"That's not the impression they left on the townsfolk," Ava said. "You checked them all out?"

"We did. The rental company sent the reservation information over." Rondeau used the remote to bring up the form. "They're all just older people with fancy bikes and a lot of time. It's some kind of travel club that arranges meetups and rides over long weekends, that kind of thing. The guy you told me about, the one who looked questionable at the market, owns a brewhouse in Carlsbad."

"Okay so not a gang of criminal bikers," Ava said. "What about the nurse at Shady Acres?"

"Her name is Debbie Whitmore," Granger said. "She's an upstanding citizen of Black Oak. No trouble. Grew up here. Her mother has a store in town. I believe she lives down in Idyllwild now, and commutes."

"Why do you think she might dose a witness right before we talk to them?"

Granger shrugged. "I believe she told you why."

Ava stilled at his tone. "You believe that Lucy fell into hysterics over the thought of helping us find her parents' killer?"

"I believe she was anxious and thought you'd make things worse," Granger said with a little heat. "From what I heard, she wasn't wrong."

The others in the room watched the exchange, tense. Ava regarded Granger. He was sheriff of this town and loyal to its citizens. Protective. She smiled softly. "Okay. Note taken. What about this vet?"

Granger looked at her for a beat, thrown. "Uh, his name is Hyde Daniels, he's a large animal veterinarian. Horses, cows, we have some emus and donkeys up here, too. Smart guy. He's on the town council. Single, but everyone thinks he's dating a guy in Irvine. An English professor. I called and asked why he made that connection between Suarez and the Thompsons. Daniels said he was guessing but promised not to spread panic around."

"Thank you, Sheriff." August turned to Talia. "What about you, Dr. Clay?"

Talia stood and handed out printed sheets to each person. "When Ava mentioned Mrs. Thompson's sleeping pills, I ordered a tox screen specifically for sedatives, barbiturates, and other sleep aids on each of the victims' blood. They're pending. As for the photos of Mr. Thompson's arm." She nodded to Rondeau. "Martin and I are working with the Black Oak ME, Dr. Wren, to get those as clean as possible."

"I know it's been less than twenty-four hours since I spoke with Wren," Ava said, "but is there anything there?"

Talia nodded. "There is a shadow on the image in the upper arm area. Could be a distortion, though, so Rondeau is running it through a few digital filters."

"It's there," Ava said mostly to herself. "Update me as soon as you know?"

Talia and Rondeau nodded.

Ava tossed around the idea of a financial angle, though she had no evidence the second victim, Marley, had engaged in similar purchasing activity that Suarez and the Thompsons had. August asked Rondeau to take a soft look at the victims' financials, nothing that required a subpoena. Granger made a disapproving face but kept quiet.

They finished up the meeting by covering the possible leak. August reiterated the importance of keeping information about the case, like the type of knife used by the killer, out of the press. Granger said he'd look into it. Once finished, Talia headed back to check on Dr. Wren's progress with the UV photos and to see if the ballistics report on the slug pulled out of the tree on Suarez's property was ready.

As they filed out, Ava hung back, catching Granger's attention.

"Can we talk?" she asked.

He nodded toward the snack machine alcove, and she followed him there. Arms crossed, he fixed her with a blank look. "Something wrong?"

"You're angry," Ava said.

"You aren't what I thought you'd be."

"Yeah, I get that a lot."

"I thought they brought you in to give the team direction. Instead, you're causing problems. I heard you sent Lucy into hysterics. That you yelled at her."

"I didn't yell at her."

"That's not what I heard."

"And Dr. Craig told you this?" She tilted her head. "Or was it Nurse Whitmore?"

Granger's mustache bristled, his eyes sliding from hers. "You didn't need to do that to her."

"Lucy knows something she's afraid to tell us," Ava said softly. "She's terrified."

"Then why push her like that?" His jaw clenched. "It wasn't necessary. That girl has been through enough. I've been fielding calls by angry residents. And now you want to look into the finances of the victims? What's that about? You're making them out to be suspects."

"It's routine, Sheriff. We're not pointing fingers—we're tracking movement."

"It looks like you're casting aspersions on the dead. People here won't take that lightly."

"Clearly." Ava considered him for a moment. "Lucy stabbed the shit out of her wedding planner and screamed that she killed them. You don't think that's worth looking into?"

Granger's chin jutted out stubbornly. "I think you're under a lot of pressure and you're desperate for something to give your bosses. I've heard rumors, you know. About some of your other investigations. You go too far."

She didn't take the bait. Didn't lash back. Instead, she said, "The CBI doesn't call me in to smooth things over. My job is to find the killer. By any means necessary. You know that, right?"

"That includes harassing victims, does it?"

"That includes anything in my power and other people's power if I can convince them."

Granger shook his head. "There are different ways to go about it."

"I wouldn't be here if that worked, Sheriff. And I'm telling you now, if I have to tear this town apart to stop any more of your citizens from being massacred, then so be it."

"The way you treated Lucy, how you asked people to point fingers at each other, all of it is making people scared and paranoid."

"There's a killer moving through the towns like a dark mist, picking their friends off one by one. Brutally. They *need* to be vigilant. Wary. Watchful. And it's working. The killer feels us closing in. You want to know how I can tell?" Granger shrugged. Ava pointed out the window. "He's been active for seven weeks and in all that time, he didn't call. Until now. He wanted to know what we know. He feels us biting at his heels, and I'm not going to let him rest."

Granger shook his head again, but his frown had softened. "I hope you know what you're doing."

"Do you hunt, Sheriff?"

"I did as a kid with my father. Why?"

"You know how to stalk a deer, then. You plan it, using checkpoints like terrain features as reference. You notice details, grazing times, where they bed..."

"Yes, okay."

"But the one thing you *must* get right is the wind. Reading it, knowing its direction, understanding the patterns. It's essential, because if you get it wrong, one whiff of you and the quarry is already gone."

"Flow," Granger said, nodding. "Like the rhythm of the forest."

Ava nodded with him. "You feel it, when you know it. After years of paying attention, wind checking while on the trail, you can sense when something... isn't right. It's like the air changes. You know what I'm talking about?"

"I do." Granger stared past her at the vending machine for a few moments, then said, "Lucy could just be in shock."

"She could be." Ava agreed. "But I don't take short cuts. I stay on plan. I check out every detail. This is how we catch him."

He sighed. "What do you need from me?"

"For one, we may need to reach out for volunteers."

"For..."

"A possible manhunt. I don't have the details yet, but I want things already moving so that we can mobilize a search party when we need it. Police personnel only. This isn't a missing kid out there."

"I'll make some calls. What else?"

Ava reached into her bag and pulled out printed screenshots from the wedding venue's website. She handed them to Granger. "I know you're opposed to looking into the victims' finances. I get why. But, I want you to see the wedding venue the Thompsons booked. It's a luxury hotel and their wedding packages *start* at fifty-thousand dollars. And that's not even for beachfront ceremonies, which I'm told Lucy's wedding was supposed to be. Mrs. Thompson had even annotated a deadline for a twenty-five-thousand-dollar deposit in her planner."

"I don't remember seeing that."

You didn't see the sleeping pills either.

"It's there. Trust me. Do you know if the Thompsons have that kind of money?"

Granger's brow furrowed. "Not that I know of."

"I also need to see Lucy's dress."

"She was wearing jeans and a sweater when she found them."

"No, her wedding dress. I want to know the brand. How much it cost."

"You really think there's a financial motive to the killings?" He looked at her doubtfully.

"I want to rule it out," Ava lied. "Tone Marley doesn't fit the money angle so it's likely a false lead, but I want to run it down and make sure. I think those kinds of questions coming from you might go over better. I'd like you to start with the fiancé, if possible. I've seen the photos of him on Lucy's social media. He looks like he's from money. And, you know, he's probably not my biggest fan at the moment."

"Yeah, well..." Granger looked at her thoughtfully. "I heard his family was more than comfortable. They could have wanted a grand wedding and helped pay for it."

She smiled. "That's what I'm thinking."

"And you want me to talk to him?"

"To clear things up. We already heard about Suarez throwing

around money. I want to make sure it was just him and not a factor in the case."

"The Thompsons wouldn't have been involved in anything shady. Jack and Stephanie were good people."

"Then help me prove that," Ava said. "Show me I'm on the wrong track with them and the money and I'll back off."

Granger stared at her for a moment before nodding. He turned to leave, but hesitated. "He shot you. The unsub. Agent Blake said he taunted you about it on the call."

"He did."

Concern flickered on his grizzled face. "Are you okay?"

"He barely grazed me. The amateur."

The corner of his eyes crinkled slightly before he said, "Where are you headed next?"

"I have to go and speak to a mother about her murdered son."

ELEVEN

Hikers had found Tone Marley at the bottom of a cliff in Pine Cove. Ava knew the scene through the photos and drone videos made by both Dr. Wren, and later, the CBI. His broken body had lain on the ground thirty feet below the ledge, and the recording provided a dizzying view of the depth of the fall. The sheriff had discovered Marley's empty backpack, metal water bottle, and phone at the top of the cliff. His phone, also found on the ledge, had appeared smashed— the SIM card removed. On top of the injuries the killer had inflicted to his liver and heart, he'd sustained multiple broken bones in the fall, including a skull fracture. Mercifully, Talia believed the young man was gone before he went over the cliff.

Due to recent rain and snowfall, August suggested Ava skip visiting the crime scene in the woods. A trail cut through the area, which is how hikers had found Marley's body. So, the evidence was likely tainted by the elements or trampled. She wanted to see it anyway. Not where they'd found the body, but where the fight had occurred.

During the initial investigation, Agent Rondeau had recorded the scene with a CBI drone and knew the area well, so August wanted him to come along. Granger ended up getting a call about a break-in at a farm. So by eight thirty that morning Ava, August, and Rondeau drove to the trail head and set off down the path. The wind sent a chill through her as fat, steel-gray clouds brooded over the horizon in the distance. Patches of overnight snow stuck to the tops of boulders and the edges of the path where the sun couldn't yet reach. Ava walked in silence, thinking about when she'd chased the killer and how he'd moved like he was hurt. Could be something there.

August glanced at her from over his sunglasses. "You're unusually quiet."

Ava motioned to the rising terrain. "The killer said something like, 'He didn't fight like a kid,' when he talked about Marley. He thought it was funny."

"Likely meaning there was a struggle." August nodded. "He thinks this is a game?"

"No idea. But he isn't acting scared, that's for sure." Ava kicked a rock off the path. "That's got to change, fast."

Behind them, Rondeau appeared to be enjoying himself, taking photos with his phone of interesting plants and explaining their alleged medicinal uses as they went. She wasn't quite sure drinking pine needle tea would help with headaches but decided he was interesting.

She fidgeted with the patrol radio at her waist and adjusted her earpiece, making herself focus on the trail. Paying attention to the sights that Marley might have witnessed on his last journey. The crispness to the air. The towering pines that loomed over the ground. Wood carved signs pointed to vernal pool hikes, artistically piled rocks lined the path, and the occasional squirrel flitted in the corner of her vision. In the distance, birds chirped, but Ava couldn't spot any up in the trees. Nothing nefarious. Though she knew what the dark woods felt like at night.

Shaking the past from her thoughts, she followed August as he led them up the rise to the cliffside. Ava walked the area where they believed the assailant had attacked Marley, spotting only rotten leaves, mud, and broken branches. Nothing seemed disturbed. No trace of the blood that had pooled there that night. As if a young man hadn't died a painful and frightening death on the ground where she stood.

Leaning over the ledge, she looked down. At least three stories. The wind whipped through the trees, swaying the branches, blowing her hair around her face. Sunlight sliced between the leaves, dappling the ground. Puffs of her breath clouded in front of her. It would've been frigid when Marley died weeks before. Still mid-winter. Ava had checked the weather almanac while reading the case file earlier. The temperature had plummeted to the mid-thirties on the evening Marley's mother called in the missing person's report. A storm had been on its way and yet he'd still gone out.

"Do you have the video from the night he was found?" Ava asked Rondeau.

"Right here." He stood next to her and pulled up the video from the CBI drone. She leaned in, watching. The video screen displayed time, location, and temperature. Thirty-nine degrees. In the recording, August stood in his field jacket talking to Chutney and Granger, both wearing heavy sheriff's department coats.

"Marley had on a light hoodie and jeans, right?" Ava asked, knowing she was right. The photo of his body in situ flashed in her mind for a moment. "He wasn't dressed for a hike that late."

"Correct," August said, his gaze on his tablet. "His mother seemed perplexed at that as well. He grew up in Pine Cove. He would've known how cold it could get."

Ava turned to Rondeau. "Did we ever find out what he was working on?"

"He'd told his mother it was a project for school," he drawled. "Granger called the dean of the community college and was told he'd ask Marley's professors what he could have been working on, but we haven't heard boo since."

"What about his mom? What did she say?"

"His mother didn't know specifics. Just what classes he was

taking. They were typical general education courses for college sophomores. Math, English, Biology, and I believe History," August said, the tip of his nose red with cold. "What are you thinking?"

"I just... I mean, what was he collecting? Biology is what... the mitochondria is the powerhouse of the cell? Life cycles? It's winter, everything is dead." She did a full three-hundred-sixty-degree turn, her arms out. "Most animals are overwintering or migrating. Just, look out here. Pine trees, rocks, dead leaves... bark. There are barely even any bugs out this time of year."

"Might be for a different class," Rondeau offered. "History or maybe English?"

Ava shrugged. "Does this area have historical significance? Was it written about in a novel? I can't even think of why you'd end up out here with a math assignment."

"His mother got the impression it was for science. Something about drawings," August said.

Rondeau held up his phone. "It could be photographic collection. Photos of non-migratory animals, winter's effects on the landscape, things like that. But without the SIM card for his phone, we have no idea if he took pictures with it."

August glanced at his phone. "And without cell service, they wouldn't have uploaded anywhere for us to check."

"He wouldn't need a backpack to take pictures though," Ava argued. "And he didn't seem to have collection containers. I mean, not even a Tupperware for small samples? No snacks for the hike?"

"The killer could have taken the samples," Rondeau offered. "He took the SIM card."

"Maybe..." Ava shook her head, bothered. "For someone who knows the area and the weather, why would Marley have been so unprepared?"

August cocked his head. "Why do you think the reason for the hike wasn't to collect nature samples?"

"It all just feels off," Ava said. "His backpack was empty. Was he looking for something specific up here? Because there was plenty of time during the entire hike to collect samples." She gestured at the area around them. "Did the killer choose Marley at random and follow him up here? Was the killer already here and Marley was just prey that wandered into his orbit? Did Marley come up here to meet someone and it went sideways?"

"You think the killer was someone he knew, don't you?" Rondeau asked Ava.

"We can't rule it out if we don't know why he was up here in the first place."

August shoved his hands into his jacket pockets. "I'll light a fire under the school."

"What next?" Rondeau asked.

Ava glanced at August. "Can I talk to the mom now?"

———

On the drive back into town, August arranged to speak with Marley's mother. Despite the hike, they were making good time to her house in Pine Cove. While August drove, Rondeau filled Ava in on the initial interview with her. He sat in the back seat of the rented suburban, his long legs angled into the footwell.

"The mom gave us permission to check the kid's electronics when we first joined the investigation," Rondeau said as Ava turned to face him. "Much like Suarez, we dumped Marley's phone records, and we checked out his social media, email, everything. Nothing unusual popped. Again, similar to Suarez. And with the SIM card gone, plus his remote location at the time of the murder, all we got was what happened before the phone was destroyed."

"Any weird calls or texts? Sometimes kids use messaging apps that look like a calculator app," Ava asked. Something didn't sit right with her. "There's one that makes the messages disappear, even. I didn't see anything in Vincent's report—"

"Hold on, now. I got you." Rondeau grinned and held up his palm. "So... like most kids, Marley preferred text. He communicated with his peers that way and used the community college's app for leaving messages with professors. The only voice calls were from or to his mother. Except for an office at the college..." He checked his tablet's notes. "Admission and transfers. Typical social media presence for his age. Daily posts about what he was doing at school, his food, outfit of the day, yada yada. But it fell off before his death."

"Was it around the time of Suarez's murder?" Ava asked as they passed by a cluster of shops surrounded by broadleaf oaks.

"Sure was." Rondeau held up his tablet for her to see a photo of Marley standing next to a welcome back sign while smiling at the camera. "He last posted when the new semester started."

"What about his gaming accounts?" Ava asked. She watched as her phone played the video of the ledge taken by the drone. Something odd about the scene floated at the edge of her mind, but she couldn't grasp it.

"Nah. The kid owned an older gaming system, and he didn't connect with any particular players. It looks like he joined teams set up by the platform."

"Did he have any friends in real life?"

"Plenty. His messages are with friends he made at the community college, mostly table-top gaming messages. Meet ups for movies in Hemet. That kind of thing. Granger and I spoke with a few of them. They didn't find anything odd about his behavior in the days before his death. And to answer your initial question, no mystery numbers or weird texts."

"You mentioned gaming. Did he do any computer gaming?" Ava asked, her gaze on the winding road. "He might have encountered the murderer online in a chat or something. I didn't see anything in the files."

"He didn't have a PC, just a loaner laptop from the college. He qualified for the program because of his family's finances. You can't play games on those. Too slow."

Ava looked at August. "We're solid on time of death?"

"As close as we can be given the state of the body," he said as he took a left turn toward town. "That hike would've taken him approximately thirty minutes from the road."

"So, he could have been there as soon as a couple of hours after his last class?" Ava asked.

"Marley's phone carrier finally got back to us this morning. They required a subpoena."

"How helpful of them."

"As always," August said.

"What'd we find out?" Ava asked.

Rondeau leaned forward. "Alright, your phone interacts with cell towers for calls and to stream data, not for GPS tracking. So, even though the SIM card was removed and his data was patchy, the phone's location could still be tracked to a twenty-five-mile radius, but nothing closer."

"Do we have that? His approximate GPS?"

"According to the phone carrier, tower pings and GPS location data both ceased around six that night. We believe that is when the phone was destroyed. Thereabout, anyway."

"Six," Ava murmured. "Before his mother even came home."

"Exactly. His phone backs up the timeline his mother gave us."

"Heads up," August said. "We're here."

The road twisted around a stand of impossibly tall pines and then a street lined with mailboxes and driveways came into view. They stopped in front of a dark green cottage style home. It sat back from the wrought iron gate, beyond a winterized garden. Two stories, with decorative gingerbread trim and a brick path to the covered porch.

Mrs. Marley greeted them at the door with the tired smile of grief. She'd pulled her hair back in a bun at her nape, gray at the temples, no makeup. She looked spent. Cried out. And thinner than the photos Ava had seen of her before her son was murdered. A small blue dot on her skin peeked out from underneath her collar, just below her collar bone. They stood in her living room. Photos of Mrs. Marley and Tone at various stages of his life sat on the mantel. A grandfather clock ticked in the corner. Flowery couches and chairs surrounded a cold fireplace. An antiseptic smell hit Ava's nose, and she glanced around. An IV pole with an empty bag and tubing sat in the corner by one of the chairs.

Mrs. Marley's red eyes looked at Ava with desperation. "I heard they brought in an expert," she said softly. "Do you think you can find who did this?"

"I will do my best, ma'am," Ava said. "Thank you for meeting with us so quickly."

"I'm on leave from work," she said. "I think you all are the first people I've spoken to in a week."

Ava understood that solitude. The buffer of death often kept people away. "Mrs. Marley, I know that Agent Blake and Agent Rondeau already searched your son's room, but I was hoping you'd allow me a quick look."

Staring at Ava blankly, Mrs. Marley said, "Sheriff Granger tried to say that Tone got turned around out there, but I knew better. He knew those woods. He never would have—" her voice cracked, and she turned away, blinking away tears. "I knew better."

"You were right." Ava leaned forward, touching her forearm. "That's why I'm here. To find out what really happened to your son."

Mrs. Marley relented. As she led August up the stairs, Ava stayed back and caught Rondeau's attention.

"Take a look around down here, would you?"

His pale brow rose. "For?"

"Anything that might look like Marley came into money. And I mean anything. Think outside the box."

He nodded and Ava hurried up the stairs to catch up. Mrs. Marley stood away from the door talking to August.

"I don't go in there. I can't yet," she murmured.

He nodded. "We'll be careful."

August pushed through the door, Ava right behind him. A typical young adult's room with posters of sports heroes and music artists hung on the walls. Shoes and books littered the carpet next to his closet. August stood by the door, chitchatting with Mrs. Marley to keep her there, asking about Tone's father while Ava perused the space. Mrs. Marley explained he'd died in a car accident when Tone was nine years old.

"Was he stressed about this project he was working on?" Ava asked toward the door.

"Uh..." Mrs. Marley's face appeared at the threshold. She hugged herself. "Not especially. Tone loved school. Things like that came easily to him. He even helped me with my insurance claims."

"Do you have any idea what he was working on? I know you mentioned the biology class, but do you know anything specific?" August asked, he caught Ava's eye and nodded to the desk by the window.

Mrs. Marley shook her head, edging inside, her gaze going to the bed. "No."

"And that day?" Ava went to the desk, scanning the papers and spiral notebooks scattered on the surface. She moved them, spotting a few drawings on thick paper underneath. "You didn't know he was headed out?"

"He wasn't supposed to. The weather was turning, and I got off work early. I thought we could... I thought we could make pizza together like when he was younger, but..." She shook her head. "He was gone when I got home from work. I'm a nurse down in Hemet."

Ava leafed through the artwork. Tone had sketched birds and rocks and cloud formations, coloring them with vibrant hued pencils. Something about the strange red shade pulled at her memory. She took photos of them all.

"Is this what he was working on?" Ava asked, holding up the sketches.

Mrs. Marley shrugged and shook her head. "I think so?"

They spent a few more minutes in the room. Ava looked under the mattress, the bed, finding some PC building magazines, flyers from school advertising events around campus, some forms from the counseling office for classes next semester. The usual debris from college life. As she squeezed between the desk and wall, leaning over to peer out the window, she stepped on something, feeling it crack. There were no sign of notes or samples for a science project anywhere in the room. Ava doubted there was an assignment at all.

"Mrs. Marley, did Tone make any recent purchases that seemed out of the ordinary?" Ava asked, bending to pick up the snapped colored pencil underneath her boot.

"No, uh, what do you mean?" Mrs. Marley crossed her arms over her chest.

August looked up from the spiral notebook in his hand. "Just touching all the bases."

"Well, it sounds like you're thinking he was into something he wasn't supposed to be."

Her defensiveness piqued Ava's attention and she asked, "Was he? Did anything come to you during the past few weeks that might shed light on what he was doing out there or how he might have come in contact with the killer? Anything at all?"

"No. I've wracked my brain trying to figure out why he was up there." Mrs. Marley rubbed her face with both hands, tired. "He was just a kid."

Ava pointed to the UCLA banner over the desk. "Was Tone going to transfer soon?"

"No... we couldn't afford UCLA, are you kidding? He was working toward an AA in bookkeeping."

"Then why does he have an IGETC form?" Ava held up a piece of paper. "This is a list of courses that community college students take specifically to transfer to California universities for junior and senior year. I took them myself. If he was taking these classes, he planned to go on to a four-year to finish his bachelor's degree."

"Well, I don't know about all that." Mrs. Marley frowned. "We have a shared account I added him to when he was eighteen, but that's it."

"No job?" August asked.

"No, he was working hard at school."

Ava took out her tablet and swiped through Rondeau's notes on the phone dump. "Mrs. Marley, it seems your son had plans to go to a four-year. He called the admission and transfers office for the paperwork." Ava held her gaze. "Did Tone believe he might have the money to do this soon? Stay at the dorms, maybe commute? Did he have his own car?"

"No, he borrowed mine or biked." She pulled her sweater closed, her lip trembling. "What's all this about? It sounds like you're trying to say Tone was somehow to blame for being attacked."

"Not at all, Mrs. Marley," August said. "We're just—"

"This wasn't his fault." She looked at them with a mixture of anger and suspicion. "I think you all are done here."

Ava snuck the broken pencil into her messenger bag's pocket while Mrs. Marley glared at August as he said, "I believe you're right."

Ava handed Mrs. Marley one of her cards as they said goodbye. Telling her to call if she thought of anything. She took it with a frown.

On their way out, Rondeau leaned in and said to Ava, "I clocked a lot of medical equipment in the main bedroom. I think Mrs. Marley is sick."

"She is," Ava muttered, looking over her shoulder. "Did you see the radiation tattoo on her chest?"

"The blue dot?" August said. "I wondered what that was."

"The equipment could be rented," Ava said. "Did you get photos?"

Rondeau tilted his tablet to show Ava the screen. He'd taken photos of a hospital bed, standing equipment, and packages of medication on the table through an open door. A wide shot with no personal information, but clearly a home health set up.

"I'd like to follow up on the equipment," Ava said. "And let's put calls in to the community college office while we're at it. If Tone was lining up a transfer, then it meant he believed he could pay for it."

"Maybe he got a scholarship," August said.

"I want to verify it's something like that." Ava climbed into the SUV, her mind reeling with scenarios and possibilities.

August slid into the driver's seat and looked at her. "You're still looking at the financial angle?"

Ava shrugged. "Getting sick in the US can be expensive. As is trying to educate yourself. Plus, they were living on one income. A nurse's salary. She didn't work a specialty, like surgery or anesthesia, either. And Tone didn't have a job according to Granger's notes. I'd like to see how they made that all work."

"She said she's on leave," Rondeau said. "I thought it was bereavement, time to grieve. You think it's medical?"

"That's another question we could answer via her bank account." Ava pulled the sun visor down. The morning burning away to afternoon.

"You didn't push her," August said. "Why?"

"She looked as perplexed as we did. Uneasy. She didn't act like she was hiding anything. Plus, I think she's medically fragile. I didn't want to give her a heart attack."

"But pushing Lucy into an anxiety attack was okay?"

"In terms of survivability, yes." Ava shook her head. "It's triage. An anxiety attack doesn't kill like a heart attack could."

He looked at her for a moment. "That's very surgical of you."

"Just let me know if you want a scalpel or a detonation, because I can do both."

"I'll call Vincent about subpoenas to take a real look into the finances of the victims."

"That's going to piss Granger off," Ava warned. "You better let him know you're doing it."

"He'll get over it," August muttered, rolling through a stop sign. "Insulted or not, Mrs. Marley got squirrely when you brought up money."

"I picked up on that," Ava said. "She senses or knows something. I just don't know how much."

"Where to next?" Rondeau held up his phone. "Talia said she has some updates."

"Good. I need to pick her brain a little. Catch up on forensics, tox screens, stuff like that."

August glanced at her. "What's that face mean, Ava? What're you thinking?"

"I think this town has some deadly secrets," she said, watching the perfect little houses flitting past the car window. "I hope they're ready for me to dig them up."

TWELVE

Delano Kester wandered carefully among the crowd gathered at the town hall in Black Oak, which was actually an old store the owner couldn't rent so they allowed the town to use it for a fee. Metal folding chairs sat in uneven rows facing a small plywood dais that had been painted green. A white plastic table with coffee and donuts stood ignored in the back. Posters depicting the recent holiday street festival curled on the walls. The town counsel's emergency meeting wouldn't start for another thirty minutes, but it was already standing room only. At least fifty people crowded the place, chatting as they waited.

A cold front had drifted in earlier than expected, dropping the temp. Nearly eleven in the morning and the winter sun did little to warm the day. People entered the room covered with snowflakes. Neck gaiters pulled up over their mouths and noses, scarves wrapped around their chins. Many people he'd never seen before, which helped him to blend. He spotted Granger and his deputy, Chutney, standing against the back exit eyeing the crowd, so he steered clear.

Delano spent the time eavesdropping on a number of conversations, staying on the edges of the groups. He kept his gaze on the itinerary they'd handed out at the entrance, seemingly oblivious to those talking around him. He paused to listen to a couple of people talking about a theft at the emu farm up the way.

"Someone just cut the lock right off the storage shed," a raggedy looking mountain man said.

He was talking to a woman Delano recognized from town. She ran a candle shop or some shit like that. Her name was Henley. Or Haley? Didn't matter. He scooted closer. Nerves on edge because he had to infiltrate the town meeting to get information. His side ached from a wound he'd suffered months ago, and he rubbed it with the heel of his hand absently.

When will this damn thing heal?

The mountain man continued. "The robber took all the feed, fertilizer for the garden, and a decent generator." He snapped his fingers. "Gone. Just like that."

"What did Granger say?" the possible Henley asked. She looked down her nose through black framed glasses. She looked like a cartoon nerd.

"He came out this morning and did the initial call, but then he put Chutney on it so, you know..." Mountain guy rolled his eyes.

She smirked. "What, you don't think Deputy Chutney can do a proper investigation?"

"Let me say this... You're not gonna find any books at *his* yard sale, if you know what I mean."

The woman nodded and Delano moved on.

Nina and Foster Chen, the lawyer couple who owned the burger joint, stood near the stage talking to the punk rock chick from the Riot Brewing Café. Her name was Velma, like the cartoon character, and he'd heard she'd been talking to the CBI. Drifting near them, he pretended to check his phone's email. He struggled to hear amid all the other chatter, but it's not like they were whispering.

"Well I ran into Yaeger's wife, Pam, when I was walking Luna this morning and she said he got a call at home from Sheriff Granger,"

Velma said. She glanced around. "The CBI is organizing some kind of grid-search out there."

"Like a search and rescue?" Foster asked.

"No, like a manhunt in the woods," Velma said, her pierced eyebrow rising. "I wonder if they'll bring in search dogs?"

Shit.

Nina shared a look with her husband. "The CBI really thinks the killer is out there in the woods?"

Velma shrugged. "Yaeger said the sheriff was asking about trail cams too."

The prickly fingers of fear gripped Delano's gut. He hadn't thought of trail cams. Hadn't seen any, but that didn't mean they weren't there. Delano weighed the risk of retracing his steps.

"Pam said she didn't want Yaeger wandering around in the forest looking for trouble. Their grandkids are coming to visit in a few days, and she has no idea what to tell her daughter. I told her to go visit them instead. Especially with a killer hanging around."

Foster shook his head. "I heard people are thinking of bugging out."

"Yeah, well, not everyone can afford that," Velma said.

Nina scanned the room, her gaze sliding past Delano. "Do they know what he wants?"

"Wants?" Velma looked at her like she was dumb. "What do you mean? He's a maniac. He wants to kill people."

"Yeah. I mean they have like motives though." Nina let out a nervous laugh. "It just seems like the Thompsons were so random."

"Not just them." Velma looked over her shoulder, then said, "I heard that Doctor Daniel's guess was right. The Suarez murder is connected. Granger told him."

Delano nodded to himself. He knew that might happen. That first hit had gone sideways on him, he'll admit that. He'd had to chase Suarez around the cabin. Things had gone better with Marley. His body hadn't been found right away. He hadn't had much choice on his timing with the Thompsons.

"The veterinarian... Hyde?" Nina's face went pale. "T-That's horrible. What made—I mean, how does he know this?"

"No idea. I think..."

Delano kept moving, his step faltering when he heard a name.

Agent Ava Cortes.

"Apparently she went too far a couple of years ago." Mrs. Walton, who he'd heard lived near the Thompsons, spoke with another woman he didn't recognize. "My sister Gale works at the station and said there was some kind of inquest or something over the death of a suspect."

"Maybe that's not a bad thing in this case," the other woman muttered. "You know what Yaeger was saying about the killer? That he was likely staying in the area. Can you imagine? What for? Isn't he afraid of getting caught?"

"I don't know, but Gale said this Agent Cortes woman is good." Mrs. Walton lowered her voice. "She's the one who was involved in that shooting over at Suarez's cabin. I heard she hit the killer in the ass as he was running away. Word is he might have a limp."

"Effin' coward," the other woman snapped. "Creeping around in the woods like a pervert."

Anger burned through Delano's chest. Ava was telling lies. And no one seemed to know about his phone call gloating about him hitting *her*. He tore up the itinerary. He'd really wanted to see the CBI give a press conference quoting all the religious shit he'd spewed to throw them off.

"What if he's here with us now?" Mrs. Wilton murmured.

Delano glanced around. A tension moved through the crowd like a fever. Everyone looked paranoid, peering over their shoulders. Eyes flitting to exits. He really had the town in his grip. A plan licked at his consciousness. He needed more fear. He needed chaos to get what he wanted.

"Testing... testing..." Neil Yaeger, the head of the council stood on the dais and fiddled with the microphone. "Let's get started, people."

The room broke into shouting. The crowd pushed up to the stage, yelling questions. Asking where the CBI was and why they hadn't found the killer yet. Yaeger's voice boomed over them.

"Order, order!" He shouted.

Delano strode back out into the cold, fighting his body to walk normally, his breath coming in ragged puffs with the pain. The vast sky hovered over him with bulging, dark clouds, crowding out the light. He forced himself to stroll casually down the street, his expression deliberately serene. That damn Agent Cortes had teased him about his hurt side. Now people were looking for a guy with a limp. He bet the manhunt idea had come from her too. And she'd likely decided to cover up the phone call. She was manipulating everything. His hands bunched into fists as he strode. An image of Ava burned behind his eyes and his gut wrenched. He needed more time.

He needed to keep them busy.

THIRTEEN

After talking with Mrs. Marley, the team went back to the sheriff's station looking for Granger. It was a little after eleven in the morning and the receptionist, Gale, told them he was still at the town hall meeting, though he'd called to say it was wrapping up. Ava, August, and Rondeau settled in the conference room talking about the hike and Mrs. Marley's interview.

"I need to call Vincent and see if we can find out Mrs. Marley's diagnosis," Ava said.

"Don't hold your breath. We have no legal reason to be snooping into her medical information." August looked at Rondeau. "The photos were pushing it."

"The door was halfway ajar, and I snapped two photos of what I could see standing in the hallway, so we're good." Rondeau spun his tablet on his palm. "The desk in the room had rows of medical packages. Tubing, sterilizing wipes, gauze... what you'd expect to have on hand for home care. Medicine bottles, too, but they were in a semi-closed room, not in plain sight, so I didn't get those. I'll jump online and see which medical equipment businesses in the area deliver up here. She might have an account with a place down in Hemet or over in Palm Springs."

August checked his watch. "We're still waiting on Vincent's yes or no on the subpoenas for the victims' financial records. She's meeting with legal this afternoon."

"Why? It's standard."

"With the scrutiny this case is getting, they want a solid reason to invade the privacy of the victims without a clear indication of fraud or a financial link to the killer."

Ava rolled her eyes before glancing at Rondeau. "What'd Mrs. Marley have in there? A bed with rails and lifting capabilities, maybe a portable tray on wheels?" She closed her eyes, seeing the equipment she'd had to learn to use as a teenager when her grandmother fell ill. "Digital IV meds dispenser. She might also have mobility accommodations for the shower and car, maybe even nutritional support like shakes or other kinds of consumables so we should include those in our query."

Rondeau nodded, taking notes. "She said her son helped with her claims. Could be rental—"

"They're not," Ava said, leaning back in the comfy chair, staring at the holes in the ceiling tiles. "My grandmother did hospice at home. Rental equipment is often out of date and a bit battered. I had to hand crank my grandmother's bed to make her sit upright. The bed in your photos looks new." She leaned over and pointed to a panel of buttons on the end of the bed frame. "See this control panel? That's expensive. This is for long-term care of bedridden patients. Mrs. Marley is ambulatory. She's walking around, moving on her own. Why have something like this in her room if she doesn't need it?"

"She could have been sick and then recovered," Rondeau said.

"Then why did she just take leave from work? She said she hadn't spoken to anyone in a week. That's recent." Ava shook her head. "I think she anticipates needing that kind of heavy-duty medical equipment in the near future."

"That's bleak," Rondeau muttered. "With her son gone, she's alone."

"It is." She sat up. "Either way, that stuff is costly."

"She's a nurse," August said. "Maybe she got some help?"

Ava looked across the table at him. "I sure hope so."

They went over some incoming reports from the field office. Ava had tried calling the killer back, just in case he was forwarding the call from another number or using an app, but the number went straight to a series of beeps and then it hung up.

"We've set your phone to record if it receives another anonymous number," Rondeau said. "Other than that, the actual number and owner are untraceable. He knows what he's doing."

"So maybe a longtime criminal?" Ava wondered. "Or trained in clandestine practices."

Rondeau updated them on the Thompsons' missing laptop. It was not connected to a cloud data storage service. He also revealed that Dr. Clay did find a secondary cord at the scene which turned out to belong to some kind of external hard drive. It was missing as well.

"The killer also took the SIM card from Marley's phone." Ava clicked her pen, working through the possible scenarios why. "He'd take their electronics to what... destroy incriminating evidence like photos, possible text conversations or phone calls proving they knew him personally?"

"They might've met before the murder," Rondeau said. "And the killer wanted to destroy the location data."

"That's good," August said, scribbling on his tablet with his smart pen. "What else?"

"Maybe there was something on Marley's SIM card and the Thompsons' laptop that pointed to his motive or the commonality between the victims," Ava said before turning to Rondeau. "Did you get anything off the phone itself? Anything in the photo gallery or messages?"

"No, it was smashed and then rained on." Rondeau shrugged. "We couldn't pull anything off it."

"The killer might believe they had something on their devices that would lead to him," August said, drumming his fingers for a few seconds before continuing. "Or he thought both of them had information he wanted."

"Speaks to a solid connection," Ava said. "All the victims have something in common. We just haven't found it yet."

They talked about Suarez's service record, and Lucy's current mental status. Dr. Craig had not returned August's phone call after their visit to Shady Acres. Ava was starting to think about lunch when Talia arrived. She came into the conference room fluffing flakes from her hair, crisp air and the scent of leaves following her. She smiled, handed Rondeau her laptop and sat down beside him. Without a word, he started typing. Ava watched them, they seemed like old friends. Rondeau fiddled with the keys and then his, Ava's, and August's tablets pinged with the update.

"I have results," Talia said, taking back her laptop. "Let's start with the tox screen on Mrs. Thompson. It came back positive for her sleeping medication, as per Ava's theory. She had a normal dose onboard." She held up a manicured finger. "However, Mr. Thompson had a large dose of that same medication in *his* system."

"You were right." August sat back, his gaze catching Ava's. "That's why he didn't have any ligature marks. The killer chemically restrained him."

She nodded. "What about the other victims?"

"The CBI expedited tests on the blood we took from Suarez and Marley," Talia said, scanning her laptop screen. "Neither had drugs in their system, though Suarez had some alcohol onboard. Not quite the driving limit but getting there."

"It's weird the Thompsons were drugged and not the others, right?" Rondeau looked at the photos. "The unsub has no discernable victim preference. We've got a thirty-something marine in Suarez, a twenty-year-old student, and an older couple. This guy doesn't operate like a serial killer looking to fulfill some kind of pathological fantasy."

"Could he be mission oriented?" Talia asked. "Or are they victims of opportunity?"

Ava doodled looping arrows in the margin of the report, thinking. "The problem with using MO to link a killer to his crimes is, they learn. Adapt. This unsub attacked Suarez on his home turf, and it looks like it went haywire. An alcoholic veteran is still a formidable target. With Marley, he chose a hiking trail, a place where he might have an element of surprise again. I think it's because he can't overpower them."

"He's hurt." August's gaze flitted to her arm. "You said he had a limp. When you chased him after the shooting."

"Not really a limp, but something. He moved wrong, like he was favoring an injury to his side." She wiggled in her chair. "He waddled a little."

"The unsub might have been injured while fighting either Suarez or Marley." Rondeau looked at Talia. "Any evidence of that? Defensive wounds on Marley, maybe?"

"Marley did have some light bruising on the skin of his forearms," Talia offered. "He likely sustained them before the fall."

"Bruises don't form after death, right?" Rondeau asked.

"It's unlikely. With lividity and lack of blood flow, he'd have to have still been alive after he hit the ground. So, it's probable he fought with the killer before he died."

"So, the unsub chose to use restraint this time instead of a blitz attack. He refined his technique," Ava mused. "Perhaps injury... perhaps he needed more control because he was dealing with two victims, not one."

August shook his head. "If control is what he wanted, why didn't he kill Mr. Thompson, the trained law enforcement officer, first?"

"And how did he dose him?" Talia asked. "I checked for puncture wounds."

"Maybe the killer forced Mr. Thompson to take the meds," Ava murmured.

"How?" Rondeau asked. "Why?"

"I don't know." Ava rubbed her face with both hands, her gaze on the files. "Did we get anything new on the bullet?"

Talia swiped through her tablet. "Let's see... ballistics on the round we pulled out of the tree on the Suarez property came back as having the size, markings, and rifling pattern of a nine-millimeter round. Likely fired from one of the most popular concealed carry pistols on the market. The one the unsub used is not in the system. But what I did find..." She pulled a manilla folder out of her bag and fanned several glossy photos onto the table for everyone. Some showed bright blue and violet images. Others displayed more natural colors. A pale arm appeared almost blue. "You've got copies in the file, but I thought the images were better printed. These are of Mr. Thompson's arm."

Ava pulled one toward her, tilting her head. A ring-shaped bruise encircled the skin above Thompson's bicep. "These are the UV photos Dr. Wren took?"

Rondeau held one up, nodding. "We did the best we could with the existing equipment, then I ran them through a digital filter for contrast."

"It goes up a little." August held one up, pointing. "Do you see that?"

Ava nodded, reaching into her messenger bag and pulling out the rubber tubing she'd taken from the ME's office. She wrapped it around her arm and then tugged on the long end. The movement distorted the loop around her arm, creating a lift at the tension point. "Look familiar?"

August held her gaze. "Dr. Wren's theory was right."

"Yeah." Ava undid the rubber tubing. "A tourniquet left that mark."

"What are you getting at here? That the unsub tried to save Mr. Thompson?" Rondeau frowned at the glossy photos.

"I'm not sure 'saved' is the right word." Ava swiveled the chair from side to side, her mind working through scenarios. Flashes of case reports, books from her criminology major, stories from cops and lecturers all whispered through her head. She'd seen something similar, she knew it, but didn't know where. Knives and ropes. Slow and fast deaths. Blood and cold. A series of images strobed behind her vision. Black and white. Stills from a scientific journal article. Old...

She stilled. "Talia, did Thompson have hilt marks?"

"You mean—"

"Yeah." Ava made a stabbing motion with her hand. "Marks from the knife's handle slamming down onto the skin." She looked through the photos of the wounds on Thompson's chest and abdomen. "Did any show up in the UV photos?"

Talia shook her head. "No, none."

"What about depth?"

"The wounds measured between five and a half and six and a quarter inches."

"So, some shallow hits?"

"Yes."

"Where's the rage?" Ava asked August, holding up one of the photos of a knife-wound. "The killer stabbed Mr. Thompson multiple times but was controlled enough to not slam the knife down and bruise the skin around the wound? He didn't hit any major arteries either."

"Maybe he's just sadistic and took his time," Rondeau offered.

"Okay, but the blood on the lampshades and walls... that's from swinging the knife up and down rapidly, right?" Ava handed a glossy photo of the crime scene to Talia. "I know we haven't blocked out the attack choreography, but that's what the scene looks like to me."

"It does have the markings of a blitz attack..." Talia said. "What are you suggesting?"

"In your experience, is it normal to have a heavy upswing, enough to throw blood around the room, but a controlled down swing in a knife attack?"

Talia looked at her, but her eyes were seeing something else. "You mean he stabbed with control, but pulled the knife up in an arc on purpose? To make it look like he was frenzied?"

"Granger asked if you thought the killer faked the viciousness... staged it, essentially," August said. "You said not exactly."

"Well, I amend that statement now that the unsub tried to sound nuts on the phone call. His rantings were utter bullshit. He wants to sound like an unhinged killer, but so far, he's been organized." Ava tapped her index finger on Talia's forensic report. "He left no evidence at the scenes and took out two full grown males despite having a weird gait that indicates injury. Is it possible he's a sadistic serial killer enacting some unknown fantasy? Yes. But I think he wants people scared for another reason..." The drone footage of the cliff had bothered her and now she knew why. Ava looked up suddenly. "Did Marley have injuries to his fingertips?"

"Uh..." Talia shook her head while leafing through the photos on the table. "There was mutilation of his fingers and other exposed skin due to weather and animal activity. I couldn't get prints even if I tried."

"I don't need prints." Ava shook her head. "I want to know if he tried to hang onto the cliff's edge."

August leaned forward. "Explain."

"The killer used coercion with Thompson." Ava hugged herself. "I think he might have done the same with Marley. Dangle the kid off the ledge and say—"

"I let go and you die, now tell me what I want to know," August finished. "How did he get him in that position though?"

"I mean, he ambushed Suarez. Who's to say he didn't do the same with Marley. Knock him off his feet, maybe tackle him and shove him to the edge?"

"And he did the same with Thompson, but instead of a ledge, it was a tourniquet. I let go and you die," August said.

"More like I let go and *he* dies," Ava said. "Mr. Thompson was unconscious, remember?"

"You think the killer questioned Mrs. Thompson... not her husband?"

"Yes." Ava rubbed her face and leaned back. "I think the killer was threatening to strike a killing blow with every wound. It was an interrogation using a loved one's life."

August stilled. "How do you mean?"

"If someone was hurting me, and I was resisting telling them what they wanted to know, that's one thing. But if someone was hurting you... for example... and every time I don't answer, you get stabbed?" Ava shook her head. "I don't think I would resist. Not with you dying right next to me."

He scratched at his temple. "And the show. The dramatic upswing to throw blood above the bed—"

"That was to sell it," Ava said. "To scare her into giving him what he wanted."

"Well, I'm not gonna sleep tonight," Rondeau said with a sour face. He looked at Talia. "You think that happened?"

She nodded slowly, her gaze on the photos of the room. "Ava's theory could explain why Mrs. Thompson only had one wound. The final killing blow. And why she was restrained, but not her husband, the larger threat."

"What do you think he was after?" Rondeau asked. "What could such different victims know about him?"

"No idea," Ava said with a shrug. "I don't even know if I'm right."

"Let's test the theory then." August nodded toward Talia. "I want you to work on the attack choreography for Suarez, Marley, and the Thompsons. I know you've got a rough idea sketched out with the forensics team, but I want it nailed down for the lawyers. You and Rondeau work out the angle of blows along with the rest of the scene. I want to see if the data supports this kind of scenario. It would change the profile for Behavioral Sciences."

"On it," Talia said, writing down notes on the outside of a manilla folder. "What else?"

Something Alfonzo had said bothered Ava. "I think Suarez's brother was right. I think this guy has military training. Statistically, military retirees tend to stick close to their last command if they don't go back to their home state with family. What's around here? Camp Pendleton?"

"And Twenty-Nine Palms. Both the city and the military base," August said, nodding. To Rondeau he said, "Let's pull crime reports involving military or former military in the area for the past six months. Concentrate on Fallbrook, Rainbow, and Oceanside. Camp Pendleton Marines spend their money in those towns."

"Also Palm Desert and Hemet," Rondeau offered. "Anywhere else?"

"Up here on the mountain as well. Black Oak, Fern Valley, and Pine Cove. We should include Idyllwild in the search too," Ava added. "If he's familiar enough with the area to lure Marley to a secluded place to kill him, then he might be from around here, or used to be. Look for stabbings and shootings, the killer used both weapons."

"Got it," Rondeau said as he jotted down the information.

"I said you could exhume Marley if we were able to see bruises around Thompson's arm," August said. "Do you still want that?"

Ava tapped the pen on the autopsy photo. "Let me think about it. If the killer changed his MO from Suarez to Marley and then again when he killed the Thompsons, I'm not sure going back will give me much. What we know now is that he used a tourniquet on his last victim. But for what reason? That's the more important question."

August shook his head, staring at the photo of Thompson's bicep. "What's he doing?"

"Torturing people," Rondeau said with a frown. "He gets off on it."

"Here's the weird thing." Talia flipped through the toxicology report. "Mr. Thompson had so much sedation in his system, I doubt he really felt all that much. He'd be fully unconscious at these levels given his height and weight."

"So Mrs. Thompson was the focus..." Rondeau began.

Ava leaned back in her chair, barely hearing the discussion between them. Instead, she followed a dozen bunny trails, their bright streaks glowing across her mind until she eliminated the scenarios when they reached impossible or dead ends. The low din of their discussion vibrated in the background as she tried to find the wisp of a memory. She'd seen deliberately placed stab wounds like the ones on Thompson before. Or maybe it was the tourniquet. An incandescent thread pulled through her nearly eidetic memory. Pages from a history journal came back to her recollection. A recounting of an anthropology professor's visit to a dig near Cambodia she'd had to read for an assignment in college.

The professor had been asked to lend his expertise to a UN forensic anthropology team that had uncovered a mass grave near a Buddhist temple in Cambodia. They believed it was the work of a paramilitary group known as Sangkat 7 which had committed atrocities against several Cambodian ethnic groups during the seventies. Sangkat 7 referred to the municipal subdivisions in Cambodia from which the group grew.

Ava had read about the torture endured by monks who'd helped to hide people hunted by Sangkat 7. They'd used brutal tactics to extract their information. One of which was called The Cold Death. It involved bloodletting, and the threat of death by exsanguination, over pure torture. The article had included excerpts of the anthropologist's journal and a rough sketch on a dusty page flashed behind her eyes. An ink-drawn man holding a length of rope around another's thigh. A hastily drawn knife plunging down. Echoes of screams filled her head and made her flinch back to the present. She gasped and caught August watching her.

"You okay?" he asked.

"He's searching for something." Ava shook her head. "And he's torturing the victims to find it."

"You're sure?"

"As the dawn." Ava bit her lip. "Our killer isn't nuts. He's on a mission."

FOURTEEN

They spent the next few hours filling out paperwork and going over the forensic reports. During this time, Ava got August to agree to stay at the Timberline Inn. For the time being. But only if police officers from the Hemet Police Department were posted at both entrances. If anything else put the team in danger, they were moving.

By midafternoon, Ava's stomach started growling and August had them break for lunch. Deciding to stretch her legs, she gathered her messenger bag and headed for the exit. August caught up, falling in step and opening the door for her.

"What's up?" he asked. "Where're you going?"

She'd forgotten about his rule about staying partnered up. "I'm sick of restaurant food. Figured I'd check out the little grocery store at the end of Main Street. Maybe get some soup or something to warm up. You wanna come or should I grab someone else?"

"Soup sounds good." He pulled on his field jacket and leather gloves, flexing his fingers as they walked. "I forgot you liked to walk everywhere."

"Puts you in the mix." Ava slipped a little on the icy asphalt on her way to the rented SUV. She pulled her coat from the backseat and shrugged it on as they crossed the parking lot to the main drag. "People might not walk into a police station to talk to us, but they'll shoot the breeze with a 'helper' out and about."

The sun burned pale and muted behind an overcast sky. Completely gray, Ava couldn't even make out the individual clouds. The wind kicked up, sending spits of wet snow down on them as they strode along the sidewalk. Black Oak used to be a boom town, according to its website, and the building façades on main street leaned into the aesthetic. Western style storefronts, a boardwalk with shop signs in carved or burnt wood, the occasional wagon wheel nailed to a random barrel trash can. Rusty farm equipment used as planters and fountains dotted the picturesque little town.

"Your theory..." his voice trailed off.

"You don't buy it?"

"You said earlier that the town had secrets," August said after a few moments. "That indicates collusion. Your theory, about the killer using the tourniquet for interrogation, points to that as well. I didn't see it. So I guess I'm asking, how did you get there?"

"I think the Shady Acres nurse did it for me. She clearly didn't want us speaking with her patient. I think the victims are connected in a solid way, we just haven't found it yet. Lucy Thompson can help with that. I know it."

"I don't think we'll get another crack at her anytime soon. Her fiancé petitioned for temporary power of attorney. Vincent thinks he'll get it."

"That sucks," Ava said, sniffling from the cold. "By the way, I asked Granger for a few things. In case you speak with him."

"Everything alright? I caught the tension between you two back there."

"It is now. We sorted it out. I asked to see Lucy's wedding dress. She wouldn't stop talking about the expensive lace. That and the cost of the wedding is sending up red flags for me. He said he'd get the dress and look into the venue."

"Why am I not surprised you got him back on your side?"

"Because my side is right."

August nodded. "Gale said he's on his way back from the town hall."

"Charming the assistants again, I see."

He smiled. "You know they run everything. Anything else?"

"I also asked Granger to speak with the fiancé for us about the wedding finances. I thought he might have better luck than the agent who made the future bride crash out."

"Good call." Their shoes crunched along the gravelly road. August kept his gaze on the tree line beyond the town. A bird call, low and melancholy, floated out from the forest. "He said you asked him to form up a search team."

"So, you already talked with him." The Big Basket Market sign across the street lit up the gloomy afternoon with dark mustard neon. "Checking up on me?"

"I don't check up on my team. I touch base about *our* plans."

"Right." Ava smiled.

"Granger called me to talk about coordinating the search team." August shoved his gloved hands in his jacket pockets. "A manhunt? Do you know something I don't?"

"In general, or this specifically?" Ava caught August's subtle eye roll. She fought another smile tugging on her lips as they crossed the grocery store's small parking lot. Nearly empty, with just a few older people and a mom with teenagers loading bags of groceries into their cars. Ava and August walked through the sliding doors and into the quaint market. The scent of coffee and oranges hit her as they entered.

"We didn't discuss this, Ava."

"That's because I don't really think we need one. But, I specifically presented it as a manhunt to Granger because I know, and you know, that Gale is going to find out what he's doing and tell absolutely everyone that we're trying to form a posse to search the woods."

"You're putting pressure on the killer," August said as they walked past the shopping carts and sale bins.

"That's the idea. I mean, if we actually do end up needing volunteers for a grid-search, we'll have things ready in the wings, but the killer is moving around in the woods thinking he's some kind of untouchable wraith. I want him to know his territory is now ours. And we're closing in on him."

"And if he's moving around in the town itself?"

"If he is, then the manhunt thing is a moot point." Ava grabbed a hand basket and scanned the signs dangling from the ceiling, looking for the deli.

"But you don't think he is." August followed her to the back of the store where the deli counter stood.

"I think he's able to slip in and out of town undetected. He's likely socially competent, but forgettable. Probably on purpose. But he's not just killing people here in Black Oak. He's going up to Fern Valley and over to Pine Cove... so he definitely has a vehicle."

"So, a moveable base. Like Westerfield in San Diego. He killed his victim in an RV."

Ava nodded. "Yeah, like that. Mobile. But not an RV. People might notice that in town."

A guy in a paper hat and beard-net greeted them with raised brows. His nametag said, Ben. "What can I getcha?"

She ordered the vegetable beef soup and then waited while August asked numerous questions about the other soups and salads, before ordering a vegetable beef soup as well. Ben offered them some fresh baked rolls that would be out of the oven in a few minutes. They agreed to wait and wandered off, looking for snacks to take back to the inn.

August's phone trilled and he glanced at the screen. "It's Agent Vincent. I'm going to float her some of our theories." He split off from her to talk outside.

Ava perused the discount bins but found only bruised fruit and stale snack cakes. She hit the deli aisle next and grabbed a package of cheese sticks. A bulletin board near the restroom sign at the back of the store caught her eye. Various flyers and printouts papered the board, and she skimmed the tacked-up notices. Piano lessons and handy man services. Missing pets and lawn care coupons. One offered free consultations for heating and air conditioner maintenance. A stranger visiting houses, Ava thought. Might be something there. Several of the little tabs with a phone number were torn off from the bottom of the paper. She took one of the few left.

She lifted the various papers to see what was underneath. One flyer, a handwritten leaflet on lavender printer paper, announced a walking tour of the area and promised a ninety-nine percent chance of a "find." Whatever that meant. It must have been posted for a while, with old and tattered edges, so Ava yanked it out from under the thumbtack and dropped it into her messenger bag. She also pulled off a book club flyer.

She kept wandering around the store, her impatience growing. Ava normally shopped at the chain grocery store by her house in Oceanside and each of their stores used the same layout. It normally took her fifteen minutes tops to buy her weekly groceries. Ava had already been in this store longer than that and had yet to figure out the layout. There seemed to be no rhyme or reason where they placed their products. She had to zig-zag back and forth across the store to find what she wanted. From the dairy aisle, to the produce on the other end of the store, to the back wall for crackers. What normally took her a short time back home took much longer here—Ava paused. *She had to zig-zag... to find things...* An errant thought began to crystallize when she heard someone call her name.

"Agent Cortes?" A woman said from the far end of the aisle. Polished, late forties maybe, long ebony hair. Beautiful smile. She moved in Ava's direction, her hand out. "I'm Nina Chen. I own the Grizzly Grill down the line."

They shook hands. "That's the burger place, right? I passed it on the way to the café."

"Well, it's more like a steak house now." Nina glanced down the aisle behind Ava. "Is Sheriff Granger here?"

"No. He was at the town hall, but I believe it's ending soon."

"I went. It got out a bit ago." Nina picked a box of strawberry toaster pastries off the shelf, considering it. "I heard you had your own sort of town hall over there at the Riot Brewing Café. I'm friends with Velma, the owner."

"Oh, yes," Ava said, eyeing Nina. She had a professional bearing, friendly but stand-offish. "Did you grow up here?"

She put the box back and smiled. "I wish. No, my husband Foster and I bought the Grizzly Grill from the original owners about five years ago. We retired early from the rat race."

"Law?" Ava guessed.

"Yeah, corporate. How did you know?" Nina asked, smoothing her hair. "Has someone been bending your ear about us?"

"I just know a lot of attorneys." Ava caught a familiar figure passing by the end of the aisle. Deputy Chutney. He didn't seem to notice her.

"Tax law, but don't hold it against me. I'm retired." She followed as Ava scooted further down to the cereal section. "So, Velma was telling me that Doc made a connection between the Thompson murders and another victim."

"How do you know Velma?"

"We're part of the community business guild," Nina said. "Anyway, I heard Doc said another victim might be a man named Rio Suarez."

Ava smiled, a Cheshire cat grin. "Are you cross examining me, counselor?"

Nina's smile faltered. "Old habits."

"We're looking into Suarez's death, but nothing is decided yet."

"I heard you also visited Tone Marley's mother. Is *he* officially part of the investigation?"

Ava shrugged with nonchalance. "The timeline doesn't fit. He went missing way before Suarez's death," she lied. People often hesitated to answer direct questions, but few could resist correcting a wrong statement.

"Oh no, he died *after* Suarez. A few weeks." Nina pressed her lips into a thin line. "At least I think."

"Did you know Suarez or Marley?"

"Uh, not really. I know Mrs. Marley enough to say hi. She's a local, grew up here, I believe."

She said it as if that explained why they weren't friends. Ava gave her the standard 'We're following all available leads and information' line. Nina didn't like that and tried asking for details about the investigation in other ways.

Ava gave her non-answers, then said, "I asked your fellow Black Oakians at the café to share their theories about the killer with me. Care to add?"

Nina thought for a moment before speaking. "I know he uses a knife and ambushes people. I also heard he might be some kind of Navy SEAL or something. Is that true?"

"We're vetting evidence, building a profile," Ava hedged.

Nina narrowed her eyes, frustrated. "Rumor has it you shot the killer at Suarez's place. Did you really shoot him in the butt?"

Ava let out a chuckle. "I hope so."

They chatted for a few more minutes, but Nina eventually gave up her interrogation. Ava watched her wander toward the frozen aisle before going back to her search for snacks. She found the beverage section and spotted some individual guava drink cans on the lower shelf. As she knelt down, a looming form walked up to her. Glancing up, she noted the furrowed brows and furious gaze.

"Deputy Chutney. I was wondering when you were going to give me a piece of your mind."

He hesitated for a moment, caught off guard. "What the hell gives you the right to terrorize Lucy Thompson?"

Ava raised a brow, her face calm. "My job. Literally. And I didn't terrorize her. I asked her what she knew about her parents' murder."

"She's a witness... a victim..." he counted the words off on his stubby fingers. "A well-respected citizen, and—"

"Former girlfriend?" She dropped a couple of guava juice cans in her basket.

"What... who told you that?"

"Well, it sure wasn't you," Ava said and stood to face him. She smelled liquor on his breath. "Wanna tell me why, as part of an investigation into the brutal murders of Lucy's parents, you neglected to tell the CBI you had a failed relationship with the daughter of the victims?"

"Failed... That's not even what happened!" His face flushed, matching the color of his blood shot eyes, and he leaned over her. "It was mutual. We were still friends—"

"Uh-huh. So, are you coming at me as a fellow law enforcement officer concerned about my interrogation techniques or an ex-boyfriend hoping to score some points with Lucy for defending her honor?"

Chutney took a step back. "I'm not doing that!"

"Then why confront me here? In public. So unprofessionally?" Ava glanced down the aisle where a woman slow walked her cart pretending not to eavesdrop. "In uniform, no less."

Chutney stared at her, his breathing a little ragged. "You had no right."

"Okay, even though I totally *did* have every right to question our only witness, Granger already chewed me out for upsetting her."

"Good."

"Okay then," Ava said and moved toward him. "You done?"

He stepped into her path when she tried to walk around him. "Not even close."

She sighed. "Deputy, Lucy's fiancé is getting legal authority for her care so you can't swoop in and be the hero. Don't blow your career over a shot you don't have."

"You don't know what you're talking about."

"I gave you a pass with that dumbass posturing when I showed up at the crime scene but if you want to tussle, we can tussle." Ava stepped back on her right heel, tilting her head. "You were at all three crime scenes, yes?"

"What?" His gaze flitted over his shoulder.

"You have history with one of the victims. A bad break-up. And suddenly your lost love's wedding is off and what... you're playing hero? That's a little suspicious, don't you think? The killer cut the victims with almost surgical precision. No hesitation. Like a hunter might field dress a kill. You hunt, don't you, Chutney?" Ava was guessing. Almost everyone up in Black Oak did according to the town's chamber of commerce site. Fifty-fifty she was right.

"What of it?" Chutney said a little too loud. "Are you accusing me of something?"

"I'm saying that I look at *everybody*. And I rule them out if they're innocent. That's all I was doing with Lucy. But Chutney... she's hiding something and it might get her killed."

"What the hell are you talking about?" He shifted on his feet, unsure. "What do you mean she's hiding something? You think she knows who the killer is?"

"Maybe... maybe not." Ava picked up the same box of toaster pastries Nina had grabbed. "But she won't talk."

"Well, I can't get her to if that's what you want."

"What *can* you get me?"

"Huh?"

"How about the names of people up here you see regularly but don't actually know?"

"I—" His face pinched into a frown. "I don't work for you."

"Sure, but I'm asking you to do more than stomp around and glare at me."

He pointed in her face, his finger a hairsbreadth from her nose. "You think you're some kind of super-cop, but I called a buddy down in Oceanside and he had a lot to say about your 'Constellation of Crime' theory everyone thinks is nuts. Oh, and I also heard you and Agent Blake were hitting the sheets between cases."

"From whom?" Ava snapped despite herself.

"A reporter. She was at the station earlier, asking questions."

"Let me guess, Ricki Rogers?"

"So, you *do* have it out for her," he said, triumph on his face. "She told me you and your boyfriend, Agent Blake, covered up a crime."

"She also reported on a UFO that turned out to be a weather drone. I wouldn't take anything she says too seriously."

"I can see why she scares you. She's got all sorts of interesting tales about you and your time at PIT. Before they kicked you out."

She looked at him with boredom. "There are breathtakingly few things that scare me, and Ricki Rogers isn't one of them. She's a wannabe news blogger drooling for a break that will make her feel like a legitimate news caster."

Chutney's face split into a crooked grin, full of malice. "Did I hit a nerve?"

"You couldn't hit water if you fell out of a boat." Ava shrugged. "Ever wonder why a reporter would bother to tell a deputy anything when the CBI is in town?"

He wavered for a second, then said, "We happened to be sitting at the same bar—"

"And she somehow got you talking about how big of a problem I am, right? She's using you to get to me. Wake up."

"You don't know what you're talking about."

"Come to think of it, there's a lot of information flowing out of the sheriff's office lately." She pointed at him with the box of pastries. "Is that you? Because feeding Ricki information on the case is a bad career move."

He knocked the box out of her hand, looming over her. "Listen you crazy—"

Ava was already moving. Hitting his hand away with her forearm, opening up his chest and throwing him off balance. She lunged in and twisted, driving the heavy basket in her other hand against the inside of his knee. His leg gave out and he staggered to the side, hissing with pain. He caught himself on the opposite shelf and looked at her with shock.

Ava leaned in. "I bite back, Chutney."

"Everything alright down here?" August walked up, passing Chutney. He stopped next to Ava, his shoulder rolled back like he might throw a punch. "We have a problem?"

Chutney pointed a shaking finger at her. "She's the problem."

August made a face. "I'll put that in the report right next to your drinking on the job."

Chutney glared at Ava. "You watch your back."

"Excuse me?" August said, stepping between them. "Say that again."

Chutney glanced at August, before turning and limping away.

"That looked cozy," August said after he'd left. "What was that about?"

"He's mad at me over Lucy. They used to date."

August's brows rose. "How long have you known that?"

"Since the café. Also... he heard about the Constellation of Crime theory and that we were a thing," Ava said absently as she stared at the box of toaster pastries on the floor and then up at the aisle signs overhead.

"Crap. I'll talk to Granger about him. You should've told me about his past with Lucy..." He paused, staring at her. "Ava?"

She looked up and down the aisle and tried to remember the map of the area she'd shown to August earlier. The irregular route the killer had taken through the towns flashed to mind, and her gaze snapped to his. "I had to zig-zag."

"Come again?" August bent down, picked up the box of toaster strudels, and dropped it in her basket.

"I know why the killer's path through the towns seems so erratic." Ava bounced on her heels. "I know what he's doing out there."

FIFTEEN

Ava and August returned to the sheriff's station and settled back into the conference room to eat. They sat together at the end of the table, chatting quietly, pitching scenarios. Flurries drifted down from a gray cotton sky outside the window. Ava fussed with her soup, dipping her roll into the broth and biting off the soggy bit. It could use a little salt, but it fought off the chill, which she needed.

"You have a theory," August said, his gaze resting on her. "I can see it in your eyes."

"I think all of this has to do with information," she said between spoonfuls. "That's what he's after."

"Okay, lay it out."

"Think about it. You can look at the unsub's behavior in a few different ways. One, he's a psycho going off his own delusional mission, literal fantasy dictating his route, and his victims."

August shrugged. "Which could explain the weird victimology."

She held her index finger up. "But... if you look at his behavior not as a killer, but as a sane person on a search, say for incriminating evidence against him, *now* it looks like he's systematically destroying proof of some kind. Something each victim had. *Then* the way he's been moving around makes sense."

"His erratic route across the towns is a process of elimination?" August nodded while crumbling some crackers into his soup. "He could be taking out witnesses."

"That would fit too. I mean, we know he was stalking them because he admitted he's been watching me, too."

August sat up straight. "Wait, what?"

"When he called me after our little shootout, he claimed that he saw Deputy Chutney arrive at the Thompsons' crime scene as a first responder, and then, days later, he said he saw me standing in the bloody bedroom."

August put his food down. "He's stalking you?"

"No, I'm stalking *him*," Ava corrected. "He's just confused who the prey is here. Besides, one of the first things I warned you about was that he was probably watching. But that's not the point I'm trying to make." She waved his concern aside. "We know by his own admission that he's a watcher. A planner. Which in my mind eliminates the psychotic or delusional aspect. Look at the lack of evidence. The way he broke into their homes."

"Alright, so he picks them out. He carefully plans his attacks..." August ripped a roll with his fingertips, his gaze off toward the evidence boxes. He got up, grabbed the map she'd used to show him the routes before and set it down between them. Pointing to the line she'd drawn, he followed it with his index finger. Moving from the marked crime scene area closest to town and moving outward toward the forest. "By your logic, the unsub should have taken out the Thompsons first, they're closer to the center of town. Then Suarez, with his cabin at the edge of town. Then Marley, out in the woods where he was found."

"Right." Ava pointed at the map with her plastic spoon. "Let's say you are of sound mind and not wandering around town looking for victims of opportunity. If the murders were just about the victim, you would stalk and kill people on the outskirts of town. There would be less chance of being noticed while walking around out there. It's also less likely that a neighbor might check in. And you definitely wouldn't move on to victims who live closer to town after everyone is on high alert. If it were me, I'd start in the center of town and move outward. That way, as word gets out, I'm already moving away from my kill zone. This guy isn't doing that. He's sticking around. He's moving toward the more populated areas. And if he's not crazy, then it's likely because he *has* to take out the victims in that order."

"You're saying he didn't have a choice on when he killed his victims?"

"Exactly. Look, when you map behavior, patterns emerge. We all live by them. Sometimes even going on autopilot. Which, if you've ever arrived at a destination without quite remembering the drive, that's what you're doing. Falling into behavior patterns subconsciously. Like, grocery shopping. When I shop, it takes maybe fifteen minutes to grab what I need every week. Easy peasy."

August nodded. "Sure."

"But sometimes, like I had to do today before Chutney confronted me, you have to shop in an unfamiliar market. You know what you want, but you don't know where to get it. You might have to go from one end of the store to the other to find things. A fifteen-minute trip at your regular store turns into a half hour of wandering around. You have to find the signs, use the aisle numbers, and interpret context clues to find what you're looking for. And because of that, making an efficient route through the store is impossible."

"And you think that's what the killer is doing?"

"Yeah. I think he's going from victim to victim."

He leaned back in his chair, his gaze narrowed.

"Maybe each of them knows a piece of what he wants to know?" Ava continued. "It's out there, the explanation, we just need more information to see it."

August's phone pinged and he glanced at it before texting back. He finished off his soup and said, "Rondeau is looking for us. He has the first batch of trail cams from Yaeger and Granger. He said to meet him at the library."

Rondeau, it turns out, had taken over the media room at the town's library. The sheriff's station didn't have the multiple monitors he needed so he told Ava and August to meet him at the room in the back of the children's library section. A grandmotherly woman in a fuzzy yellow sweater unlocked the glass front doors for them and they followed her through the modest library. The yellow fuzz on the sweater bounced like feathers. The library faced the main road, and the sound of wet tires on asphalt drifted through the large windows as people rushed to get ready ahead of the snow.

"We'd normally be open," she explained as she led them back. "But we're closed at the sheriff's request as you all had to use the TV screen we use for movie night." She gestured out the large windows at the wisps of snow drifting down. "But with the temperature falling, we probably weren't going to see anybody today anyway."

Ava unzipped her black trench coat, shaking it before folding it over her forearm. The scent of books hit her as they walked. With only half the lights on, the dim ambiance gave the well-worn rugs and overstuffed chairs a cozy feel. Everything shrank a foot or two when they entered the children's section. The shorter shelves held colorful books, games, and wooden puzzles. Tattered stuffed animals sat atop a few red and blue plastic tables. They crossed a foam puzzle floor to the media room entrance at the back wall.

Once inside, Ava realized why Rondeau needed the media room. The huge display monitor hung on the wall, its screen split into a four-section view. Several more monitors sat underneath the internal window. A rickety coffee maker gurgled and hissed in the corner. Rondeau worked on hooking up his laptop to the system while Granger spoke with a stout man. Tall, faded brown hair, cowboy mustache, weathered skin. He wore a corduroy jacket lined with fleece, thick winter slacks, and weathered cowboy boots. The hat in his hands, a pale beige Stetson, had seen better days.

"Agent August Blake and Agent Ava Cortes," Granger said as

they walked in. He gestured formally to the man next to him. "This is Councilmember Neil Yaeger. He rounded up the private trail cams from the residents."

Yaeger nodded and they all shook hands. August thanked him for his help in gathering the footage and speaking to the people of Black Oak, Fern Valley, and Pine Cove. They chatted a bit, catching Yaeger up on the case with what they could reveal, and then Rondeau spoke up from behind his laptop.

"The trail feeds started trickling in early this morning," Rondeau said. "I've been scrubbing through them, but so far, I haven't seen any images of a guy sneaking around out there. This is the next batch." He hit a key, and four videos popped up on the large screen. Black and white, green and sepia, all of them showing recordings of wildlife. "Most people mount the cameras at hip level so that's the view."

They all spent some time just watching. It was addictively numbing to stare at the goings-on of busy woodland critters.

"Now, that's over on the Milliped's property," Yaeger said, pointing to a video of a raccoon scratching its belly while leaning against a tree. "It's pointing in the direction of the Thompsons' home, but it lies more than a hundred yards through the forest, so can't see much. Not even in the day."

Rondeau fast forwarded the recording, and they watched birds, a stray dog, and lots of snow falling or forming drifts on the ground, but no human. The final thirty seconds showed a mountain lion sniffing the camera, its wide eyes flashing green in the darkness. Ava pulled out a chair and settled down at the desk. "What else you got?"

They spent the next couple of hours going through the recordings they'd received so far. Aside from one video in which they'd seen a weird shadow at the edge of the frame, likely a trick of light, they came up with nothing. After that, they decided to take a break before starting the next batch. Ava headed to the soda machine in the librarian's lounge and cheered up a little when she spotted the cream soda.

Not quite the day-saver, but close. She inserted her coins and watched it tumble down to the bottom.

"You know you bought some healthy guava juice at the market. They're in the cooler in my trunk," August said, walking up.

"They're probably frozen then. It's too cold out there. Whereas this soda is perfectly chilled. Big difference."

"Ah yes, pure logic." He held up two vending machine snacks. Both of them giant, likely stale, cookies. "The machine in the front gave me double. You want one?"

"Absolutely," Ava said and bent to grab her soda from the machine. She cracked it open as she stood and said, "I should've mentioned Chutney and Lucy."

August, tearing open a cookie package, handed it to her, and nodded. "Yes. You should have. We can't do the 'keeping secrets' thing. Not this time around, Ava. I can't protect you, or the team, if I don't know what you're doing."

"I know." Ava bit into her cookie. It was the chewy kind of stale, and she made a mental note to grab more later. "Okay, look. I know he looks bad on paper, but I don't think he's involved. I mean, sure, maybe he was one of the first responders at all the crime scenes. But it's just Granger and Chutney for three towns up here. Of course he was there. He had a one-year relationship with Lucy, but it was a long time ago."

"But she's getting married. That could've been a trigger."

"Sure. That's true. But he and Lucy Thompson only dated for a year or so before she met her fiancé. One of the café owners, Cole, said it was over five years ago when the relationship ended."

August gestured with half of a cookie. "He does have a temper though."

"He was drunk and sad. He wanted to fight because that's all he feels he can do right now to make things right. He knew the Thompsons. Likely quite well." Ava shrugged. "It's not him. So, I didn't think it was relevant that he dated the daughter of two of our victims.

It's a small town. A lot of overlap happens with numbers like that. Besides, Granger obviously didn't think it was important either."

"Or he didn't know."

"Yeah, well..." Ava popped the last bit of cookie in her mouth. "You can ask him about it if you want. I just got him back on my side so that's all you."

"Gee, thanks." August wiped crumbs from his sweater. He took in a long breath. "I have to ask Granger if he knew, whether we think Chutney is involved or not. And if he did, why he kept it from a CBI investigation. I should do it now before we reconvene."

He turned to leave, but Ava caught up to him. "Wait. If he *did* know, ask him what his impression was of the relationship. I'll bet you it was bland city."

"You mean healthy? Normal?" August looked down at her with a smirk. "Those are possible, right?"

She smiled, tipping back her soda before saying, "You tell me."

Ava went back to the trail cameras while August went to find Granger. Another hour in, Rondeau got a call. He took it, nodding as he murmured, thanked the caller, and hung up.

"US Forest Service is sending us six months of cached recordings from the networked cameras in the area."

Ava sat back, already exhausted. "Let's start from seven weeks ago. Right before the first murder."

Everyone agreed and Rondeau set the search parameters for the first video. It played on fast forward. They raced through mostly gray mornings. Hazy days with minimal activity outside of birds and rodents. And dark, still nights. Deep winter with visible snow on the ground, piled up against boulders, resting on tree limbs. Finally, after another hour into their search, they caught something. A man lumbered past a mile marker, clearly walking with difficulty. His camouflage parka and watch cap looked almost white with the night vision filter. Rondeau stopped the recording.

Ava sat forward, squinting at the sepia video. "Where's that?"

Rondeau pulled up a map with the various camera locations, checked the meta data on the recording, and zoomed in on a section of the mountain. Ava typed a message to August.

> Come look at this.

A few minutes later, he returned from talking with Granger and leaned in. "Is that a hiking trail?"

"Uh-huh," Rondeau said. "In Pine Cove."

"Yeah," Granger said as he walked in after August and sat next to Rondeau. He pointed to a terrain marker on the map. "That's the cliff where we found Marley's body." He ran his finger along a line leading down the south side, away from the crime scene. "We came up the main trail, but that mile marker is part of an old maintenance road, I believe. I don't even think it's included on the newer maps of the area."

"So, the killer knows Pine Cove and Black Oak well," Yaeger said. "You think he grew up here?"

"He's definitely spent some time up here." Ava kept her gaze on the figure. "He could have been from around here and moved. So, he knows the area, but isn't a local, per se.

"Or he could have spent some time up here scoping out the terrain, planning his attacks," Rondeau said. "If he's camping out there, hunting and what not, he might have come across the road by accident."

Ava pointed in his direction. "Also, true. Either way, the killer used this back road to his advantage. What's the time stamp on the recording?"

Rondeau checked his computer. "He goes up the trail about two hours before Marley's phone died. Which is when we put the approximate time of death."

"He went up there and waited for that kid." Ava shook her head.

"Another ambush," August said.

"Does the feed show him coming back down?" Ava asked.

Rondeau tapped on the keyboard. "Let's see."

They sped through the recording and caught the camouflaged figure walking back down the path, passing the same trail marker, about a half hour after Marley supposedly died. The camera, waist-high to capture animals, did not record his face. But he walked with even more difficulty after killing Marley. His breath clouded out in front of his torso as he walked, face down. The watch cap, glasses, and neck gaiter came into view from the side as he walked further from the camera.

"I wonder if he knew about the trail camera." August pointed with his smart pen. "He kept his head turned down and angled his body away. He also wore full face coverage."

Ava sat back, her gaze on the figure. Tall and bulky. Same get-up as when he'd shot at her. Wearing sunglasses despite it being overcast. Wheezing with effort like he'd done when she'd chased him down at the Suarez scene. This was the same guy. No question.

"I think he's hurt somehow, maybe even disabled," Ava said. "That's why he has to ambush his victims and bind them. It's why Suarez had been able to put up a fight, even after being stabbed."

"And why he drugged Mr. Thompson," Rondeau said.

Ava nodded. "He can't control them physically. We should check ER visits in the past six months, and I think we need to release this video to the public. That and a refined description." She pointed to the screen. "Someone has seen this sucker in town. Watched him walk like that while wearing camouflage." She turned to Rondeau. "Can you get a good screen capture of him for me?"

"I'll try." His gaze shot to August.

Ava caught it. "What?"

"There's been some debate about when to release the description," August said. "Behavioral Science thinks it might make him run to ground."

"I can call Seth," Ava said. "He'll listen to me."

"It's not just them. The sheriff's office is worried about causing panic given how vague it is."

Granger nodded in agreement.

Ava opened her mouth to speak, but August shook his head slowly. "What are we going to release? The killer is tall with a camouflage jacket? We passed twelve guys with that kind of print on our way to the market. We don't have body-type because of all the layering. We don't have hair color, eye color, or even a definite skin color either. Him potentially having a disability that makes him limp is not a specific enough description." He nodded to the window. "Almost everyone up here is armed. They'll be shooting at shadows and hitting each other if they panic."

"Then we better make sure we word it right."

"We wait until we have more." He turned back to the screen, ending the conversation.

Ava let it go. He was right, it was his call. Even if it was the wrong one.

———

At nine PM, they broke for the night. Ava got up, her back screaming at her for sitting for hours, and decided to get some fresh air. The soup she'd eaten for lunch seemed like forever ago. August was typing out an email to Agent Vincent about the identity release when she wandered over and asked for the keys to the SUV. Keys in hand, she headed for the door and threw on her trench coat to go and retrieve her guava juice and snacks from the cooler.

After rifling through the bags in the SUV, she pulled out a toaster pastry package, a guava juice can, a couple of cheese sticks, and a chocolate bar. Shoving them into the pockets of her coat, she started back toward the library. Already deeply involved in unwrapping a chocolate covered granola bar with her gloved hands, she heard a voice by the front doors that made her miss a step. Ava rolled her eyes when she saw her. Tall. Blonde. Evil.

"Well, if it isn't the huntress herself," Ricki Rogers said with her signature thousand-watt smile. "You do look like you're in the thick of things, Ava."

Ava sighed. She hated that title and it was Ricki who'd coined it in her damn article. "What do you want?"

"What do I ever want?" She asked, strolling to meet Ava in the middle of the parking lot.

"Innocent souls... the blood of virgins... to disappear in a plume of black smoke—"

"You're still sore about my little article. I get that," she said smoothly, her perfect, white teeth glowing in the parking lot lights. "Let me make it up to you."

Ricki Rogers was a beautiful woman, Ava had to admit. Not on the inside, by any means, but definitely on the outside. She had a face that had catapulted her news account into the millions. Though calling it a news account might be a bit of a stretch. Mostly opinion, gossip, and "anonymous source" backed reports. She was a decent writer, had great connections for up-to-the-minute videos, and her prose kept her followers loyal. Not a dummy. Not exactly decent either. Her pink, fitted parka, black leggings, and tawny-colored snow boots with fur puffs on the laces made her look like she was going to a rooftop ski party— not covering brutal murders.

"It wasn't a *little article*. It was a hit piece. While I was under investigation. You kicked me while I was down. I don't forget shit like that." Ava walked around her toward the library's entrance.

"What's the difference? You were totally cleared." Ricki ran to catch up, falling in step with her. She frowned, a fake pout on her cherry red lips. "Come on. Give me an exclusive. Remember when you were a rising star? The CBI's bright new weapon against the crazies? I can bring that back. You help me. I help you..."

Ava shook her head. "I wouldn't help you if you were on fire and I needed to pee."

Ricki smirked. "There's that famous temper."

"Not liking you is fact based, not emotion based. You professionally suck. To post lies about people also probably means you person-ally suck, as well, if I'm being honest." Ava sped up, trying to get to the door. "Leave me alone. No comment."

"Are you going to murder this one too? Maybe I should repost that article. You know, bring the public up to speed on the great Agent Cortes and her corrupt practices."

Ava stopped, turning around slowly. "Make sure you include your arrangement with Deputy Chutney while you're at it. Let everyone know you're *somehow* getting classified information from him and interfering with a murder investigation."

Ricki shrugged, her face blank. "I don't know what you're talking about."

"I'm sure that comes out of your mouth a lot," Ava said.

She pointed a boney finger at Ava, her face going red. "Everyone thinks Agent Vincent brought you in because the case is crumbling and they wanted someone to hang it on if the killer gets away. No one would be surprised if you screwed up another big case." Ricki raised her brows, but her forehead remained smooth. "I heard they sidelined you to White Collar Crime because you couldn't hack the real cases anymore. You don't know what you're dealing with."

Ava pointed at her chest a little too forcefully. "I *know* what I'm hunting. I'm the one who wanted to release the description from the video—" she snapped her mouth shut, eyes widening.

Ricki leapt at the reveal. "You have a description?"

"I didn't say that."

"Yes... you did." Her grin widened. "What camera? From where?"

"Everything I've said to you was off the record."

"No, it wasn't." Ricki pulled out her phone, tapping on it with glossy nails.

"I'll deny everything."

"Then I won't say it's you." Ricki shrugged.

"Don't—"

Ricki blew her a kiss as she backed up. A fire behind her eyes as she smiled. "I'll send you the piece when I'm done."

Ava covered her mouth, silent as she watched Ricki drive away. August stepped out of the library, pulling on his field jacket. "What was that all about?"

Ava handed him his keys, her mind racing. "I'm not sure yet."

SIXTEEN

Later that night, back in her room at the Timberline Inn, Ava sat in her sweats on the fluffy down comforter watching TV on her personal laptop. She'd had a nice hot shower and now sipped licorice tea out of the Sheriff's Station mug she'd taken. She always carried a box of it in her go-bag. The show, a local news update, droned in the background while she perused her relics. That's what August used to call them. Her tokens, taken from places along an investigation. She collected them as a sort of mnemonic device. A memory aid that helped her keep conversations, theories, places, and people straight. Spread out on the comforter, they reminded her of the steps she'd taken thus far.

The honeysuckle from the Thompsons' house. Why had the husband been drugged? What did the killer ask Mrs. Thompson? Ava lifted the dried plant to her nose, taking in the warm scent. What had they known that brought a killer's wrath down onto their happy home?

She pushed the medical tubing from Dr. Wren's office aside. It didn't matter anymore. She'd proved her theory to August. The Cold

Death torture images flittered at the edges of her vision. Ava shook her head, banishing them.

Flyers and advertisements she'd gathered from the Riot Brewing Café's bulletin board sat by her knee. She'd called the numbers but had to leave messages as most of them went to voicemail. A couple just rang until Ava eventually hung up. If the people she'd talked to at the café were right, the killer could be moving among them freely. Blending in. Possibly military trained. Definitely not aliens though, Ava thought with a chuckle.

She added what she'd taken from the Big Basket Market cork board, as well. The HVAC, book club, and tour flyers. Nothing jumped out at her. Nina, the lawyer who'd tried to question Ava, had seemed nosey. Ava remembered how she'd been worried someone was talking to the CBI about her and her husband. Which could be paranoid attorney thinking, the result of having been burned by small-town gossip, or something else.

She set the mug down and slid the paper doily she'd taken from Lucy's food tray closer. Holding the delicate lace-like edge between her fingers, Ava thought back to that meeting. Lucy had seemed fixated on her dress. The lace. Granger had said he'd get it and talk to the fiancé. She hadn't heard back about either yet. She wasn't sure if he was dragging his feet, but she didn't want to wait around to find out.

The colored pencil she'd taken from Tone Marley's room sat on the side table. She used the pointed end to scribble on the complimentary pad of paper by her lamp. The deep salmon, almost red color, reminded her of something, though she couldn't place what. It was an odd shade.

Why would Marley be drawing something that color in the winter?

Holly? That would need more of a true, cherry red. A bird? She looked it up on her phone. California didn't have Cardinals. They had red-winged black birds. They were black birds with a stripe of red on the wing, but it was more of an orangey-red. She'd taken photos of his drawings and pulled them up on her phone, swiping through them. Stopping on his sketches of the rock formations, she realized that not only did they cover every inch of the paper but he'd gone over and over the lines of the rocks. The paper looked to be nearly worn through. What could he have been thinking about while he did that? Ava traced his pencil marks with her finger on the screen.

Sighing, she tossed her phone on the bed and stared out the picture window. Nothing but dark night pushed back against the glass. They still didn't know what Tone Marley was doing up on that cliff. Did he voluntarily go to meet the killer? Was he up there doing something else and was ambushed? Mrs. Marley had grown defensive when Ava asked about money and her son. She swore Tone had none, but they were making by somehow. Rondeau needed to push on finding out about the medical equipment.

And finally, the fishing lure from Suarez's cabin. Dangling it in front of the lamp light, the silvery blue reminded her of the ocean. Of boats and plans he'd suddenly had money for. He was the one victim who'd seemed up front about a windfall. Ava dangled the lure in front of her eyes, the laptop screen flickering behind it. He was the first victim. The killer had zeroed in on him for some reason. Why? The file she'd read about Rio Suarez's friends and coworkers fluttered behind her vision. No one had said anything to Sheriff Granger about enemies or bad blood with anybody when he interviewed them. Maybe they hadn't known anything or hadn't wanted to get in trouble. But the victim's brother, Alonzo, was blunt. He'd freely admitted Suarez's misdeeds. And the landlord had said Suarez often got involved with get-rich-quick schemes. Maybe that's where the killer had picked up his scent. Ava put the fishing lure down. She needed to speak to the brother again.

Round and round, she went. Moving the relics, reordering them to test timeline theories, going over her interview notes in her notebook, rehashing brainstorming conversations with August. She poured over the flyers again. Trying the numbers of the ones who hadn't called back yet. By eleven, fatigue caught up to her and she was done. She had just started to drift away, thinking about the trail cameras and the video of the killer, when her phone pinged. Bleary eyed, she peered at an incoming call from an unknown number. Sitting up, she answered it.

"Ava." Denny's deep voice sounded in her ear. "Your nemesis, Ricki Rogers posted something you're going to want to see."

Ava rubbed her eyes. "What— are you tracking her?"

"Not her, you. After your data request, I set up a crawler for your name and a few other key tags. Looks like this was posted about an hour ago. I'm sending you the link."

"Hey, I found some flyers and announcements for services around here. I was wondering if you could check them out. The piano teacher and HVAC guy specifically."

"I live to serve," he said. "I'll get some preliminary information to you in a few hours."

"Thanks, Denny."

"Hey, you know I got your back," he said, and the call ended.

Two seconds later, a text message with a link pinged through and Ava clicked it. It launched her to a news website called *RickiLeaks*. Flashing arrows announced a new post by Ricki Rogers.

A RickiLeaks Exclusive Report: CBI Insider Confirms – "We Have the Black Oak Killer On Camera!"

Ava pressed play.

Ricki stood on the side of the road underneath a streetlamp, her coat collar straightened up dramatically as she spoke into a camera. Hair and makeup perfect, the light overhead caught the snowflakes falling around her nicely. She looked like a femme fatale detective on the cover of a noir thriller. Brows furrowed, she spoke in an urgent tone as if announcing the arrival of flying saucers over an old timey radio.

"Fellow fans of the truth, I have an update on the serial killer stalking the sleepy mountain town of Black Oak. Not only has Ricki-

Leaks confirmed that there are two more victims in neighboring towns, but we have learned that there is a recording of the killer!

During a late-night clandestine meeting between myself and a highly placed CBI official, RickiLeaks uncovered a growing rift between the CBI and the local authorities. According to my source, her efforts to convince the powers that be to release critical information about the maniacal killer stalking the residents of these small towns has fallen on deaf ears. Will this affect the investigation? On top of this troubling news. I've also learned via another source that one of the CBI agents on the case now stands accused of pushing a possible witness to hysterics during questioning. This same agent, I'm told, was at the center of a scandal and internal investigation into unlawful use of force and possible misconduct issues, due to the death of a suspect in an earlier case. Stay tuned for more exclusives!"

The video ended with a montage of Ricki's news reports in different locales before closing out. A graphic popped up urging Ava to join Ricki's paid tier of fans before fading to black.

"The Black Oak Killer?" Ava groaned. She hated when they named them. Dropping her phone next to her on the mattress, she said, "August is going to be so pissed."

SEVENTEEN

Delano Kester stood in the middle of the dark road holding his phone over his head, trying to catch a few bars of a signal while freezing his ass off. He hated shitty mountain towns. The wind felt like it was made of cold needles, and it bit at the exposed bridge of his nose. A storm was moving in. Faster than they were saying, and he thought he might have to risk going into town again for some supplies to ride it out.

The maintenance road he stood on dead-ended ten yards behind him, and no car had ever come down the dusty path during the weeks he'd spent in the area. He pulled his glove off and checked local social media accounts. He did it daily, usually at night to be sure no one saw him. Local news, mentions of the town names, stuff like that. Delano had learned how to do thorough searches during one of his stretches in jail. He'd set an app to grab news links and posts containing information on the investigation and his victims and send them to a ghost email, one with no real identity tied to it. It kept him anonymous on the web, something he'd also learned while incarcerated. The correctional facility he'd stayed at in Riverside would sometimes let inmates use computers if they didn't get into fights. In fact, he'd picked up more survival skills from his fellow inmates than he had during his entire two-year stint in the marines before they'd kicked him out. Delano thought that said a little something about the military as a whole.

He found a spot with a patch of signal and stood still, checking the alerts one by one. No real updates since the day before. Shifting on his feet, he shook his head. He needed a lead on the next person in the chain. Something. Maybe the cops had figured out a connection he hadn't.

A face flashed behind his eyes. Thompson's wife, the nurse, her eyes wide with terror as she looked up at him. The husband had just up and died mid-questioning. He wasn't sure if the dose had been too much, or if the guy's heart had given out. He *was* sort of fat, Delano thought. Maybe he'd lost too much blood? Either way, she wouldn't stop with the crying. He couldn't get anything out of her, not even a name. Suarez had given him Marley. And then Marley had coughed up "a cop with a nurse wife, who live in Black Oak." Not too hard to figure out he'd meant the Thompsons. In turn, they were supposed to have given him the next name in the chain. Only they hadn't.

At first, Delano had thought she was just being stubborn or that she secretly hated her husband. He'd realized after a while that her husband had told her lies. She was useless. At one point he'd debated drugging the wife and then questioning the cop, but there had been two problems with that. He hadn't known how to wake the cop up and he wasn't sure that he could make the nurse take the medicine. Not now that she'd seen what he was going to do to her. Also, he'd lost track of how long he'd been in the house, and his nerves were building. She'd mentioned a device, an electronic wallet, so he'd decided to just go with that and offed the wife. Quick and merciful. One blow, and she was finally quiet. He'd grabbed the device and laptop next to it on his way out.

Since then, he'd stalled out. Unable to get into the password protected laptop, and therefore unable to figure out the device. Then the CBI had shown up. Relieved that they'd seemed to have nothing on him, he'd stalked the investigation, always staying ten steps ahead of them.

Until Agent Cortes.

Delano kept clicking through the links, looking for progress in the case. Halfway through, he paused. A blonde bombshell-looking chick stood talking under a streetlamp. The video's title made his gut lurch. They had a video of him? He licked his lips, his mouth suddenly dry despite the beer he just had and rewatched the report a few more times. He'd already heard about the possible manhunt, and now they might know what he looks like. It had to have been a damn trail camera. He'd been so careful in neighborhoods and around town. Kept his face hidden whenever he was out. Not so much while in the woods.

A noise in the bushes made him jump and then anger burned through the fear. This was all her fault. He thought back to when Ava had first arrived. At the time, he'd thought she was just a little thing, but she was fast when she'd chased him at Suarez's place. He remembered when he first saw her on TV, that he'd wanted to pay her a visit. See what she knew. Delano checked the clock on his phone. He needed more time, and a messy tragedy might keep the cops busy long enough.

Time to set up another ambush.

———

The Timberline Inn sat tucked back from the street and he crossed onto the property using the gravel path behind the dumpster. He walked past a storage shed and entered the dried-up garden via a locked side gate. He climbed it, stopping on top to peer into the inn's windows on the east side, gritting his teeth when metal creaked beneath him. Delano knew Ava was staying here. Everyone in town knew. Someone at the laundry place had mentioned seeing the CBI Agents coming and going at all hours and Delano had overheard. So he'd watched the inn. Finally clocking her the day before.

He crept over the gate, his gaze roving, looking for security. He dropped down onto the ground and froze, listening, before he moved again. When Delano had watched the inn, he'd made sure to watch the windows. Which rooms had lit up when different agents arrived and went. He'd narrowed her room down to the one in the corner with the big window overlooking the grass, and that's where he was going.

Slipping behind a tree trunk, he paused again, thinking he'd heard a dog, but it sounded far away. Her window sat underneath a tree branch and even the patio lights didn't reach it. Creeping up underneath the sill, he sat in a crouch for a few seconds, then chanced poking his head up for a look through the curtains. Pitch black inside. No movement or noise. He'd waited until after midnight, hoping she'd be sleeping. The shadows covered his movements as he tapped on the window softly. He waited, tapped again, a little harder. Waited again. Definitely asleep.

Unsheathing his hunting knife, he pried at the lock where the panes met in the middle. Stuck at first, he thought it might have been painted shut, but then it gave. The lock slid around, out from under the latch, and he pushed the window up an inch. It made a cracking noise, and he ducked down, ready to split.

Silence.

He popped up again, and pushed the window open further. Far enough for him to climb through. Only, he realized it was too high off the ground. He needed something...

Delano scanned the dark forms in the garden, spotting an angular box-like shape and snuck over. The planter lay against some edging. Ten inches across and fairly solid. Probably resin because it wasn't heavy. He dragged it over, under the window, and then hoisted himself up and into the window in one motion. He slid like a snake, using the strength of his legs to slow his entry while his hands found the floor below the window. He listened, letting his eyes adjust. The window opened into the far side of the room by the bed. Not hearing anything, Delano angled first one leg in, then the other.

The lump on the bed didn't move as he crept over, holding his blade at his thigh, but something was wrong. He didn't hear breathing or see any hair on the pillow. Delano yanked back the covers. Nothing. Confused, he checked the bathroom. Empty. With growing frustration, he moved quickly through the room. No Ava. He stood in the dark, thinking. Could she be in that other agent's room? Agent Blake or whatever? They'd had a thing, he'd read. He stopped breathing when he heard a female voice outside the door. He couldn't shoot without the other agents hearing. He needed a distraction to disorient her.

Delano, in his quest to prepare, had shoved quite a few things into his coat pockets. One of which was bear spray, something everyone carried out in the woods. He pulled out the cannister, slipping his finger over the gun-like trigger just as the door beeped and pushed open. Squinting, he made out the form of a gun and lunged, grabbing it with his free hand. He thought he could just yank it from her hand, but it didn't move and then the larger form registered. *Not the chick. Not the chick.* Delano squeezed off a few shots of the bear spray while stumbling backwards, coughing as the mist filled the room. The figure shouted too. A man's voice.

Through tearing eyes, Delano recognized the bulky form of her boyfriend, Agent Blake. Without warning, the guy ran at him like a freight train. A hefty shoulder pummeled into Delano and sent him flying into the wall.

"Go! Call 911!" Blake, backlit by the hallway light, gun still in his hand, coughed and then shouted, "Find Agent Cortes!"

Delano registered a woman running away from the door as he scrambled to his feet. She was the one who worked at the inn, and she screamed as she ran. He tried to get to the window, but Blake was already running at him, bumping and tripping over furniture, unable to see either. Delano picked up a crystal vase from the table and hurled it at the agent. It bounced off his forearm like it was plastic, and the guy kept coming. In a panic, Delano shot another stream of bear spray in Blake's direction. Nearly to the open window, Blake hit him with full force, wrapping his meaty arms around him as they went crashing through the frame in a hail of glass.

Delano landed a foot from Blake, gasping for breath. Sirens and dogs barking in the distance made him move. He reached for the gun in his jacket. Blake rose first, rubbing his eyes. His hands now empty. A look of utter fury on his face. Delano gasped and aimed at the standing agent, firing as he scuttled backwards. Blake twisted away, going down as Delano climbed to his feet. A patrolman and a dog ran through the garden toward them. Breaking into a sprint, Delano headed toward a group of buildings. Ava was here. Agent Blake had thought she was in her room, which meant she was nearby. He spotted a bright window in the sea of darkness and headed in that direction. Blue and red lights flashed from the patrol cars. The sound of pounding boots and radio chatter behind him. He focused on the light. The building loomed ahead. Made entirely of glass. Someone moved inside.

EIGHTEEN

The big man stalked her in the woods, children's laughter echoing in the distance as she walked carefully through the dried grass. It was twilight. Cold. The light dying around her as she peered into the forest beyond. She stopped at the tree line, her gaze on a form scurrying from tree to tree. Dirty face. Tattoo tears. Hair jutting out at odd angles. Ava froze. Unable to breathe.

Gunshots ripped her out of her dream, and she rolled out of the chair, hitting the floor. She hadn't been able to sleep so she'd gone to the solarium. Police lights flashed overhead, dogs barking and men shouting in the distance.

Reaching for her phone, she found her trench coat pocket empty.

Rising, she slipped her weapon out of her other pocket and ran for the door. A shard of dread stabbed through her.

Flashlight beams danced across the windows of the solarium, sending stark shadows across the ground. Ava peered out at the lawn, but the moisture from the heated solarium obscured her view. She hit the lights by the door when she spotted a figure running along the glass wall toward the entrance. Ava locked the deadbolt and backed up just as the figure stopped at the door, rattling the handle. Climbing up behind some large plants, her gun out in front of her, she stilled. Controlled her breathing. The figure stepped back from the door and then gunfire erupted from somewhere outside.

"Ava!" August yelled and then the door crashed open, the metal frame dangling from the hinges. He flipped the lights on. Busted lip, red, tearing eyes, blood on his neck and white t-shirt. He rubbed his face with his forearm, trying to look around.

"I'm here," Ava said, hands up as she stepped carefully down from the mound of plants. "I'm okay."

He leaned back, slumping against the door frame. "He's here. The unsub broke into your room."

"The shooting?" Ava stepped closer, taking in his bleeding lip and swollen eyes. "Did he hit anybody?"

"I don't know. The guy fired wild after we crashed out of the window. He would've gotten me if I hadn't seen him reaching for his gun. I think he got his own bear spray in his eyes. He was big though, solid." August leaned out of the ruined doorway and spit blood. He looked back at her and slowly exhaled. "You weren't in your room."

"No." Ava reached up and pulled a small chunk of glass from his hair. Then winced at a nasty cut near his ear. "I think you might need stitches."

He nodded, taking her hand and holding it against his chest. His gaze rested on hers for a moment before letting go. Standing up straight, he raised a police radio to his lips "This is CBI Mobile 1, I have eyes on Agent Cortes. She's unharmed. I want a status on the suspect, ASAP."

Chatter came back. *Suspect moving eastbound, approximately six foot, wearing all black... shift your perimeter, suspect sighted near the back street... K9 unit on scent trail... negative contact... possible perimeter breach near a culvert on Taggert street... suspect might've doubled back...*

No time to establish a real perimeter, the stunted visibility from the overcast sky, and the lack of boots on the ground in the area all worked in the killer's favor. Despite Rondeau getting the drone in the air within minutes, thermal filter on... They lost him.

NINETEEN

Dangling patio lights swayed in the icy wind casting shifting shadows on the lawn. Ava's cheeks burned as she stood on the Timberline Inn's porch next to August. Still in the sweats she'd gone to sleep in, she had to wait outside because the CBI forensic team wouldn't let her back into her room. Talia worked inside with Dr. Wren and the forensics team. Paramedics had arrived and looked over August who did not need stitches, just skin glue and a bandage. They had him change out of the sprayed clothes and then rinsed his eyes out and told him they'd be sensitive for a few hours, but the symptoms should resolve completely in twenty-four hours.

Vincent and August spoke on the phone about relocating the CBI team. She said her office would work with local PD on logistics. Rondeau stood next to the patio stairs watching the forensic team work the area outside Ava's window. Figures in white paper Tyvek suits collected evidence, their cameras flashing in the dead of night like lightning. A crowd of looky-loos wrapped in thick fluffy robes and oversized puffer jackets had set up across the street, filming with their cameras, and talking with each other. A sense of curious worry permeated the crowd.

Rondeau nodded to the window. "He's getting bold."

"He's terrified," Ava countered.

"Attacking a CBI Agent in their own room doesn't sound scared," Rondeau said. "Psychotic, maybe."

"The CBI is looking for him. I already shot at him. He likely heard we have a video of him because of the RickiLeaks post so—"

"What?" August looked at her with alarm. "What post?"

"Uh, here's the thing..."

She explained how Ricki Rogers had accosted her in the parking lot, they'd traded insults, and then Ava had seen an opportunity and mentioned the video. "The press named him The Black Oak Killer, apparently. Which is dumb because he's been slashing people in all three of these little towns up here, but whatever." She pulled the video up on her phone and held it up for him to see.

"You told her we had a video of him? The one I said we were *not* releasing?" August's gaze snapped to Rondeau, who walked off without a word. When he was gone, August said, "That was a direct order."

"It was a judgement call."

"Yes. Mine."

"You know what I mean," Ava said and folded her arms. "You didn't have a problem with how I did things when Vincent was in charge of PIT."

He stepped back, shoving his hands in his pockets. "First of all, yes I did, and I told you that often."

She tilted her head back and forth. "Did you?"

He raised his brows. "And second of all, I was your fellow agent back then. I'm in charge of PIT now. It's different."

"But the suspects aren't, and sometimes plans need to change in real time, you know that. We need to keep the pressure on. The report from RickiLeaks that we have his image does that. We're closing in and he knows it. He'll make mistakes."

"Is that what this attack was? A mistake? Because it sounds like it was you who made the mistake." He pointed to the window. "If you had been in your room, you'd be dead."

"I take offense that you assume I'd be the one to die in that situation," Ava snapped back. "I mean, you didn't."

August looked at her for a beat, then shook his head. "Unbelievable."

"Look this is what—"

"This is what you do," he finished for her, turning away and rubbing the back of his neck with his hand. "I know. I just..." August faced her, his gaze intense. "I didn't know what I was going to find in that solarium."

"We never know, August." She took in his bloody lip, the bruises forming on his face, the cut to his neck from the window, and her throat ached. "That's the job."

CBI Senior Special Agent Lee arrived along with a California DOJ Forensic Services van. He took their statements and supervised the scene after the shooting. They started a 3D scan of her room. Agent Lee, a soft-spoken man, with a discerning gaze and genuine smile, wore the same cologne her grandpa had. After taking August's statement, he informed them that Agent Vincent was on her way and took Ava into the front lobby of the inn to talk. After her report, he filled in some of the gaps for her.

One of the patrol officers assigned as security for the inn had witnessed movement inside the garden area. A figure walking back and forth wearing all black. He'd alerted August and then left his car with the K9 to investigate. He did not see the open window due to the shadows and, having heard the metal clang of a gate, had walked around to the other side of the building to investigate further. August, after getting the alert from the officer, had called Ava. It'd gone to voicemail.

"That's because my phone was in the room," she admitted. "It's probably still on the mattress where I dropped it."

Agent Lee nodded as he jotted something down, then continued. "Agent Blake proceeded to your room while alerting other agents as he went down the hallway. His movements alerted the inn keeper, Theresa Ballard, who joined him in the hallway with a pass card to enter your room for a wellness check."

"And then the killer ambushed him with bear spray and a knife," Ava said.

Lee then explained how, after going through the window, August had lost sight of the killer because of the spray in his eyes. The initial patrol officer who'd called in the prowler had been on the opposite side of the property with the K9 and did not see the unsub cross behind him on the pathway leading to the solarium. The dog did not alert.

Theresa, the inn's clerk had previously told August that Ava used the solarium, and he'd headed that way only to hear shots fired. He'd thought they were coming from inside the solarium and kicked in the door. The gunfire had actually come from a different patrol officer the next street over who'd been racing toward the scene. It is believed the suspect had run out into the street, nearly got hit by the officer's vehicle, and then had fired on the patrol car as he ran through an area thick with brush, disappearing into the night. The officer in the patrol car suffered a graze wound above his ear but was otherwise unharmed.

After the interview, the CBI agent running the forensic team told Ava they'd documented and processed the scene to the point where they could grab a few items for her from the unaffected areas.

"Find anything?" she asked him as she jotted down which items she'd like them to get.

"We're still working through the debris. There might be a few pieces of glass to work a trace lift."

A few minutes later, a tech came in with a bag of Ava's things, including her phone and charger. When she went outside, she found August standing with the rest of the team in the garden and wandered over. Her phone buzzed with an attachment from Denny, but she ignored it. Talia and Rondeau were debating something about the killer. Rondeau said he'd had both a knife and a gun but had chosen to try to kill Ava with the knife That meant he was after the ritual of it. Talia argued it was about the noise. A gunshot would have alerted everyone, and he'd have been caught. In this scenario, the knife was more efficient.

"I don't know about efficient." August shook his head. "He didn't know what he was doing. The patrol guy said the gate was creaking enough to call his attention." He glanced at Ava. "If you'd been in your room, you would have woken up."

"And shot him for his trouble." Ava hugged herself against the cold. Delicate flakes fell on the charcoal gray river rocks lining the fallow garden beds, bright white against the dark stone. She breathed in deep, and the biting wind brought with it the scent of snow and pine. She wondered out loud, "But why even try? Why take such a substantial risk to kill one agent?"

"He blames you," August said. "You've been the face of the CBI to the public. You arrived and then we started making some serious progress..."

"I agree," Talia said. "I also think the knife being his first choice, particularly with a woman, says something about his psychological profile."

"If he had the knife out, he wanted answers," Ava said. "He's task oriented. I don't think he's delusional at all despite the crap he tried to feed us with his phone call. I think he's desperate to find out what we know about him. I just don't get why."

August cocked his head to the side, leaning closer. "Elaborate."

"Okay, look. If I was going around slashing villagers to death, and then not only does the CBI move in, one of them shoots at me. I'd think about leaving. Then, let's say, I also hear via the rumor mill that the authorities are starting to connect the Thompsons' bodies to other murders I've committed. We can assume he's also monitoring the case, he made a point of letting me know he's been watching. Then it comes out there might be a recording that can identify me. Again, I'd be getting the hell out of town. Putting as much distance between myself and the area as possible." Ava blew on her cold hands. "What

I *wouldn't* do, is crawl into the window of an inn filled with armed agents. Something is off about his choices. He's not acting with even the least amount of self-preservation."

"You did shoot him in the ass, according to the people of Black Oak," Talia said. "Maybe he feels like you've shamed him or made him look incompetent."

"Maybe," Ava said, unconvinced.

"He could just be stupid," Rondeau offered. "I find that explains a lot of people's behavior."

Ava smiled. "We should consider that."

August's phone trilled, and he glanced at the screen. Turning to Ava, he told her to wait there and went into the inn without saying another word.

"What was that about?" Ava asked Talia, who shrugged.

A minute later, he poked his head out of the inn's door and motioned with his hand. "Forensics found something you need to see."

She joined him, walking down the hall by his side. "What is it?"

August rubbed his forehead with his fingertips. A stress tell. "The killer left a note, or he dropped one. They aren't sure."

The room looked like a storm had raged through it. Broken chairs, a two-foot hole in the wall from the killer's body flying against it during the fight. Blood on the windowsill. The smashed window. She stood at the threshold for a second, taking it in.

Ava chewed on the inside of her cheek, thinking. "What did the note say?"

"It's in a manilla envelope. Sealed. We haven't opened it." August looked at his phone and then leaned back out of the door, talking to someone in the hallway. When he came back in, he said, "I'm having Rondeau run it to the Black Oak Medical Clinic to X-Ray it for powder or wires. You know the drill. He used to do some kind of hazardous substance detection and containment for the military, so he'll also run swab tests for substances on the surfaces before we get it back. Talia and one of her forensic techs will go with. I've asked that they work with Dr. Wren on it up here to protect chain of custody and get quicker results."

She glanced through the busted window, looking for light on the horizon. Nothing. "Did any cameras catch the unsub?"

"We're seeing what's around the area, but you know small towns. They still leave their doors unlocked at night. I did request a few more agents, they came with the forensic services team. I sent them out to contact the owners of the little shops up and down the road here. I'm hoping one of them has a camera facing out at their street parking. We might get something." He hooked a thumb over his shoulder. "The gas station down that way is our best bet, but we'll see."

Ava shook her head. "How does he keep getting away? He can't even run right."

"Like you said, he knows the town. He probably has every egress point figured out ahead of time. He stalks his victims, including you."

They watched the techs work silently for a moment.

"We should be reading the note already," Ava complained, fighting the adrenaline crash she felt coming on. "I doubt he laced it with anthrax. He's not the Unabomber."

They spent the next hour talking with the supplemental patrol officers from Hemet about witness statements from the looky-loos. None of them had seen anything. She grabbed her leather notebook and pulled on her long black trench coat. Agent Lee provisionally cleared both her and August since neither of them had fired their weapon.

After a bunch of digital paperwork, Ava checked her watch. It was nearly three thirty in the morning. "Maybe we should go see how it's going with the killer's note."

August's phone rang and he answered, listening for a moment. He nodded and then caught Ava's eye, shaking his head. "We're on our way."

"Was that Talia?" Ava hefted her messenger bag over her shoulder. "Did they open the envelope?"

August took her carry on from her hand and carried it down the stairs. "That was Granger. Someone set a fire at the sheriff's station."

"That's... unexpected." Ava followed him past the garden, the forensic team still working outside of the bedroom window, and the patrol guy watching the sniffer dog poop under a tree. "Is anybody hurt?"

"Well, no one can find Chutney, apparently."

———

Ava saw the smoke before they got there. Black and billowing, it curled up around the lone streetlight illuminating the sheriff station's small parking lot. They'd taken August's SUV, parked on the street, and walked across the asphalt toward the scene. Yellow caution tape blocked off part of the building and the walkway along the south wall. Acrid fumes whirled in the growing wind. An old firetruck and a half dozen volunteer firefighters milled around the wreckage, poking it with metal sticks and then spraying it some more. Granger, and what looked like the fire chief, given his white helmet, spoke near some equipment. The sheriff nodded as they passed.

When they approached, the stench of burnt rubber and foam filled her nose. What had been an SUV, parked in the back lot for staff, now looked like a steaming, hulking mess of melted plastic and rubber on the asphalt. It listed to the left, windows blown out, bumper deformed and sagging, grungy water puddles surrounding it. They stopped just outside the cordoned off area and waited.

"This is an interesting development." She stared at the scene, letting the map of the area and route possibilities flit behind her eyes. "No matter the scenario, the killer coming to the station wasn't on the way out of town. Not by a long shot."

"What the hell is going on, Ava?" August muttered, his gaze on the smoldering wreck. "It looks like he's panicking, spinning out."

"I don't think he is," she whispered tightening her coat belt against the frigid temperature.

"Why?"

"I can't explain why. I just..." In the distance, hidden by the night, tree limbs creaked in the wind. "Whose vehicle was it?"

"Deputy Chutney's."

"Huh." Ava frowned. "And they still haven't found him?"

"He's not answering his phone. Granger sent somebody to check the cabin he rents in town."

Ava regarded the scene, looking for meaning in the chaos. A fire at the enemy's gate meant what? An insult to cover embarrassment over his failed attack or something else entirely?

"August, help me out here. The unsub attacks you, shoots at patrol cars, gets away on foot. Then, having escaped capture, again, doesn't disappear into the forest. He comes to the sheriff's station that is smack in the middle of town to commit destruction of government property *and* arson? Both felonies, by the way. Why would he do this?"

August got the fire chief's attention, who nodded his head at the wreck and signaled to one of the volunteer firefighters. "You tell me."

The volunteer who wandered over looked familiar. Ava thought she might've recognized him from the Riot Brewing Café. He gave her a friendly nod as he lifted the yellow tape cordoning off the scene, letting them in. She strolled around the hulking mess, crouched and peered at the driver's side door with her phone's light, her mind working the evidence. Burn pattern, chemical odor, the missing windows. All of them blown out except for the one at the rear and the windshield. All four doors locked. Too much damage and buckling to see into the rear footwell and cargo area. The lack of sunlight wasn't helping.

She looked up at August. "You smell that?"

He nodded. "Gasoline."

Ava pointed to what looked like small pieces of glass down in the driver's side footwell and across the front bench seat. "Inside. Not out on the asphalt."

"The driver's side window could have been broken before the fire blew out the others."

"He smashed it in." Ava walked around peering into the windows. "You think he was trying to steal it? Or maybe something that was in it? Did Chutney have evidence in the cargo area or something?"

"He shouldn't have. The CBI has been handling evidence since we arrived."

"Then why—"

"Tell me what you see, Ava." August pulled his tablet and smart pen from his jacket pocket. "Why did the unsub do this?"

Her gaze traveled over the burned vehicle. "Well, the fire caused a lot of damage to the SUV. Strategically, the unsub took out one of only two patrol cars out here. But that wouldn't do much to hinder the investigation. The CBI has their own vehicles, and we can call in more patrol cars from other departments. So, what did he gain here?" She spotted what was left of the security camera just under the eaves. She couldn't even recognize any parts on the solid lump. "He almost lit the station up."

"Yeah, they were lucky."

Ava walked around the SUV. "But why didn't he?"

August paused his writing. "Come again?"

"Why not light up the station? If you want to take out your enemy, you burn down their base, right? Why just the SUV?"

Granger, on his way over after talking to the fire chief, frowned and said, "You're mad he didn't do enough damage?"

"I'm surprised he didn't do more damage." Ava waved her arm at the building. "I would've burned down the whole shebang. Most of the evidence is in there."

He looked at her for a beat and then said, "The fire chief said it was arson. His name is Captain Andrews, he covers Idyllwild, parts of Hemet and the towns up here when needed. The volunteer firefighter training goes through him. He'll come over and talk with us when they have things tightened down."

"This is Deputy Chutney's vehicle," August said. "Do you know where he is yet?"

Granger shook his head. "I left a message. Haven't heard back. He was off today, and he usually visits his family's property on his days off. That's probably why he wasn't at the inn after the break in."

"We should still do a wellness check." Ava peered at the charred SUV.

The bakery around the corner had seen the blaze as they'd baked for the coming day and sent over hot coffee and donuts. Ava, August, and Granger stood around eating, drinking, and talking about the fire. They spit balled about where Chutney might be and speculated about whether or not the melted security camera on the roof would contain anything useful. August took some calls, and she read through the information Denny had sent her earlier. The follow-up info on the local flyers. Most of them were just home businesses. He'd marked one of the numbers as utility and she wondered if that meant public. She'd have to get back to him. She closed her phone thinking that the conversation with him seemed so long ago. After the fire chief cleared the station, the group moved inside.

"She's structurally fine," Captain Andrews said, gesturing at the ceiling with his helmet. He'd taken off his turnout coat, and his bottle-brush mustache and matching brows had flakes of snow on them as he spoke. "It'll smell like hell, but you're cleared to continue operations in here. The fire charred a bit of the stucco and wood siding but the roof's fine. You're gonna want to get a proper inspection in the next day or so."

"Do you know how the fire started?" August asked.

"Looks like a road flare and an accelerant. Likely gasoline, and a lot of it. Do you keep that kind of fuel here at the station for the cars, Sheriff?"

Granger shook his head. "We fill up at the Gas and Go like everyone else out here. I think I might know where the gas came from, though. A lot of fuel went missing after a recent theft at the emu farm."

Ava grabbed a second cup of coffee to fight the fatigue while she and August spoke with Captain Andrews a bit more. Rondeau and Talia arrived half an hour later.

"Not sure I'm a fan of the smoky vibe," Rondeau said to Ava as he strode in and wrinkled his nose. "I'm more of a 'clean linen' guy myself."

Ava grinned as Talia pushed through the door waving an evidence baggie, her face hard as stone as she handed the note from the killer to Ava. "This asshole is getting on my nerves."

"Any issues with the seal?" Ava asked, reading the note with a frown.

"No. We swabbed for drugs, particulates, and toxins. Which all came back negative. The X-Ray showed no wires or ridges either. I checked for prints as well. It's clean. After the tests, we still opened it in a controlled setting under a containment hood. It's just plain paper."

The note consisted of a photocopy of a newspaper article that came out over two years before. An exposé of Ava, complete with a photo of her being led away in cuffs from a decrepit brick building. Angry strokes of red sharpie crawled across the paper.

I WARNED HER TO STAY OUT OF MY WAY. AGENT CORTES GOT WHAT SHE DESERVED. THERE WILL BE MORE.

Granger frowned. "He's talking about you in the past tense."

Ava held the paper up to the ceiling light. "That's because the note wasn't meant for me." She looked at August. "You were supposed to discover it. When you found my body."

He stepped back, his jaw working. "Did he intend to use you as a distraction? Have us chasing him over your death instead of trying to figure out why he killed the others?"

It wasn't a *terrible* plan, Ava thought. The death of a team member would definitely have thrown the survivors. But it smacked of a Hail Mary, not strategy.

She handed the note to August. "Whatever his reason to attack me, the killer screwed up. I'm still alive, and now I'm pissed."

They wrapped up the meeting and then Chief Andrews and Sheriff Granger went back outside to continue supervising the scene. Ava and August met with the rest of the CBI team in the conference room.

"Do you think Chutney's involved?" Talia asked as she pulled off her pink angora scarf and sat at the table. "A lot of indirect evidence supports the idea."

"I don't think he's good for the murders, no," Ava said. "But he's definitely the leak. He's been slipping information to Ricki Rogers."

"I saw her post." Rondeau raised a brow at her. "What were you talking about? We don't have a solid description."

"True, but we can say we do," Ava countered. "The killer doesn't know we have squat."

"Did the sheriff know about Chutney's past with Lucy?" Talia asked. "That's something we should've been told. It offers motive. And now with this fire..."

"He said he didn't think about it since it was so many years ago." August stood at the head of the table. He put the note and his phone down. "That's a non-issue. This escalation is a problem. The killer's taking risks that don't track."

"He does seem to be fixated on you," Rondeau said to Ava.

"I'm just the messenger. We're breathing down his neck and he lashed out."

Talia tapped a slender fingertip on the note. "I agree with what Ava said earlier. This unsub must feel threatened. The note is supposed to be him gloating, right?"

August nodded. "It is. But his actions broadcast desperation. Both the attack at the inn and the fire here at the station put him at enormous risk of getting caught and yet, he did it anyway."

Rondeau sipped from his Styrofoam cup, a thoughtful look on his face. "His failure to kill Ava might be a tipping point for him. This whole scenario feels... explosive. You know, rife."

"Rife?" Ava asked, a smile tugging at her lips.

"Yeah, the whole case is rife with bad energy. Like right before something goes wrong."

"Well, that's helpful, Martin," Talia said. "Will you read our palms next?"

"Don't dismiss the unknown, my brainy friend," Rondeau said with a grin. "Let me tell you, I have *seen* some things..."

As they sparred like old friends do, August leaned close to Ava.

"The killer researched you. He figured out where you were staying." He caught her gaze. "He knows about the Ghost Town Killer case."

"Good," Ava said, looking out at the worsening weather. "Then he finally knows what he's up against."

TWENTY

Agent Vincent cleared Talia to help the forensic team, and they worked through the night but ultimately didn't get much from the note or the fire. The two-second recording taken by the security camera's motion detection showed nothing but black paint spraying onto the lens. The unsub had been careful.

By five in the morning, August sent Talia and Rondeau to the new hotel to get some sleep.

"Are you leaving?" Ava asked.

"No, I'm wide awake. You should go, though," he said. "You look exhausted."

"Aw, thanks," Ava said and smoothed her hair. "Ever the flirt."

August yawned. "You know what I mean."

"I won't sleep anyway. This guy has me on edge." Ava rubbed her sore neck. "I'm gonna go over some of the newer stuff. Try to stay on top of things."

Grabbing her carry on from August's SUV, she changed into a pair of black jeans and a blue ski sweater in the bathroom, washed her face, and tried to wrangle her hair. When she walked back out,

August was on a call with Granger about the gas station down the street.

"They did have a camera," August said afterwards. "Sheriff Granger already retrieved the recording without trouble. He's on his way back."

Granger returned with the footage and she sat in the conference room going over the video, looking for how the killer got to the inn. After rewatching the feed several times, she concluded he must have parked and walked in from the back of the property. Dead on her feet, she tried to get some candy from the station's vending machine, but the dispensing spiral didn't rotate fully, and the candy got stuck. She blinked at it for a few seconds, the fatigue and sugar cravings taking over, before swearing and banging on the front of the machine. Granger wandered over and without a word, used Gale's key to open the machine, gave Ava her candy bar, and then offered her his office couch to rest.

She took him up on the offer, turned off the lights, plugged her phone charger into the wall, and sank onto the hard couch. Using her trench coat as a blanket, she leaned back, resting her head against the wall, and closed her eyes. The adrenaline of the night had been long burned through, and she drifted, half asleep, thinking about the killer. At some point August came in and said something, but she didn't register what it was.

At seven in the morning, her phone bleeped, startling her awake. A message from her boss, Agent Vincent, popped up on the screen.

AGENT VINCENT

Mandatory 11 AM meeting this morning at the Black Oak Sheriff's Station.

"Crap," Ava said under her breath.

"Probably about the RickiLeaks post. She sent me one too," August said from the door.

Ava jumped at his voice, then said through a yawn, "She knew who I was when she called me in."

He gave her a tired smile and then leaned in, flicking on the lights. "Isn't there a folk tale about a frog and a scorpion that said that?"

"Very funny," Ava said, getting up and stretching.

"We're all grabbing breakfast. Rondeau and Talia are meeting us at some place in Pine Cove he read about online."

"Do you think they'll have breakfast sandwiches?"

"Only if it's a decent place," August said.

They walked out to the SUV and Ava, groaning with the ache in her bones, searched the pockets of her coat for her gloves. Morning brought with it a crystalline cold that felt like a slap to the face. At least it woke her up, she thought. A headache brewed at her temples from lack of sleep, and she fished out a bottle of aspirin from her messenger bag and took three. She had to rally. Another long day was just starting.

The Quilt and Kettle was indeed a decent place. A log-cabin-style diner, the rustic feel and bear-themed décor gave it a family friendly feel. The river rock fireplace in the back held a roaring fire and the air smelled like good food and wet coats. Pine chairs painted red, and tables covered with red and black checkered tablecloths took up most of the floor space with a couple of booths near the windows.

Ava lifted her nose to the heavenly scent of bacon grease and baking bread. The display case offered pre-made ham and cheese croissants, English muffin sandwiches, and cheesy veggie panini melts. Talia and Rondeau sat opposite each other at a booth against the wall and waved them over. A decent crowd. More than a few souls braved the increasingly frigid weather.

They ordered some specials. Ava decided against a breakfast sandwich once she'd perused the menu. She ordered an egg, ham, and cheddar omelet with toast. They chatted about the case as they ate. Ava mostly listened, sipping her coffee, her gaze going to the television screen mounted on a wall. It played the local news on mute.

When the conversation died down, she said, "You know, we should get a protective detail on Ricki Rogers. She'll accuse us of trying to control her reporting, but we should at least try."

August cut his egg white veggie omelet with his fork. "I know you think the killer watched her report and went after you."

"I think that's exactly what happened. Ricki, in her lust for viewers, made it sound like she had inside information on the killer."

"Doesn't she, though?" Talia asked, raising a brow. "She's been working Deputy Chutney for information."

"Her landing page on the video site promises she'll release more information soon," Rondeau said. "I'm keeping tabs on her posts. Nothing yet. Maybe Chutney isn't talking to her anymore."

"Well, the promise that she knows something secret about our investigation might make the killer seek her out. What if he thinks she's seen the video we have? He could want to question her." Ava added more sugar to her coffee, stirring slowly. "I would."

August took out his phone and typed out a text. "I'll send someone to speak to her about her contact with Deputy Chutney. We'll warn her about a possible threat to her life, but whether or not Vincent will authorize personal security is up in the air."

They chit-chatted about what each of them were doing next. Talia said she was going to go back to the DOJ lab in Riverside. They found blood on various pieces of the window that August and the killer crashed through.

"It'll take some time to run the blood DNA," Talia said, rewrapping her scarf around her neck. "But we'll run Touch DNA samples we took from the room. Those will be faster. August said the killer bounced an ashtray off of his hard head."

"Vase. And it hit my arm." August corrected, leaning back in the booth. "He hit the wall too, if you want to swab that."

Talia gathered her things and stood. "Fingers crossed we get a decent sample to test. Even better if the killer is already in the system."

"Hey, watch the road," August said as she was leaving. "They're saying something about black ice."

Talia frowned. "Awesome. I'm from San Francisco. We don't deal with much snow."

"Meh, it's barely snowing," Rondeau said. He'd explained to Ava earlier that week that he'd grown up in the mountains. "I'll drive."

As she was leaving, Talia caught Ava's gaze. "You've got this guy on the ropes. I have to say, you're tougher than you look."

"I try," Ava said with a tired smile.

Rondeau walked up to the counter to pay for the group with the CBI card, and Talia left with him. When they were gone, August handed Ava his tablet. A tipline form appeared on the screen.

"Someone called the station earlier this morning. They wanted to speak with a CBI Agent about the Black Oak Killer and Granger came and got me. I told you about it in his office."

"I think I barely registered that."

"The tip is from a local bartender. She works at the Prickly Pear in Fern Valley and says she might have seen the guy we're looking for."

"The bar where the first victim was buying rounds of drinks and promising fur coats to the waitress?" She handed back his tablet.

"The very one."

"How would this bartender know what the killer looks like?" Ava reached for her messenger bag. "We don't even know. And we didn't release the video yet."

"No idea," August said pushing up from the table and leaving a generous tip. "I hate small towns."

————

The Prickly Pear was exactly how Ava imagined a cactus themed dive bar would look like. It sat at the edge of Fern Valley's scant downtown. Though still closed, the door was unlocked, and they walked in. She smelled fried tortilla chips, salsa, and limes the second she walked in. Dark and slightly shabby, the black and brightly colored stripes of serapes tacked to the walls, the myriad ceramic cacti sitting on the bar and depicted in salt and pepper shakers on the tables, and even a sound activated dancing one on the old-timey jukebox gave it some cheer. Dusty foil Christmas tinsel still hung two months after the holiday and really added some sparkle.

A woman worked at the bar, wiping the counter as she stared straight at them with a curious look. "You the feds?"

Ava followed August over, her gaze on the scrappy surfboard mounted over the bar. They were nowhere near the beach. August pulled out his badge, as did Ava, and they introduced themselves.

The bartender was a dirty blond with faded star tattoos at the corners of her eyes that wrinkled into crow's feet when she smiled. She wore a tight leather vest over a band tee, and some acid washed jeans. Pretty, a little melancholy maybe. Ava guessed late thirties. She had the tired expression of a woman who had seen more than she'd wanted and didn't care to see any more. She introduced herself as Dream Taylor.

"You're the one Rio Suarez promised a fur coat to," Ava said with a smile. "I've been hoping to catch up with you."

"Well, I've been here the whole time," she said, her big blue eyes a little tired. "But yeah, Rio was turning into a regular here. Always buying rounds of drinks, appetizers too. He seemed cool."

"Did he seem bothered at all?" August asked.

Playing with the damp bar towel, Dream said, "No... at least I don't think so. I didn't really know him that well. He had only just started coming to the bar a month or two before he died, so I can't tell you for sure." She shrugged. "He seemed happy though."

"I heard he was bragging about his big score. Telling tall tales about how he got it," Ava lied, watching her.

Dream shook her head slowly. "Well, he didn't do that here. He was all about how it was such a big secret, how it would blow the town apart if people knew what he knew."

"And he never mentioned what he knew?" August asked.

"That's all he would say. 'If you only knew what I knew, you'd look at this town different.' He said if he revealed anything it would, 'bring a raging shit storm down on the town.' His words." Dream's lips pulled down in a frown. "I guess he wasn't lying."

August shot Ava a look. The victims had known something that got them killed. She walked them through Suarez's short time as a patron, and then when they couldn't get more they moved on.

"You called the station and said you had some information about the suspect?"

"The Black Oak Killer. Yes. I think so." She looked at Ava. "I was at the Riot Brewing Café when you were talking with Velma—" She stopped herself, eyeing August with interest. "Is there a reward for this information?"

"A reward?" August repeated, his eyebrows raising slightly.

"I got bills so... Like, if I tell you guys what I know, do I get a reward?"

"Yeah," Ava said with a smile. "If your information ends with the capture of the suspect, you and your friends don't die."

Dream frowned. "That's cool too, I guess."

August let out a slow breath. "There's no reward, ma'am. Other than helping the CBI catch a killer."

Dream shrugged. "Okay, so, I heard you guys were looking for a big guy, sort of gimpy, right?"

August made a face. "That's not really the proper—"

"Yes," Ava cut across him. "Doughy white guy, waddles a little when he runs."

Dream nodded. "Well, I didn't see him run, but the guy I'm thinking about sure did have a weird walk. Kinda like he was hurting."

Ava's gaze went to Dream's rose quartz necklace. Tattoos of zodiac signs and depictions of goddesses, plants, and the moon in all its phases covered both arms. An earth child or green witch, maybe.

She tilted her head. "That's hard to pick up on when someone's hiding it. You must really know people. Is it the job?"

A blush of a smile lifted Dream's face. "Actually, I sort of get these intuitions about people. My sister thinks I'm an empath."

August opened his mouth to say something, then shut it, a look of total loss in his eyes.

Ava nodded sympathetically. "I get that. It must be hard. Dealing with everyone's baggage. Draining?"

"The world's a dark place, sometimes, you know?" She looked around the empty bar. "So much loneliness."

Ava agreed and pushed on. "So, this guy you saw. What kind of vibes did you get from him? Did he give off good guy energy or... did you pick up on any red flags?"

Dream's perfectly plucked brows pulled down. "You know, that's what got me thinking I should call." She pointed to the corner of the bar. "There was this guy who came in a few times before Rio died. A couple weeks before, maybe. Quiet. Polite, but only the basics. Didn't ask how my day was, didn't want to chit-chat. He just ordered and said thank you."

"Okay." Ava sat up straight. "You took his order, so you saw his face, right?"

Dream grimaced. "Kind of... he had on one of those thick winter scarves all wrapped up around his mouth. It was really cold each time he came in. At the beginning of winter, we had a lot of storms."

"And he just left it on?" August asked.

Dream pointed behind them. "See those little like, kiosk thingies on the tables?"

Ava looked over at the small touch screens with the menu and bar offerings. Games too. She'd used them before at bars and cafes. "Yeah."

"The owner got them so he didn't have to hire another waitress. Customers can just order and pay at the table."

August walked over. "He ordered from there?" He jotted something on his tablet. "After weeks of cleaning there'd be no prints, but I'll see about pulling the receipts from credit card customers."

"He paid cash." Dream pointed to the kiosk on the table next to the bar. "The way it works is you order first. I bring it. Then when you're done eating and want to close out your bill, you tap the 'Ready to Pay' button and then you can choose cash, credit, gift card... whatever."

"And he paid cash?" August asked, walking back over.

"Yes, the exact amount all three times he came in. He even left the tip in change. A bunch of quarters."

"What about an accent?" Ava asked.

"No, he sounded like he was from California."

Ava jotted information in her notebook. "Did he order the same thing each time?"

Dream nodded. "Yeah. A beer and a beef burrito plate. Four-dollar tip in quarters."

"What about when you brought his order to him?" August asked.

"I mean, it gets busy here on the weekends and he tended to have the sports section of the paper open in front of him," Dream said. "I think I saw his whole face maybe once."

"The sports section?" Ava asked. Thinking her first impression of the killer had been right. "Did he get the paper here or bring it with him?"

"He must've brought it with him because we don't have newspapers delivered here. And, honestly, when people bring in things to read and just leave them, I toss them out when I close."

Ava gazed back at the corner booth. A dark corner with no window. No real light except what was coming off the bar. "Do you think you could describe him? If we got a sketch artist to work with you?"

"I don't know..."

Ava caught Dream's gaze. "Hey... What are you worried about?"

Dream sighed, fear creeping across her face. "I heard he went after you."

"He won't know you spoke with us," August promised.

She bit her lower lip, her hand shaking. She looked like she was going to change her mind and not talk, but then she said, "The last time the guy was here, Rio was hanging out with friends. Buying drinks, ordering appetizers for everyone. You know, a party. And the guy just stared at him from the booth. Like he was studying him. Neither of them came back after that."

"Had he ever done that with anyone else?" Ava asked.

"No. Just that one time. I thought he was mad that Rio was being so flashy and loud, but he never said anything. Just ate his dinner and left." She started wiping the already clean bar again, a little lost. "I didn't think anything of it until I heard about the limp thing. This guy definitely had one. It's like sitting in the booth for so long made the guy feel worse. He had more trouble walking when he left."

Ava talked her through the serving of the guy's food, trying for more information. Dream verified the guy appeared Caucasian, a little on the pudgy side, and tall. He might have brown eyes or hazel. "What color were his eyebrows? This will help us determine hair color since he was wearing a cap."

August nodded, writing on his tablet as they spoke.

Dream glanced up at August's hair. "Not, what is that... deep brown with red undertones? This guy had, like normal to light brown. Medium, I guess? I'm sorry I don't remember better."

"Well, we didn't know his hair color before." Ava smiled. "You're doing great. Just a few more questions. If you had to describe his body type in one sentence, like one image... how would you?"

Dream thought for a minute, then said, "You know those high school guys who go from totally cut to a little soft. Not fat, but..."

"Yeah," Ava said, thinking. "What would you guess is his age, roughly. Old guy, college aged, thirties... middle age?"

"I wanna say late thirties to early forties. I don't know why though." Dream stared past Ava for a moment, lost in thought. "I think it was his voice, if I had to guess. He didn't sound like an old fogey, but also not young. He gave off aggressive energy, too. You know those guys who enjoy brawling? He'd scan the bar, really check out whoever walked in, sizing up the competition." She sighed heavily, looking at Ava with defeat. "I don't know. Maybe I'm remembering wrong because he might be the killer."

"He's just a person of interest," August said with no real conviction.

Dream nodded, catching Ava's gaze. "I heard you catch these guys."

"We've encountered criminals like this before," Ava said with a reassuring smile. "You've been a big help."

"Everyone is jumping out of their skins," Dream whispered. "I just want this nightmare to end."

Ava placed one of her cards on the bar. "I still want you to talk with a sketch artist. You might know more than you think. Our artists can work with you here, after your shift, so you won't be seen going into the sheriff's station. Or we can set you up for a video call right here in the back room."

Dream agreed and August arranged a meeting with a CBI sketch artist during her lunch break in a couple of hours.

On their way back to the car, August said, "The unsub picked up Suarez's scent somewhere else. I'd bet my paycheck. He was waiting for him here. That's why he came in multiple times and then stopped once he saw Suarez."

"My bet is he followed him from here to his cabin." Ava blew out a cloud of vapor as she glanced around at the other small shops. More appeared open since they'd gone into the Prickly Pear, the town slowly waking up. Coffee and baking pastries scented the air. She checked her watch. "We should try to talk with Suarez's brother again while we're in Fern Valley. I think he's still cleaning out the cabin. I wanna ask him if he's ever seen anyone like the customer Dream just described around his brother's place."

"I'll call in the description to Rondeau and tell him about the sketch artist." August unlocked the car. "Hopefully we'll have a sketch early this afternoon and can send the description and other info out to local law enforcement ASAP." He checked the dashboard clock. "It's ten right now. Depending on how long the artist takes with Dream, we might make the afternoon news, definitely the evening. Vincent will want to do a live news conference to get the word out." He looked at her. "Hey, this is good. We're closing in."

Ava stared out of the window, the thrum of the chase in her chest. "Not fast enough."

TWENTY-ONE

They took a winding road out of town toward the denser forest near Suarez's cabin. The meager sunlight peeked out from between the gray clouds, dappling the windshield through the branches. Ava stared out at the trees and bushes dusted with snow as they drove and decided that Fern Valley looked a lot like Black Oak, only sparser. The description they'd taken from Dream would move things, Ava thought. Hopefully. A thrum moved through her again. She was gaining on him.

"So, August, you're a jock," Ava said, scribbling in her leather notebook. "What's happening in the sports world during the winter?"

August looked over as they pulled up to a stop sign. "You're thinking he might be a gambler?"

"All three times he brought in a newspaper it was the sports section. Then he made a high risk move by calling one of the CBI agents hunting him. Come on. That's not a coincidence. Think about it. If you see me at a café with the newspaper, what section would you guess I'd have?"

"The crossword puzzle." August took them back down the rutted road leading to Suarez's cabin. The towering pines behind the houses on the street loomed like brooding giants against the overcast morning sky. Sunlight slipped between the clouds sending shards of brilliance onto the frosty grass lining the driveway. "Where are we taking this?"

"I don't know. I'm just trying to figure out why the killer focused on Suarez first. Like you said, he was obviously already onto Suarez when he went to the Prickly Pear to wait to see if he'd show up." Ava fidgeted with a cardboard coaster she'd picked up from the bar. "The killer picked up Suarez's scent somewhere else. But where could they have crossed paths?"

August glanced at the Prickly Pear logo on the coaster and shook his head. "Are you still stealing relics?"

"They help me think." Ava dropped it into her messenger bag. "Besides, you can't steal things if they're free."

"Yes, but your idea of free is a little vague."

They pulled up to the shabby cabin just as Alonzo walked out with some boxes and dropped them onto the open tailgate of a beat-up truck. Other boxes sat in groups on the lawn. Some labeled trash. Others donate. The ones in the truck bed said *keep*.

He spotted Ava and hesitated, then shoved his hands in his pockets as they walked up to him. "Why're you guys back?"

"We have a few more questions," August said.

Alonzo frowned. "I'm in the middle of something—"

"The last time we spoke you were incredibly helpful," Ava said with a disarming smile. "We'd like to run something by you, Mr. Suarez, if you have a minute."

"Yeah, okay." Alonzo gestured listlessly at the boxes. "I'm just organizing which stuff to toss and which to give away. I have no idea what Rio would want."

"I think whatever you choose to do with his things will be honoring him." Ava looked down at all the boxes. "You guys seemed to understand each other."

"We did." Alonzo nodded, his tension easing in his shoulders. "What do you need to ask me?"

"I think we've come across something about your brother's

death." Ava blew into her cold hands. "Agent Blake and I just received information that an unknown male might have been stalking your brother at the Prickly Pear."

Alonzo looked at her with surprise. "I know the place."

"Did he say anything to you about that?"

"No... what do you mean stalked?"

"A man may have been waiting for your brother at the bar," August said. "Did Rio ever say anything about being followed?"

"No, he—" Alonzo shifted on his feet. "You're saying this guy hunted my brother?"

"This is what we know about the suspect," Ava said. "We know he's over six feet, white, medium brown hair with brown or hazel eyes. He speaks English like it's his first language. Keeps to himself, possibly hides his face with a neck gaiter or scarf, and may carry parts of a newspaper to obstruct his face. He might also walk with a limp or favor one side enough to notice. We believe he is either camping or living on the outskirts of town, and may have a vehicle, but that last part is just a theory given his movements."

Alonzo looked at her with surprise. "You found all that out in two days?"

"I said you were helpful." Ava caught his gaze, trying to get him to focus. "Mr. Suarez, does the man I just described sound familiar? Maybe someone Rio met in one of the get-rich-quick schemes his landlord mentioned."

Alonzo frowned. "The landlord said that?"

"Think... you might have seen him walking in town. Maybe loitering around where Rio hung out."

"I don't think so. Who is he?"

"We don't know yet," August said. "The individual in question showed up at the Prickly Pear but kept to himself. Our witness also said that when Rio was partying with friends at the bar, this man was watching him."

Alonzo rubbed his eyes with a calloused hand. "You're sayin' this guy is the killer?"

"No," Ava said. "We're asking if you recall seeing a guy with the description we just gave you around here or with Rio at any time. Maybe at his work?"

Shaking his head, Alonzo put his hands on his hips and stared back at the cabin. "No. I can't remember ever seeing a guy like that."

Ava blew out a breath, shaking her head. She was still missing a nexus between all of the victims. Their connection point.

"Did your brother ever gamble?" August asked.

"I mean, he'd go blow off some steam at Soboba once in a while."

"Are you talking about the gaming casino down in the foothills?" Ava asked. She'd read about the Indian gaming resort on her flight back from Hawaii. "Did he go there often?"

"Not really. He went for the shows. You know, old rock stars we couldn't afford to see when they were hot. He'd go to concerts there and get himself a shirt. It was nothing. He didn't really like to gamble as far as I know. Maybe some slot machines? Why? Do you think he owed someone money, and they killed him?"

"We're still putting things together, but we're building a picture. He's not going to be able to hide for much longer." Ava took Alonzo around the subject a few more times, but he didn't have anything more to add. His brother, Alonzo insisted, didn't mention anything about money before he died. He talked about their boating trips and the last thing they'd caught. And then they listened to him complain about the overwhelming task of emptying someone else's house and Ava sympathized. Memories tended to pop out of nowhere just to rip you open all over again.

The boxes on the lawn sat between them and she looked down as Alonzo recounted the last time he'd talked to his brother. "Rio was excited. He was looking at boats."

Her gaze slid over their meager contents. The last pieces of Suarez's life. Photos in cheap frames, mismatched plastic drinking cups, old clothes. A metal bucket with a hammer, chisel, and some work gloves. They weren't mechanic's tools. More like... landscape equipment. She scanned the property. Unkempt piles of leaves and dirt peppered the front lawn. No discernable garden beds. She spotted an old-timey metal canteen in a belt sleeve. Ava wondered if Suarez hiked like Marley had.

She pointed. "Mr. Suarez, can I see what's in that box?"

Alonzo shrugged. "I guess so. I'm throwing those things away. What about the ones in the truck?"

"No, I just..." She dug in the box. "Was your brother into hiking?"

"No way. When Rio had a spare weekend, he spent time on the water if he could, not getting sweaty climbing up hills."

She held up the work gloves. "What about gardening?"

"Look at this dump. Do *you* think he was into gardening?" Alonzo scratched at his sideburn. "Why?"

"Because of the equipment." A camera lens, partially wrapped in a red cleaning cloth sat in the bucket next to the tools and work gloves. Had they missed something? She searched the rest of the boxes. "Have you come across a camera during your packing?"

"Rio didn't have a camera. He used his phone to take pictures."

August tilted his head. "Let me see it." She handed it over and he nodded. "This is a magnifying loupe."

"Like for jewelry?" Ava asked, taking it back.

"For anything. This one sits on a frame so that you lean over and peer through the lens at the object."

Ava sat back on her heels and looked up at Alonzo. "Any idea what he was doing with that?"

He shook his head. "Does it mean something?"

"I'm not sure..." Something caught her gaze in the depths of another box. A piece of watermelon, wet and glinting in the dappled sun. Ava frowned. Watermelon in winter? And why was it in a box next to a couple of old remote controls? She reached over and picked up the watermelon. Only it wasn't. It was a wedge-shaped section of shiny rock. She held it up to Alonzo. "What is this?"

"I think that's uh..." He snapped his fingers, thinking. "Tourmaline. Watermelon tourmaline, as Rio called it. You can see why. It looks like a piece of watermelon."

Ava stared at the pinkish-red center and green outer edge. "I know this color…"

"I mean, yeah. They're all over the town," he went on. "Every souvenir shop, hotel lobby store, even the gas station. They aren't worth much. I think there used to be a mine or something around here."

"Do you know where your brother got it?" August asked.

Alonzo shrugged. "No, he always had weird stuff around, though. He has a water ionizer here too if you want that. I loved my brother, but his landlord was right. He was always tangled up in some kind of scheme."

Ava held the stone up to the sun and a flash of the same color in Marley's room flitted through her mind. The colored pencil.

"Once is chance. Two is a coincidence…" Ava murmured, letting the tendrils of the thought unfurl. What had the kid drawn with the color? In her mind's eye, she flipped through the sketches she'd found on Marley's desk. He'd drawn cloud formations, birds, but the only thing he'd drawn in this color had been angular rocks. She startled, her breath catching. "Three is a pattern."

"What've you got, Ava?" August asked.

She'd seen this gemstone somewhere else. Not just there at Suarez's cabin and the kid's sketches. Someplace high. A tinkling sound drifted through her memory and her gaze snapped to August's.

"We have to go back to the Thompsons' house," she said, the words rushing out of her.

His eyebrows shot up. "Now?"

Ava bounced on the balls of her feet, her mind racing. "Yes, if not sooner."

They left Alonzo with his brother's things surrounding him. He'd given the stone to Ava for evidence, and she'd thanked him while dropping it in an evidence baggie.

Back in the car, August said, "What's brewing in that brain of yours?"

"I think I know how the victims all know each other," Ava said and held the tourmaline in the bag up to the sunlight. "I just want to make sure."

Half an hour later they stood back on the porch of the Thompsons' house. She again used menthol under her nose before entering the home, slathering it as she took the stairs to the bedroom two at a time.

"Hold on there, Speed Racer," August said behind her. "What are you doing?"

"I feel like I saw something before..." Ava went straight to the bedroom, veering left toward Mrs. Thompson's side of the bed. She stopped in front of the shelf of trinkets she'd noticed that first night and searched through the crowded knick-knacks. Glass butterflies, porcelain frogs with leaf hats, little ceramic mushrooms painted to look like fairy cottages, bears carved out of obsidian, and one marble-sized piece of crystalline gemstone. The green edges and inner reddish center looked exactly like Marley's drawing.

Ava pulled a nitrile glove from a pocket inside her messenger bag, slipped it on, and picked up the stone. She showed it to August. "Watermelon tourmaline."

August stared at it. "They all have this?"

"This could be the nexus, August, how they're connected."

He shook his head, a wisp of a smile on his lips. "Tell me you're sure."

"I know Alonzo said this rock was everywhere and okay, maybe it's coincidence, but other than dying violently, this is the only other thing we've found that connects the victims."

"We need Rondeau on this. We should have the victims' financials by now. The subpoena came in earlier. Let's see if we can find out how each of them got the gemstone." He took out his phone, punching in a number, but paused. "I need to speak with Vincent."

"Oh, crap." Ava checked her watch. "I have a meeting with her in like two minutes."

"Where?"

"The sheriff's station." Ava shook her head. "It's a waste of time. We need to keep pushing."

"Call her and I'll drive you back. We need to tell her about the sketch and the gemstone anyway—" His phone rang, and he looked at the screen. "It's Granger." August answered and stilled, his gaze finding hers. The expression on his face made her stomach drop. He nodded, murmuring assent. "We'll get there ASAP." He hung up, his face pale. "We need to get to Shady Acres right away. Lucy Thompson was just found dead."

TWENTY-TWO

August and Ava pulled into the parking lot of the facility, parking next to several sheriff cars from other jurisdictions as well as a forensic services van. Biting wind moved through the old trees with a low, woeful howl, as if mourning the loss of one of their own. It chilled Ava to the bone, and she shivered despite her thick sweater and trench coat. Clouds blotted out the wan sun as fat snowflakes floated like cotton balls to the gathering drift at their feet. The storm was almost on them.

A sole ambulance parked close to the recovery center. A young man sat hunched over his knees, a shock blanket wrapped over his shoulders, oxygen mask on his face. Nothing behind his eyes except grief and shock. A paramedic tended to him, nodding to Ava and August as they passed.

"Was that the fiancé?" Ava asked. She'd only seen him in photos from Lucy's wedding planner. He looked ten years older.

"Trevor Stevens," August said, folding a piece of gum into his mouth as they mounted the stairs to the entrance. "We need to question him."

"Good luck with that. He wanted to move her, and the doctor wouldn't let him."

"That wasn't us."

"He won't see it that way," Ava muttered. "Especially not after I sent her into hysterics."

Inside the lobby, Rondeau stood leaning against the front counter talking to the receptionist behind it. He wore jeans and a band t-shirt under a green, old man cardigan. He turned when they entered, walking over to meet them in the center of the floor away from earshot.

"Bring me up to speed," August said. His phone pinged and he glanced at the screen, then said, "Vincent is on her way here from the station."

Rondeau scrolled through his digital notes. "The facility called the sheriff's office who forwarded them to Granger. He had Gale call us on our phones to avoid people listening in on the radio scanners and causing a panic."

Looking around, Ava asked, "Where's Granger?"

"Out behind the recovery center where they found her," Rondeau said, his expression grim. "Talia too. She's directing the forensic team. She had the one from the Timberline Inn scene resupplied and it just got here." He indicated for them to follow, and they did, through the lobby and into the main facility via a locked door the receptionist buzzed open. "The whole place is freaked."

"What happened?" Ava asked, as they strode down the hallway heading toward the rear of the building. The polished floors reflected the afternoon sun shining softly through the skylights.

Rondeau told them the gist. "Lucy's fiancé, Trevor, arrived at the center to have breakfast with her. When he realized she wasn't in her room, he wandered around to look for her. He checked the art and music rooms, the exercise room, and cafeteria, thinking she'd maybe woken up early and was out and about. She didn't turn up, so he had reception call on the overhead speakers for her to meet him. After twenty minutes and still nothing, the staff started searching. They found her in the fountain out back. Drowned. Talia says time of death looks sometime after two or three in the morning. There's evidence of a struggle. It looks like he held her under."

"So after the killer attacked Ava's room and set fire to the sheriff's SUV, he came here?" August asked.

Rondeau shook his head. "Balls of steel."

"Or a head full of rocks," Ava said.

"Now, remember, this is essentially a private retreat for the people staying here, so no actual rules," Rondeau said. "The nurse who helped the fiancé look said the patients come and go as they please. Oh, and we're pulling what security cameras they have, but I wouldn't hold my breath. This place traffics in discretion."

"I don't understand how he got to her," Ava said. "The CBI arranged for a guard or patrol officer to watch her room, right?"

"We did. Rotating guards." August's jaw worked as he punished his gum. "Where is the officer who was assigned to her room last night?"

"There's some confusion as to where her guard was during the incident. And we don't know where he is now." Rondeau pushed through the exit to the back garden. "Granger will explain."

A meandering lawn with noble pine trees, some oaks, and evergreen bushes sloped gently toward an elaborate fountain area near the perimeter of the property. Wooden signs marking the garden path read, Fountain of Tranquility.

That's gonna have to change.

As they approached, the horror of the scene came into view. Granger, and several other sheriff's deputies huddled on one side of the towering granite fountain. On the other side, nestled between a set of white wrought iron lawn chairs, a prone form lay on the frosty grass covered with a body sheet. Forensic techs worked the scene in their white paper suits as she and August approached.

The ornately designed pedestal fountain, made of three carved, red stone bowls, sat in a clover shaped basin. A top nozzle embedded in a softball-sized conch shell dribbled water into the top section. A tech worked with the controls on a nearby panel that was artfully hidden within the manicured hedges. Ava stood at the edge of the scene, taking it in. The icy ground crunched under her shoes, a biting wind chafed her cheeks, and the sun shrouded everything in an eerie, muted light. How much colder and forlorn had it been out there in the dead of night?

Did Lucy come out here on her own to find the killer waiting for her or did the killer force her down here? She looked back from where she'd come, searching for drag marks and saw Agent Vincent walking down the lawn toward Granger and August. Ava wandered over herself, joining the group as Agent Vincent approached. High heels, a cashmere coat in a sedate camel color, and black leather gloves. She nodded to Ava, then August.

"Boss," August said in greeting.

Glancing over at the body, Vincent said, "We screwed up."

He nodded. "I'll find out how."

"Did we find the patrol officer assigned to her?" she asked.

Granger shook his head. "No. But I know the guy. His name is Officer Manafort. Twenty years on the job with Riverside."

"We need to track him down, now," Vincent said. "Find out what he knows."

"Already on it," Granger said.

As August and Granger gave Vincent the most recent information, Ava wandered away, going to Lucy's body and kneeling. Talia, who'd been conversing with a forensic tech, came over and stood next to her.

"This poor woman," Talia said in greeting, genuine compassion behind her soft eyes. "You want to take a look."

"I think I owe it to her, no?"

"What do you mean?" Talia knelt next to Ava.

"I missed something, and she died," Ava said.

"You can't think that way. This guy is unpredictable and rash. He's running scared."

Ava shrugged. "I should have seen this coming."

"Do you really believe that?"

Ava cleared her throat. "Show me what he did to her."

Talia looked at her for a beat, like she was going to say more, but then reached out and gripped the edge of the body sheet. "Ready?"

Ava nodded and she pulled it back. Lucy lay on her back, her vacant eyes stared out from under a mat of wet, tangled hair. Deep abrasions marred her forehead and nose.

Talia pointed at the injuries with a gloved finger. "We think that's from the edge or bottom of the fountain. They discovered her bent over the edge of the basin as if someone held her head under."

"How is the water not frozen? We passed a creek on the way here, and it looked solid."

"According to the director of the facility, they refurbished the fountain twenty years ago. That included a heating element to keep the inner pipes from bursting."

The fountain stopped working, the hum of the inner motor suddenly silent.

Ava looked over at it. "Who found her?"

"The fiancé. During their initial search. Granger said her head and shoulders were still submerged. When the fiancé saw her, he pulled her out and tried CPR. But she'd been gone for hours." Talia looked stricken. "The staff had to pry her out of his arms."

"I saw him in the ambulance." Ava glanced down at Lucy, her skin so pale that the blue of her veins showed through on her neck. "Any sign of stab wounds?"

"No. But we found this."

She pulled the sheet back further, then, with her hands on the body's shoulder and hip, rolled it over to show Lucy's back. The imprint of a muddy boot in the center of the pink pajama top made Ava's blood boil.

"That bastard," she whispered. Anger she thought she'd learned to manage long ago flared awake. Talia set Lucy's body back down and laid the sheet back over her. "She has a nasty bump on the crown of her head. Possibly a hit to disorient her or knock her unconscious."

"Explains why she didn't scream."

"He also left bruises on her upper arms and some of her hair was ripped out. It's in the water."

"This brutality. Out in the open." Ava looked off at the approaching clouds. "He's coming undone."

"We're draining the fountain now that we shut the pump down. Then we'll dismantle it, and I'll check the filter, water, and components at the DOJ lab in Riverside. The medical clinic here isn't equipped for this kind of thing. Hopefully he lost some hair or something in the struggle."

"What did Lucy know? And why wouldn't she tell us?" Shoving her hands into her coat pockets, Ava chewed on her inner cheek. "She must have known he might come after her."

"There's something dark and twisted going on in this town," Talia said quietly. "And this guy is in the center of it."

"Yeah," Ava said, thinking about Lucy's cries last time she'd seen her. *I did it. I killed them.* "I'm going to need a straight-on photo of Lucy in situ."

August called her name and waved her over. She rejoined the group, standing next to him.

"The unsub is on some kind of spree," Vincent said. "First, he attacks the CBI, then the sheriff's SUV, then this?"

"All within hours," August added.

Vincent looked at Ava. "What's his end game?"

"Other than taking out a possible witness and escaping again?" Ava shrugged and glanced at Granger. "Did you ever get a chance to speak with the fiancé?"

"We were arranging a time for today or tomorrow. He's been busy dealing with cancelling the wedding and taking care of family that flew in. They're all scrambling. Plus, you know, Lucy wasn't doing well." Granger hiked up his pants and sighed. "So, no. I didn't meet with him yet. He was going to bring me the dress too, but then this happened..."

"Have we found Deputy Chutney?" Ava asked.

"Not yet," Granger said. "You still think he's innocent?"

"Yeah, but he also might be incredibly dumb." She looked back at the building. Its ornate façade seemed a little haunted in the subdued light. "We need to find him."

Vincent regarded her silently, then said, "I've seen that look before. What are you thinking?"

"I'd have to speak with Chutney to be sure, but I think I know why the killer hit the SUV." Ava shook her head. "I just didn't see it in time."

"Explain," Vincent said.

"Let me check something first," Ava turned to Granger. "Can I get a count on the police radios? All of them. Even the ones you loaned to the CBI team."

He looked at her for a beat before running a hand down his face. "Dammit."

August stilled, his gaze snapping to Ava's. "The fire was to cover up a theft."

She nodded. "I think the killer busted the driver's side window to get to a police radio in the vehicle. Then covered it up with the fire. It's why he didn't light up the entire station."

"And he used it to get to Lucy," Vincent said.

"Yes. I think it's why he hit Lucy so fast afterwards. He was rushing in case we noticed a radio missing."

Anger flashed across August's face. "He played us."

"So, we regroup." Vincent's phone pinged and she checked it before adding, "Stop using radios and switch to cell phones until we clear this mess up. Ava, where do you see this heading?"

"I don't think he's done causing havoc. I think he's just getting started. Lucy knew something, was involved in all of this somehow, and now she's dead." Ava looked back over her shoulder at the body. "We should check on the nurse who dosed her. Whitmore, was it?"

"You think he'd go after her?" Vincent asked.

"I would," Ava said. "I'd shut all of them up."

Granger lifted the radio to his lips. "I want a twenty on Deputy

Manafort and Deborah Whitmore immediately. And someone figure out where the hell Chutney is!"

———

The director of the recovery center, an officious man named Harold Warner, started making noise about private property and warrants as soon as the CBI agents closed down Lucy's room. Armed with a google search of the law, he requested documentation, though for what, Ava didn't know.

"This is private property, and our guests expect privacy and discretion. Besides, that one," he said and pointed at Ava. "Caused such a problem last time, a few guests checked out."

The facility didn't have standing to block their investigation. Still, August said he'd speak to his bosses to give the guy time to cool off.

"We need access to any cameras in this place," Ava said.

"We'll get it."

Unable to reach the Shady Acres nurse with her phone, Gale located her by calling her church's prayer tree which eventually reached Whitmore's mother. She explained that Whitmore was working on her physician's assistant degree at UC Riverside and normally kept her phone on 'do not disturb' while on campus. She'd gone in for morning classes and was still there in a study group. Her mother, designated as an emergency contact, called and it rang through. She was fine. Granger then called and asked her to head to the school's security office and to wait there until Riverside PD could send someone out to get her.

Officer Manafort turned out to be at the Timberline Inn crime scene. They pulled him and sent him back to Shady Acres where he met with Granger, August, Vincent, and Ava in a family counseling room. Blue wallpaper with puffy clouds, soft lamp light, an obnoxious number of frilly accent pillows on the couch. He sat on a cushy sofa, sweat sliding down from his temples, as he answered their questions.

August and Ava sat on overstuffed chairs facing the couch. Vincent stood behind them, watching silently. Granger at her side.

August leaned in. "Relax and just tell us what happened."

"Alright, uh, I received a radio call from Deputy Chutney about 2:30 this morning. He told me about the attack at the Timberline Inn and that there had also been another incident at the Black Oak Sherriff's Station, a fire. He said you all were getting slammed, and that several officers were down." Manafort licked his lips, his gaze darting from Ava to Vincent and back. "He said they needed backup desperately. A killer was on the loose taking out police. I mean, fellow law enforcement told me all hell was breaking loose. What was I supposed to do?"

Ava, who'd been writing in her notebook, held her pen up, stopping him. "What happened when you got to the inn?"

Manafort shrugged. "It was chaos, obviously. They put me to work cordoning off a street that locals were using to drive by and gawk."

"He called you on your police radio?" August clarified. "Did you know his voice?"

"He said his name, and I believed him. Who else would call me on a police radio and know what had just happened at the inn?"

"The killer, clearly." Ava regarded Manafort. He looked genuinely confused. And scared. "How did it work? Chutney called you and you just took off, or did you wait for a replacement?"

"I didn't 'just take off'." He stiffened, sitting upright. "I wouldn't do that. I saw Deputy Chutney when he got here. He'd said over the radio that he was on his way up to alert the facility's security and that he'd be right behind me. I passed him on my way to the car."

"You saw him?" Granger asked. "It was definitely my deputy, Chutney?"

"Yes..." Manafort paused, blinking for a few moments. "Uh, I mean, I think so. It was cold, and he had on one of those neck gaiter things you pull up over your mouth and nose. But, I mean, he had his sheriff's jacket and cap on. Also, when he passed me, he waved his radio."

"So, you didn't see him at all," Ava said. "You saw someone you thought was him given the situation."

"He had on a sheriff's jacket and hat, like I said. It was him," Manafort insisted. A vein bulging in his forehead. Ava hoped he didn't stroke out in front of them. "I didn't... I wouldn't have left a witness unguarded if I thought she wasn't in safe hands."

"Did he walk funny?" Ava asked.

Manafort looked at her confused. "I don't—"

"Yes or no, officer," Vincent said.

"Uh, he was hurrying, hunched over with the cold." He glanced at Ava, then August, a pleading look on his face. "I don't even think I noticed him all that much. I was running out. My mind was on the shooting at the inn. The officers who were down..."

They talked with him for a little longer, but he didn't have much to add to what they already suspected. The killer stole a radio and a sheriff's department jacket and cap, impersonated Deputy Chutney, and then murdered Lucy Thompson.

Vincent asked Manafort to give them the room, then said. "Next steps?"

"I want to see what the cameras caught," Ava said. She remembered seeing them in the hallways and lobby. "If they recorded the killer sneaking through the recovery center, then the sheriff probably knows Chutney well enough to confirm if it's him."

"I can do that." Granger nodded.

"I want to see the way Lucy's killer moved." Ava twiddled the pen between two fingers. "If the suspect was stressed, he might not have self-corrected the way he walks."

"We'll get the security cameras pulled. I have to head back." Vincent started typing on her phone, then looked up. "What do you need at this moment?"

"Honestly?" Ava said and glanced behind her at the closed door of the family room. "I need a few minutes in Lucy's room without the director hovering. He's causing a stink."

Vincent checked her watch and then stood. To Ava she said, "Screw the director. You're chasing a killer. We have probable cause to check her room. Her property is relevant to the investigation as well. Do what you need to do. You're covered."

Ava stood with her. "And our meeting? The RickiLeaks post—"

"I knew what kind of fire I was playing with when I called you in," Vincent said. "Now go hunt down this asshole."

TWENTY-THREE

Granger left Shady Acres to speak with the nurse, Debbie Whitmore, at the sheriff's station. They decided to encourage her to stay at a friend's house for a few days until they sorted things out. He said he'd return to watch the recovery center's security recordings as soon as he got her situated.

Before she returned to LA, Vincent took the director of the facility aside to explain his position and authority on the matter of their investigation. When she was done, she caught up to Ava by the coffee machine.

"I secured written consent from the director on site. Legal said that will hold until the paperwork catches up. He agreed to let us in with their security guard to go over the camera footage from last night. Maybe they caught a better image of the guy than the trail cams did." Vincent paused. "Logistics is telling me there's a record-breaking storm moving in. You need to stop this guy soon."

"Dead in his tracks," Ava said and then put her hand up. "Figuratively speaking."

"Do what you do." Vincent pulled her gloves back on. "If you need anything, call."

After she'd left, August tasked Rondeau with the surveillance cameras on the property and then went with Ava to inspect Lucy's room. On their way, they stopped and spoke with the charge nurse, Linda Keely. A tall, solid woman with strawberry blonde hair and a stern face, who told them that, other than her fiancé, Lucy had wanted no visitors and received no calls. She'd barely eaten, had nightmares for which she'd needed sedation, and refused to go on walks or visit the garden.

"She'd just sit and stare out of her bedroom window," Keely said. "Sometimes, she cried but tried to hide it when I came to check on her."

"Did she talk with anybody here?" Ava asked.

"No. She barely spoke. Occasionally, she asked for more juice. All she wanted to do was sleep, bless her heart. Losing her parents, so suddenly and so violently... it's like it broke something inside her, I think."

Ava tended to agree.

Though she'd visited Lucy's room previously, it had a pall now, an echo of death that hung in the air like a scream cut short. She thought about how Lucy had died as she snapped on her nitrile gloves. In the cold. In the dark. Shaking off the thought, she looked in the nightstand drawers and sifted through intake paperwork, complementary pairs of grippy socks, snacks, and small cans of apple juice. Without words, they searched like they used to. Ava from the door inward. August from the far side of the room, working toward the center.

"The footprint on her back matched the one at the Thompsons' crime scene," Ava said quietly. "He killed her parents and then stomped the life out of her."

August glanced over his shoulder. "We'll get him."

"The way he killed her... the drowning. It fits with the coercion angle. He used the tourniquet, the cliff, and Mr. Thompson's life as means to force his victims to tell him something."

"You think this smacks of waterboarding?" August turned to face her.

"The killer thought she knew something. So did I. Whether she actually did or not doesn't change the fact that she's dead." Ava scanned the intake form. "I should have pushed harder to get in the room with her again."

"Don't take blame that isn't yours. You're the one who requested a guard for her." August went through the desk and pulled out the flat middle drawer. "Her fiancé, doctor, and the director of this place were working to quash any chance of us speaking with her."

"Yeah, but that usually doesn't stop me. This whole case is just..." She shook her head. "The pressure of being back on the team since the Ghost Town Killer scandal messed with me. The hit to your career last time we worked together keeps looming over everything."

"Ava, I'm head of the Priority Investigations Team. I think I landed on my feet."

"Ricki said we covered up a murder."

"The CBI cleared both of us. End of story." He peered into the back of the drawer. "Besides, I think I found something." Bending over, he reached deep into the back and pulled out a phone. He held it up for Ava. "Maybe Lucy can still tell us something."

She strode over. Mercifully, it didn't have a passcode. However, the message app appeared to have been sanitized. No texts whatsoever. From anyone.

"You have this kind of phone, right?" August handed it over.

"I do." She checked the social media apps and found messages between Lucy and her friends about the wedding, the bridal shower, etc. All of whom had already been questioned by the CBI before Ava arrived on the case. Nothing out of the ordinary other than the missing messages. "Why would Lucy erase all of her texts with her parents and fiancé? There wasn't a falling out as far as we know. She expected them at her rehearsal dinner and went to check on them. Her fiancé, by all accounts, is doting and protective. And yet, she got rid of her text conversations with them. With everyone, actually."

"You were right. She was definitely hiding something," August said at her ear.

Ava checked the photo gallery and found nothing recent. The photos still there bore dates of more than six months prior.

"No pictures of friends, the bachelorette party... Not even her dress?" Ava turned to face him. "I don't buy that a bride didn't have a ton of photos leading up to her big day."

"I'll tell Vincent we need a subpoena for Lucy's cloud memory." August pulled out his phone and typed a message.

"Can we get Rondeau in here?" Ava asked. "He's your digital guru, right?"

"The team's, yes." August finished his text, then called Rondeau in from the fountain crime scene.

Ava handed him Lucy's phone as soon as he entered the room.

"I read that you can find deleted messages on this kind of phone. I know it's a feature, but I don't see it."

Rondeau took one look at the phone in question and nodded. He set his laptop on the table and then stood there, perfectly still except for his thumbs navigating the phone. "Yeah, I see some texts here in the deleted folder." He tilted the phone for them to see. "And there are some pics in the deleted photos gallery, but let's be sure that's all there is." He handed the phone back to Ava. "I have some adapters in my bag out in the SUV," he said, opening his laptop and pulling up an unidentifiable black program window. "Those photos and messages we recovered are less than thirty days old so I could get them back just with the phone. But we should take a look and see if she had older ones. I'll be back."

Ava and August perused the photos while Rondeau went out to the car. Images of the wedding dress caught her eye, and she zoomed in on the design. She studied several photos from every angle as it draped over a mannequin. The dress took her breath away. Elegant, silk organza, hand stitched details and beading. And the Italian lace Lucy had bragged about.

August was reading something on his phone, and she nudged him with her elbow. "Remember that one case with all those runway models and the cocaine smuggling ring?"

He grinned. "I'm never forgetting the case with the runway models."

"Oh, for Pete's sake, focus." She pointed to the wedding dress. "The show runner kept talking about the craftsmanship and skill, remember? He pulled out stuff on the rack and pointed out the details, the sewing? It was like a crash course in haute couture, right?"

August stared at the dress on the phone. "Yes, I remember."

"Lucy's dress is exquisitely made. It's custom. Expensive." Ava set the phone down next to Rondeau's laptop. "The money is the issue. I can feel it in my bones, August. That's what all this is about."

He opened his mouth to say something, just as Rondeau came back with a large equipment bag. He rooted around in his cache and pulled out a cable. Sitting at the small desk, he attached Lucy's phone to his laptop and started typing in the program's window. "Give me a sec."

They continued their search of the room while they waited. Lucy's toiletries now sat in the shower and on the sink, so she'd been making progress. Dirty clothes stuffed into a sturdy plastic laundry bag hung on a hook on the back of the bathroom door. Ava searched through it, but didn't find anything except old pajamas, underclothes, and socks. Back out in the room she checked under the mattress, then the bed. Nothing.

"You gave me a look," Ava said, standing up. "When I was talking about a financial angle to these killings."

He looked up from a drawer. "It wasn't a look."

"Well, you didn't pull on your chin, but you didn't agree, either."

He chuckled. "What?"

"One of your many tells." Ava tilted her head, catching his gaze. "I know you. You have... I don't know, reservations or something. Come on, spill it."

His gaze wandered her face for a moment before he said, "Vincent sent me a preliminary analysis of the victims' finances from the forensic accounting report. I got it a few minutes ago. It's not a full breakdown, just what they gleaned at first look."

"And..."

"Well..." August frowned. "Let's start with Tone Marley's mom. She didn't have anything suspicious. Tone, the son did. She'd said he had no bank account of his own. Our forensic accountants found out that wasn't true. Marley had opened up a bank account in early September. It's down in Hemet. A credit union for teachers and students."

"With what? I thought he didn't have a job. Unless he had a scholarship. He had great grades from what I understand."

"We don't know where the income came from." August slid his finger across his screen and Ava's phone pinged. "Maybe he had a job that paid cash under the table."

She scrolled through the report on her screen. "What was he buying?"

"Her medical equipment," August said. "And some computer parts. They think he was trying to build a gaming PC, but he was doing it piecemeal. The parts were being shipped to a PO Box, also in Hemet. Most of the money went to the equipment."

She looked at the purchases. He'd been taking care of his sick mom. "How much was in his account initially?"

"Initially a couple hundred dollars, which was the minimum to open that particular type of account. He kept depositing small amounts of cash every few days with the ATM machine. A few hundred at a time only to drain it down to a hundred bucks each time. Total, he'd be around twenty grand as of his last deposit. Mostly after hours, late at night. Vincent had them pull video from the machine. They show Marley by himself."

"Risky walking around Hemet at night with cash. Plus, he was willing to drive down the mountain every time he wanted to make a deposit." Ave checked the little trash can by the bed. Facial tissue and protein bar wrappers. "It's almost like he didn't want anyone from home to know what he was doing."

"I don't know why. He used his card online to order medical supplies and equipment like the bed, some pharmacy charges, alternative medicine teas." August held her gaze.

"What?"

"The look was because I don't know how you leapt to money so early, but you were right. How—"

"The tourniquet." She told him about Sangkat 7 and the Cold Death torture she'd read about. "The killer wanted something from the victims. Information, evidence, money? Something ties them all together. Going with information, what would be worth killing over out here?"

"A crime?" August flipped through a folder.

"Okay, if they'd witnessed a crime, then why did none of them come forward? Especially an officer of the law."

"They could be afraid."

"Of what?" Ava shrugged. "The CBI is here. If a killer is picking them off and they have information on him, why not tell us. Even anonymously? Think about it. If the killer thought the victims had something on him, like evidence or blackmail... But how would such varied individuals have this damning information, and it doesn't get out? We can't place them in the same location with any certainty, but somehow they're all aware of the same crime? Witnessed it together, and no one talks?" Ava shook her head. "Doesn't track. It's like a bad joke. A cop, a nurse, a college kid, and a mechanic walk into a crime scene..."

"Okay, so it had to be that no one *could* talk," August said. "For whatever reason."

"Exactly. Whatever they know or have must, logically, be bad for them as well. So, the silence while their friends are slaughtered makes a little more sense."

August dropped a can of apple juice in an evidence baggie. "You're saying that if it were information or evidence, they would have us go after the killer to save their own skins."

"Right. That's human logic. But they sat silent while a killer picked them off one by one. There were weeks between Suarez and Marley. Plenty of time do something. And they didn't."

"But money?"

She shrugged. "Vincent and the CBI brass may think that they were keeping a lid on the murders, but literally on my first day here, I went to a random café and someone there had already connected Suarez's death to the Thompson murders. Following that premise, whoever was involved knew they were being hunted, but couldn't ask for help. Outside of like a hostage situation, which this doesn't appear to be, what would make someone do that?"

"When telling implicates you as well," August said. "Do you think they all were involved with the killer in some way before their death?"

"I think they're all inexorably linked with him. I just don't quite see how yet, but money is a good bet. Could be something else entirely, but if you look at the pattern of behavior all these victims share, and Marley's financials, it looks like a solid motive." She looked through the makeup bag in Lucy's suitcase. All soft pinks and champagne sheer. An ethereal bride who will never be. She dropped the bag on the bed. "What about the Thompsons?"

He'd been staring at her, his head slightly tilted as he tracked her movements. Clearing his throat, he said, "It's weird. Neither the wife nor the husband made large deposits or withdrawals. No purchases of stock or other financial products. They'd paid off their house a year before he retired. They were living comfortably off Mr. Thompson's retirement from the police department and Mrs. Thompson's salary as a nurse. Nothing overtly suspicious."

"They weren't comfortable enough to pay for a wedding like that. I looked up the wedding package. We're talking seventy grand total for the wedding and reception. That's without the cake and dress."

"Here's the odd thing," August said. "We had agents calling around, getting background information from the various vendors. Checking on who actually paid, if there was any friction within the party, staff impressions of the Thompsons' state of mind at the time, etc."

"And?"

"The concierge at the hotel said that the Thompsons had paid with a BytePay card. That's a platform that allows users to pay with cryptocurrencies using a debit card. The service converts crypto holdings in a virtual wallet into legal tender at checkout. I think that the missing external drive we found the cord to at the Thompsons' crime scene actually belongs to a crypto wallet."

"You're probably right." She looked through the dresser and nightstand for the wedding planner but couldn't find it. "That still supports the money angle, so I don't see a problem."

"The problem is we can't prove Thompson had any extra money without the stolen digital wallet. We don't know how he bought the currency in the first place."

She raised a brow. "Your dad is a hedge fund manager. Don't you chat about hiding money while sailing on his yacht?"

"It's not a—" August glanced over at Rondeau working on the laptop. "It is a wood schooner, Ava. You've been aboard. And no. We don't talk about work. He's still angry I chose criminal justice."

"But you know things."

August sighed. "Cryptocurrency is designed to be anonymous."

"So how did he get the crypto-whatever in the first place? Say I have a ton of cash, but I don't want it in the bank. How do I convert it to cryptocurrency and then... how do I pay with it?"

He thought for a second. "He could've opened a peer-to-peer platform, visited a Bitcoin ATM... He'd have to go into LA or something for that, or used an exchange."

Ava rubbed her temples, a headache brewing. She needed to sleep. "Okay, forget I asked. It doesn't matter. He had and used money he shouldn't have."

"I'll give you that. We also have a problem with Suarez. He had a couple of thousand in a savings account designated 'Boat,' and twelve hundred in his checking. CBI agents called and spoke with the bank.

He would cash his check from the garage for cash. Just under a thousand dollars a week. Records indicate he threw between fifty and a hundred dollars into the boat account a month."

"When was he going to buy it, in the year twenty-fifty?"

"The point is, there's no evidence other than his promise to drape the bartender in furs that he had any money at all."

"He had boat catalogues and an account waiting to be filled titled 'Boat,'" Ava said. "What more do you need?"

"The money, for one."

"He had the money. No one circles boats without thinking they have a way to purchase one. And just because Suarez didn't leave an electronic trail for that money doesn't mean it wasn't there. He had it. He just wasn't dumb enough to deposit it in the bank."

"You're saying it's likely all cash."

"That'd be my guess. Or something else liquidly valuable like gold or diamonds."

August scratched the stubble at his chin, thinking. "We need a paper trail. We barely have one with Marley. Nothing on the Thompsons without that stolen crypto wallet."

"Guys," Rondeau said, looking up from the laptop. "I got something."

His screen displayed Lucy's phone screen, only bigger. Other windows with information surrounded the phone's screen, but Ava didn't know what they did or meant. Rondeau pointed to a file icon.

"This is her recent memory cache. It holds what you delete on your phone for thirty days before final deletion. So, if you accidentally put a special photo in the trash, it's not gone forever. In this model, trash files are kept in the system programs area, here. And this folder is the messaging trash." He double clicked the folder and a list of contacts with a number next to the name popped up.

"These are the message threads she deleted?" Ava asked, leaning in.

"Yes, the individual texts are still intact."

"Look up her mom."

He did and the three of them huddled together, reading the text thread. It started with a message from Lucy telling her mom that she thought she saw "that guy" following her again as she was out in town running errands. To which her mother replied with a series of exclamation marks and that she was going to tell Lucy's father. The exchange mentions that Lucy had thought she'd seen the man before but wasn't sure. Now she was.

Over the following two weeks, Lucy's texts take on a worried tone with her questioning if she should just cancel the wedding and venue. Her mother assures her it's nothing. Jitters. And that cancelling the wedding this close, and without explanation, would be rude to those flying in. They also would lose all the deposit money. Not to mention putting her relationship with Trevor at stake. Lucy argues that he'd understand, but her mother promises that her father will look into it and to just sit tight for the moment.

The text thread between Lucy and her father read much differently He'd seemed immediately alarmed that she thought someone might be following her and had asked for a description and other details.

DAD

Where do you see him? At home in Irvine or just here?

Just here. I keep seeing him around the postal place. And when I had lunch at the breakfast place mom likes. I swear he's following me.

DAD

Does he say anything to you or try to make contact?

No, but I'm sure he's watching me.

> It's a small town but what are the
> odds, dad?

DAD

> I'll check it out. Why don't you go and stay
> at Trevor's just to be safe. Don't go to your
> apartment until I know what's happening.

The next message came a few days later.

> Dad. I'm getting creeped out. Someone left
> this on my windshield. What does it mean?

Her message contained a photo of a rock the size of a lighter. Its reddish hue familiar to Ava. An image of the notepad with the sketches she'd found with Marley's colored pencil flashed behind her eyes.

"That's a rough tourmaline," she said to August. "See the green outline at the edges?"

The photo also contained a written note.

TELL YOUR FATHER I WANT WHAT'S MINE

> Dad, I don't know what's going on but I'm
> worried. Where are you getting all this
> money for my wedding? Is there something
> you want to tell me?

DAD

> Don't worry about the money. I made some
> good investments. Concentrate on
> planning.

> I don't know. This all feels like too much.
> The dress alone is making me nervous.

"Too much." August's gaze snapped to Ava's. "She was suspicious about the money."

She nodded. "That's why Lucy felt guilty. They'd spent it on her."

DAD

Stop reading into things. It's fine. You know his family expects a certain caliber of things. All of their rich friends are going to be there.

Are you sure?? What about the note?

DAD

I'm sure. See you at the dinner.

Rondeau sat back. "That was the last text before he died."

"I'm assuming the dinner he's talking about is the rehearsal dinner he missed," August said.

"This was the week between when Granger found the second victim on state land, and when the Thompsons were killed," August said.

Ava sketched a timeline in her notebook. The unsub was already moving fast.

"We need to run this by Granger," August said. "I also want to speak with the fiancé as soon as possible."

Rondeau closed his laptop. "I'll get started on the gambling angle, but if it really was an illegal game, we might not find it."

"Okay, but..." Ava lifted her phone to show him the photo of the rough tourmaline. "This is something we need to look into."

Granger pushed into Lucy's room, his face flushed. "Gale called. Chutney just walked into the station and, according to her, he looks like he's been through hell."

TWENTY-FOUR

They stepped into the station and Ava spied Chutney slouched at the long table through the conference room windows. Ratty hair, bags under his eyes, rumpled sweater and jeans. He caught her gaze and froze, his worried eyes tracking their entrance.

The normally bustling station felt still and cold. Gale and other staffers worked quietly, talking with hushed tones. A solemn, sad vibe permeated the space. Ava didn't blame them. Another one of their own townspeople had died and a member of their department looked guilty.

Granger met them at the front desk and nodded at the conference room. "Apparently, Chutney tied one on last night and ended up staying at a friend's house to sleep it off. He finally checked his messages when he woke up and came in voluntarily."

August peeled off his jacket. "We'll need to verify that and speak with the friend."

"I know him. His name's Judah Biggs. I'll get you his information."

"Does he know about Lucy?" Ava asked.

Granger combed his mustache with his fingertips. "No. I told my staff to hold off."

"Good. That information could be useful during questioning. How he reacts to it." Ava slipped off her trench coat, hanging it on the hooks behind the reception counter. "I need you outside that room and out of sight. Can you do that, Sheriff?"

He looked at her, surprised. "What is that going to do?"

"It'll make him feel alone." Ava pulled her leather notebook from her messenger bag.

"Now, wait a second. You don't believe he killed Lucy, do you?"

"No, I don't. I'm trying to clear him, but I need to go in there by myself to do that."

"Why—"

August put his hand up. "If you aren't in there, then you're not backing him up. You know he accosted Agent Cortes earlier at the market. He was intoxicated and aggressive. And that was before Lucy was killed. Do you understand, Sheriff?"

Granger shook his head. "No. I don't. He's angry with her."

"Which makes him off balance in the situation," August said.

"He already thinks I'm the bad cop," Ava said. "I'll use it."

Ava took her time before she went in, refreshing her makeup and hair, organizing a file folder and tablet. She even grabbed a soda. As she walked up to the conference room door, she took a deep, centering breath, and turned the handle.

When she entered the room, cleaned up and put together, she looked down her nose at Chutney with disapproval. "What happened to you?"

"Nothing." Disheveled and sweaty despite the cold, he subconsciously tried to fix his flannel shirt as she sat down. "Where's the sheriff?"

"He's not coming."

His brows furrowed. "Listen... I don't know what's going on, but somebody better tell me something—"

"Drink this." She cut him off and slid the can of ginger ale over to him. "You look like death warmed over. It'll help the stomach."

He glanced out of the conference room window to the reception area. "I need to talk to Granger."

"You can't. We're keeping him at a safe distance. You're radioactive, right now." Ava fluffed her hair and fixed him with a stern look. "Drink. Your breath smells like booze."

Chutney scowled but pulled the drink close and opened it. "I should call a lawyer."

Ava shrugged. "Do it. I have plenty to tell them. But I encourage you to recall, if you can, our conversation at the market about how good you look on paper for these crimes."

He sat back with nonchalance, staring at her defiantly while he gulped the soda. When he was done, he burped, pushed the can toward her, and said, "Here's my DNA. I told you I didn't have anything to do with the killings."

"What about the break-ins?"

"The—what?" Chutney froze, confused. "What are you talking about, break-ins?"

"You, first. How did you know about the fire?"

"Everyone at the station apparently felt the need to message me about it."

Ava pulled out her CBI tablet, turning on the screen. A video of the burning SUV taken by Granger played without sound. Chutney leaned forward, watching with widening eyes.

"This is your vehicle. Did you know that?"

"I heard it was Granger's truck that burned."

"It looked that way at first. But no. It was your vehicle."

He tapped the table next to the tablet. "I didn't do that."

"Even if that's true, you left it unlocked," Ava said.

He shook his head, crossing his arms. "No. I didn't."

"How do you know?"

"Because I was careful."

Ava raised a brow. "Like you were earlier that day when you

confronted me? You were already drunk. In uniform. Are you telling me that despite being in that state you're *sure* you locked it?"

"I wasn't drunk." His eyes went to the windows, then back to her. "Did you tell Granger that, because—"

"How do you know you locked it?"

"I just know."

"Did you make an effort to specifically?" Ava reached into her messenger bag and pulled out her police radio, setting it between them. "Was it because you left something inside?"

Chutney opened his mouth, his lips flapping like a fish on dry land. "I... I may have left my radio in there."

"And your jacket and cap?"

"What... No. It's freezing outside." He thought for a moment and then his gaze slid back to Ava's. "Wait, I changed into my civvies before I left the station. My uniform is in my gym bag."

"Where is that?"

"I don't remember," Chutney snapped, a flush crept up his neck. "Why do you care about this crap? What the hell is going on?"

Ava took out the tourmaline she'd taken from Suarez's brother and set it on the table. "Do you know what this is?"

Chutney shrugged. "A rock?"

She scrolled to the photo of the rock Lucy had found on her windshield and showed him. "What about this one?" she asked, watching his face. Then she flipped to the text messages of Lucy talking to her dad about being followed. "Any idea who did this, or why?"

He read them and his face drained of color. "What's going on? Where's Lucy?"

"Where were you all night?" Ava asked, showing him photos of her broken window at the inn. The crime scene tape and busted furniture. "Did you pop by my room for a visit?"

"No!" Chutney pushed the tablet away. "I need to speak with Lucy right now."

"Where were you all night, Deputy?"

"I told Gale. I was at Judah's sleeping it off."

"How did you get there? Do you remember?"

"I... yes, I left the market." He rubbed his temples with shaking hands. "I parked at the station, changed, and then... Judah picked me up to watch the game."

"Leaving your radio and clothes in the SUV?"

"Enough with my truck and my clothes!" Chutney stood, knocking his chair against the wall.

August pushed through the door and pointed at Chutney. "Settle or I'll do it for you."

Chutney sagged into his chair, his head in his hands. "I didn't do anything."

"I know. And you did lock the SUV. It just didn't matter," Ava said and waited for him to look up at her. "I have some tough news to share with you, Deputy." Leaning forward, she pulled up a photo on her tablet. The one she'd asked Talia to take of Lucy's body. A kind one, with arranged hair and closed eyes. She slid it across the table to him and said, "I'm sorry. She's gone."

"No, no, no," he breathed as he stared at the photo unblinking. A strangled sob escaped his chest before he slammed his fists on the table. August moved closer. In a raspy voice Chutney asked, "I don't understand how we could let this happen. W-Where was her security?" His gaze found Ava, eyes filling. "What did he do to her?"

"She drowned." Ava pulled the tablet back and flipped it over. "I am so sorry."

Chutney covered his face with his hands, rocking back and forth slowly, a silent cry on his lips. August caught her gaze and shook his head. Unless Chutney was a world class actor, he wasn't involved. She could ease up on him now.

"We think the killer believed she knew something." Ava nudged the tourmaline from Suarez's cabin closer to Chutney. "She complained of being stalked."

"Why didn't she come to me with this? I could have..." He wiped his face with his hands. "What did she know?"

"We have no idea. All we have is this." She showed him Marley's drawing of the gem from her file, took out Mrs. Thompson's tourmaline from her trinket shelf, and set it next to the one from Suarez's cabin, then pointed to Lucy's text with the photo of the same kind of rock. "Four instances of these stones. They're some kind of gemstone as well."

"They all had one of these?" Chutney asked through sniffles, his eyes flitting from rock to rock. "I mean the town is lousy with them, but the odds…"

"The odds of all the victims having this exact kind of stone as well as dying by the same hand is not high. In fact, it's astronomically small," Ava finished. Opening her notebook, she pulled out the bulletin board advertisement for a tour of the area. "I found this at The Riot Brewing Café, and another one at the market. I think the 'guaranteed find' means the participants will likely find something to take home. I had someone gather information on the small businesses up here, the ones offering services…" Ava ignored August's exasperated look. "No one makes these homemade flyers for their business. They have websites."

Chutney shook his head, confusion on his face. "Okay, what does that have to do with me?"

"You want to help find who did this to Lucy, then start cooperating." She tapped the handprinted flyer. "You grew up here, right? You know the people of your jurisdiction. Does this ring any bells?"

He held his head in his hands like he was trying to keep it from cracking apart as he stared at the paper, his lips moving while he read. "I don't know."

Ava thought he might be on the edge of falling apart. She held up the tour flyer. "Okay, let's try this. For argument's sake, connect each of the victims to the tourmaline, and then to this tour flyer. It's hokey. Homemade. Almost childish. Whoever made this is not a business guru."

He squinted his eyes, shaking his head. "Okay, so why even believe him?"

Ava paused, staring at Chutney, then through him as the possible reasons churned behind her eyes. Trust. Fear. Reputation? No, something else.

"What's wrong with her?" Chutney asked with a frown.

August leaned in. "Ava?"

She blinked, her face flushing hot. "Studies have shown that if people believe someone has special knowledge, they tend to override their caution and follow. Even if they don't show acumen in one area, something convinces them to trust them in another area. Like the flaky brother-in-law who plays video games in his mother's basement but can actually fix your computer problems." She pushed out of the chair, pacing a few steps. "You know what I mean? The context matters."

August nodded. "The teenager acting stupid in the mall is also who you turn to if your child is drowning at the beach. He's the most capable person in that instance. His lifeguard training defies his age."

She pointed at him. "Exactly."

"Okay, I get it," Chutney said.

Ava sat back down. "Now, Deputy Chutney, considering all that. Think about who around the three cities would fit that scenario. Not really a brainiac but trusted in this one thing." She slid the rocks toward him again. "Who would do this kind of tour, be believable for some reason, and lead them to these stones?"

"What about the souvenir—"

"We can look at the stores," Ava said, nodding to August. "But if I were leaving threatening objects on someone's car, I wouldn't buy it retail where there are cameras. Especially if I've already killed two people. Now, I can't prove it yet, but I think this tour and those rocks are connected." Ava leaned forward, catching his gaze. "Who pops in your head when you think about that? Look at the flyer. There isn't an address or even a working phone number. I've called it. A scattered person made this. And yet, savvy people— a cop, a nurse, a military trained man— all met with him." Ava held up the tablet with the unfinished tourmaline photo. "And, I believe, followed him down a deep, dark path." It hit her like white-hot lightning. Where they'd followed him. "Somewhere like a mine."

"A mine?" Chutney asked.

"Yes."

August leaned forward. "I'm sorry, what?"

"Yes. It fits. I mean, it's starting to." The hum of the chase returned as the idea unfurled in her head. Flashes of old photographs, yellowed wanted posters, and wagon trains flitted behind her vision. "I read about the mining history up here on the flight over, but from what I remember, there aren't any operational ones in this area. Active claims are more toward Anza, right? Which means, if it is a mine, it's likely abandoned." She tapped the tabletop, catching Chutney's gaze. "Knowing which defunct mines still have veins is specialized information. Access to it is another kind of privilege. Who do you know in the three towns or beyond that fits the bill? There can't be that many people in such a small population."

Chutney searched the ceiling for answers, then his gaze snapped to Ava, his brows raised. "I think I heard something about a walking tour, but it was this past summer."

"A tour of what?" August asked.

"Historical sites, I think. Like you said, this used to be a boomtown. A lot of people up here take pride in that whole founding members type of thing." He scratched his ratty head. "Let's see... There's a mill on a small lake about a mile from the edge of town. Dyer Mills? Something like that. Granger would know, his family is from around there. Also, there're a lot of old family cemeteries. A few buildings still standing from back when Fern Valley was first built." He shrugged. "I mean there're mines all over the San Jacinto Mountains that haven't been active for more than a hundred and fifty years. But they're supposedly sealed up for safety."

"What if they missed one?" Ava asked, spinning through possibilities. "What if they couldn't get to it for some reason?"

"What do you mean, couldn't get to it—" Chutney sat up. "I think... I need to look at a map."

Ava pulled out a folded map from the depths of her messenger bag. The one she'd used to discuss the case with August. She unfolded it between them. "Show me."

According to Chutney, he'd grown up listening to stories about mines. Silver, copper, semi-precious gemstone like tourmaline, and even uranium. Though some were still active, they were small finds and nothing like the boom that had established the towns decades before. Chutney, Ava, August, and Granger, who'd come in after the initial interview, worked on the different gemstone claims. After a while, they whittled the possibilities down to four in the area that might be relevant to the towns of Black Oak, Fern Valley, and Pine Cove.

"Wait, I know that one," Chutney said, pointing to Wart Wood Prospect Mine. "I had a run-in with someone who said they lived near there." He looked at Granger. "Boden, I think? Someone called the station to report loitering or nuisance. I can't remember."

"You're right. It was a dispute at the Gas and Go." Granger looked over at Ava and said, "They're an older family. They had property all over the mountain."

"And now?" Ava typed the mine name into her phone's browser.

"Russell Boden is retired. He moved into town with his wife, sold the big house. I think they still have a parcel north of town."

"Yeah, they do. The land is worthless though. Sloped with huge boulders." Chutney said, his red-rimmed eyes catching Ava's as he stabbed at the tour flyer with his index finger. "The son, Cody Boden. He'd do something like this. Make a crappy flyer and charge people to walk around his dad's property."

"Tell me about him," Ava said.

"He's a burn out. Drugs or something. He lives up there on the parcel in an RV."

Ava considered the location of the property on the map. A secluded area in the woods. Camping in an RV would be better than a tent in these woods. That could also explain how the killer has been able to stay under the radar for so long. "What does he do out there?"

"Whatever he wants, I guess. He keeps squatters off the land. I think he does grocery deliveries sometimes. He's a weird dude, but not dangerous."

"That you know," August said.

"He has a vehicle other than the RV?" Ava asked.

"Yeah, a beat-up truck." Chutney shook his head. "Unless he has an office in that old camper, he has no way to print out a flyer. Unless he goes to the library, and I've never seen him there."

Ava sat back and looked at August. "I want to speak with Cody Boden."

August checked his watch. "The storm is moving in."

Ava stood, gathering her things. "Then we better find him fast."

———

The storm front moved in, dropping sporadic fits of snow from the steely sky. Ava and August sat in the back seat of Granger's SUV as they drove to the property. Ava insisted on Chutney coming and he sat in the front passenger seat with Granger. She caught his gaze flitting toward her every few minutes. He probably wasn't her biggest fan at the moment, but he knew the people and the area better than anyone, including Granger apparently, and she wanted him there.

As he drove, Granger told them about what he'd found in the Shady Acres security files. The killer had definitely impersonated a deputy. Hat, jacket, radio, even a holstered weapon. He'd walked boldly down the hall, entered Lucy's room, and then left with her slumped over in a wheelchair. Though the killer's face had been covered, Granger said he was sure about one thing— he hadn't moved like Chutney.

"She looked unconscious," Granger finished.

"You guys really thought it was me?" Chutney genuinely seemed hurt.

"He favored his side like your shooter," Granger said over his shoulder. "Like he had a broken rib or something."

August looked at him askance. "I didn't see wheelchair tire marks in the grass."

"He could probably manage carrying her to the fountain," Ava said. "It's a short downhill walk."

"I'm surprised at the lack of night staff," August said.

"And Debbie Whitmore, the nurse?" Ava asked. "Did she say anything when you told her she might be in danger? Better yet, did you ask her why she dosed Lucy?"

"She wouldn't answer anything. She clammed up and tried to hide behind not wanting to talk to me without a lawyer, but I can tell she is scared out of her mind." Granger craned his neck to look at her. "You must get tired of being right."

"That's the thing," Ava said, staring out the window. "It never feels good to hear that."

As they drove through the snow coming down in light waves, she perused the file on Cody Boden that Rondeau had cobbled together before they'd left. His photo sat tucked into a paper clip on the next page and she slipped it out. Spikey brown hair, big blue eyes, freckles like the sun hated him. A pea-sized mole at his temple. He looked young for being twenty-eight. Like he'd never quite grown out of adolescence. They hit rough road, and she put the file away, holding on to the door handle as they bounced over rutted dirt and potholes.

They took a path into the woods and had to park at a chain strung between two cement pillars barring the rest of the way. Granger got out and walked up a grassy knoll to make a call. He shook his head, his mustache undulating as he spoke. Ending the call, he shook his phone at them as he strode over.

"Finally got ahold of Cody Boden's father, Russell. He says he can't get in touch with his kid. In fact, he hasn't heard from him for months, but that's not unusual. Cody only comes into town for supplies once in a blue moon and he doesn't have a cell phone. He thinks they cause brain cancer. Apparently, he goes to the medical center and uses the public phones there if he wants to make a call." He nodded to Ava. "That's the number on the flyer you found.

Russell said Cody will stand by the phone and wait for a call, then leave. They sometimes take messages for him, but Gale called over there and they haven't seen him in a while."

Ava let her head fall back and groaned. "That's why no one ever answered it."

"Either way, we have permission to enter the property and to enter the RV if we find it. The father owns both."

"How are we on time?" August asked Granger.

"The storm will probably fully hit tonight or tomorrow. These flurries aren't what I'm worried about."

They set off, walking past the "No Trespassing" sign and into the thickening woods. Though still early afternoon, the chill in the air now felt bone-deep and Ava hugged herself as they hiked. Chutney mostly whispered back and forth with Granger. He was taking Lucy's death hard but having something to do seemed to help. The trail twisted through pine trees, their astringent fragrance sharp on the wind. Snow dusted the tops of boulders and settled on branches. Finally, they reached a rocky outcropping that jutted out from the hillside. Ringed with rusty metal and rotted wood planks, a yawning shaft opened down into the depths of the mountain.

"That's it, then." Chutney stopped at the entrance and appeared to have no intention of proceeding further.

"You're not going in?" Ava asked.

He looked at her like she was nuts. "It's supposedly haunted."

"Are you serious?"

Granger cleared his throat. "Someone has to stay out here in case of a cave-in."

Ava glanced at the dark hole carved into the mountain. "Didn't that already happen like a hundred years ago?"

"We have no idea when it happened. Or when it will again." Chutney said with raised brows.

"Fine, we'll go in," Ava said as she pulled a mini flashlight from her jacket and turned its beam on the shaft entrance. "See if you can get ahold of Agent Rondeau."

As they approached, August leaned in and whispered to Ava, "I'm not sure this is a good idea."

"Historically, that has never been a problem for you." She leaned into the entrance, listening. Water dripped somewhere within, and the air smelled of damp earth and something faintly like firecrackers. She ducked inside, panning her flashlight on the craggy walls. They walked for a few yards, carefully testing the ground as they went. The light caught her breath puffing out in front of her. On the ground, she spotted a few iron nails and picked one up.

"There's a sharp decline here," Ava said over her shoulder. "Watch the sides. There's literally tetanus everywhere."

"Slow down," August's voice floated to her in the dark.

Ava stopped suddenly. Cold, stale air wafted past her, and she pivoted her flashlight beam toward the ground. Beyond the level area on which they stood, a gaping maw opened up.

"Hold on, there's something wrong." Ava peered over the ledge. Where there had once been a tunnel floor with tracks, only torn metal remained. "The floor caves in here."

August's hand closed gently around her arm. "Careful. Do you see anything?"

Leaning over, Ava shone her light into the darkness below. Wet rocks, dirt and leaves, and then a flash of bright orange. She ran the beam over the color, it had a familiar shape, and then she saw the face. White, slightly mummified, holes where the cheeks should be. She stared at the body lying just beneath the edge and her gut sank. A raised lump on the skin by the temple confirmed her suspicion.

"I think we just found Cody Boden."

TWENTY-FIVE

The rest of the afternoon went quickly. Talia had arrived at the mine with a fresh crew, but with the light fading and the temperature dropping they'd decided to cordon off the area with tape and start fresh in the morning. Granger had called in some help from Hemet to guard the scene until they returned, then went to inform Cody Boden's father. The rest of the CBI team checked into the new hotel, which lacked the charm and solarium of the inn. At least it was still in Black Oak, Ava thought. That night, she fell asleep to thoughts of deep dark caves and lies that killed.

At seven the next morning, a wakeup call stirred Ava. She threw on the last of her clean clothes. Black sweater, dark blue jeans, trail runner shoes. August met her in the lobby and handed her one of the many coffees he held in a to-go carton. He sipped tea that smelled like wet grass, and she thanked him for not getting her that. His deep brown hiking pants and rust-colored shirt complemented his coloring in a way that made her remember him from when they were together — astride a thoroughbred, looking down at her, the sun picking up the gold in his eyes as he smiled.

Talia came down looking polished as ever, even after just waking up. Her dark blue field pants and camel turtleneck complimented her graceful neck and slender arms. Rondeau shuffled out of the stairwell wearing a dark orange cardigan and olive colored T-shirt. His black jeans rounded out the weird Halloween vibe he had going on. August handed a coffee to each of them.

Talia left for the lab at the California Department of Justice's Bureau of Forensic Services, which CBI worked closely with on complex cases. Vincent had asked her to perform Lucy's autopsy there, to avoid risking something going awry in the Black Oak medical center again. August, Ava, and Rondeau headed back to the mine. This time, with Rondeau's surveillance drone in tow.

The temperature had dropped further since yesterday, the sky a little gloomier. Snow that had fallen the night before glistened in the pale morning sun. Icy wind whipped through the woods, throwing dead leaves and twigs around, howling across the cavernous mouth of the shaft. Ava's scarf, gloves, and trench coat took the edge off the chill, but she found herself shivering all the same.

The CBI had called in a specialized rescue unit. Equipped and trained to deal with confined spaces, hazardous environments, and vertical rescue, they spent an hour or so assessing the mine shaft. They checked structural integrity, tested for gas, you name it. Once cleared, a couple members of the rescue team, carefully reinforced with equipment, descended into the mine with body cameras and lights to document the scene before they removed the body. Rondeau had set them up to view the operation inside one of the surveillance vans, and Ava and August piled in to watch on the monitors.

August leaned down, speaking quietly to Ava. "Granger said word of Lucy's murder is filling the town up with press. They're setting up a roadblock to keep people out of the area."

"How do they even know already?"

August shook his head, eyes on the screen. "This is why I hate small towns."

"The story's heating up again now that another body dropped,"

Ava said with some anger. "What do you think will happen when they hear about Boden here?"

"Vincent halted the exhumation request for Marley's body. We need people working on this one first."

Squeezed next to August and an equipment rack, she sipped her coffee while looking over Rondeau's shoulder at the screen. A microphone let them talk to the team leader in the shaft and they could hear him over his live body cam view. His name was Carter, and he had rough, calloused hands and a friendly smile.

His tinny voice came through the speakers as he was lowered into the mine. "Yeah, the tunnel must have completely collapsed over a cavern of some kind. Looks like a twenty-foot or so drop onto jagged rocks." He panned his helmet camera, showing the slick rock walls, picking up swirling dust in the light. Touching down, he tilted the view so that they could see the body.

Ava leaned forward. The body lay on its back, arms up over his head, legs bent at wrong angles. He wore what looked like a safety vest and what had once been an aqua t-shirt. "Can you zoom in on the face?"

Carter did and the semi-mummified face of the victim came into view on the monitor. Ava held up her phone with a photo of Cody Boden, comparing the bone structure, skin anomalies, and hair. "That's definitely him."

"We'll wait for fingerprints or dental," August said, his arms crossed over his chest as he chewed another innocent piece of gum to death. He pointed at the screen. "What is on his T-shirt? I see a logo or something."

Carter moved, adjusting his helmet light onto the fabric. An RV flying over trees with the words, "Boden Tours," underneath came into view.

August tugged at his chin. "Probably him though."

"Why are his arms up?" Ava asked. "Would he fall like that?"

"That's a question for Talia," August said, the smell of mint brushing Ava's nose. "That, and how long he's been down there."

They took notes, watching while the descent team collected evidence into protective bags and raised them up to the surface on ropes. Flashes flared inside the shaft as they took photos and collected samples. About an hour into the collection, the walls of the shaft shifted. Dirt and debris rained down onto the body and rescue team. The recovery paused for another assessment and then restarted after they put up more support structures. Finally, they were ready to move the body. Enclosing it in a body bag, they lifted it onto the rescue stretcher and hoisted it up.

"You're going to want to see this," Carter said and pointed with a gloved hand at the ground where the body had been. Lying in the dirt, still semi-wrapped in plastic wrap, were faded strips of paper.

August tilted his head, staring at the image. "What are those?"

Carter bent down and picked one up, holding it in better light for the camera. "Are these—"

"Paper bands," Ava said. "For holding stacks of cash together."

———

August sent the body and evidence to Talia at the DOJ science building, with a rush on drug testing the paper strips. Ava declined his offer to go down into the shaft and waited on solid ground while August strapped into a harness and descended with the rescue crew for a final look. Ava scanned the area around the mine, taking in the growing storm clouds on the horizon and the dropping temperature. They needed to find the RV soon.

While August lived out his adventure, Rondeau set up the drone a few yards outside the crime scene tape. He looked like a mad scientist in his virtual flight goggles. They sat in comfortable silence, Rondeau putting the equipment through a diagnostic check.

"You keep strange company," Rondeau said without looking over.

Ava smiled, the travel cup of coffee warming her hands. "What makes you say that?"

"You know I monitor incoming data to the team. Especially their tablets," Rondeau said.

"You saw what Denny sent me."

"That's sensitive information. Especially the military records."

Rondeau sent the drone up, circling overhead to record a bird's-eye-view of the crime scene. Ava watched on the laptop he'd set up for her.

"Are you concerned about the information, or that I bypassed you?"

He smiled. "Straight shooter. I like that about you. But I have heard some things."

Ava scoffed.

He turned to her, but the sci-fi looking goggles made her lean back involuntarily. "You have a reputation for your comfort with criminals."

"I have a vested interest in curating relationships with them."

Rondeau tapped the flight control console in his hands and lifted his goggles. "Do tell, mystery lady."

"I'm sure I'm not a mystery to a man with access like you have. How about you tell me what you found out about my *reputation*," she said with air quotes.

"Really?"

Ava nodded and he slipped his goggles back on and went back to the flight controls. "Okay, your parents and twin brother were murdered by a drifter when you were ten. You lived with your grandmother for a time, but she passed, and you went into the system."

"I did." Ava sipped her cup. The faces and smiles of kids she'd met in foster care floated up from the past. "I lucked out and stayed with some good families before going to college. If my grandmother hadn't left me what she did for school, I'm not sure where I'd be."

"I heard that's how you met Agent Vincent, at a seminar or something, right?" Rondeau fiddled with the controls on his goggles. "I'm curious what her first impression of you was. A friend of mine said he worked with you back then and that you're scarily good at predicting criminal behavior and mentioned something about a Constellation of Crime theory you have? Full transparency, he thinks you're a little nuts."

Ava found the way that Rondeau operated fascinating and realized it was much easier answering questions without looking someone in the eyes. Almost like a distracted confessional. Might be a tactic she could use in the future. She finished her coffee and set the paper cup on the ground next to them. "I get that. I'm not everyone's cup of tea, but what he's talking about, the constellation thing, is not a kooky concept. It's a field of study called Social Network Analysis. I studied it for my complex systems degree, and it's solid."

She went on to explain that the field of study tracks how individual groups, including underground organizations like criminal networks, don't really operate like they do in the movies. There's no strict chain of command with rules. No "us" vs "them". Rather, each group relies on connections with others in similar fields. They have shared goals, strategies, and resources like money cleaners or weapons dealers.

In her theory, each criminal operation is a constellation made up of connected people working together. And each constellation has several key individuals that connect to other constellations. A forger, for example, will work for numerous criminals who are willing to pay for their services. A crooked cop takes money from everyone in his territory. These people connect constellations. They know the players and what is going on in the crime world, but they aren't loyal to one group. Which means they can be turned.

"And this works?"

"Oh yeah, they can't help it. Out of necessity, all of these connections occur at a deeply personal or face-to-face manner because of the lack of trust all around. This makes tracing them via connection patterns not only possible, but inevitable. But you have to know where to look. Like I tell August all the time. The devils are in the details. Their habits. Their timing. All of it means something if you find it." Ava leaned forward, watching the drone fly in a grid pattern over the ground. "I worked on a predictive model using this theory in college and found that taking out a given star or key person, if you will, often creates disruption across the entire swath of criminal networks."

"The crime world is connectedly unstable, you're saying." Rondeau swooped the drone down into the mine, taking a video of the cavernous crime scene. August glanced up as it passed over him.

"That's what I'm saying." Ava rooted around in her messenger bag. "The way they work is efficient and adaptable, but vulnerable if we can target someone who's a pivotal connector. Take a sheriff for example. Replace a corrupt one and suddenly supply routes are in jeopardy, they have to beef up lookouts and spend more money and manpower just to keep from disrupting their operation. Everything gets destabilized."

"So, it's kind of a whole commerce system, beneath our own. A hidden, overlapping one that ties criminals together without them knowing."

"Uh-huh. They're forced to use shared infrastructure, and that makes them weak."

"And you researched this theory because..."

"Because I'm going to find my family's killer. Every connection I make, every new constellation I worm my way into gets me closer." Ava hugged herself. "I'll find him. It's only a matter of time."

"Well, I hope you do find him," Rondeau said. "In fact, given what I've seen of you, he's already toast."

She smiled at that. He navigated the drone away from the crime scene and back toward the way they'd hiked in. At ease with the equipment, it soared between trees and over berms like he was playing a video game.

After a few minutes he said, "Didn't Granger mention that Cody might've parked the RV near a small creek on the property? Can you check the map for me?"

Ava pulled a paper map from her bag and scanned the area. She found an unnamed sliver of water running cattycorner across the edge of the property and he steered the drone in that direction. She sat next to him on a boulder, eating a snack bar and listening to the buzz of the rotors as it navigated the woods. The broken, weirdly positioned body in the mine kept popping up in her thoughts.

Bumping Rondeau's elbow with hers, she asked, "If Cody is dead, then that makes him a victim, not the killer. But who killed him? And who killed Suarez, Marley, and the Thompsons?"

"And Lucy," Rondeau added, tilting his body like he was piloting a fighter jet. "He looked a bit mummified, don't you think?"

"*That's* what bothered me." Ava chewed on her bar, ruminating. "Cody looks like he's been dead for months, not weeks. And what's with the currency straps?"

"Looks like you were right about the money angle," he said.

Ava nodded slowly, thinking through the new evidence. "We should do a search of cash and drug crimes in the area, including the military bases. This is starting to look like a heist gone wrong."

"That, I can do. I'll add in anything I can find on Cody. Arrests, complaints, you name it. We might come across an accomplice if we're lucky." Rondeau worked the flight controls, weaving between stands of trees. "I mean, unless you want to ask your mysterious hacker friend to help out."

Ava grinned and tossed her wrapper at him. "Now you're sounding like August."

She spotted a flash of white between the branches as he directed the drone over the woods behind the mine. "Wait, is that—?

"Yup, I see it." Rondeau hovered the drone over the pale structure tucked between the creek and a rise of boulders. "We found the RV."

Ava called August and by the time he joined her and Rondeau, he'd already submitted a request for additional help locking down the scene. They'd worked out that she and August would go to the RV with Rondeau directing them from the air through an earpiece. The RV creaked in the wind as they walked up to the rusty, decrepit trailer. They walked the perimeter of the motor home taking in the condition. Bald tires, a broken satellite dish on the roof, thread bare aluminum lawn chair in front of the door.

"I don't see a truck."

"I noticed that."

"Something feels off about this set up." Ava pulled some nitrile gloves from her bag. "I want to take a look inside before forensics moves in. I won't touch anything."

August pulled on his chin. "A quick look."

She tried the door, finding it unlocked. Pulling it open, the smell of cigarette smoke hit her. She stepped inside and glanced around the squalid home. Dirty clothes littered the floor, takeout packages and other trash took up most of the galley kitchen's small counter, and beer cans filled with cigarette butts sat lined up along a window. August checked the mini fridge. Broken and empty.

Ava flicked aside some stained curtains. "There's no way this guy ever saw a dollar of the money that was in that cave."

"Maybe he had an accomplice."

"They'd have to be the brains." She spotted a cabinet over the stove full of nudie magazines, comic books, and monster truck magazines. Not a single book in the place. "It looks like Cody didn't have the brains to pull off his own pants, let alone a heist with stacks of cash."

"You'd be surprised how far sheer balls and rank stupidity can get people."

"You have a point." Ava picked up a flannel shirt draped over a towel rod. It seemed larger than it should be. Shirt still in hand, she went to the closet and slipped another flannel from the hanger. Holding them up with her gloved fingers, she smiled. They were two very different sizes. "Check this out."

August walked over. "What happened to not touching?"

"These clothes are for two different men, look." She showed him jeans in the closet and then pointed to the ones laid out on the eating nook bench. "Cody is the smaller one. He was skin and bones, but this one... he's hefty."

August nodded and held up a rumpled fast-food receipt from a week before. "The killer might be using this RV to hide out."

"Yes, but he had to have killed Cody a while ago. So, what was the unsub doing during the months between killing Cody and killing Suarez?"

He scanned the filthy interior and then shrugged. "It'll play out. Keep looking."

Wind whipped through the trees, shaking the RV and making it squeak. Cold air pushed through the cracks and crevices with a low moan. Ava went to check the bathroom, basically a closet with a toilet and miniscule wall mounted sink. In the bottom of the sink, the light brown whiskers of a man. Just like Dream Taylor had described. Ava kept wandering, making it to the bedroom. A rumpled, unzipped sleeping bag draped over the bed like a comforter. Lavender paper on the bedside shelf caught her eye and she went over. Another hand-written tour flyer. Only the number on it didn't match. She grabbed her notebook from her bag and flipped through it, looking for the flyers she'd taken. Finding one, she held the two versions up in front of her, her heart racing.

The handwriting breaks the pattern.

"August."

He walked up behind her, leaning over her shoulder. "It doesn't match."

"Better sentence structure, a phone number that probably isn't a payphone at the medical center, and he has a mustering point." She scanned the note. The block letters, organized layout, there were even little tabs with the number written on it to take. Crisp and clean, the note appeared much newer than the ones Ava had. It also promised that tours often ended with a souvenir to take home. "This says Saturday the fourth."

August checked his phone. "First weekend in December was the seventh and eighth... January was the fourth and fifth. February was the first and second."

"So he was going to put it out for January... why didn't he?" Ava asked.

"That would be around the time Suarez died so maybe he didn't need it anymore."

"He found a thread and followed it to the next victim." Ava nodded. "That tracks with the timeline."

"He meets them at the pond just before the public land starts," August said, showing her the address on his phone's map.

"The unsub was using the tours to what... get information from the town's people? Maybe find a lead on his next victim? Not a bad idea actually."

"What happened to make him switch gears?"

She went back out to the living space. Her gaze jumped along the piles of trash. Too many things to look at. She ran her gloved hand along the clutter, touching things to focus on the area. Right when she was about to turn away, she saw it. Shoved in a wicker basket. Heavy, pale blue material peeked out from behind the papers.

"What is that?" She strode over and August followed.

"Hold on." He took a few photos with his phone first. Ava picked it up with her gloved hands, unfolding it to reveal a work shirt, the kind mechanics wore. The logo on the back read "Spiffy Oil". On the front, a single red patch with a name.

Suarez.

Ava smiled. "There's the connection between the victims and Cody Boden's RV."

August unfurled an evidence baggie and tucked the shirt inside. "Suarez's boss complained that he would misplace his hats and shirts a lot."

"This has to be where the killer picked up Suarez's scent." She looked around the interior. "The question is, who's living here now?"

August turned, dialed a number, and paced up and down the small space. "Rondeau, I need a priority check on this number..." Ava held up the flyer and he read out the digits. "I want a warrant to tap the phone." He listened for a moment, then said, "Hold off on calling it for now, we don't want to spook him."

Ava caught his attention. "We need to lock up this place. Dust for prints. I doubt Cody had a lot of visitors inside. If Suarez's or any of the stabbing victims' fingerprints are in here, we eliminate them. Cody's as well. What's left could be the killer's."

"Not yet. We should pull back," August said, looking out of the door's small window. "Maybe he'll come back. You can't see the mine from here. It's half a mile away. There's a chance the killer won't know we found his squatting ground. We should set up and watch for him."

"I don't care if he knows. We need to secure the RV. Chain it, I don't care."

"You should." He dropped the phone from his ear, brows pulled down. "You might think that will flush him out, taking away his base of operations, but that might drive him further out of our reach."

Ava stared out of the grimy windows to the whipping branches. "He wouldn't be out of the storm's reach."

August's brows shot up. "Is that your plan?"

"One of them."

"And how many of them end with us catching him alive?"

"My job is to stop him." Ava held his gaze. "Will we stop him? Yes, just give it a few days. A week, tops. Will he leave these woods alive? That's up to him, isn't it?"

He looked at her for a beat, then lifted the phone again. "Break it down. We're leaving before this storm hits. Seal off the RV with tape and whatever else we have until morning."

A tv tray stood by the couch, holding a plastic Christmas themed plate with a jumble of objects. The kind of thing you empty your pockets into. Poker chips, cigarettes, change, and gas station lighters filled the cheap container. She'd been right. He was a smoker. A gambler too. Rondeau's voice sounded outside, and August stepped out of the RV to meet him.

Ava slipped a poker chip and the cigarettes from the basket. Flipping the coin along the knuckles of her hand like a magician, she took a final look around the place.

I'm coming for you.

———

Back at the hotel, they had to use the back entrance to avoid the news people milling in the lobby. Once on their floor, before they'd turned in for the night, August had asked why she'd slipped information to Ricki in the first place.

"I wanted to see something," she'd said.

"And?"

"Any sane criminal would've left after I gave that description. But he didn't. He doubled down. He tried to kill me. He set a police vehicle on fire at the station. He *did* kill Lucy. Only one reason seems to make sense for him to do all that."

He looked at her, tilting his head. "Which is?"

"He can't leave," Ava said with a wicked smile. "He's stuck up here for some reason."

"That's bad news for the whole town."

"That's bad news for him."

Once in her room, after a long hot shower and a room service dinner of lasagna, Ava stepped out onto the terrace wrapped in the thick robe she always packed. At three stories up, it provided a panoramic view of the town. Patrol officers sat in the parking area and walked the hotel grounds below. Cold, crisp wind whipped over her, stinging her face. It woke her up, made her feel the thrum of nature. Ominous cloud cover slid over the sky like a blanket from the horizon, partially blocking the full moon.

Her phone showed it was just past ten and she hadn't slept much the night before. She started to see two blurry moons as she slipped her fingers into her robe's pocket. She lifted a single cigarette to her lips and lit it. Inhaling deeply, she let out the stream of smoke with closed eyes, thinking of the days she used to run wild as a largely unsupervised teen. Before she had a purpose. Holding the poker chip up, she covered the moon with it, blotting out the light. Another drag. She let the smoke out slowly, watching the wind snatch it away as she mused. What would scare a killer into staying up on a mountain full of cops and state agents? And more importantly, was that threat already up there with them?

Ava went back inside, shivering as she dialed August.

He picked up on the first ring. "What happened?"

"Nothing. I just think we need to pull the trigger on the manhunt. Take away his hiding places. Push him from his comfort zone."

August was silent for a beat before saying, "You're sure?"

"He's been out there recently. You saw the receipt. We fan out from the RV and the mine, overlapping the area and pushing toward the town. I want him to have no respite. No safe place to go. I want K9 units barking in the woods, making him move."

"I'll call Granger. He already has the other departments on alert that we might need them for this." He paused for a moment. "There is one main road out of here."

"We set up a roadblock. Call it a sobriety checkpoint, whatever, but we check every vehicle leaving the mountain."

"And if he heads into Black Oak?"

Ava clicked her tongue. "That would be unfortunate for him."

TWENTY-SIX

Granger pulled the search together overnight, it seemed. At least forty members of supplemental law enforcement showed up at the staging areas near the RV and mine sites by seven the following morning. August went to the crime scene near the mine with Deputy Chutney to handle that search. Ava went with Granger to the RV staging area, in the hopes of getting back inside after forensics finished processing it. A K9 officer named Meg and her partner, a black German Shepherd named Rex, stood on the search line together. Meg let Rex sniff a baggie holding what they believed to be the unsub's clothes. He whined and tugged on his leash before they took off, ahead of the human search. A sheriff's deputy following after them.

Ava stood next to Granger in front of the RV search group, holding a rough likeness of the suspect on a flyer in her hand. "You all have our composite sketch. This is what we know. He's a six-foot, Caucasian male, solid build, with light brown hair. He is likely armed and dangerous and has already attempted to murder a CBI agent." A murmur moved through the crowd. She let them settle. "We locked him out of his hiding place so he may be camping out there. Use your poles to check under brush and dense foliage before you get close. He was hiding in the bushes and shot at me the last time I encountered him."

Granger stepped forward and handed out search grid maps. "I want to remind everyone about disturbing evidence and trampling crime scenes. Don't do that." He held up a bundle of survey flags. "Mark your finished sections or anything you think needs a closer look. Also, don't forget to check the dense vegetation layer and look up once in a while. The guy is cagey, so stay alert at all times," Granger said and then nodded at Ava.

She held up her radio. "All of your police issued radios should have the encryption features enabled at this point. This will lock the unsub out of our communications, so double check. They're in settings and the card you received has the key code you'll need."

A bunch of people lifted their radios to check as Granger clapped his hands a couple of times and said, "Okay, let's get going. Stick to your search grid map. If you see something, tell your group leader or radio in and we'll come to you. Remember, we need to maintain chain of command and document evidence, so don't touch or move anything."

For the next few hours, Ava walked with her group. Side by side, they swept and prodded the underbrush and tree litter with sticks, canes, and collapsible hiking poles they'd brought for the search. They shone flashlights up into the trees and peered under fallen logs. The dog barked in the distance with periodic messages from the K9 unit coming through the radios.

Group D, hold back—K9 actively tracking in dense brush... false alert... possible scent loss... recent campfire located, marking location on GPS... Rex is showing fatigue, will return to staging area for rest and water...

The overcast sky never burned off, and the muted light overhead offered poor illumination. The temperature dropping every hour as the storm moved in. An occasional gust of wind brought with it a stinging cold, and wet, sloppy snowflakes. Ava clung to the hand warmers she'd stuffed in her pockets before leaving her room. The only respite against the chill.

Sporadic shouts came from the different groups and then they'd hear something about possible trash dumps or footprints, a freshly chopped sapling. Nothing solid. By noon, Ava and her group headed back to eat. They handed out sandwiches from the market deli and juice or bottled water. She called August and he filled her in on the search fanning out from the mine.

"It's rough going. The other K9 unit from Riverside is delayed due to a paw injury during a takedown. They'll be up after lunch. Also, I'm hearing murmurs of the weather turning. We might need to call this off for a few days."

The darkening sky overhead backed up August's words. Ava said, "Granger's saying the same thing. Looks like we can keep going another couple of hours, but he wants us out of here by at least three."

They didn't have to wait that long. At one forty-two in the afternoon, while out with her group again, Ava heard the frantic baying of Rex. Meg shouted up ahead, her arm waving at Granger a few yards from her. Ava took off running toward them, eyes scanning the area, hand at her holster. Rondeau's drone screamed past her as Granger's gruff voice came over her radio.

"All units. All units. We have a body out here…"

TWENTY-SEVEN

Delano Kester's skin crawled with the icy wind. Something was off. A forest energy he'd somehow tapped into while living among the wild. The birds maybe? He thought he heard barking but wasn't sure. Did wolves bark? His hand went to his half-full can of bear spray. He heard barking again. No, that was Huskies, he told himself. Though he'd never been in a room with either animal. Wait, did southern California even *have* wolves? He tried to remember as he adjusted the rucksack on his back. Still, once he hunkered in, he'd be fine. He left the truck ditched under some brush off a back road and walked up toward the RV site, his mind on Ava and what her face probably looked like when she'd found Lucy's lifeless body floating out in the open like a dead fish. Killed right under her nose for the world to see. Not really the huntress the press had made her out to be. He smiled thinking about it.

Lucy hadn't even really put up a fight. She'd tried to jump out of the room window, but a good punch took her out. The rest was cake. She hadn't known much, like her momma. Just a rumor of a name. Apparently, Thompson hadn't told the women in his life a thing about the money. What an asshole.

The barking started up again, pulling him from his thoughts. Not like before, but frantic, excited. Like his father's hounds had sounded before a kill. Delano froze, searching the woods with a narrow gaze, holding his breath. He should get to the RV and out of sight. He'd been about to walk across an open meadow when a high-pitched buzz sounded overhead and then a drone shot across the field going somewhere fast. Slipping behind a stand of dense, dry bushes, he watched it. Across the meadow, people broke from the tree line and ran after it. Safety vests, sticks. Cops. He spotted Granger and a K9 unit.

Dammit.

He hated dogs. His heart rammed in his chest as he backed up, aware he'd almost walked into an ambush. He shifted the rucksack. Full of food and beer, the straps made the muscle between his neck and shoulder ache with the weight. Why had he bought cans of stew? Delano leaned against a tree, his mind reeling. The wind shifted and he panicked that he was giving off a scent.

He'd been messing with the police radio all morning, but they must've figured out what he'd done because all he could get was dead air. Then it died. So he'd chanced a trip into town early, when the one market cashier also helped with restocking. With the storm moving in, he needed supplies. He needed that RV.

He set the rucksack down and dug out his binoculars. Peeking over the bushes, he scanned the area. A group formed just under the canopy of trees to his left, waiting for something. A figure shot out from the trees and streaked across the field, dark hair flying behind her, weapon at her thigh. Ava.

Delano growled. She did this. The man hunt. Wait... he backed up, confused. Something was going down over there, but if it wasn't him, who did they find? Stomach knotting, he licked his lips, reaching back into memory. Past the haze of blood loss and pain that had muddied it. Trying to gauge where they were looking. They weren't at the mine, so it wasn't that Cody dude. It must be...

He stilled. Sweat falling into his eyes stung the skin already irritated by the bear spray. No, that can't be—that was further south, right? Delano lowered the binoculars and looked at the area with his own eyes. Months had passed. He'd been dying. He was almost sure he'd driven further than that to dump her. Hand over his mouth, he tried to remember, but it was a blur. He hadn't been familiar with the area yet. And he'd never bothered to go back to find her. Jaw clenching with old anger, he knew that woman would be the death of him.

Granger walked back out from underneath the canopy of thick trees with Ava at his side. Delano raised the binoculars, watching. They faced off, their breath clouding between them during a heated exchange, her arms flailing. It looked like she was the one giving orders. Then his heart stopped as she turned her head in his direction, her dark eyes scanning the brush like she'd done the last time he'd watched her. The binoculars made her seem close. He could feel the pull of her. The need to make her scream tore at his insides. Delano shook his head, banishing the thought for now. The last time he'd done that without a plan... well, he still had the limp.

Backing up slowly, he turned and trekked through the vegetation rather than taking the well-worn path. He didn't know how far the search spanned so he headed back to the truck hidden just off the road. The pressure of the cops at his heels, he hurried to pull off the branches hiding it, sweating despite the cold. Once done, he pushed his rucksack through the door and then settled behind the steering wheel, thinking. He had to get someplace with shelter. Where he could hide from the cops *and* the storm. Staring out the window, his mind racing, he wondered what Bailey looked like now. She'd been a smoke show. Hot, funny, and full of chaos. Right up until he'd killed her.

TWENTY-EIGHT

Six months ago...

The heat of the night had made it hard to sleep. Still in a fitful dream, Delano woke and his hand automatically went to Bailey's side of the bed. Empty. Where was that woman? She'd been acting the fool for days now. Moody, quiet. Not anything like when they'd first met. When he'd first laid eyes on her, she'd been at a house party. Blonde hair, blue eyes, a leather mini skirt showing legs for miles, and dimples. Man, a girl with dimples always did it for him. On the way out, his buddy had told him to steer clear of her. That her father and brother were in deep with a motorcycle gang out of the low desert. The Jackal Saints. They ran drugs, guns, people. Real bad guys. She was trouble waiting to happen. That had only made Delano want her more. He got up, wandering the cabin to look for her. It was small, but warm, and it reminded him of the reformatory camp in the woods that a judge had sent him to when he was a teenager. He had to admit, the past few weeks back on the mountain had been nice. She'd sunbathed and read trashy novels. They drank wine on the little deck. Sometimes they'd gotten high and watched the stars streak across the sky. He walked into the kitchen, scratching his head, and picked up the empty coffee pot. He looked out the window over the sink and froze. Bailey had taken his truck and not her little sports car, and the alarm bells immediately went off. She hated the truck and would only need to use it to get around the rougher roads up there. She wasn't going to town.

She was going for his money. No question. This chick was as untrustworthy as an alley cat. He quickly got dressed and got into her car, only to find it wouldn't start. He kicked the crap out of the tires, shouting with rage. Then he remembered the dirt bike he'd stolen, intending to sell it down the mountain for cash. Running into the small, detached garage of the cabin they were squatting in, Delano tried to start it only to find the gas tank was empty. Again, he lost his shit, but not for long. He had to get to the mine before her. Gut burning as the time ticked away, he filled the tank with the gas he had left in the garage and siphoned some from Bailey's car. He burned himself on the hot bumper, the sun already scorching. Then he suited up and took off.

Delano tore up the terrain, not sure of where he was going since he'd only been there a few times before. He'd never had to get there without a map. Much less on a bike going mach-stupid without a helmet.

"Dammit, Bailey!" He yelled at the trees. "What are you doin'?"

He should've heard her out instead of shutting her down when she'd tried to talk to him. They'd had a fight about her father, and she'd shifted a little. Her and her father had been on the outs and hadn't spoken.

Mostly because Delano had killed him.

He made sure she didn't know and had said that he and her father had gotten into it at the bar. He'd learned all of her insecurities and had told her that her father said she wasn't fit to be in the business and that, if Delano wanted to rise in the ranks, he needed to cut her loose. She'd lost it, as he'd hoped, and they'd skipped town with money he said he'd gotten from an outside job. Another lie. It was her father's money. And drugs.

. . .

The cabin they had been staying at belonged to some couple that only used it for Christmas, but it was too risky to hide anything there in case they rented it or showed up unannounced. He'd sold Bailey on the romantic hideaway thing. She wasn't running away from her family, Delano had told her, they were just on a mini vacation. Letting things settle.

"Someone must've figured it out and told her," he muttered.

Delano weaved in and out of the trees, racing toward her and the money faster than the road would have allowed. He hit a rut in the forest and almost went down. Righting the bike, he checked his watch. She had at least a twenty-minute head start, and Bailey drove cars like they were stolen on a good day. He hit the throttle, trying to make up time.

Almost there, he climbed the dirt path leading up the back way to the mine, his wheels skidding as he took the corner when his red truck came tearing down the road in the opposite direction. She swerved and looked over at him through the passenger side window, flipping him off as she passed. Delano skidded out a turn and chased her. The uneven road took away her speed and steering as she weaved around the bumps and holes. He chanced slipping past her as she veered to the right. He raced ahead, took the gun from his waistband as he stopped, and shot the windshield three times. The truck slammed into a tree as her scream reached his ears. Then nothing but dust in the air and the ticking of the truck engine. He stayed still, his gun still out. But she didn't even moan.

"Bailey?" He shouted, looking around. They were far enough out that no one would've heard, but he'd seen someone in the area about a week before. A skinny, ratty looking dude. Just walking around like he was lost or something. When she didn't answer, he said, "Babe, you alright?"

Moving closer, he popped up to peer into the passenger side window. Through the dusty air, he spotted her slumped against the seat, thrown back by the air bag. Blood poured out of a wound on her chest, and she wasn't moving. He walked around to the driver's side and hit the window with his palm. She didn't flinch. Satisfied, he opened the door. Blood covered the seat and her legs. He'd gotten her good, he thought, and put his fingers to her throat.

Her eyes snapped open and she lunged, burying a knife in his side as she screamed.

Delano reared back, firing as he stumbled backwards, the pain shockingly deep. The world blacked out and the ground raced up to meet his face. Eyes fluttering open, he saw Bailey hanging out of the truck, still stuck in the seatbelt, her eyes wide and unblinking. He waited ten minutes trying to catch a breath or a blink before he believed she was really dead this time.

Struggling to his feet, he touched her gingerly, the warmth from her skin spreading through his fingers. He hadn't been out long. A wave of nausea moved through him when he looked at his wound, and he nearly passed out again. He felt the hole in his shirt with his fingers and then carefully looked at the wound. It streamed blood steadily. Lightheaded, he leaned on the crumpled hood of his truck and tried to clear his head. A branch cracked and fell in the woods, snapping him out of the fog. Unsure of how much time had passed, and if anyone had heard the shots, he needed to move. Bailey's sweat-shirt sat crumpled at her feet. He wrapped it around his waist and pulled it tight, shouting with the pain of it.

He walked the dirt bike to the edge of the path and shoved it down the rocky hillside. It bounced its way down, slamming into jutting rocks, before falling off a ledge into the thick brush and trees below. Then he pushed Bailey over after it and climbed into the driver's seat. His hands shook and he knew he was breathing wrong. The truck started after a couple of tries, and he took the road back up the rear of the mine slowly, feeling every rut in the dirt.

Dragging the two gym bags back into the mine shaft was the hardest part. He had to stop and rest several times despite it only being a couple of yards. He left the bags around a bend in the shaft and covered them with the tarp she'd left behind. Once done, he stumbled back to the truck and drove himself home.

He thought about going to the hospital. But that would bring questions. So he used Bailey's vodka to clean the wound and the first aid kit from under the sink to wrap it. The bed seemed too far away, so he sank into the couch with a bag of ice on his side and a handful of Percocet. Delano thought about those long legs as he let the black take him.

What a waste.

He woke up thinking he was bleeding, but it was the melted ice running out of the bag. He drifted off again. A fever chill woke him, and he shook under the couch blanket, his skin on fire, sweat pooling off him. He wasn't sure how many days had passed, but he wasn't hungry. He took more pills and went away again. It was like that for who knows how long. Go to the bathroom, change the bandage, grab more ice, take more pills, drink water, pass out. When he could, he'd just piss in a bottle and then go back to sleep. Eventually his fever broke, and the hunger hit him like a train.

He ate all seven of the instant noodle bowls, drank a crap-ton of water, and then watched television until the pain pills took him again. He found some antibiotics in the medicine cabinet and took those. There were only fifteen, but better than nothing. After he went through all the food in the fridge, he found he was still too weak to go anywhere. Thankfully, the cabin had all sorts of canned soups, stews, and vegetables.

By the time Delano had to leave the cabin for supplies, it had been a month and a half since Bailey had died but he hadn't heard a thing about it on the news. He tried going to the Gas and Go first, grabbing burritos and juice and smokes, watching for wanted posters or whatever they did now to catch killers. Nothing. Later that week he went to the market. No one noticed.

It occurred to him that he still didn't know what had set Bailey off in the first place. Why that day?

Months passed, and the pain started to subside, and his strength returned. One day at the market, as he stood in the dessert aisle counting out change to see if he could afford eggnog ice cream, he got a call on his burner.

"You know Macho? From back in the day?" A young female voice asked through the phone. "He said to give you a message."

"Who is this?"

"He's at Presley. He says he owes you."

Robert Presley Detention Center was the jail in Riverside. Where Macho, an old acquaintance, ran with his crew. Delano had met him during his time there.

He gripped his phone. "Who is this?"

"He said to tell you this." A bunch of kids laughing sounded on her end. "Ryder Coats is asking around about you. He put the word out. You're marked. There's money on your head."

Dread crawled through him at the name. Bailey's brother, Ryder, was unhinged. "Did he say why?"

"He's talking like he thinks you killed his dad. He said someone had proof the fire was a cover up. He wants revenge and he wants his stash. He said you took it and his sister, and now he can't get ahold of her. Macho said some guy is running his mouth about you. A guy that goes by Stand."

Morton Stand. A sometimes friend and former drug dealer he knew. "What's he saying?"

"That he remembers you talking about some time you spent up in the mountains. I heard Ryder is sending people out to look for you."

Delano closed his eyes, fear moving through him. "Where abouts is he looking—", he started to ask, but the caller was gone.

He stood in the freezer section, the lighthearted holiday music playing overhead, the peace he'd found dissolving as his legs went weak. He knew he was running out of time. He'd tried to get back out to the mine several times already, but the truck was toast. Something had leaked out underneath it from the crash. He'd even tried to hike there and almost fainted after the first half mile.

Delano needed to keep lying low. Or better yet, take a plane anywhere but this crappy town he'd been stuck in. Both required money. The holidays were nearly here which meant the owner of the cabin might come back any day. He had to move, and he had to get rid of his truck. It had Bailey's DNA all over it. The last time he'd tried to hike to the money was over two weeks ago. He should go again. He left the cart in the aisle and walked out.

Six hours and a lot of pain later, Delano looked over the ledge of the collapsed cave, absolutely mystified at the body he found there. Who the hell was that? His head lamp drifted as he looked for the bags that he'd left there four months earlier. Shock and panic burned through him.

"Where the hell is my money?"

TWENTY-NINE

After finding the body in the ravine, the forensic team, led by Talia, worked as fast as they could to haul up the remains. They worked until it got too windy and cold before everyone packed up and sealed off the RV and the mine again. August sent the remains to the California DOJ's Bureau of Forensic Services to process once they'd finished Lucy's autopsy. Around four thirty in the afternoon, and already darker than Ava could believe, they called it a night and tried to beat the snowstorm back to town. They barely made it into the parking lot before the storm hit. Dodging questions from the press while striding across the lobby of the hotel, Ava let the elevator doors close on them. Reporters always made everything more chaotic.

She skipped dinner downstairs for that very reason. Instead, she dove into the stash of snacks she'd bought at the market. She submitted a request to Vincent for Lucy's cloud data storage and went over the incoming info from Rondeau. Several packages of chocolate-covered macadamia nuts later, not having found anything new from the data Rondeau had sent, she called the front desk to arrange a laundry pick up and then hit the shower. She fell asleep as soon as her body hit the bed. The storm outside rattled her window, waking her up, but Ava buried herself deeper under the covers and drifted off again.

She woke before sunrise the next morning to a blanket of pristine snow outside of her window. It had settled on the manicured bushes and grounds. Being from the coast, she'd probably never get used to the otherworldliness of snow. By five thirty, she heard a quick knock on her door and went to look. A garment bag with her clean clothes sat in the hall. She got dressed in a deep plum sweater, black hiking pants, and her trail runners, then poured herself a mug of hot coffee from the room's maker. Drinking it out on the terrace, she frowned at the worsening weather. The low gray clouds from the day before had grown dark and thick, spreading out across the sky like a shroud. Her weather app predicted a larger cold front moving in right behind the first.

A flicker of Lucy and her nearly frozen skin flitted in her head and Ava wondered where the unsub was hiding out. Somewhere miserable and cold, she hoped. Stomach growling, she wandered down to the lobby, avoiding a group of reporters huddled near the business center, and picked at some things from the continental breakfast.

August came down around seven thirty, and paused, glancing around the room. She was on her third cup of coffee and finishing off a plate of hotcakes with sausage. She'd been reading through the updated reports from Rondeau and Talia when he walked into the lobby, catching her attention. She sat at one of the chair groupings by the fireplace watching him. He wore the deep navy fisherman's sweater she'd given him one Christmas, charcoal field pants, and black hiking boots that looked expensive. The sweater surprised her. He hadn't known they'd be working together when he'd packed it. Interesting.

He spotted her, pointed at the breakfast buffet, and went to serve himself. He came back with a tray containing a huge bowl of oatmeal, a bowl of fruit, and some kind of greenish tea in a mug. Psycho. He slid into the chair opposite her.

"How long have you been up?" He asked with a yawn.

"A while." She held up her tablet. "The tests on the strips we found in the mine came back this morning."

He nodded. "Talia called me last night from the lab. She stayed late."

"Did you know we started testing large amounts of cash for drug residue?"

He nodded. "With how lethal fentanyl has been for first responders, they added it into protocol." He picked at his fruit cup. "Good thing, too. Apparently they found cocaine residue as well as fentanyl."

"And then there's this." She pointed to the photo of the strips on her screen. "They weren't official bank issued straps. They were cut out of printer paper."

"I heard." August sipped his grass water. "Talia also mentioned she found a phone in the back pocket of the victim's jeans. Rondeau's working on it as we speak."

Ava sat up. "Really? Does he think he'll be able to get in?"

"It was dead and likely too damaged by the fall, but we got the serial number and he's working on it." August pushed his bowl of fruit closer to her, and she stabbed a grape with her fork. "After this, we're headed out to speak with Talia about the body we pulled out of the ravine last night. She gloved a finger and rehydrated it to get a mostly complete print. She's running it now, so we should know soon if the victim is in the system. Talia also said she has news about Cody Boden's remains too."

"Two more victims since I got here... I'm getting tired of pulling bodies out of this town."

Shaking his head, he said, "Things are moving, Ava. You did that."

"We need to move faster." She ate more fruit, thinking about loose ends. "We need to identify the body we just found to tell if she's a part of this mess."

August's tablet pinged and he glanced down before catching Ava's gaze. "We have a name."

———

Icy streets led down to those with sleet, and eventually just cold wind and rain when they drove down the mountain into Hemet. The heavy traffic and noise assaulted her senses after being on the quiet mountain. By the time they made it to Riverside, it was almost ten in the morning.

The California Department of Justice's Bureau of Forensic Services was a blindingly white, Spanish hacienda-style building in the historic part of Riverside. Located near other restored municipal buildings and the courthouse, they reminded Ava of the old mission churches they made all fourth graders in California visit. Despite its façade, the inside held a forensic facility unrivaled by any in the area. They'd found Talia in a sleek glass and metal autopsy theater, the three of them now stood near the draped body of a young woman who'd been ravaged by the elements.

"Her name is Bailey Coats." Talia folded down the sheet to expose the partially skeletonized body above the shoulders. Her skull, nearly devoid of skin, bore bits of flesh and hair on the surface. Her body, better protected by her clothes, had fared a little better. "Decomp and insect activity put her death somewhere in the summer, but the southern California heat may have sped up the time-line a bit."

"Best guess?" August asked, writing on his tablet with the smart pen.

"I'd say late July to mid-August."

"She's been out there since last year?" Ava considered the victims clothes splayed out on the medical tray. Designer jeans, expensive running shoes, a few rings that looked real. She'd had money. "Did we check missing persons?"

"I did," Talia said. "We got a hit. Her brother, Ryder Coats, reported her missing in December."

"But she'd been gone since the summer."

"Yeah, weird," Talia said and shrugged. "That's more your department. I deal with science, not personalities. Thank goodness."

"We'll do the notification this morning," August said.

"How did she die?"

"Someone shot her. Twice. Once in the upper left arm." Talia pointed to a groove in the skin and then lifted the sheet to show a hole in her chest. "And once a few inches from her heart. Medium range. She bled out in minutes."

"She was dead before the killer tossed her down into the ravine?"

Talia nodded. "Just like the second victim, Marley, and the guy from the mine, Cody Boden."

"Speaking of Cody," Ava said. "His arms bothered me."

Talia smiled. "You don't miss much, do you?"

"It looked weird."

She walked them to the metal table holding Cody's body, then pulled back the sheet to expose his head and upper torso. The mummification had twisted and warped his features, and he looked nothing like his photo. A large depression on the front of his head appeared to have been the main injury.

"Did he get that from the fall?" Ava asked.

Talia shook her head. "No. Someone did this guy dirty before he fell in there."

She explained that the victim showed signs of blunt force trauma to the forehead and believed it might have been from a rock or brick, given the deep abrasions. He had also suffered breaks in his legs and one arm that went through the skin, but the injuries showed little to no evidence that he'd been alive or had bled from those wounds. He had no drugs in his system aside from what was on his body. No stab wounds. No gunshot wounds.

Talia pointed at his arms. "It appears as if his body was thrown into the cavern and then dragged further inward which is why his arms ended up above his head. Postmortem retraction would have moved them a little, but I don't know that he would have fallen that way naturally."

"Is there any way to say for sure that he was killed by the unsub?" Ava asked.

"Not physically. No DNA. The method of murder wasn't a match to the more recent victims either, but something does tie him to Bailey." Talia pointed at the tray of Bailey's belongings. "Her body and clothes had the same drugs we found on the bank strips. It's an exact chemical match. And we found this." She reached into a metal tray on the counter and held up a bundle of cash, weathered and wrinkled, but still intact with the strip of paper.

Ava's eyes widened. "Where was it?"

"Her underwear," Talia said. "This woman was *intent* on keeping at least some of that money safe."

"How much are we talking about?" August asked.

"No idea. The seven paper strips we found, if they match the stack of twenties discovered on Bailey Coat's body, would add up to fourteen thousand dollars. There may be more though."

"So, we *can* connect all the bodies in some way," Ava mused, her mind winding through the possibilities. "We know that Cody was living in the RV. The same RV where we found Suarez's work shirt. And we know Suarez was connected to the other victims because, well, they're all dead. And they'd all come into money recently. Which we found Cody with evidence of money and drugs near his body. The same money and drugs we found on Bailey. She's definitely tied into this somehow."

August pointed with his smart pen. "But he killed her much earlier than Suarez. That wouldn't make her just one of his victims, that means she's his first victim. And Cody Boden his second."

"Interesting," Ava said. "So he's been up here dropping bodies even longer than we thought."

"I'll finish with the autopsies and then try to get back to the RV later, if the weather holds," Talia said. "We might find more there."

August looked up from his tablet at Ava. "Rondeau sent me Bailey Coat's arrest records. You're gonna want to see this."

They went to find Rondeau who'd set up in the digital forensics lab. A large room that resembled a high school audio-video class. Equipment hung on racks, machines she didn't recognize filled the back shelves, and Rondeau sat hunched over a bank of laptops at the wooden worktable. He waved them over.

"I downloaded what I could from her phone. It's a burner, no surprise given her background. We have a warrant pending for her financial records." He tapped on his keyboard and Bailey's DMV photo as well as several mugshots appeared on the various screens hanging from the wall. "Our victim has some interesting history."

Bailey Coats was the second child to Tucker Coats, the known leader of the Jackal Saints motorcycle club. A suspected drug trafficker, he was violent, smart, and dead. Apparently, a victim of homicide. Her brother, Ryder Coats, was believed to be continuing his father's activities with the Jackal Saints. Though by all appearances, he ran the family HVAC repair shop in Riverside. Her mother had died when she drove into a bridge abutment going sixty with sky-high blood alcohol. Bailey had been eleven. Since then, she'd been in and out of juvenile detention and mandatory drug rehab places around the city since the age of thirteen. She looked mad and lost in her mug shot. The brother, Ryder, on the other hand, stared out from his mugshot with pale, dead eyes.

Rondeau held up her phone. "The last call she took was in August."

"Who called her?"

"Oh, lots of people since then. Her brother, friends, but I think whoever called in August talked with her right before she died."

"Whose number is it?" August asked.

"It's more of a where," Rondeau said. "The call came from the Robert Presley Detention Center in Riverside."

"Jail?" Ava asked. "She got a call from an inmate there?"

"Apparently," Rondeau said. "I started bugging them yesterday when we got back from the scene. Vincent finally got them to cough up the information on who called Bailey that morning. And get this, it didn't come out of the inmate calling system. According to the detention center, a low security inmate made a three-minute call from a library desk to the victim's phone. He's assigned there as a trustee worker. Turns out he's a well-known associate of her father, Tucker Coats. His name is Morton Stand. He's awaiting trial for cooking meth in his mom's garage and blowing it up. No bail."

In his mugshot, Stand had that ratty, thin-jawed look of malnutrition growing up.

"I want to talk to this guy," Ava said. "I want to know what he said to Bailey before she died."

———

It took a couple of hours to clear it with his lawyer, and then they spoke with the prosecutor handling his case and cleared what they could offer for information. Vincent gave them the go-ahead to make the video call. As she waited, Ava went back to the autopsy theater, took photos of both Cody and Bailey, then returned to the secure room to read about Morton Stand. A low-level cook and dealer for local gangs, he was often in trouble from sampling his own product too liberally. He was known to work for Tucker Coats and had been arrested with the son, Ryder, at one point, though the grand theft charges had been dropped.

Morton Stand appeared on the screen in an orange jumpsuit. Balding with gray, scraggly hair and a goatee, tattoos snaked up his neck and skinny arms. A nasty burn, covered the right half of his face. He sat with his attorney inside a room at the jail, tapping his fingers on the metal table. August spoke first, going over the rules and caveats with the lawyer. A serious but young public defender named Jay seemed more intimidated to be speaking with the CBI than his client was. He and August hassled each other over the prosecutor's deal and then got down to business. Ava pulled her notebook and pen out, then waited.

August told Stand that he'd been the last call to Bailey's phone that she'd answered, and that the CBI believed she might be involved in a serious crime.

Stand waved his hand, the audio cutting out as he interrupted August. "Yeah, I called her. But it wasn't about no crime. I tried to warn her about that loser she took off with. I told her that I heard her dad wasn't killed in the fire at his house. He was stabbed."

Ava perked up. "Which loser?"

"Some dumbass named Delano Kester," Morton said, a metal tooth peeking out from behind his chapped lips. "I knew him from..." He glanced at his lawyer. "A separate business venture. I recommended him to Tucker when he called to check him out. Delano was seeing Bailey and Tucker was considering him for a job."

"Doesn't sound like you two were super close," Ava said.

"Meh, we worked together sometimes. But he met Bailey at my house party and from what I learned, she introduced him to her father pretty quick. After I vouched for Delano, he worked for them nearly a year before Tucker died."

"What kind of work?" August asked.

"Sales." Stand smiled at his own joke. "Driving. Whatever."

"Did something happen between them for you to think Delano killed him?" Ava interjected.

"Yeah, I was there at the house earlier. Delano and Tucker were fighting. They were out in the backyard shouting at each other, so I couldn't really make out what they were saying, but I saw. They started throwing punches and I got out of there."

"You knew the family," Ava said. "Records show you have for years. But you just left him there while he was getting beat up?"

Stand's eyes widened like she was nuts. "You don't interfere with Jackal Saints business. And no one beat up Tucker. Delano was the one getting his clock cleaned."

"And you have no idea what they were fighting about?" August asked.

Morton shifted in his seat, his mouth pulled to the side. "I don't know how much I wanna say here. Like I said, you don't interfere with Saint's business."

"Tell us about Delano, then," Ava said. "What could he have done that would piss off Tucker?"

Morton smirked. "Plenty. I know Delano wanted to join the Saints, but Tucker was blocking him. Said he had to make his bones first. But I think it might have been something else. I heard Tucker yell something about missing cash. Which I wouldn't put past Delano. He took whenever he thought he could get away with it. Not sure if that's what started what I saw. I didn't stick around long enough to find out. Then like a couple hours later, a house fire turns Tucker into a crispy critter and Delano takes off with Bailey. Sorta coincidental, no?"

"But you vouched for him." Ava said, writing in her notebook. "Why would you do that if you thought he'd skim off the top?"

"Tucker wanted to know if he would do what was asked of him without questions. Which he would if something was in it for him. Delano is a deal closer, you know what I mean, he's good at getting things out of people and leaving them thinking it was their idea. So yeah, I recommended him for what Tucker wanted. Something wrong with that?"

Ava looked at him for a beat, then brought up the photos she'd taken of Bailey on her phone and showed him. "We found Bailey yesterday. Shot and dumped."

His smile vanished. "No way."

"Way," Ava said. "Do you think this Delano Kester would do that to a woman he was dating?"

"I think he'd enjoy it, actually." Stand said with a rueful look.

Ava leaned forward. "Who is he afraid of?"

"Bailey's brother, for sure. Then again, everyone is. Ryder is pushing everyone for information. He put a price on Delano's head. I heard something about stolen money and, uh, inventory. They've been searching places Delano liked to go. Casinos, things like that, but I think they're also heading up the mountain."

"What makes you say that?" August asked.

"Because I told them to. I called Ryder a few weeks after it came out how his dad died. I heard the Jackal Saints were looking for Delano and Bailey, so I told him that when Delano and I were cellies at the Vista Detention Center a few years ago, he'd told me about this program he'd been ordered to do up there when he was a kid. Said he'd always wanted to run away to the woods again. Back to Black Oak. He wouldn't shut up about it."

"He liked it?" Ava asked. "The program?"

Stand nodded. "Said learning all those camping skills was the best time he ever had."

Ava tilted her head, observing Stand. "Did you care about Bailey's safety because you were close to the family, or did you just want to win points with Ryder?"

Stand smirked. "Why not both? Besides, Bailey was a good girl, considering. I mean she had some run-ins with the law, but it was for petty shit, not murder. Delano, on the other hand, got kicked out of the military over someone's death. At least that's what he said. Some kind of training accident that looked suspicious. And I liked Bailey. A little wild and nuts for me, but she was fun. So, when I didn't hear back from Ryder, I called the number I had for Bailey. She didn't even know her dad was dead. She flipped out. She said that Delano had a lot of money and drugs, and that she suspected it might be her dad's. I told her to leave it, but she wanted to get the money back to Ryder and the gang. Even she knew to be scared. Her boyfriend probably killed their dad. She thought if she at least came back with his shit, Ryder wouldn't kill her."

"Was she right?"

Stand shrugged. "Part of Ryder's charm is how unpredictable he is. Especially when he's mad."

"How much money are we talking about?" August asked.

Morton shrugged and shook his head.

"When was this?" Ava asked.

"Mid-August, I think?"

That tracked. His call to Bailey's phone had occurred on August thirteenth. "Why do you think they haven't found him?" Ava asked.

"Ain't no one going to find him out in the woods if he doesn't want them to. That guy loved camping. He thought of himself as some kind of commando or something."

August and Ava prodded and poked at Stand's story, but it seemed legit. They finished the interview and closed the call, then sat at the table staring at each other.

August rubbed his forehead with his palm, his eye twitch back. "He just said he directed armed drug dealers on a blood vendetta to Black Oak."

Ava stood, gathering her things. "Then we better give the people of these towns a profile. They need to be on the lookout. For all of them."

THIRTY

With the impending storm, Talia opted to stay in Riverside to finish up her work. She told August she'd come up the following morning to go through the RV. August drove Ava and Rondeau back to Black Oak a little after two. On the way, they spoke with Agent Vincent on speaker phone, filling her in on what they'd learned from Morton Stand. Everything from Delano Kester to the possible presence of Ryder Coats and his armed Jackal Saints brothers looking for the killer up there.

When they were done, Vincent said, "We need to get that name and photo out. I'll have a team pull together a packet on him for your news conference. Every law enforcement officer on and off the mountain should know what this guy looks like."

"I'm grabbing everything I can find on him," Rondeau said from the back seat. He tapped on his computer. "But I'm losing service. So far all I have is a DMV photo and his criminal record."

"We'll send you more information." Vincent spoke to someone with her before saying into the phone, "Release as much as you deem necessary without causing panic. We need the people of those towns to be on the lookout. I'll have media services contact the local news and see about getting the word out as soon as possible."

"We're headed back to the station," August said. "I want Sheriff Granger and Deputy Chutney standing next to me when we release a statement. There are rumors of a rift floating around between the CBI and local law enforcement and we need to show the people of these towns we've got our act together."

"Make it happen," Vincent said. "Catch this guy before he kills anyone else."

Ava opened her mouth to say something but the call dropped. They rode in silence, the only sounds were the clicks of Rondeau's keys and the rain pelting the car. The snowy landscape slid past the window as she grappled to put the information they'd just gained into play. Delano had taken off with money belonging to Tucker Coats and the Jackal Saints. He'd likely planned to hide out in Black Oak until things cooled down, but then Morton Stand had called Bailey and told her about her father's murder. Delano must've caught her and killed her when she went after the money. But then... how do Suarez, Marley, and the Thompsons figure in? How did the money get in their hands? And why did Delano wait months between killing Bailey, Cody Boden, and Rio Suarez?

"We need to check hospitals for major injuries to a John Doe this past summer," Ava said.

Rondeau quirked his eyebrow at her. "Context?"

"The lag between murders bothers me. No one knew about them yet, so why lie low?"

August nodded. "Something slowed him down."

"Yeah, that could be lack of information too," Rondeau said.

"But we can check on the other," Ava countered. Something Morton Stand had said stuck in her head. She turned to face Rondeau. "Do you think he could be camping. There're campgrounds around here, right?"

"They're closed for the winter, we checked," he said. "We included them in our initial canvas when August and I arrived.

Empty. The rangers who run the campgrounds stop by every week or so but that's it."

"And they're primitive. Tent camping only. No water. No electrical hook-ups. Most only offer a portable toilet," August said. "No structures to weather the storm in. No bathrooms." She shook her head, and he sighed. "We'll sweep them again."

Rondeau squinted out of the window. "If the guy is out there in a tent, he's already a popsicle."

The storm buffeted the car as they climbed the mountain, the weather getting wetter and windier the higher they drove. Halfway up the mountain to Idyllwild, a Riverside County Sheriff's Deputy stopped them at a law enforcement checkpoint. He warned them to watch out for black ice on the road leading up.

"There's a bit of a fender bender up a ways. It's on the descending side of the road, but we're working to clear it out," he said. His dark hair drenched, even under his hat. He nodded at August. "You're gonna need snow chains for your tires, sir. You can't go further without 'em."

He directed them to a pullout. A mechanic who was helping with the crash offered to help. He threw the chains on the CBI SUV in just a few minutes. Ava caught August slipping the guy a hundred for his trouble. Once up the road at the crash site, August used his badge to get past the delay, and they ushered them up without having to wait in line. They passed dozens of cars heading off the mountain. Full of kids and grandparents and couples, they seemed deadlocked with the storm building over them.

Granger met them at the door when they walked up the steps to the station a little after four in the afternoon. He looked haggard, leaning against the wall as they came in flapping their coats of snow.

"I just got off the phone with your Agent Vincent. She filled me in on your interview with Stand." He shook his head, looking at Ava. "Delano Kester? Never heard of him. You think he's been up there the whole time?"

"I don't think he has a choice. There's a price on his head, according to Stand. Kester needs money to get away and stay hidden. I think that's why he stayed. He's been looking for his money and using torture techniques to interrogate the victims."

"Why would they know about his money?" Granger asked, following them in.

Ava slipped off her trench coat, heading for the conference room and the maps. "Because they took it."

———

They didn't have time to dig into her theory before the press conference. Needing to prepare a statement, August sat next to Ava while he talked on a conference call with Vincent and media services. They hashed out the wording of the press release. What to reveal. What to hold back. What to insinuate and quell. Like the rage of Ryder Coats and his Jackal Saints brothers if they were already up in Black Oak. How to warn the public without inciting panic yet convey the gravity of a killer trapped in their midst. A delicate dance Ava was happy she didn't need to worry about. August, with his leading man looks and cultured upbringing, inspired confidence. They should run with that.

Rondeau, tasked with the media package, worked on a laptop at the end of the table while Ava studied the paper map of the three towns out in front of her. She nibbled on a gloriously warm meatball sandwich, savoring it as she studied the terrain and ruminated about Delano Kester. One of his mug shots captured a malicious glint in his eye. Something that fit the voice she'd heard on their call. He liked drugs, but they didn't get on top of him. It looked like his temper is what mostly got him in trouble. Several aggravated assault charges stemming from bar fights and football games. He didn't have any family to speak of. Never married. Kicked out of the military dishonorably for gross negligence resulting in death. Sporadic jobs from which he inevitably got fired or quit. Delano, it seemed, was just an all-around shit magnet. Bad choices and worse reactions.

After talking with Vincent, August interviewed Lucy's fiancé over the phone but didn't get much. He was told the money for the wedding had come from investments her father had made. He never questioned it and thought her nervousness had just been wedding jitters. Granger verified the fiancé's alibi. He'd been at his parents' during the time of her and her parents' murders. A doorbell camera proved it.

Granger followed up on Chutney's friend, Judah Biggs, who'd verified Chutney's story about staying the night. He'd been drunk and sad and slept it off on the couch.

Chutney checked out the local gambling den and private games, but no one noticed a new player or admitted to seeing one.

Ava got through to Marley's academic advisor who'd spoken to his professors. No one had assigned a nature or science project. Desperation clawed in her chest as she tried the number the killer had used to call her phone that night. It didn't go through.

By the time six rolled around, members of the press that were already in town gathered in the foyer just in front of the Black Oak Sheriff's Department seal. More reporters had remained in town than Ava had thought. Which was a good sign they'd get the word out quickly. A blast of arctic air followed the stragglers, one of which was Ricki Rogers. She winked at Ava while filing in. August, spiffed out in his CBI windbreaker, stood at a wood podium with Granger and Chutney at his side. Ava settled next to Rondeau to the left of the screen. He sat with his laptop on his lap, working the display monitor behind August.

August's low voice boomed over the noise of the crowd, and they all went silent. The whir of cameras and the phones in the station the only sound. Ava squinted against the flashing cameras.

"The CBI has identified a person of interest in the ongoing investigation into the Black Oak, Fern Valley, and Pine Cove murders," August announced. A mugshot appeared on the screen. "His name is Delano Kester. Furthermore, within the past twenty-four hours, we've discovered additional remains in the surrounding forest which we believe may be connected to this man. A Black Oak resident named Cody Boden and a Riverside resident, whose identity we cannot disclose at this time. We believe he is driving a work truck belonging to Cody Boden." Rondeau flashed a photo of the vehicle behind August with the make, model, and specs. "We encourage anyone with information to come forward. Please be warned, this man is dangerous. Do not engage with him yourself. Call the sheriff's department and steer clear. Shelter in place. Especially with the storm coming. And don't open your door to anyone..."

The press conference wound down with August answering a few questions. Ricki Rogers raised her hand, and Ava closed her eyes, willing him not to call on her. He didn't, to Ava's great relief.

August thanked the press and went to step off the podium when Ricki stood and pointed her fuzzy microphone in his direction, but her gaze slid to Ava.

"Agent Cortes, after you caught the Ghost Town Killer, many in the press dubbed you the Huntress. What do you have to say to the terrified towns people about the Black Oak Killer?"

August looked at Ava and then motioned for her to come forward. She walked up to the microphone, pulling it down, the eyes of the room on her.

"First of all, the CBI's Priority Investigations Team caught the killer. Secondly, what I have to say to the people of this town is this..." She paused, her gaze bouncing from face to face in front of her. "You know this man. You've seen him out of the corner of your eye on the street. In coffee shops. At the Gas and Go. He has a weird gait, like he's hurt. He smokes and has a crackling cough when he laughs. Possibly military trained, but he couldn't hack it. He doesn't engage, doesn't make friends. He's quiet. But you've seen him around. At the market. Maybe walking into the woods with a rucksack. He dresses like you. Wears his hair like you. But he's odd. Slipping between the layers of town life like an extra in a movie. He's surrounded by woods and snow and people looking for him. He can't hide for long."

"The killer called you. Threatened your life. Even attempted to kill you," Ricki pushed. "Anything to say to the man responsible for so much suffering?"

Suarez's bloody tub, Marley's broken body, the Thompsons' gory bedroom walls, Lucy floating in the icy fountain, Boden thrown down a hole like trash. Their faces were forever burned behind her eyes. Their anguish. Sensing her pause, August moved to end the questions, but Ava leaned forward, gripping the podium with white knuckles.

"I know who you are, Delano. I know what you're looking for and who you're running from. And guess what? They're here." She stared right into the camera. "You better hope they find you first."

THIRTY-ONE

Delano shivered in the ranger station he'd broken into that afternoon. The campground was closed, so the small station sat nice and empty. They barely had a lock. He'd pried it open hoping to wait out the dogs Ava had sent after him, expecting to be warm at least for a little. He'd quickly realized they cut the power to save money in the off season. The place was basically a one-room office with a small bathroom. The station had those plastic wrapped bundles of wood they sold to campers in the back. He debated making a fire in one of the pits outside but thought it might draw attention and decided against it, even if he could literally see his breath inside.

He sat huddled in the office chair, looking out the window blinds and listening for the sound of snarling hounds. Despite his fear, with the adrenaline burned through and exhaustion from the constant running taking over, he drifted off.

A rattling gust of wind shook the station, startling him awake. He flailed in the dark and checked his phone. He'd been out for hours. Though it was only six in the evening, it looked dark as pitch outside. Rubbing out the kink in his neck, he decided it was still too risky with the building storm to go and see about the RV. He should hunker down, ride it out. His weather app said it could pass as soon as overnight. Starving, Delano used his little one-burner camp stove to heat up water for some of the dehydrated meals he'd taken from the cabin. While he waited for it to boil, he doom-scrolled social media looking for news on the murders. Several accounts for the towns themselves had posted updates. They'd found Cody. So, the RV was probably a bust at this point. That was okay, Delano told himself. He could still find the money. He'd seen one of the thieves in town when he'd gone to get gas. The one he'd found through Lucy.

A video with Ava's face slid onto his screen from a local news outlet. He watched it with growing fury as she outed him. She had his name and face big as a billboard behind her, putting his injury and smoking on blast. Calling him weak, saying that he "couldn't hack" the military. A ticker tape running beneath her on the video said that he was wanted for questioning in connection with the death of a Riverside woman. Delano's gut dropped. If Ryder saw that video... The camera zoomed in on her, snagging Delano's attention, and she almost smiled while blatantly threatening him on live television.

"No, no no!" He threw his phone down, pacing the ranger station. All he wanted was his money and to get out of town. Why was that so hard?

Movement outside the window caught his eye. A ranger truck pulled up next to Delano's. He cursed inwardly, knowing he should have hidden it. But he'd been too cold and tired from hiking back to his truck to think of avoiding the CBI.

He watched the ranger through the blinds of the office. The younger man peered into Delano's truck, the brim of his hat collecting falling snow. He walked to the front of the truck, looking down at the license, his back to the station's door as he lifted his radio. Delano crept forward, his hand going to the gun at his waistband. He'd never shot through glass and wondered if it affected accuracy.

Raising the gun, he whispered, "Guess we'll find out."

THIRTY-TWO

After the news conference, they stayed in the Black Oak Sheriff's Station for a while, fielding calls on the tip line the news stations flashed every ten minutes on their newscasts and social media accounts. So many tips poured in that they had to call in volunteers. People seemed to see Delano Kester everywhere. Fern Valley. Pine Cove. Mostly in Black Oak. They spotted him at the market, the Gas and Go, slipping out of the back of bars. Literally every place she'd mentioned. Some tips had the air of legitimacy. Granger and Chutney left to check those out but ruled one a jumpy neighbor and the other the result of cataracts. Ava volunteered with the call bank to escape the stony silence from August. Although he hadn't brought up the things she'd said to the press, he hadn't brought up anything else to her either. And he'd kept his distance. He always put space between them when he was upset. But he'd heard Vincent. *Do what you do.* Well, that's what Ava was doing.

By seven thirty, the storm rolled in. Driving wind whipped snow at the windows and forced itself through cracks with low moans. Riverside Sheriff's Department sent deputies up to help local law enforcement deal with additional fender benders caused by unprepared tourists racing to get down the mountain before the storm trapped them.

By nine at night, with Granger and Chutney back from their various goose chases and the calls dwindling, Ava and the rest of CBI team headed to the hotel to ride out the storm. August stayed behind to "finish off paperwork" but he was brooding. So she left with the team for the hotel.

When they got there, they ran into reporters. The front desk attendant told Ava that they'd trolled the restaurants, cafes, and stores till they closed. Now they were congregating in the hotel lobby like vultures. The team, muttering no comment as they made a beeline for the elevators, rode in silence out of sheer exhaustion.

Back in her room, she re-heated coffee in the microwave and sat at the desk to go over the tips they'd received. She sorted out the ones they should check out first thing in the morning. A few minutes in, her phone rang and August's number flashed on the screen. She picked up, relieved he'd come to his senses.

Wind buffeted the phone microphone making it hard to hear even while he was yelling. "Ava, there's a ranger down at one of the campgrounds."

"What?" Her heart rammed in her chest. She'd ordered that search.

"Granger got a call from the Chief Ranger saying they hadn't heard from one of their men in a few hours. He went out to look and found him."

"Where are you?"

"I'm on my way now. Five minutes out. I was still at the sheriff's station."

She bit her lip. "Please say he's not... Is he likely?"

"Granger says he's alive, but unresponsive. There's a search forming up here with Riverside sheriff's deputies and the Rangers. I need you here, Ava. Overwood Campground. It's on the map. Delano left all his things. I want you to go through them, but we have to preserve chain of custody. You still have your SUV, right?"

"I'm on my way," Ava said, running around her room, trying to locate her shoes and gloves. "How is this ranger even alive in this weather?"

"Granger thinks Delano shot him through the window, then dragged him inside and took off with his truck. He did it to cover his tracks, but it saved the guy's life."

She found her muffler, grabbed her weapon, and threw her messenger bag over her head. "I hear the road out of town is closed. Something about a downed tree."

"Yes. Ice and wind did a number on some of the older trees out here. Rescue is going to try to get the ranger down the mountain with one of their four-wheel drive trucks. I see flashing lights at the ranger station—"

The call dropped. Ava redialed but got a fast tone. No service. She spotted her keys on the desk and ran to grab them, but commotion on the street outside pulled her gaze. People ran up and down in the snow, their arms flailing. They were gawking at something down the road.

She rushed out of her room and onto the street in time to see a massive fireball roil against the inky sky in the distance. An inferno just beyond the tree line at the edge of town. The map of the town flickered behind Ava's eyes.

Suarez's cabin was in that direction.

She dialed August, but it didn't go through again. Then she froze. The RV. If the killer was trying to destroy evidence, then he might hit the RV next. Forensics hadn't gone through it yet. Fingerprints, everything was in there. She texted a message as she ran for the SUV.

> I think the Suarez crime scene is on fire.
> Heading to Boden's RV.

She drove up the way the forensic van had taken earlier. An easier back road that did not require a mile of hiking. The wind rocked the SUV, and she followed her lights through the shifting storm. Just missing the turnoff, she had to back up and pull between a stand of trees.

Icy needles flew at her face and stung her cheeks as she climbed down from the SUV. Pulling her weapon and flashlight, she walked the rest of the way to the camper. It stood under a canopy heavy with snow, the boughs whipping with the frigid gusts. Snow blew into her eyes. Pulling a knife from her bag, she cut through the layers of tape plastered over the door and went in. The smell seemed worse somehow, maybe it was the cold. The RV appeared untouched. Ava stood in the center of it, her eyes closed, getting the feel of it. If she were Delano, lazy and big and hurt, where would she hide stuff?

She spent an hour going through the place inch by inch. The wind rocked the trailer with huge gusts that seemed to rattle Ava's teeth. Losing hope, her fingers getting stiff from the cold in her nitrile gloves, she reached behind the bathroom toilet and her hand hit something. Stiff paper. Pulling it away from the tape keeping it there, she opened the manilla envelope and pulled out the stack of papers within. She looked through them, her stomach twisting. Delano had compiled an impressive dossier on each victim.

He had notes about their comings and goings. Places they frequented. Photos of them walking, in their homes through the windows, and standing at ATMs in Hemet. He'd collected other things. A public blotter report for Suarez's arrest for fighting at the Christmas parade in December. A copy of Marley's community college schedule. The wedding announcement for Lucy Thompson in the paper. A flyer for the grand opening of a candle and soap shop in Black Oak called Mystic Meltings. The announcement said the owner, Henley Morris, would be handing out raffle tickets for a complete home illumination set.

Ava tried the radio and got static, so she pulled out her phone, her heart racing. Henley Morris was Delano's next victim. August's phone still didn't pick up.

"Come on!" She bounced on her toes, texting him again. Snapping photos of the documents and sending those too, but they didn't upload. Ava let out a yell and shoved open the RV door, running toward a rise with her phone held up to the stormy sky.

Something flashed behind her, and she turned just as the RV exploded. Windows blew outward, sending shards of glass and fire at Ava. She tumbled backwards with the blast, landing in the snow. The wind knocked out of her. Shrapnel sliced through her trench coat and raised arms. From the ground, she saw movement. Someone was running into the woods. Scrambling to her feet, she pulled her weapon and took off after the figure. The flickering fire lit up the woods with shifting light as she tracked her target.

"Stop, CBI!" Ava shouted, gaining on the figure as they struggled through the snow.

One of their legs sunk deep, trapping them. Ava didn't hesitate. She sprung, tackling them at the waist like a linebacker. They tumbled together, the figure screaming and Ava realized it was a woman. Flipping her over, Ava trained her weapon on the suspect and gasped. Nina Chen, the owner of the Grizzly Grill, the former lawyer who'd tried to question Ava at the market, stared at her with terrified eyes.

"It was an accident! It was an accident," Nina screamed, her hands up.

"Oh yeah, and the money?" Ava asked as she grabbed her cuffs.

Nina hesitated. "It made everyone crazy."

"Who?" Ava helped her to her feet and cuffed her hands behind her back. "Who went crazy?"

"All of us." Nina stumbled. "We all lost our damn minds."

"Who? Suarez, Marley, Jack Thompson, you. Who else? Henley Morris?" Ava asked, leading her to the SUV. Heat from the burning RV hit her as they walked past. All that evidence, gone. "Why does the killer have her information?"

"Sh-She was there." Chen's eyes locked on her, a look of terror on her face. "My husband. Does the killer know where I live?"

"I don't know." Why *didn't* Delano have information on Chen in the envelope? "I didn't exactly get the chance to examine the evidence. What the hell were you doing? Was that a Molotov cocktail?"

"I-I'm sorry. But, Agent Cortes, we have to get back to town!" Chen climbed into the SUV with Ava's help. "Please. My husband thinks the money came from a dead aunt in China. He has no idea what we did."

"And what *did* you do, Nina?" Ava asked as she climbed into the driver's seat and started the SUV, heading back. "How did all of this start?"

"I think I might need a lawyer."

"You are one," Ava said, glancing at her in the rear-view mirror. "The killer had another name. He's targeting Henley Morris. Tell me what's going on."

"Not Henley." Light from the fire played across Chen's tortured face as she hesitated. "I don't know…"

"Your collective silence cost lives, Nina," Ava snapped. "Five to be exact, about to be six. So spill it. Now."

———

On the drive home, Nina told Ava what happened. One weekend in September, a random confluence of people from the three towns happened to take Cody Boden up on his flyer's offer to tour the historical areas. Tone Marley had joined the walking tour to have one last summer activity before school started. Nina and Henley, close friends through a local businesswomen's group, regularly exercised together. They took walks and that weekend, seeing as how beautiful the early fall weather was, they'd chosen the tour as a way to get some extra steps in. Thompson, he'd heard people often found a little stone to take home and wanted to see if he could get something fun for his wife's collection. Her birthday had been just around the corner, and she'd loved trinkets. Static from the police radio broke Nina's concentration. The weather still blocking its signal.

"And Rio?" Ava redirected.

"Rio was there to see if he could do the same kind of tour himself," Nina said as they drove through the storm. "He was inside peppering Cody with questions on how to set up tours and where to get mining equipment cheap when we got there. Like Cody did something other than post a phone number and tell people to meet at his RV." Nina's voice broke. "Which, I guess he did. He had snacks for us, even let us leave our stuff in the RV during the tour. He was a really nice guy."

"Then how did he end up with his head caved in at the bottom of a mine?"

Nina explained that Cody had led the group into the mine looking for tourmaline but had instead stumbled upon two huge bags stashed inside. The group debated what to do until Thompson eventually opened them.

"Once we saw the money, it was over," Nina said, shaking her head. "We all had our reasons, and it was just lying there."

"What went wrong?" Ava asked as the lights of Black Oak's main street came into view through the falling snow.

"I don't know. Everyone was arguing about what to do, but then Cody found the drugs at the bottom of the bag," Nina struggled to catch her breath, her eyes filling. "It freaked him out. He started yelling that the drugs had to belong to some bad guys and that we should just pretend we hadn't found any of it."

"Then what happened?"

"We couldn't do it!" Nina cried. "How could he think we would just walk away from all that money? Rio said the bags looked abandoned, all dirty. He said whoever left them was probably dead or had forgotten." Nina sniffled, her breath hitching. "I mean, it made sense. But Cody wouldn't listen to us."

Ava's chest tightened. "What did you guys do, Nina?"

"We all had reason to take it," Nina said as she stared out at the town passing by. "Tone's mother was sick. Dying, I heard. She needed treatment, and he needed money for school. Jack said his daughter was getting married. His only kid. And they were struggling on retirement after some bad investments. I have a huge balloon payment on the loan for the Grizzly Grill, and we were going to lose our house. Our retirement. Everyone had a legitimate reason. Except for Rio. All he wanted was a boat to go fishing with his brother."

"Who killed Cody?"

Nina shook her head. "It was half a million dollars, at least. And the pills. Thompson said they could bring in just as much, and we were all drowning in debt," she whispered. "It was a gift from heaven."

Ava pulled the SUV over and shot a text to August, Rondeau, and Talia.

> I need a hard room. I have one of the suspect's possible targets. Nina Chen. Put out a BOLO for Henley Morris, another possible victim.

"Answer me," Ava said, as she pulled back onto the road and started driving again. "Who killed Cody Boden?"

"We were all screaming at each other. And Cody, he said he wanted to call his dad and started getting really loud about it. He said we should tell the cops, and then next thing I know..." She shook her head, tears falling down her cheeks. "Thompson hit him with a rock, and he just crumpled. Thompson told us we were all accessories now, and they all believed him."

"But you knew different," Ava said. "You're a lawyer."

Nina sniffled. "I *really* needed the money. And with him dead, there was no choice. So they... they dropped him into the shaft, but you could still sort of see him. So Rio and Tone jumped in and pulled him further back, but as they did, the track thing collapsed. They barely got out alive."

"Let me get this straight. You all decided to dump his body in the shaft and, then what? You split the money five ways?"

"No, Henley thought she could sell the drugs to her arthritis support group, so she gave up some of her share. Must've worked out because she opened the store a few weeks later." Nina took in jagged breath. "Oh, we screwed up. We all screwed up so bad. You have to stop this Delano guy from getting to Henley."

"Do you know where Henley is right now?"

Nina hesitated again, this time squeezing her eyes shut. She looked at Ava after a few moments. "She was the one at Rio's cabin. We thought he might have something that exposed what we'd done."

"Is that why you were at Cody's RV? To destroy evidence?"

Nina nodded. "I waited until you were a safe distance though."

"Yeah, thanks for that." Ava slowed as they passed the sheriff's station. No cars in the lot. No lights inside. The streetlamp stood there, dark as night. Delano had likely already scoped out the building when he'd lit up Chutney's SUV... Ava went with her gut and kept moving.

"Where are we going?"

"To the hotel where the CBI is staying. I think the electricity is out at the station."

"We sometimes lose power in storms like this. It goes out in patches."

Ava started to make a call just as her phone rang. She set it in the car holder before answering on speaker.

"Ava, its Rondeau. I got your text. Are you okay? We just heard there's a fire at the Cody Boden scene."

"Yeah, I got that." Ava checked the scratches on her face from the explosion in the rearview mirror. She told him about Nina Chen and what she'd found at the trailer on Delano's next victim. "I have Nina with me and you're on speaker. I'm back in Black Oak, but I don't want to go back to the sheriff's station. Delano has been there. Knows his way around."

"August is on his way from the ranger station."

"Tell him to get ahold of Debbie Whitmore," Nina said. "She'll know where Henley is."

"The nurse? Why would she know that?" Ava asked.

"Debbie is Henley Morris's daughter.'"

Well, that explains why she dosed Lucy.

"Debbie Whitmore," Rondeau said. "I'll get on it. I've got a hard room to stash her, too. Did you know the library media room has no windows and reinforced walls?"

A smile tugged at Ava's mouth as she rolled her eyes. "I did not."

He hesitated, then said, "I'll meet you there."

"Listen, Rondeau, the killer had a dossier on Henley. He already knows her routines and may still be looking for her. Make sure the feds know to be careful."

"Do you think he'd risk coming into Black Oak right now, after the ranger shooting and fireballs? Just to kill her?"

Ava caught her dark eyes and bloodied face in the mirror and nodded. "I would."

They got to the library and Ava pulled around back, scanning the parking lot before turning off the SUV. The metal door pushed open, and Rondeau leaned out. He and Ava ushered Nina inside the library and toward the media room without turning on any lights.

"The librarian gave me the keys so I could work here after hours," Rondeau said, sticking a key in the media door and winking at Ava. "I think she's sweet on me."

"She's an octogenarian," Ava said, her gaze going to the people still milling around outside gawking at the fire consuming the Suarez crime scene closer to town. Her phone rang—August. She put him on speaker so Rondeau could hear.

"You're on speaker in mixed company," Ava warned.

"You're safe?" he asked. "Where are you?"

"Rondeau and I are at the library with Nina Chen. Delano has to be here in Black Oak. He had information on Henley Morris. I think he's going after her."

"I sent someone. Listen, Ava," August's voice pitched down. His tone making the hairs on her neck stand. "Someone just called and said they spotted the stolen park ranger truck on the road. Delano's on the move."

"Where did they see him?"

"He's there, Ava," August said over screeching tires. "He's in town right now."

Rondeau pushed through the door, turning to help Nina, when the constant buzz of the building fell silent. The lights outside winked off. Streetlights, houses, all of it went black. Ava instinctually crouched, dropping her phone. She pulled her weapon, eyes adjusting to the dark. In the quiet of the library, a rustle of material sounded.

Delano's raspy voice floated to her from somewhere behind the librarian's counter.

"I see you, Ava..."

Rondeau moved, but Ava was already firing. Blasting light as they dove into the media room with a screaming Nina.

Then everything went quiet.

THIRTY-THREE

Delano limped as he ran away from the library. His foot dragging behind him, shock dulling the pain in his calf. How could she do that? Aim in the dark? He'd thought he'd finally had some good luck when he saw the skinny agent walking to the library like he was late for something. He'd waited a few minutes and then snuck around the side of the library to the maintenance door. He couldn't believe they were bringing Henley right to him, but then they'd pulled some Asian chick into the back of the library.

He'd crept along the children's books, listening to them talk. He should've just left to find Henley. But he hadn't been able to help himself. He'd wanted to look into Ava's eyes when he shot her and so, he'd called out. Taunting her.

Only for her to start blasting like a lunatic without seeing who it was. She'd shot the night vision goggles right off his face, then hit his leg, and he'd run.

He wiped blood from his eyes, wincing with pain as he trotted awkwardly toward the stupid soap and candle shop a few streets down. According to Ava, Ryder was already in Black Oak. Him and his brotherhood of assholes. Delano flinched at an old truck back-firing but kept going. He pushed himself to go faster. He had to get to Henley before the agents. Ryder would skin him alive, literally, if he caught him.

THIRTY-FOUR

Ava waited a couple minutes, then used her phone light to look around the media room. Rondeau sat against the far wall wiping his cheek with his sleeve. She noticed a stream of blood trickling down his face. Nina sat next to him with a weirdly blank expression.

"Are either of you hit?"

Rondeau shook his head. "No. I hit my face on the table going down."

"I'm good," Nina said. "I think my brain is fritzing out though. Shouldn't I be scared?"

"Shock," Ava said, then gestured at the door. "I think he left."

"Did you hit him?" Rondeau asked.

"No idea, I just tried to screw up his night vision goggles."

"How did you know he had them?" Nina asked, huddled against the wall. "I couldn't see anything."

"Exactly. We couldn't see anything, but he recognized me." Ava crawled to the door, slammed her hand on it, and crouched lower. Nothing. No bullets came flying at them. "I think he's gone."

She called August. He picked up on the first ring, breathless. "What happened?"

Ava cracked the door open. "Delano was in here with us, but he took off. I think he's headed for Henley."

"I'm thirty seconds from you. Run out and we'll head to Henley's. She's in her apartment, above her shop. The patrol we sent is almost there."

Rondeau stayed with Nina in the media room. Granger and Chutney were still dealing with the ranger shooting. It was just the two of them.

Ava hurried to the back door and August skidded to a stop, his flashlight and weapon out as he covered her. She ran to the SUV and they took off. She told him what Nina had confessed. That Thompson had murdered Cody and all of the victims had helped cover it up. August moved through the town, avoiding the people who'd been drawn out by the shooting, the magnetic light on the roof swirling red and blue onto the snow.

"What a mess," August said. His phone bleeped and he tossed it to her. "What does it say?"

"It's from the patrol," she said, trying to read the text while bracing against the dash. "They're breaching the shop now."

"I told them to wait." He took a turn too wide, and the tires slipped a little. "Something must've happened."

"Rondeau and Nina are covered," Ava said, her gaze at the town speeding past. "But where's Talia? If he's going after us—"

"She's still down the mountain. The road is closed but they're working on it." August pulled onto the main street. All the lights, including the streetlamps, sat still and dark. The Mystic Meltings Shoppe sign came into view. A patrol car parked in front of it, door open, lights going. A flashlight slashed the darkness within. August turned to her. "See if the radio works now that we're closer."

She grabbed it from the dash. "CBI Mobile One on site, identifying Agent Blake and Cortes, request status update and location of all units."

Suspect fled with a young female hostage, pursuing now on foot toward east side of street.

"Holy hell…" August murmured.

Ava shook her head, her gut knotting. "Initiate immediate broadcast alert for abduction," she said. "All units on high alert. Suspect is armed and dangerous. Establish a perimeter…"

They searched for over an hour, but it was no use. Though blood in the snow initially had led them north, his training must've helped him cover up his path. They lost him and the girl.

August and Ava took a look around inside after their search. The violent scene fractured her focus, pulling her attention everywhere at once. The acrid smell of gunfire, sweat, and smoke hung in the air. Bullet holes in the bedroom door, smashed glass and overturned chairs. Broken dishes and knocked over plants. The silent wake left behind after violence.

One of the responding officers standing nearby pointed to the blood smeared on the floor. "Our witness said he was hit."

"She hit him?"

"We don't know quite yet. She broke her ankle trying to get down the stairs."

Ava regarded the blood. There wasn't much, so he wasn't going to die anytime soon of his wounds. The pain would slow him down. Make him frantic. He'd make mistakes. The question was, would one of those mistakes take the hostage out as well?

In the aftermath, August and Ava set up a command center in the sheriff's station. They moved Rondeau there with Nina, who was screaming for a lawyer and no longer talking. Chutney had hooked up the generator for lights, but the grid came back on shortly thereafter. Ava and August spoke with the first responders as they waited for Granger to get back from the ranger station. The patrol officers who'd gone to check on Henley arrived, an older man with gray hair and a younger man who'd pointed out the blood to Ava. They questioned them separately. The older guy first and then the younger. They said the same thing, more or less.

When they'd arrived to check on Henley, they'd heard a woman screaming inside, which had prompted the officers to breach the shop from the front, smashing through the glass door. They'd cleared the area, finding Henley hysterical and struggling to her feet. Her sixteen-year-old granddaughter, Melody, had stopped by for dinner when the lights went out. She'd gone down to check on the breaker when Henley heard her scream. They believed Delano had grabbed her on a whim.

"Grabbed my gun when I heard her scream," Henley said, her lip quivering. "But I fell running down the stairs. By the time I got to my feet, he was dragging her out the door and heading toward the woods. I tried to run but my ankle—".

"I'm told it's broken. There was nothing you could do." Ava put her hand on Henley's forearm. "Did you shoot him?"

"No, I mean I shot at him, but I hit the wall and window. He was moving too fast. I did see a truck. I could have sworn it had a municipal seal on the door."

"He stole a ranger's truck," Ava said, her gaze out the window at the falling snow. Delano had drowned the last woman he'd abducted.

When they'd left the room August said, "He was already hurt. You got him in the library."

"I hope it slows the bastard down or makes him pass out so Melody can get away."

Granger showed up a few minutes later. He'd sent Chutney out with the back up patrols to ride around town, while he and August worked out the intricacies of abduction. How to deal with the weather, when and where to start a search, if she was still alive... The weather got worse by the minute, so Delano had limited places to go.

Ava listened, her eyes on Henley, who sat in the conference room with Dr. Wren. When she was done getting her ankle stabilized, Ava moved in. Nodding to Wren as they passed each other, Ava sat next to Henley at the conference table and slid a mug of hot cocoa over to her. Henley stared at it with vacant eyes, sniffling. She'd folded into herself, her shoulders rolled forward.

"It's just powdered, but there're marshmallows," Ava said.

"Studies show that heat and sugar have been known to help with shock."

"Thanks." She touched the bottom of the mug with her fingertips but that was it. "Dr. Wren gave me a Valium."

"That'll probably work faster," Ava said, leaning back, giving her space.

"This is all my fault..." She put her fingers over her lips.

"Listen." Ava looked over her shoulder and then leaned in and whispered, "Nina told me everything. The money, the drugs. That's what he came for. He wanted what you stole from him. If we get a ransom call. It'll be for that."

Henley covered her face with her palms and cried. "There's none left."

Ava tried talking with her for a few more minutes, but she was barely holding it together.

She found August just outside the interview room and couldn't shake the feeling that she was spinning her wheels in mud. There was no mystery as to what was happening anymore. They knew what Delano wanted and what he was willing to do to get it. They could only wait for his next move.

Granger caught her eye, waving from the reception desk and frantically pointing to an office phone in his other hand.

August leaned in. "Go. I'll get Rondeau."

She hurried over and he handed her the phone. Rondeau ran up out of nowhere and stuck a recording device on the handset receiver. Delano's rapid breathing filled her ear and then she hit speaker.

She took in a slow breath, quashing down the nerves, and said, "Delano Kester. How's that limp now?"

"Oh, you think you're so smart, but who has the hostage, huh? Who has all the cards?" He was practically yelling. She heard a panic in his voice, adrenaline or fear still running through him. "I know you're all listening in so pay attention. I want—"

"I don't care what you want. I need to talk to her. Proof you didn't accidentally kill her on your way out."

"She's a little dinged up but fine."

"Proof."

Granger looked at her, exasperated. "Easy," he mouthed.

A rustling sound came through and then the shaky voice of a young woman. "I'm here."

"Are you hurt—"

"That's all you get!" Delano growled. "I want what they took. All of it, or this girl dies."

"What happened, Delano?" Ava asked, trying to ignore Melody crying in the background. "Marley gave you his share, right? You threatened his mom, or something vile, and he agreed to meet you. His backpack was empty, so you took something. What about Suarez? I never found any cash on him."

"He spent it, just like the rest of them. In months. How do you go through 100K that fast?"

Ava kept pushing for time. "But Jack Thomspon was smarter. He used a crypto wallet."

"This isn't memory lane, Ava. I want my money. All of it. By tomorrow morning."

"Have you seen your buddy Ryder yet?" Ava asked, nodding as August motioned to her to keep him talking. "How much do you think it'll cost to convince him not to murder you for killing his father *and* his sister?"

"Well, he ain't ever going to see me again anyway," Delano growled. "I'll text you the location at sunrise. I want the money in large increments, and I want you to come alone, Agent Cortes." She could practically hear him grinning through the phone. "You do what I say, and the kid lives. Screw around, and she dies like Lucy," he said before disconnecting.

Ava set the handset down and looked at August. "I'm not arguing about this."

He shook his head. "He'll set a trap. He doesn't just want the money, Ava, he wants to kill you."

The cry of a terrified child was the worst sound Ava could think of. "Let him try."

THIRTY-FIVE

They'd spent the night working on the ransom money with Vincent. She'd called in favors with the FBI. That had gotten them some of the funds. Then they'd tapped local law enforcement from Riverside who'd sent three patrolmen up with more cash. It wasn't all of the money. It was two hundred and fifty thousand dollars with a lot of dummy stacks mixed in. They hid a tracker and a dye-pack inside as well. The stuffed backpack had landed in front of Ava in the conference room by three in the morning.

After that, Ava looked through the things Delano had left behind at the ranger station. Bagged and tagged, she pondered the junk of his life. Cans of soup, beer, dehydrated packets of food. Why would he leave them behind? Maybe he'd thought the ranger had already called in for help and he had no time to repack. The bullet in his leg would slow him down more. She hoped he was still bleeding from it. After going through his things, she sat around the conference table with everyone else, drinking coffee, eating, and discussing the case to pass the time.

Ava was pacing the floor by six, her thumbnail chewed to the nub, when her phone buzzed. Everyone froze as she looked at her phone. The same number Delano had used to call her had sent one text.

UNKNOWN

Dyer Creek Mill – one hour

They got to work. Nestled between Pine Cove and Fern Valley, the map showed a substantial waterway called Dyer Creek that cut a swath through the mountain reserve. A sawmill that had once been used for early logging ventures before the steam engine pushed logging further out into the wilderness still stood in ruins on the shore. Closed off to the public due to structural concerns, it sat deep in the woods, isolated, with only one way in. Perfect for an ambush.

———

Six thirty in the morning brought the sunrise with a hint of silver through the trees. A fresh shroud of snow covered the terrain with pale softness. Ava and August drove out to the mill property with Granger, Chutney, and Rondeau in the truck behind them. They all stopped just before the gate blocking the entrance to the mill road. Rondeau got out to set up the drone. Ava and August jumped out of the SUV to talk with Granger and Chutney. Snow fell steadily, the wind building. They stood a quarter of a mile from the actual mill with the frozen lake running parallel to the path. Granger updated her on the forest rangers moving toward the location through the woods, and the deputies positioned further down the creek past the mill. Both teams ready to head off Delano should he run.

She listened as she adjusted the straps of her bulletproof vest, slapping them down and tugging on the sides before closing her trench coat.

"These are voice activated. You don't need to push to talk," Rondeau said. "That should help with the gloves."

"You just have all the bells and whistles, don't you?" Ava asked.

She fidgeted with the earpiece Rondeau gave her. Beeping it to respond.

August stood next to her. Silent, grinding his gum, listening to the chatter on the radio. Flakes piled on his shoulders and eyelashes. Chutney pulled a pair of bolt cutters from the sheriff's truck and cut the rusty chain barring the entrance. All four of them pushed the chain link gate to the side. It creaked with ice and rust but eventually moved. Ava took in the stark terrain. Bare trees and frozen water that reflected the wan light of a hazy sky. They hadn't seen a truck or any other way Delano would get to the area, and that made Ava wonder if his leg was that much of a problem after all. Especially if he'd hiked in through the woods.

"I don't like this. It's too unprotected." August looked down at her, his gaze intense.

"We'll be ready."

His jaw worked, and he caught her eye. "Play it safe, Ava."

"I will." She turned and walked toward the mill, her gut tight. Something pulled her forward, like when she stood on the shore and the wave around her feet pulled back out. A disorienting optical illusion from the snow driving down. The path curved around the bend of the creek. Trampled snow blanketed the ground, and it crunched beneath her feet. She'd strapped crampon cleats to her trail runners at Chutney's urging. "The compacted snow could act like ice," he'd said.

"Someone's already been here. I see boot prints but they're filling fast." The mill finally came into view. A tattered silhouette against the coming sunrise, deeper in the woods than she'd thought. Tall, silent pines scratched at the brooding sky. Icy wind slid across the lake, stinging her cheeks.

August's voice whispered in her earpiece. "Look up if you can hear me. We're watching you on the drone." She did. "We have some guys on a road leading down the west side of the reserve. They found the ranger's truck parked just off the road. We're sitting on it."

"Do you see Melody?"

"Not yet, Rondeau is running a grid overhead. We're using a thermal camera due to the lack of light, but we're worried the battery might freeze up there."

"What if he hears it?"

"We're betting he suspects anyway and I want the visibility."

Her gaze fell on multiple footprints, the ground around them disturbed with pine needles and mud. "Looks like a struggle here.".

She walked along the trampled snow, almost to the mill, the creek to her right forming a lake. Larger than it seemed on the map, it sat still and silent. Branches and other debris from the storm lay scattered on the frozen surface, along with mounds of piled snow. Icy flecks stuck to her eyelashes, and she blinked them away.

The high pitched, rotors of the drone overhead gave her comfort. She started to adjust the backpack on her shoulders but froze when she heard a voice nearby. Glancing around frantically, she spotted the walkie talkie. It stood upright, shoved on the top of a snowdrift like a candle.

"I said, stop right there. Drop the money." Delano.

She picked up the radio, scanning the property while depressing the talk button. Visibility was poor with the falling snow and low light. "When I see Melody."

"She's getting ready for a swim."

Ava's head snapped to the lake. A figure sat in the center of the ice behind a fallen branch. Her hair rustled in the wind, flakes falling at angles toward her. She must be nearly hypothermic.

"Let her leave, and I'll drop the money and walk away."

"You're not calling the shots here!" Delano screamed. "I'll show you I'm serious."

A small patch of ice near Melody exploded and then a weird, echoing crack resonated in the woods and rattled across the lake.

"He's shooting the ice," Ava shouted. "He's in the woods."

"Don't!" August's voice sounded in her ear.

Ava turned and sprinted for the lake, carrying the backpack with her, screaming into the radio. "Keep shooting, dumbass. I'll take your precious money with me!"

"Stop!" Delano yelled, and more shots sounded from his end. "Drop the money!"

Ava pulled off the backpack once she reached the ice, the spikes on her shoes digging in as she raced for Melody. The girl sobbed, her eyes wide with fear as bullets chunked up the lake around her. Ava veered left, away from her, as she ripped open the zipper. Pulling out stacks of money, she threw them ahead of her as she ran, drawing his fire.

"What are you doing? Stop throwing it!"

"Come get your money. I dare you!" Glancing behind her, Ava spotted a figure running out from the tree line fifty yards away. His leg lagged behind him, but his arm was out, shooting as the snow drove down around him. She slid the backpack across the ice, throwing it as far as she could ahead of her, then sprinted back toward Melody.

"You just killed her!" Delano's voice screeched from the radio as he pointed the gun at Melody, the rounds reverberating over the lake.

Ava jumped for the girl, flying at her like a starfish, blocking as much as she could. A bullet slammed into her back, and she tumbled with Melody to the ice. Wheezing, Ava gasped for breath against the pain of the impact. Despite the vest, her back was on fire.

"Talk to me!" August shouted in her ear. "I'm hearing shots, Ava. What's happening?"

"I can't see him—the snow—visibility... maybe fifty yards." Ava rasped. She aimed her weapon with one hand and slipped a knife from her pocket with the other. Her spine aching, pulse racing in her head. She couldn't get a visual. He was using the debris on the lake and the snow to hide. She crawled to Melody who was curled in a fetal position, her mouth wide with a silent scream.

"You're okay. Hey, Melody, right? Look at me," Ava said, slicing through the rope at her wrists with one slash. The girl looked at her with wide-eyed terror but nodded. "Go hide. Now. And *stay* there."

Boots sounded behind them and Ava whirled to see Delano charging at them, his arm raised, muzzle flash lighting up the falling snow.

"Run!" Ava yelled and pushed Melody toward the far shore. The girl slipped and slid, going down on the ice and crawling away.

Ava fired back as she ran behind her.

"You have company," August said in Ava's ear. "Three figures running through the woods toward the lake. They're going to reach you before I do."

"Friendly?" Ava squinted through the falling snow at the shore from which she'd come.

A crack resonated in the air and Delano fell, yelling as he rolled on the ice clutching his arm.

"Not friendly!" Ava screamed as she ran in a crouch off the ice.

Scrambling behind a tree, she glanced around for Melody but couldn't see her. She hissed her name but only the howling wind answered. Ava scurried from trunk to trunk, creeping closer to where Delano had gone down. Then she saw them a few yards out on the ice. Ryder Coats, uglier than his mugshot, walked over to Delano, standing over him with a gun in his hand. One of his buddies, a bald guy wearing a military parka, held an ax. The other one, a weaselly looking dude with black hair down to his shoulders, held a rifle.

"I want what's mine, Delano!" Ryder said. He grabbed the ax from his bald friend and swung down, barely missing Delano's leg.

"I have it!" Delano cried, cradling his bleeding arm.

"And I want blood for blood. My father..." He hit the ice again. The very ice he was standing on and Ava wondered if he'd finished school. "And my sister—"

"There!" Delano shouted, pointing past them at the backpack and cash on the ice. "That's it there!"

The three thugs followed Delano's gaze and then looked at each other. Ryder shouted for them to go and get it. Ava crept closer to a stand of trees almost at the lake front. The weaselly thug held up a stack of cash and shouted Ryder's name.

"This one's fake!" he yelled, just before the dye pack exploded in his face. He went down, taking the bald guy with him. Delano moved, pulling a hunting knife from his boot and lunging at a distracted Ryder. He stabbed upwards, getting him in the gut, and Ryder started shooting down at Delano as he stumbled backwards. Bullets cracked the ice and ricocheted in wild directions. Ava ducked behind a tree, looking for Melody. She spotted her blonde hair behind a trunk a few yards away.

"Stay put, Melody. Do not move. I'll come for you," Ava shouted and then depressed her earpiece. "We've got Delano down, I think Ryder, too..."

"We're almost there," August said in her ear as she ran down to the ice between Delano and the other men.

"CBI, freeze!" she shouted from behind a fallen trunk.

Ryder answered with several shots in her direction and Ava returned fire before taking cover. She peeked out from behind the trunk and spotted Ryder walking toward Delano as he tried to crawl away. The bald guy, who'd been helping the now blue-faced one get up, dropped his friend when he saw Ava. He took the rifle and raised it in her direction. Ava shot him without a second thought. Unfazed, Ryder ambled across the ice leaving a red trail, dragging the ax behind him. He limped over to Delano, who was gripping a large branch half-buried in the ice. He fired, hitting Delano in the knee, sending him shouting in pain. Dropping the ax from his other hand, Ryder groaned as he grasped Delano's ankle, trying to pull him away from the branch.

Ava stepped out from behind a pile of debris, her weapon up. "Let him go."

"You're going to have to take him from me, darlin'," Ryder drawled. "And I think you might be out of bullets."

Ava shot at his feet. "I said back off."

Ryder reeled, shooting as he stumbled. Ava ducked behind the tree but saw him go down. Her gun racked open. Grabbing the extra clip, pain seared up her wrist as she fought with it. She chanced a peek at Delano.

He lay still on the frozen lake, snow falling on his face, blood pooling and freezing on the ice around his leg. Years of experience told her he wouldn't last long. To her right, Ryder struggled to his feet, taking cover behind a group of branches and debris. She had trouble tracking him through the snowfall, but what she could see in front of her... the ax.

Ava ran and grabbed it, raised it over her head, and slammed it down on the ice. She groaned from the pain shooting up her arm. Another hollow crack sounded beneath them, like the whipping of steel cables. She hit it again, and a crack split away from the blade. Water rose up in the fractures.

"What are you doing?" Ryder screamed, fighting for footing behind the debris. He shot in her direction, but it went wild. "Are you insane?"

Gritting her teeth, she swung a third time and the ice shifted beneath her. The snow making her slip.

"I personally don't think I am but..." Panting, Ava gestured at the cracking ice and shrugged. "I mean, look at us."

He steadied himself, his gut bleeding, as he listed to the side, his aim wavering. "I'm taking him."

"Over your dead body." Ava raised the ax again when a resonate crack tore over the surface of the lake. "Heads up, August, I have a feeling the ice is about to go." Then she slammed the ax down a final time.

A fissure opened and skittered between Delano, Ryder, and his crew. Ryder tried running at her, but she threw the ax at him. The handle tangled with his legs and took him down. Ava scurried for Delano and grabbed him by the collar. Using the last bit of adrenaline coursing through her body, she slowly dragged him toward the shore as the ice let off a series of deep cracks.

"We're coming around the shore. West end," August said in her ear.

"We need to get to shore," she said, struggling to pull Delano across the ice behind her.

He swung at her with the knife. Blood trickled from his lip, and she caught a glimpse of his pink teeth. "You did this! You did all of this!"

She let go. "It's me or him, Delano. Come with me or sink to your death with him. That's if you don't bleed to death first."

Delano screamed and threw his knife across the ice. "You're the devil!"

Ava smiled, cuffing his wrists. "I get that at lot."

THIRTY-SIX

Melody had hidden inside a rocky crevice and broke into tears as Ava helped her out.

"You came back," she cried. "I saw you leave and thought…"

"You did good, Melody. You stayed safe," Ava said, smoothing her hair. Her throat ached as an image of birthday pajamas flashed behind her eyes. "You stayed safe."

It turned out the reason Ava couldn't load her clip was because her hand was broken. She'd fractured her second and third metacarpal hitting the ice while trying to shield Melody. Dr. Wren took X-rays, set the fractures, and then gave her a cast at the medical center. August hovered in the waiting area, punishing gum and bugging the nurses.

In the following days, the CBI and Sheriff's Department wrapped up the havoc Delano had caused in the three small towns. As the storm moved off the mountain, Vincent and an entire team of CBI, along with additional local law enforcement, descended on the scene. Henley Morris and Nina Chen were arrested. They were the final people in the group who'd killed Cody and taken the money. They lawyered up and had already started pointing fingers.

Ryder made it to surgery, as did the bald guy Ava shot. They were sent to recover in a correctional facility with a hospital wing. The weaselly guy had to get his eyes flushed but was otherwise okay. He'd gone to Presley Detention Center to await arraignment.

Delano had miraculously survived his injuries. The surgeon said the ice must have slowed down his bleeding. Last Ava had heard, he was making deals with the California Department of Justice's prosecutor for leniency on the murders in exchange for information on the Jackal Saints.

Granger and the wounded park ranger both received commendations for their valor during the crime spree. Chutney kept his job.

———

Two weeks after the Black Oak Killer case, as the news dubbed it, August dropped by Ava's home in Oceanside. He stood in her kitchen, hands in his pockets and shoulders up by his ears.

"I need to talk to you about something."

"You okay?"

"I want you back," August said.

Ava's eyebrows shot up.

"On the team," he clarified. "I want you to consider working for me at Priority Investigations again."

She tilted her head, searching his face. "What does Vincent say about this offer?"

"She said it's my team. My choice."

"And you really want to do this to yourself? I drive you nuts." Ava handed him a mug of powdered hot cocoa.

"We're good together... at this," he said and took a drink. "Think about it."

She didn't have to.

———

They talked for a while about logistics, how August would be her boss, but she'd retain her special agent status under him as his second in command. After he left, Ava went to her office where she kept a locked filing cabinet. She unlocked it and pulled out a drawer, fished out an empty manilla envelope, and dropped in her relics, thinking about each victim in turn. The honeysuckle, the paper doily, the fishing lure, the colored pencil... slipping in the fake twenty dollar bill she'd taken from the lake ice last. Closing the flap and sealing it, she wrote across the top.

The Black Oak Killer

She filed it with the other envelopes she'd made after every case. Although Delano Kester had worked alone, he was connected in an unexpected way to another constellation of crime, the Jackal Saints. Ava had already started sifting through the tangles of their network.

A single unsealed envelope sat in the back of the drawer.

Cortes Family

She reached in and pulled out the piece of her brother's blanket she'd kept after a madman had taken her whole life.

Holding it in her fingers, feeling the softness of the material, she whispered, "I'll find him, Tomás. I'm one step closer."

———

The story continues in *Dark as Pitch*, click here to order your copy now or keep reading for a sneak peek!
https://a.co/d/oe2ZgG3w

Did you enjoy *Deep Dark Lies*? Leave a review to let us know your thoughts!
https://a.co/d/o7CRof5e

DARK AS PITCH: CHAPTER 1

Shards of sunlight sliced through the rusted metal roof of the warehouse, catching the fine dirt disturbed by Sky's feet. She hummed as she stood in the shaft of light and tilted her face toward the warmth before spinning lazily again. Her dress flared out, creating a gossamer shadow that showed the shape of her legs. She caught sight of it and giggled. A light, tinkling laugh she knew others loved, especially men. The woven crown of dandelions atop her head slipped, and she grabbed it, squishing the flowers to her nose to crowd out the smell of pee and trash.

A moan behind her drew her attention, and she rolled her eyes, turning to face the bound man on the filthy floor. Beaten and semi-conscious, he struggled against his bonds. She frowned, kicked dirt into the man's face, and sighed.

"Babe, he's waking up!"

"Just hang on. This is *really* hard to do with my stitches." Hunter grunted from the shadows. "My hand still hurts, you know."

He dragged the barrel closer to the light, fighting with its shifting contents as he sucked down air. Sky grinned as she watched him. She liked the way the sweat glistened on his forehead.

The man on the floor twitched. Likely the drugs wearing off. "You better hurry. If he wakes up, he might scream or do something annoying."

Hunter let go of the barrel with a grunt and dropped it on its side, sending murky fluid onto the ground. Growling, he kicked the container, his sweaty hair spiked up around his head. He glared at Sky, panting.

"I don't know what we're even doing anymore!"

"What we're doing?" Sky tilted her head and gazed up at him. Broad shoulders. Great hair. Big. Like a TV show football player. She liked how delicate she felt next to him. And how well he listened. She stepped closer to him, sliding her hand across his heaving chest. His heart thundered under her palm. She smiled. "We're surviving, baby. We're fighting back, doing what's necessary."

He made a face, but Sky couldn't tell if he was puzzled or if the scar on his cheek just made it look that way. Either way, the scar was hot. It made him look like a badass instead of the golden retriever he was.

Gesturing around them, he looked at her with wide eyes. "Doesn't this feel like too much? I mean—"

"Nothing is too much to protect what we have!" Sky said. She took a breath. "Look, I'll do it, okay? I just need help after."

He shook his head. "Why can't we just leave him here?"

"He'll start to smell and someone will find him. We need him to disappear. He did that a lot anyway, from what I hear. Why do you think I had you bring out a barrel?"

"I guess I was just hoping..."

"What? What is it?" She didn't mean to shout, but he was starting to irritate her. Hunter didn't do well with yelling. His eyes got all shifty, like he wanted to run. She drew a slow breath. Cleansing. Centering. "I'm sorry, babe. I shouldn't have taken your voice. What's the matter?"

"It's just that sometimes they don't fit and I have to..." He lifted his knee and made a stick-breaking motion with his hands.

"They don't feel it, if that's what you're worried about."

"But it's still gross." He looked down at her, eyes pleading. "Do we have to do this?"

"He threatened us, Hunter. He said he had evidence and everything!" She pointed at the man still groaning on the floor next to them. "This is the only way to keep us safe. You *know* that."

"Yeah, but—"

"Hey, I've been passing by that area for years. For literally years. It's abandoned and all covered in weeds. There's trash everywhere. People use it as a dump. No one is going to go sniffing around out there."

"Are you s—"

Their prisoner's head lolled toward them as he tried to push himself up.

"Time's up, Hunter," Sky whispered as she turned and picked up a small revolver from the chair in the corner.

Hunter saw it, and tried to step back, but she caught his T-shirt and pulled him close. She kissed him until his breath hitched. Then she turned Hunter's face with her palm, kissing his neck as she slipped the gun into his hand.

He pulled back, eyes swimming. "Y-You said you would do it."

"We will. Together." Sky wrapped her hand around his. Aiming the gun at the bound man, she slipped her finger over Hunter's on the trigger. "As always."

"As always," Hunter whispered as he closed his eyes, turning his face away.

Sky kept her gaze steady. She wanted to be sure this man who'd threatened to hurt them died. She waited until his eyes fluttered open, until the moment his gaze refocused and landed on her before she pulled the trigger.

DARK AS PITCH: CHAPTER 2

The lights of the patrol cars slashed red and blue down Mission Avenue, capturing the dried weeds and trash-filled gutters in bright snapshots against the night. The flashing property once housed a multiple-screen drive-in theater but now sat razed and partially leveled for a giant 'California Playground' scheduled to open in a couple of years. The developers promised a state-of-the-art wave pool, green energy luxury housing, and upscale shops.

At least, until a body had been found in one of the many trenches that scarred the property. Special Agent Ava Cortes strode in her running shoes across the soft dirt toward the construction site, cordoned off and guarded by a patrol officer.

She didn't get it. Why would people need a wave pool when the Oceanside Pier and an actual beach were only three miles down the road? Still, she'd read that it would revitalize an older neighborhood filled with retirees and sixties-style homes. Wondering what such a grisly discovery would do to the optics of the project, she flashed her California Bureau of Investigation badge at the young Oceanside Police Department officer. He nodded and lifted the crime scene tape for her to duck under.

A forensic tent in the distance shrouded the scene, and the late June mugginess made her T-shirt cling to her skin as she approached. She'd just finished a run and sweat poured out of her like she had dengue fever. It didn't help that the temperature lingered at an unusual seventy-five degrees despite the nine o'clock hour.

During her run, she'd received a call from Detective Manaia, an old colleague, who'd asked her to meet him at the crime scene in the older part of Oceanside. She tightened the band holding her long black ponytail in place and smoothed down the wispy bits. A car sped by on the street behind her, music blasting, the neighborhood still humming.

Laughter and loud voices floated to her from a group of people gathered across the street, watching the police activity. They called out questions about what was going on, but she ignored them.

A mercifully cool breeze kicked up and fluttered the green, tattered construction material still clinging to the chain-link. She made her way toward the tent, passing night crew workers leaning on their shovels or sitting on drink coolers watching the forensic techs in white protective suits working in the distance.

A medical examiner's van blocked most of the tent from view. She walked through the rusty chain-link gate. The smell of dirt hung in the air. Earthmovers, used to grade the property, sat silent. All construction had been shut down for who knew how long this time. Another length of crime scene tape, strung between a debris pile and two stacks of wooden pallets, cordoned off the inner area. She ducked under, holding up a hand against the glare of the halogen lamps. They stood on tripods like alien sentinels, lighting up the scene. Moths circled, bumping and fluttering around their warmth, casting flickering shadows on the ground.

She spotted Detective Tony Manaia talking to an officer. She and Manaia had worked together two years before on her first case after getting punted to White Collar Crimes. The joint Oceanside Police Department and CBI task force investigation turned out to be a wild case. Manaia, talking with a field evidence tech, saw her and waved.

The wind shifted. Ava braced herself when the smell hit her. The unmistakable stench of decay.

"Ava!" He hurried to meet her, his smile just as charming as it had been two years ago. He wore a Hawaiian button-down shirt underneath a black blazer and trousers. His Samoan heritage gave him thick, dark wavy hair and deep brown eyes, but he lacked the bulk of his brothers. His mother gave him both his dimples and the nickname Runt, which Ava had learned one night at a family BBQ. Though compared to her own five-foot-five height, being *only* six feet didn't strike her as a disadvantage. "Thank you so much for coming."

"No worries." She looked around. "Where's your partner?"

"Oh, his daughters have this big dance competition in Las Vegas," Manaia said with a shrug. He tended to speak with a staccato delivery that made him sound like he was always in a hurry. "You met them. The twins."

"Vegas? Aren't they nine?"

"That's what I said." He nodded toward the scene. "Lemme show you why I called you."

Manaia led her toward the forensic tent. "I wasn't sure at first, because of the state of the body, but it's him. It's Brent Cutler."

Ava's gut dropped. "You're sure?"

"I'm positive. I stared at his face for hours at a time when I debriefed him." Manaia put his hand up. "We'll run his prints and dental to be sure, but I'd bet money it's him."

The screech of tires floated over from another street as Ava counted at least six Field Evidence Techs wandering in and out of the tent. That much staff meant word had already spread about who the victim likely was.

"How'd they find him?"

"This site, it's been stop and start for the last few months. They pass one hurdle. You know, with the city or EPA or whatever and ten days later, they have to stop again. Some other environmental agency files another court order." He pulled a jar of menthol rub out of his jacket pocket, unscrewed the lid, and applied some beneath his nose.

Ava gestured for him to hand it over and then did the same. "Anyways, with work starting and stopping so much, we get a lot of vandalism. Also, theft, and trash dumps in between construction. It's a nightmare for the crews, to be honest." He showed her a photo on his phone of a padlock that had been cut on the gate. "I talked to the construction manager on the phone an hour ago. He's at the hospital with his kid. I'm meeting with him tomorrow. He said the gate gets locked when they have to shut down operations. No one really checks on the place. Except maybe an additional pass by local patrol. So no one walks the site while it's shut down."

They stepped around a pile of heavy-duty bins filled with trash.

"So, the morning crew starts up the job again after months, everything is normal, no signs of vandalism, nothing," Ava said. "Then they have a shift change, and the night crew starts over there." She nodded toward the tent next to them. "Is that right?"

"Yeah. They were excavating dirt and whatever else they do for grading."

"But since the company didn't pay for security and the site had been shut down for months... the body could've been buried there at any point."

Manaia shook his head. "The body isn't in the best shape. Lemme show you."

An excavator sat next to the tent, its two boom arms and front-mounted bucket nearly tucked underneath the structure.

Ava and Manaia pushed through bug netting that blocked the pulled-back entry flaps, and, despite the strong menthol smell, the stench of the body hit her like a cloud bank. Inside, lit by more garish light, a fifty-five-gallon blue plastic drum lay on its side in the dirt. Black sludge pooled around it and had drifted underneath a body sheet. The cracked lid sat next to it. A couple more techs worked at a portable table with samples. One looked over, her eyes catching Ava's, and she nodded.

"Dr. Alicia Cooms," Manaia said in introduction. "This is Agent Cortes, the one I told you about."

"Agent Cortes." An older woman, soft sixties with short hair and thick black glasses, Cooms looked smart and serious, with the sinewy arms of a runner or swimmer. Given the greenish cast to her gray hair, Ava guessed the latter. She nodded to Ava and moved closer. "San Diego County Medical Examiner."

As head of the entire office, Dr. Cooms wouldn't normally be the one to come out after hours. Ava greeted her as Manaia squatted next to the body.

He looked up at her. "You ready?"

She nodded, and he lifted the plastic sheet. Covered in dirt and the oily black sludge, she barely recognized him. Filthy and flopped over, he lay chest down, his face turned toward her, lip split, eyes swollen shut and slick with muck. His arms and legs were bent at odd angles like a discarded toy. A single bullet hole marred his smooth forehead. A recent death, given the state of decay. A sliver of guilt moved through Ava. Something had been going on with Brent during their case, but she'd never found out what. Now she wondered how things would have played out if she'd pushed.

She scanned the ground around the body. "No casings in the barrel?"

"Dr. Cooms is guessing it was a revolver," Manaia said. "We'll confirm with ballistics."

Ava eyed the tractor boom. Affixed straps dangled from the bucket. "Tell me what happened."

He stood, fanning away the smell. "So, the night crew out there got the go ahead to start grading in a new location. They noticed disturbed ground and thought it might be buried trash again." He gestured at the excavator as he spoke. "They used the straps to hoist it out, but it slipped. Apparently, the barrel was already leaking. It fell from a good height and popped open. They said he spilled out with the oil or whatever's covering him. Not a lot, like a gallon or two maybe."

Ava walked a circle around the body. Brent had been a handsome man. Tall, athletic, strong. He ran marathons and hit the gym often if her memory of surveilling him served. When he wasn't face-down in powder or enjoying the company of a paid date. He'd also turned against some of the most powerful people in Southern California. Rich and ruthless friends often made the worst enemies.

He still wore his wedding ring despite Ava having heard his marriage had broken up. She pointed to his discolored wrist. "His watch is missing. He wore that big square one, remember? A vintage piece I think."

Manaia nodded. "We'll send out a bulletin to all of the pawn shops."

"I think it was an heirloom. You should ask his father if he had an insurance policy on it. They'd have excellent photos of the piece." She took in the rest of the details. For his testimony, Brent had worn an expensive couture belt to court. He wore it now. Titanium buckle, textured black calf leather, classic quiet luxury. Subtly expensive. "Did you find a wallet?"

"We haven't gone through his pockets," Dr. Cooms said, turning around. "But I patted him down. Nothing. Not even keys."

"He had a driver. His license was suspended."

Ava pointed at the victim's hand. "They took the means of identifying him but didn't recognize the big-ticket accessories. His wedding ring looks platinum, and his belt is couture, if I recall."

"Meaning?" Manaia asked.

"I don't think this was a robbery gone bad." Ava turned to the ME. "Am I right in thinking the time of death was a few days at most?"

Dr. Cooms nodded, glancing at her digital tablet. "We estimate the victim was in the oil for at least two days, possibly three, due to skin slippage and other decay. I believe he died shortly before going into the barrel"

Ava ground her jaw. "If I asked you to guess at the caliber?"

"I'd say a twenty-two-caliber round to the head caused him to expire, but we'll put a pin in that until we get back ballistics, toxicology, and the autopsy."

"I'm assuming he was killed elsewhere?" Ava glanced at the loose dirt. "Anyone find a shovel?"

Dr. Cooms shook her head. "And the crew's equipment was locked up and accounted for. The killer must've brought their own."

"So, he just picked a spot and started digging?"

Manaia shrugged. "I mean, yeah. The crew told me they filled up the holes a few months ago when they had to pause operations. Some kind of safety thing."

"Also, there doesn't seem to be a significant amount of blood near the victim or in the barrel, but again, we'll have to test the fluid inside."

Ava took in the site once more but agreed with Dr. Cooms. They needed more data.

Manaia thanked the ME, who went back to her table of evidence. He nodded for Ava to walk to his side of the body, then, "What do you think?"

She glanced down at the body in front of them. "Whoever dumped Brent didn't know about the construction starting up again. Which is usually announced in papers and radio, even community email blasts. The person who did this isn't really plugged into the city."

"He knew about this place," Manaia argued.

"Yeah, but... that's a different level of assimilation." Ava scanned the area around the property. Nothing but a field to the west, the San Luis Rey River and trail to the north, and Highway 76 to the south. With the piles of dirt and debris, you couldn't see the dump site from the main road, but it wasn't really that far *from* the road. A field length away. The killer would have had to scope it out on foot to know about the covered up holes and loose ground. It wasn't a huge leap of logic. People would know construction disturbed the earth. It just seemed like an odd choice to dump a body right by a busy street. She glanced at Manaia. "But you're right, whoever it was knew the area, that's for sure."

"How do you think Brent's connected?"

"I have no idea. The guy came into our orbit via a money laundering scam and a madam. He seemed to have turned his life around over the past few years, so I have absolutely no idea *what* Brent got himself into this time." She shook her head and sighed. "Unfortunately, the fact that I knew the victim from another case doesn't make it CBI jurisdiction. It's not, uh—"

"Complicated enough?" Manaia asked. "What if I told you we pulled two other bodies out of blue barrels a couple of months ago over at the Oceanside Pier, near the jetty."

Ava frowned. Her job with the CBI took her out of town often to consult on other cases that didn't hit their desks. Had she missed something? "I remember hearing about bodies washing up on shore. The paper said they were likely swimmers from up the coast. It didn't mention anything about barrels."

Manaia nodded. "Two victims did wash up on shore, a young guy and a girl. That part is true. But they were also in blue barrels. A fisherman out on the jetty at dawn saw them and called it in so we were able to get a tent up pretty quick. Good thing. The surf camp was starting up around there. Those kids didn't need to see that. But the victims hadn't drowned. They were shot. With a twenty-two."

"You guys lied?" Ava tilted her head as she looked up at him. "That's refreshingly sketchy of you, Detective Manaia."

He put his hand to his chest, shaking his head. "Not my doing. Someone spread a rumor before we could release anything. Probably a rookie or staff at the station. The news ran with it, and we just didn't correct anyone. And when they realized the victims were homeless nobodies, they lost interest."

"Were they?" Ava asked. "Homeless?"

"Neither had a current address. We know the female victim was arrested for solicitation, but the charges were dropped. The ME's office sent out some queries on the second victim, but that's about all we've got on them. You know how slow things run out here," Manaia muttered, glancing over at Dr. Cooms.

"So, aside from the blue oil drums and the caliber, did anything else connect the victims to each other?"

"I mean, Brent and the female victim both have a connection to the sex industry."

"Did he still? Wasn't he on probation?"

"Right." Manaia raised his brows. "That always stops them."

Ava smiled. "Did the other male victim have tracks on his arms or signs of drug abuse?"

"No." He shuffled on his feet. "Still not enough?"

"Two of the victims came in from the sea, their origin could've been miles north of here, making the barrels a coincidence. Those blue drums are at every garage, mechanic shop, and industrial facility around here."

Manaia nodded. "I get that but hear me out. I agree that the barrels are a bit of a stretch. And while they *were* shot with the same caliber, a twenty-two is a common target and recreational weapon. But if you add in the markings, the cases have to be connected."

"Add in the what?"

"They were on the first two victims' torsos. Brent's body has the same markings, just on his hands." Manaia slipped a flashlight from the inside pocket of his suit jacket. To Dr. Cooms, he said, "Alicia, hit the floodlights, would you?"

She did, and the tent went dark. His flashlight lit up with the blue of UV light. The tiny parrots on his shirt glowed. His teeth, white as the moon, disappeared as he lifted the sheet once again. He shone the light on the back of Brent's hands. A pattern etched into the skin glowed to life. Strange and glyph-like, it reminded Ava of intersecting fractal shapes and geometric lines, almost mathematical.

"Well, that's interesting." She took out her phone and snapped a few pictures. "Any idea what the substance on top of the wounds is?"

He shrugged. "Some kind of pumice?"

"Poultice," Ava murmured, thinking. Flashes of things she'd read about homeopathic medicine and ritualistic symbols flickered behind her eyes. Nothing she'd come across in that field matched the ones on the body. "What did the mixture contain?"

"For the first two victims we found traces of salt, ink, some oil. We'll have to wait for the tests to come back to confirm the same mixture is found here," Dr. Coombs voice floated in the darkness.

"Huh. What's the glowy part made out of?"

"It's some kind of UV reactive binder," Dr. Cooms said from further away in the darkness. "I'll have to verify the one on this victim is the same substance, but it appears to be at first glance."

"Ava," Manaia began, his face glowing like a specter in the dark tent. "I now have three bodies and when the press puts that together all hell will break loose. Some wacko is carving glowing symbols on victims, dumping them in public spaces, and we've gotten nowhere. We sent the symbols off to the FBI as soon as the first two bodies were found. Who knows when we'll hear back from them. Add in Brent's past with OPD and the CBI? Just wait til his dad gets involved."

She nodded. "What *is* Dane Cutler doing lately? I heard he's on the chamber of commerce or something now."

"He's a city councilman and old friend of the mayor. The Chief of Police was asked to personally notify him about his son. He's probably there now."

Her gaze snapped to his eerie purple one. "Your ME didn't even make a positive identification yet."

"It's just a matter of time before the media vultures screech up to the curb." He switched off his flashlight. "Can we get the lamps back on?"

Dr. Cooms lit up the tent again.

"The markings got my attention, I'll give you that," Ava said, blinking in the bright halogen light.

"Is that a yes or no?" Manaia looked over his shoulder at the Field Evidence Techs swabbing the bucket, then at Ava. "Given Brent Cutler's history with our madam and now he ends up killed in the exact same way as a sex worker was two months ago, I mean..."

She took one more look at the barrel next to Brent's body. A sweetheart deal had kept him out of prison, one she'd helped broker. Only to have him wind up in an oil drum like two other bodies.

"I'll bring it up to my team lead, but I can't promise anything. I'm not in charge of PIT."

"I didn't ask for the Priority Investigation Team or whatever you call yourselves. I want you, Ava. I've seen what you do out there." He looked at her with that earnest, good guy face.

She gave him a slight nod and walked away, looking up a contact and hitting dial. As she paced, she spotted a coin in the rubble. Old and caked with dirt, she picked it up to examine it under the halogen lamps. A shooting star carved on the surface brought back memories of arcade games on hot summer nights. Her lost days.

August picked up after a few rings, the sounds of a restaurant behind him. "Everything ok?"

Ava closed her fist around the game token. "I need a favor."

DARK AS PITCH: CHAPTER 3

Ava woke the next morning still thinking about Brent and the strange, glowing shapes carved into his skin. She'd tossed and turned all night. Now the aches and pains of staying too long in bed when she should have given up on sleep needed to be dealt with. She got up, ate a couple of dry waffles, and decided to go for a run to clear her head.

Ava donned her swimsuit, a tank top, and a pair of athletic shorts, then wandered the house looking for her running shoes, checking all the nooks and crannies of the old home. A pretty blue and white cottage a block from the beach, Ava had moved into it with her grandmother after her family had been killed. Sofia Cortes had lived in the cottage with Ava's grandfather, raised Ava's father there, and stayed through widowhood with her walking buddies and conservation efforts, finally passing away at home after a long battle with cancer.

The home, paid off, had remained in a trust with a rental company managing the property until Ava had aged out of the foster system. The practical choice would have been to sell it and move to a smaller, cheaper apartment closer to the airport. A place easier to leave when she got a new case. But she had no intention of selling. She loved it here.

After locating her missing shoes under a chair, Ava slipped them on and strode onto her porch, squinting in the bright morning sun. She did some stretches, glancing down the sloping street straight toward a strip of sparkling blue ocean, then set off on an easy jog toward her favorite spot a mile down the coast.

The smell of the sea hit her as she took the sidewalk path overlooking the shore below, passing stairways every quarter mile that led down to the sand and ocean waves. She'd never forget her first time seeing the ocean. That had been a time filled with uncertainty and fear. After moving in with her grandmother, she'd learned to love the ocean. She walked and walked the beaches in her grief, letting the forlorn calls of the birds be her voice. One place where she always found solace was a small section of beach carved out by a rocky outcropping that jutted out over the sand.

She called it Alcove Beach, though it had no real name. Ava bounded down the steel stairway leading to the shore and found a spot near the wall of stones next to the railing. The beach was rocky, not great for sunbathing or for kids to make sandcastles, so it usually remained empty. Joggers and roller skaters used the street-level sidewalk above. Other than that, Ava had the small section of beach to herself.

Perched on a large boulder, she listened to the waves crash and let her heart rate slow. Her mind still circled around the image of Brent, slick with muck, staring up at her from the dirty asphalt. After she'd left the scene the night before, Detective Manaia sent her an invitation to the secure network, and she'd taken a peek at the case, looking for a different angle to try. He was right. They had nothing. Despite all her time digging into Brent's life, she still had no idea what he'd gotten himself mixed up in this time.

She thought back to that time right after getting kicked off the PIT team, not taking anyone's calls, still under investigation. She hadn't been in a great headspace. She'd been convinced there was something Brent had been hiding, but his father was too connected. Thrown off after her very public lashing, she'd backed off, intending to pursue it after more evidence surfaced, but that never happened. The brass wanted the case closed. So they shut her out. Brent got a deal, and Cartwright went to prison. She should have pushed to keep the case open.

Movement down the beach caught her eye, and she spotted her former partner turned boss, Agent August Blake, walking on the sand toward her, looking like a rugged movie star. August couldn't hide that he was from money if he tried. He wore a white button-down shirt, his cuffs rolled to the elbows, charcoal chino pants, and perfectly styled dark espresso hair that fell slightly over his light brown eyes.

"Hey!" Surprised, Ava rose from the boulder. "What are you doing here?"

"You sounded off on the phone last night." He leaned against the rock retaining wall. "You always come here when something's bothering you. And while you hate morning workouts, you hate standing still when you're grappling with something more." He crossed his arms. "What's going on?"

"Nothing." She adjusted the messy bun atop her head, shaken loose by her run. "Really. You didn't have to drive almost two hours to check on me."

"You asked for time off." He shook his head. "You don't do that."

"Maybe I do now."

He slipped off his sunglasses. "We've consulted on at least five outside cases since you've been back on the team, and since Black Oak, you're ready for the next official PIT one. Practically champing at the bit. You wouldn't take time off and risk missing it."

Ava crossed her arms over her chest. "You mean chomping?"

"Horses champ at the bit. It's an equestrian term."

"How many ponies did you have as a child?"

He narrowed his amber gaze at her. "What are you doing? Is it PIT? I know we've been waiting awhile for our next case, but I thought you were finding your footing with the team."

"No, it's nothing to do with you or the team. I just need some time off to work an old case."

"You don't have any old cases. You're physically incapable of moving on from a case until it's solved." He tucked his sunglasses into his shirt pocket. "And you don't close a case unless you know you completely tied everything off." His dark brows furrowed. "In fact, I've never seen you look back. Not once."

She smiled. He never missed a thing. "Okay, technically it's a new case, but with some old players. I didn't want to get you involved."

He shook his head. "That's not how we do things anymore. No secrets, remember?"

"Okay, you first. How was dinner last night?" Ava covered up the pit in her stomach with a grin.

He blinked at her. "That is personal. This is work."

"So, a girlfriend, then," Ava teased.

He cocked his head, scrutinizing her face. "Quit stalling."

Ava chewed on the inside of her cheek. "Look, I don't want to pull you into something that could blow up. I think I may have missed something before, and someone might be dead because of it."

"Walk me through it, Ava."

The sound of the waves rumbled through her, and she let out a breath before looking up at him. "I worked on a case with the Ocean-side Police Department two years ago. We were investigating sex trafficking, prostitution, and money laundering. My partner at the time was Detective Tony Manaia, with the OPD's Crimes of Violence Unit."

"This was when you had just started with White Collar Crimes? You cleared that case if I recall."

"Yeah, I helped solve it, but looking back, I was messed up, August. *Angry.* I couldn't shake what had happened with the Ghost Town Killer." Ava paced along the wall, then stopped in front of him, her eyes on the sea. "I think I should've pursued something at the time. I should've listened to my gut and I just... I didn't."

August pulled a piece of gum from his pocket and shoved it into his mouth. "Tell me about the new case."

She shook her head. "You need to see it."

On the way back to her house, Ava brought him up to date on her conversation with Detective Manaia the night before. The previous two bodies, the one they'd found at the drive in, the markings, everything. She ran into the house to grab the tablet while still talking. He followed her inside, leaning against her counter, his hands shoved in his pants pockets, as he watched her move around the kitchen. Ava found the tablet, pulled up the file for him, and handed it over. "I couldn't shake the feeling that Brent was hiding something. He was acting strangely nervous for someone with an immunity deal."

August's gaze slid across the screen, his jaw working as he read. She paced in front of him, chewing on the inside of her cheek, thinking about those strange markings.

"I can't concentrate when you're circling me like a vulture," August said.

Ava put her hands up and wandered over to the couch.

After a few minutes, he said, "And this Detective Manaia asked you specifically for a CBI consult last night?"

"He asked me as a friend, I think. We'd both worked with Brent when we took down Eliza Cartwright. He made detective first-grade off the case."

"I remember. The Sea Sirens Escorts madam." August nodded, handing the tablet back. "What's your connection to the other victims?"

"I only know the latest one. Brent Cutler." She explained that Cutler had found himself involved in some kind of escort situation and brokered a deal with the CBI to bring down Eliza Cartwright in a sting targeting her escort service. "Eliza, real name Lisa Carter, is currently serving ten years in the Metropolitan Correctional Center,

San Diego. She could've gotten less time, but she wouldn't give up her black book names."

"So, Detective Manaia thinks the victims are connected and part of a series. Do you think he's onto something?"

"He's spooked, and that's saying something. He's a solid investigator. One of the best I've worked with."

"Do you know him well?" August didn't look at her when he asked.

"Enough. We kept Brent steady when he was spinning out. I guess you could call that a bonding moment."

"Now he's dead in your backyard."

"We all live relatively near the coast, but I don't think where he was found had anything to do with me. Not yet, anyway."

August rattled the keys in his pocket, chewing his gum. "And you think you have to make it right."

"I have to figure out what I missed back then."

He nodded, pushing up from the counter. "I figured. Come on. We have a meeting."

"A meeting?" Ava followed him into her house. "Is that why you're in town?"

"I told you why I was in town." August took his phone from his back pocket and handed it to her. Then he went to the kitchen, pulled out a mug from the cabinet, and poured the dregs from her coffee pot. Just like he used to. No one would ever suspect it'd been over two years since he'd been in this house. Ava forced her attention to the news website on the phone screen while he sipped his coffee. A headline across the top read: *Political Scion Found Murdered and Stuffed in an Oil Drum...*

"Oh, crap," Ava said.

"The Brent Cutler case isn't a solo quest anymore. It's an official CBI case, thanks to the mayor's call last night. Apparently, the Chief of Police is pissed Detective Manaia went over his head."

"You'd think the Chief would welcome our help."

"Yes, well, he remembers you."

She chuckled. "That's fair."

"Vincent told me about the investigation first thing this morning when I was already on my way and wouldn't you know, you're already up to speed."

Ava grabbed his mug, took a sip, and smiled. "I guess you should work on keeping up then."

———

She took a quick shower, dried her hair, then dressed quickly. Dark slacks and a cotton, sky-blue blouse she wore when it was hot. Tailored to both hide her weapon and to allow an unobstructed pull when she needed one, the outfit met the CBI's business casual regulations. Ava kept her long hair loose because research showed it made people appear more approachable. She grabbed her personal phone, a burner not connected with the day-to-day of her work cell, and dropped it into her purse. Finally, she slipped on the Doc Marten boots she wore in the field, and they headed out in his SUV.

They hit the I-5 freeway south. August slipped them into the carpool lane as they hit traffic. The ride offered ocean views and the occasional peek at the Pacific Surfliner commuter train. Oceanside Police Department used the San Diego Medical Examiner's Office for forensic needs their in-house team couldn't handle. Forty minutes away in Kearny Mesa, the office provided lab work, autopsies, and other specialized forensic services for the County of San Diego, in which the City of Oceanside was located.

Ava sat in the passenger seat, reading the rest of the newspaper article. The press already seemed to know everything the police did.

Well, that's not ideal.

"At least they didn't mention the bodies being carved with markings," Ava muttered. "That would definitely freak people out."

They talked about what Manaia had shown her, with Ava holding up photos on her secure tablet for August to see as they sat in traffic.

"You're the queen of obscure knowledge," he said. "What do you think?"

"I am sort of amazing."

August rolled his eyes. "What do the carvings mean?"

She looked out the window, thinking about the gunshot, the broken bones, the darkness of the barrel. It meant a brutal, broken mind. Shaking her head, she said, "I'm not sure yet."

Ava switched to perusing the case file, reading out the notes on Brent Cutler to August. After the Sea Siren case two years ago, Brent had done a stint in rehab. According to Manaia's notes, he'd gotten into working out. He'd also opened a wine tasting room with backing from his father, called Bramble Wood Cellars. Though why anyone with a substance abuse problem would open up and work at a place that sold alcohol was beyond Ava's comprehension.

"It's apparently pretty good, from what I hear," she said. "My friend, Christy, went there for her mother-in-law's sixtieth birthday and said they had great farm-to-table dishes."

"Is that the one with the fairy hair??"

Ava chuckled. "The pixie cut, yeah,"

"Tell me about Detective Manaia. It's not every day you throw out compliments like, 'Best detective I've ever worked with'"

"He's a good guy. A family guy. He was the youngest homicide detective in the county back when he started. So, when they wanted a liaison to work with the White-Collar team, he came highly recommended. Manaia knows this town. He helped me get Brent Cutler to crack."

"Brent didn't have a lawyer?"

"He had a team. The Cutler family is loaded. They own land and a few mid-tier hotels in the area. His father rubs elbows with the other rich mucky mucks in San Diego County. But Brent wasn't exactly a stellar decision maker. His father kept a tight grip on the finances, especially after his legal trouble. He didn't want his father to know all of his dirty deeds, so he talked with us instead of his lawyers." Ava jotted down a note in her leather notebook. "Which reminds me, is Rondeau in town yet? I need to ask him to check on life insurance for Brent. He's not married anymore so who gets his millions?"

"He and Talia are driving down this morning. They'll set up at the police station." August took the offramp toward Overland Ave. "Who brokered the deal?"

"I did. Working with his attorney and the Department of Justice, the three of us put together a solid case. Brent, our confidential informant, agreed to wear a wire during multiple meetings with Eliza Cartwright. He did, and we got what we needed, so he got a pass on his soliciting prostitution charges."

"But you think you messed up."

"Eliza said some things to him during their conversations. She kept alluding to how everyone has their dark secrets. Something like that."

"And you think this might have something to do with his death?" He pulled into the parking lot of the Medical Examiner's Building.

Ava grabbed her messenger bag and slung it over her shoulder. "It was enough to get my attention last time and I ignored it. I'm not going to make that mistake again."

———

Enjoying *Dark as Pitch*? Click here to order your copy now!
https://a.co/d/o3dsMJnM

AVA CORTES: CRIME THRILLER SERIES

Deep Dark Lies

Dark as Pitch

Fade to Dark

Gilt Edge

A Willow Grace FBI Thriller by C.C. West

Shadow of Grace

Condition of Grace

Hunt for Grace

Time for Grace

Piece of Grace

Flight of Grace

Rite of Grace

Ava Cortes CBI Thrillers

Deep Dark Lies

Dark as Pitch

———

Join Without Warrant's private reader group on Facebook!

https://www.facebook.com/withoutwarrant

ABOUT THE AUTHOR

Raquel was a military brat who grew up on Marine bases throughout the United States. An avid stargazer, she often travels into the desert near her home to view the meteor showers or throws launch parties for major NASA events. When she's not writing she can be seen geeking out over movies, reading anything she can get her hands on, and having arguments about the television series Firefly in coffee shops. She lives in Southern California with her husband, six kids, and her beloved Huskies, Zena and Keanu. Raquel is known for pulse-pounding fiction with a breathtaking pace, and she continues to bring riveting characters and epic worlds to life in exciting new thriller series.

JOIN WITHOUT WARRANT'S MAILING LIST

Follow the link to stay up to date with Without Warrant!

https://BookHip.com/QKWGDKS

You'll receive a **free** copy of

Girl Awakened: A Dana Gray Prequel.